The Revels

THE
REVELS

STACEY THOMAS

ONE PLACE. MANY STORIES

HQ
An imprint of HarperCollins*Publishers* Ltd
1 London Bridge Street
London SE1 9GF

www.harpercollins.co.uk

HarperCollins*Publishers*
Macken House, 39/40 Mayor Street Upper,
Dublin 1, D01 C9W8, Ireland

This edition 2023

1

First published in Great Britain by
HQ, an imprint of HarperCollins*Publishers* Ltd 2023

ISBN : 9780008566661

MIX
Paper | Supporting
responsible forestry
FSC™ C007454
www.fsc.org

This book is produced from independently certified FSC™ paper

to ensure responsible forest management.

For more information visit: www.harpercollins.co.uk/green

This book is set in Centaur

Printed and Bound in Australia by McPherson's Printing Group

To Saskia, for reminding me that I could do anything.

Chapter One

London, late January 1645

Death is a song. I've known its rhythm since birth, but still I flinch from it. The drapes of the first-floor window twitch. Moments later the door to my father's townhouse opens and Stephens, my father's valet, is quick to bridge the distance between us. He has aged in the months since I saw him last, and shrugs off his stoop as though it's an unwelcome weight.

'Nicholas,' he says gently, his fingers brushing against the black mourning band that circles his arm.

'He is gone?' Stephens's sombre expression steals my hope and I let my valise fall to the ground.

It was he who had written to me of Francis's illness from camp fever. 'The roads from Oxford were flooded. If not, I would have arrived before . . .'

'The delay was a kindness,' he murmurs. 'You would not have known him.' He shivers and pulls at his servant's livery. He is cold and I am tired from a day's travel, yet neither of us suggests we retreat indoors. This is what death is. Stilted greetings and pleasantries that do little to hide the truth: Francis is dead. My brother is dead.

He grimaces and shepherds me past the silver horseshoe nailed to the threshold, counter-magic believed to prevent witches from entering. Such sights were rare when King Charles still resided in London. Most of England's witches were culled during the reign

1

of his father, King James. War has made people desperate, and the news-books are filled with accounts of people selling their souls to the Devil for magic.

Inside, the reflective surfaces of the hallway are draped in black silk. When I left for Oxford last year to continue my studies, I paid no thought of ever returning. King Charles had abandoned London following a failed attempt to arrest his most vocal critics in the House of Commons for high treason. In the three years that have passed under his command, his headquarters in the city of Oxford have become a palatial ruin, overrun with sewage, soldiers, courtiers and death. Despite this, I have not missed home. Yet here I am, caught under its shade.

I straighten up at the nudged reminder to stand tall in a place where I have spent most of my life shrinking into the shadows. Satisfied, Stephens ascends the winding staircase.

A sweet cloying scent in the air sticks to me like honey and pulls me towards the parlour. Father and his wife, Mrs Sophie Pearce, are seated across from each other, heads bowed towards his greatest achievement, who now lies between them. I step closer to my brother, forever seventeen, crowned with hyacinths and enthroned in a coffin of dark elm. The air is thick with his decay, despite the cold that bites at my skin like an icy draught. I lift my head and blink into the light where my father acknowledges my presence with a brief glance.

'You are here,' notes my stepmother, and I take a cautious step towards her. Bereavement has rattled her rigid poise and prematurely silvered tendrils of her brown hair.

'Madam, I am sorry for your loss.' And the others, the infants who died too early for Father to allow them names.

'You are kind,' she says, her tremble a hint at the resentment she's always felt for having to raise me alongside her legitimate son.

Father locks eyes with me again. 'I will speak with you privately.' He turns to his wife, who clasps her hands and presses her head to Francis's coffin. 'Our son needed spells, not vigils,' he snaps. It is said that a person's soul departs in pieces upon their death. Witches were believed to trap what remained and revive the deceased with a whispered enchantment through a loop of thread and a sealed knot. The late King James has seen to it that such arts are now a hanging offence, leaving the bereaved only with their prayers for comfort.

A burning look, but Father does not recoil from it. Defeated, Sophie stands and from underneath her dark petticoats, the rosettes on her shoes are a pink, unhealed wound.

'He is gone,' says Father once we are alone and wonders at both me and my dead brother. We were only six months apart and, despite having only our father's blood in common, were close enough in looks to pass for twins. My presence is an unwelcome reminder.

'I am sorry.' His clenched curled fists are a soft warning. He has never looked to me for anything, not even comfort.

He runs his hand through thinning grey hair. 'His treachery was a costly thing. His death more so.'

I look upon my brother, unwilling to believe that Father is still angry over the money he paid for Parliament to overlook Francis running away to join the Royalist army.

When I raise my eyes, Father's grimace has turned into a sneer. To ground myself, I press my boots against the Turkish carpet. 'My son has died a soldier's death, while you have wasted your time writing plays.'

How easily the dead are forgiven. 'Words are not to be scorned. Battles have been fought over them,' I say, a pointed reminder of the brutal resistance King Charles faced when he tried to force a revised prayer book on his Scottish subjects.

'It is not words they fight over,' he argues, and we both reach for a respite from the loss that lies between us.

'The war isn't about money,' I retort before he can repeat his worn criticisms of the King's penchant for illegal taxes. 'Nor is it about the King overstepping his authority, or his failure to further reform the Church of England. It's about power, regardless of the arguments Parliament and King drape over it. His Majesty has hoarded more than his fair share and we are all fighting for a taste of it.'

'You have never fought for anything,' he says, a familiar taunt. I am no more than a beggar to him, well dressed and well educated, but a beggar nevertheless.

'I have been offered work,' I counter, clenching my fists to calm myself.

'Doing what?' he asks in surprise.

'Writing.'

He scoffs. 'Where? The London playhouses have been shut these past three years. The Queen is not likely to return from France and the Royalists in Oxford are in want of bread not entertainment.'

He folds his arms and I force myself to elaborate. I tell Father of my friendship with Mr Dodmore Roper. A contemporary of mine at Oxford who abandoned his studies in favour of devising the Queen's entertainments. 'He purchased one of my plays and has promised me work at the Royalist court in France.'

He sighs. 'You are like your mother. She too pinned her hopes on pretty words and false promises.'

I keep my face still to hide my surprise. I know hardly anything of my mother. She died within days of my birth and Father has never cared to reveal enough to make her real.

A flickered memory of Francis causes me to arch my head in the same manner he would have done. 'Is that how you won her?'

4

He laughs, but I know I've unsettled him from the way his eyes bore through me.

'I met her on my travels and brought her home with me.'

'And?' I ask, the yearning creeping through.

'I married your stepmother a month later. Your mother and I parted ways once she found out. She had a grander role in mind.' He shrugs off the memory.

'Her name?' I beg, but he raps his knuckles against his chair, refusing to be drawn further into the past.

'My tolerance towards your poetic ambitions was a kindness to her memory, forfeited by your brother's death.' He pulls a sealed parchment from his doublet and declares, 'Everything that was once Francis's is now yours.'

The parchment is feather-light but my hands tremble from its weight. My legitimacy is marked by Father's scrawled signature and Parliament's seal, yet this prize does not elevate me. It is a reluctant gift brought about by my brother's death, but I am slow to let it fall from my hands.

'Your wife will never let me replace him.'

'Sophie has accustomed herself to the situation,' he imparts, and I notice the bite mark on his hand. Father's eyes meet mine and I recall Sophie's ginger posture with a wince.

'There will be gossip. People will not accept me.'

'I will show you how to battle your way through,' he scoffs. Father had been quick to voice his support of Parliament when the war began. Their encouragement of men from the middling ranks has given him the chance to fashion himself into something new, something regal. He has dubbed himself the merchant king and will not be checked by anyone.

'You intend to accept Mr Roper's offer?'

I meet his stare and wonder how he can make this offer with the dead laid out between us.

'What else?' At my look of surprise, he continues, 'I have made you legitimate, what more could you want?'

Stephens made my life here bearable, but Francis made it a home. Without him, it is a tomb and one I have no wish to be trapped by. 'I am sorry I could not be a better son to you.'

'Your mother,' he says and smiles when I raise my head. 'Ask me one thing of her. Her favourite poem, playwright . . . her name,' he tempts, and in the ensuing silence he retrieves a quill pen and paper from a nearby cabinet. He scratches something onto the blank parchment and hovers it above Francis's body. 'Her name,' he repeats when I stand to retrieve it, 'began with a G.'

His fist is a paperweight and I settle with tracing the letter's curve with my finger. 'You will earn the rest in the years it will take you to learn the business.'

Father's reticence has seen to it that I am unmoored from my past. That I am alone. He wets his lips in anticipation and loosens his grip. But then I catch sight of Francis's coffin and the shamefulness of it causes me to draw back. 'You are still minded to a refusal. You have taken my son from me. Now, I shall have all of you in return,' he commands and tosses another document towards me.

It is the letter I wrote to Francis last spring, my words encouraging enough that he slipped away from London to join the King's army, taking with him our father's musket and our family's good standing with Parliament.

The closest I've been to war is the staged skirmishes in the play-houses. Those exhilarating battle scenes had never been tinged by the loss I feel now. 'I did not wish for this.' I look to Francis for forgiveness, but his face is immobile. I pass the letter back to Father as though it's a loaded weapon.

'Men go to war and die, leaving the ones left behind to profit from their mistakes.' His mouth thins. 'I paid Mr Roper to humour your ambitions.'

My youth has been a backdrop to the violent feud between King and Parliament, but in the face of his revelation all I can do is stand. 'You are lying,' I say, my voice unsteady.

He shakes his head slowly. 'I wanted you safely occupied. I had an heir already and did not want you under his feet.'

I recall my interactions with Dodmore and the victories I thought so hard-won. 'You have toyed with me my whole life.'

He shrugs. 'I pandered to your vanity . . . I have not told your stepmother that you have killed our son.' His words see me seated. Sophie would never forgive me for the loss of Francis. 'I am offering you wealth and safety,' he finishes.

'The same thing you promised your wife.' His face hardens at the reminder. My stepmother traded away her privilege for my father's wealth. A loss she regrets, no matter that she and her family have done well by it. 'A Devil's bargain you are both trapped by.'

'Better my trap than hers,' he counters, and from the lines of his face I see he will not give way.

I have made words my profession, but Father's betrayal has robbed me of my trade. If he tells Sophie, her family will prevent me from finding another honest way of making a living. I snatch my mother's initial from his hands. 'One year and you will also tell me the town where my mother was born.'

His expression eases. 'Four years for me to mould you into my replacement,' he bargains, 'after which you will have my wealth and all I know of your mother to do with as you please.'

The transformation would leave me too much like him to want to seek out her history. 'I will not be moulded to your likeness,' I swear.

His scorn is fleeting. 'Francis bore my name, but you are already much more like myself. To gain an advantage, I too have steered people towards misfortune.'

I burn inside. I am nothing like him.

'The funeral is tomorrow. You will keep to your chamber.'

I raise my head. Am I to be denied the right to mourn my own brother?

He sighs. 'I have made arrangements for you to leave in three days' time. Your stepmother's family assumed I would choose a replacement from her line. Your temporary absence gives me time to smooth over the announcement.'

I am no more than a tool to him. A blunt one, I gather, by how easily he assumes my acquiescence with a dismissive goodbye.

'Where am I to go?' I ask.

He pauses near the door. 'Your stepmother has graciously availed upon her connections. You are to clerk for Judge William Percival.'

'But he is a witch-hunter,' I protest. For centuries royal scribes were charged with recording the scant history of witches. Guido Bonatti, Nostradamus and John Dee made a science of their discoveries and used their knowledge to secure appointments as astrologers and necromancers in royal households. King James's determination to eradicate magic was no barrier to their advancement. At the King's urging, they abandoned their borrowed arts and established the commission for witch-hunters, where Judge Percival spent his youth eradicating witches.

'A judge now,' he replies.

'I will not suffer such a man's company.'

'Judge Percival is the scourge of witches, not murderers,' he says by way of a departing remark.

*

The parlour is a testament to my father's youth spent sailing for riches around the world with the East India Company. These panelled walls of dark brown mahogany house a collection of treasures he has gathered over the years: golden plates, paintings, Chinese porcelain gourd vases and swathes of vivid-coloured silk and cotton from his recent ventures into China and India. I tilt my head to the Greek wall tapestry near the bay window. The embroidered eyes of Castor and Pollux are drawn to Francis, who remains a-slumber. Even in the dark, he is a bright countenance, his dark hair touched by strands of gold. My hand traces my scar, a faded circle of raised white flesh on my right palm. I have played hundreds of roles in my lifetime and cut off pieces of myself to fit the requirements. But I could never be Francis. My fingers dig in until my brother is a bleeding outline.

Stephens enters the parlour and with a brief look in my direction strides towards the fireplace. 'You have acquiesced,' he says, crouched down and with his back facing me.

I stare at Francis, my chest tight. The flush of fire does nothing for him. He is gone.

'Well?' Stephens presses.

'You were listening in,' I accuse.

He shakes his head. 'I guessed your father's intentions when he asked me to prepare Francis's room for you. You should return to Oxford.'

'I cannot. I have given him my word.' My face hardens as I recall Father's threat.

Stephens stands to face me. 'He has taken it.'

Stephens would absolve me, I'm sure, were I to tell him of the role I played in Francis's death. I turn away from him. I have spent far too many hours as a boy imagining myself in Francis's place to think myself innocent.

'Please,' he continues, almost pleading. 'Were it anyone but Judge Percival, I would not stop you. Lord Howard was his master.'

'Judge Percival is too young to have had any involvement with the Pendle witches,' I mutter, unwilling to meet his gaze.

'He is still of their ill ilk,' he spits, and I raise my eyes to his. In the brittle silence I recall his stories of the witch trials that occurred in Lancaster almost thirty years ago when Alizon Device bewitched a pedlar to death. By the time the witch-hunters had descended upon Pendle, the young witch had implicated her immediate family and another rival clan. The Pendle witches were tried, found guilty and hanged, but their deaths did nothing to sate Lord Howard, a former scribe and alleged author of King James's *Daemonologie*, who founded the commission for witch-hunters to comb the country for more. Stephens's mother was caught in their net.

'Leave with him and you'll return an orphan,' says Stephens. Unsteady words, but he does not recall them. Like many relatives of accused witches, Stephens found himself tainted by his mother's legacy. His practicality prompted him to make his family name a fruitless one. The same mindset spurred him to make a son out of his master's unwanted bastard.

He has been a watchful shadow my entire life, but I force myself to study the blow. 'I have been orphaned once. I will survive a second turn.' His flinched departure takes with him everything that was once between us. I rise after him, only to be stopped by a wayward look at Francis. You cannot revive what's gone.

'Father and Stephens each want me to go their way,' I whisper. 'I imagine you would advise me to choose myself and run off to New England.' His stillness cuts my laughter short. 'I do not know myself enough to choose anything. I fear I will lose all the good parts of myself by the time Father is done with me. I already lost one, have

lost most already when you died . . . I did not wish for your death.'
My words are coloured by doubt. Father's accusations have set in like
rot and I raise my head to the tapestry of Castor and Pollux standing
proud in their helmets and spears.

Francis and I had seen much of ourselves in the myth when we
were children. The half-brothers and somewhat twins who even death
couldn't part. We were too young to see the darkness in the tale. In
his published treatise of witchcraft, King James made a distinction
between the two classes of magic: low-level magic and knot magic.
The former was the sphere of wise women who used what meagre
magic they possessed to read and write charms, tell fortunes and sell
subtle poisons and healing cures that kept maladies at bay. The latter
was the domain of thread witches who whispered spells through
threaded knots to cast powerful love charms and illusions, summon
wind or fire and even raise the dead.

When his prayers to Zeus went unanswered, Pollux used an
entwined knot of their hair to tether his brother's spirit to the earth.
I study the frayed knot the brothers hold between them and the knife
in Pollux's hand. His brother's mortality weighed upon him. The
immortal Pollux had no wish to be dulled by it.

I lean over Francis, my unsheathed dagger a flash of lightning in
the dark. Of all the spells, death knots are the most abhorrent. I shear
off locks of our hair and weigh them up in my hand. A hesitant first
step, one any practitioner would be damned by. I am damned already
as I recall Father's words and without hesitation loop the strands of
our hair together. My dark overshadows his light as I seal the loop
with a pulled whisper and wait.

Chapter Two

I slip into the dead man's life like a thief. Framed by a gold-trimmed mirror I stand corpse-still while Stephens dresses me in my brother's clothes. Through the bay window, I'm afforded a slanted glimpse of St James's Park, the white winter view marred by the moving outlines of passers-by. A grey light trickles in from the outside and through the mirror, I study the blue veins spread across Stephens's throat like a spider's web. His mottled fingers are brisk at their task and his mouth a tight line. He has hoarded his words since our last encounter, only breaking his silence to inform me of Judge Percival's expected arrival. My brother was buried yesterday. Now, I stand in his place, a shapeless thing waiting to be rendered for a purpose.

'The red one.'

At my clipped command, Stephens sidesteps the yellow canopied bed and pulls out the doublet from the cupboard.

'Cavalier colours,' he admonishes.

'Francis's colours. Now my colours,' I say, flinching at the memory of my vigil by my brother's side until dawn's approach forced me to concede I was no witch.

Stephens clicks his teeth and, at his urging, I put on my breeches and raise my arms for him to fasten me into Francis's red-pearled doublet. The business of dressing unfolds like a dance with me hesitantly performing half-remembered steps to the music of my own heartbeats. It is a jarring process, my brother's scent growing stronger with each piece of clothing that's layered upon me like a winding cloth.

My fingers grace the knot of Francis's hair entwined with mine that rests inside my shirt and I look around me at his belongings. My brother's bedchamber has been made a mausoleum in his demise. Apart from his clothes, everything is as he left it. The mahogany cupboards bear the smudged traces of his touch and the initials 'FP'. The desk near the window is scattered with loose parchments, a book of jests and a tobacco pipe half hidden amid a collection of kickshaws. The room is burdened by his presence, but I am unwilling to rid myself of the weight.

Stephens inclines his head to mark the end of our dance measure. The connection between us is severing, the moment he leaves will see it dissipate completely.

'Stephens.' He rests his hand on the doorknob. 'Father has promised me my mother's name.'

He sets down my valise and turns to face me. 'Her name will be a cold comfort,' but there's a gentling to his tone I snatch at.

'Is there nothing you can tell me of her?' I beg.

'I knew her only as Mrs Pearce. I met her once – the day you were born.' He shies away from the memory and quickly hands me a rolled-up letter from his shirt. 'I meant to give this to you earlier. Francis's last letter to you. He entrusted it to my safekeeping until your return.'

A deathbed letter.

'I will not let you feed it to the fire,' he warns with a pointed look at my diary that I'd placed in the fireplace ashes this morning.

'I will keep it safe,' I murmur, and tuck it inside my shirt.

'Nicholas,' he says with a finality to his speech. 'Your mother . . . she was fair enough to take your father's smiles with her when she died.'

'Not all of them,' I contest. The few smiles remaining were saved for

Francis. 'I would not want the same for you.' For a moment he moves to ruffle my hair like he used to when I was a child. He'd only ever given the young heir his deference, and his dropped hand marks the loss of our rough father–son relationship. 'Sir,' a muttered departure, but he turns away with an expression that seems to separate the boy I was from the man I have become. Whatever's left of that boy he takes with him.

I turn to study Stephens's handiwork in the mirror. I'm encased in heeled shoes, dark breeches, a red doublet, a black cloak, and a rapier sheathed inside my scabbard. I lift my head to face the dead man who looks back at me through the glass.

A succession of footsteps, akin to the flutter of birds, nears and I head towards the door. Esme, Sophie's maid, stumbles over her loose pattens and into my arms. Once she is steady, I release her, while remembering that Francis would have teased the embrace out long enough to elicit a blush. Esme's cheeks are pinched red from the outside air, and she tucks her chin to her shawl while she studies me from behind lowered eyes. My resemblance to Francis is uncanny. It is made more so by my rich attire, and Esme is slow to hide her surprise at my bold display.

'The master told me to fetch you, sir,' she relays.

She leaves, her exit slowed by her full woollen skirts and a final look she favours me with from over her shoulders. I add it to the growing list of things I've stolen.

The footsteps of the downstairs servants and the whinnying of horses are like the beating of a drum. The door to my former chamber is ajar and I study the narrow bed, worn rug and ransacked cupboard. Through my brother's eyes, I'm forced to take stock of its mean and uninviting appearance.

The windows near the top of the stairs overlook the entrance where Stephens is fastening Francis's valise to a stranger's carriage. My valise.

I fight the urge to run out of the open doorway and keep running. The thought that Francis had the same urge, only to run into an early grave, propels me to the parlour where I hover on the threshold, unseen.

Father and Sophie trade low murmurs with Judge Percival, who has finally arrived to cart me away. The judge had already made his reputation by the time King Charles abolished witch-hunting eighteen years ago. Since then, witches have crumbled into a lost history, a night-tale for children. The present discord has seen them resurrected.

With his back towards me, all the judge reveals of himself is the whiteness of his collar and his thick auburn hair. The fireplace blazes behind Father and Sophie, who melt into the ember background.

'The Hilary Assizes sit in York twelve days hence.' Percival's bland announcement carries across the room.

'That is far,' Sophie remarks.

'I must administer justice across the court circuits no matter how far afield,' explains Percival. 'I have not the liberty to object, not while my hopes are so diminished.'

Sophie offers her sympathies. The ousting of the King from London had seen Percival dismissed from the now-dissolved Star Chamber while Parliament assessed where his loyalties truly lay. He only recently began to recover his fortunes by charming himself a commission as an assize judge.

'A mere stepping stone,' Stephens had sniffed last night. Parliament claims the supernatural has grown in our idleness and there's gossip the King himself is a witch. If Parliament has its way, it won't be long before Percival re-establishes the commission for witch-hunters.

Father coughs an interruption. The North has suffered much during the war and a small part of me hopes he will express his concern at another son getting caught up in the conflict. Instead, he voices his annoyance at losing a timber shipment during Parliament's siege of York last year.

Sophie impatiently tugs at a tendril of her hair. Her hands, shaped similarly to her dead son's, are long and graceful. They move to caress the miniature of Francis that dangles from a thin black ribbon around her neck. Father clenches his teeth and at this silent command, she regains her composure and lowers her hands. Father's fingers, calloused from his apprenticeship days, graze his pointed beard until he sees me, his eyes sliding from my face to the red half of my attire. He retains a stoic expression, but his eyes darken as though remembering the coins he'd parted with for the city's aldermen to overlook Francis's betrayal.

I am honouring the dead as I make my presence known. Sophie clutches the miniature around her neck even tighter. Percival turns his head and steals my breath with a look. Francis had once met the judge years ago, yet his cool assessment of my features convinces me that he is able to discern the slight differences between us, such as the cut above my eyebrow and the darker shade to my eyes and hair.

'You are much like your brother,' he remarks when I doff my hat in greeting. It is a quick reprieve that allows me to catch my breath.

With grey eyes and long hair, his appearance puts him firmly between my seventeen years and Father's fifty. He could have come straight from court with his purple cloak. An anti-witch charm dangles from his neck, a green liquid in a pendant glass form. The charms are said to grow hot at a witch's approach.

He turns away and a flash of anger flares inside at his dismissal. Francis would not have hesitated to show his displeasure at being made to serve a man out of favour. I am not my brother, but I am no longer myself and I will not be so disregarded.

'I am taller,' I point out.

Father glares at me. *You are baiting him*, he says with a pinched grimace.

Percival is amused by my retort, and I bear his scrutiny, fully aware of the trick of fate that has paired him with the natural son of one of the city's wealthiest merchants. He is the first to look away, but not before inviting me to call him Will. I incline my head and notice Stephens's spying from the hallway. He disappears, just as I catch his dark look at the ease in which I place myself in the witch-hunter's company.

Sophie gets up, pleading a headache. She grasps my shoulders, her eyes hard as she rearranges my features in her mind until I'm wholly Francis. Her cracked lips are thorns against my cheek when she leans in for a farewell kiss.

'Watch him,' she says to Will with an almost playful caution. 'My stepson is worthy of your inspection.'

My eyes narrow. The Devil is said to have a hand in the good fortune of men and a careless remark is all that is needed for people to suspect me of using a spell to engineer my brother's death.

To Father's disappointment, Will declines his offer of claret. 'I will leave you to say your farewells in private. You have my condolences for your loss,' he says, a rushed formality which Father is quick to disregard.

'Nicholas would not agree with you. He has profited from it.'

He is disarmed by Will's unaffected smile. His familiarity with harsh speech conveyed by the ease of his leave-taking.

My father shows no reaction to the departure of his last remaining child. I have been a nuisance to him from the moment I was born. Now I am something more, yet I doubt he will ever reconcile the two versions of me.

'I am not grateful.' I gesture to my clothes. 'I am making myself a dumb-show, abandoning everything I am to be a mime of Francis's life. I will not thank you for it.'

'I did not expect you to,' he snaps, and I deflate from his easy retort. His attention shifts to the window behind me. 'Nicholas.' I wait. 'The light . . . you could almost be Francis.' I brace myself for another set-down. His voice turns hoarse. 'My toying with you . . . It was not malignly meant. Your mother loved plays far more than she loved me. For a while I loved her for it. It was just a moment, but a look at you and I find myself chained to it.'

I stare at him wordlessly. A trade, not kindness, I realise. One I'd refuse were it not for the thought of him witnessing Francis's slow death. I step closer to the window until I am enveloped in the morning sun. Something in his countenance breaks as I adopt Francis's posture. I have never been so far from myself, but in this moment I am enough. 'Father.' But the receding light robs him of his softness and he turns his back to me. 'The dead do not disappoint,' I tell him. 'Neither will I.'

My presence is a shackle, eased only by my exit from the family home. Outside, Stephens waits by the carriage door. He is careful not to look in Will's direction. He presses bread and cheese wrapped up in a cloth into my hands while I choke out an awkward farewell. He grasps my hand, a silent warning that leaves a greyish trace. The horses grind their feet into the ground and at their eager snorts I step inside the carriage where Will, impatient to be off, raps his knuckles on the side before I have even sat down. We lurch forward. Stephens, along with the sturdy brick townhouse where I have lived like a shadow most of my life, fades from view.

Chapter Three

London is a dragon's hoard of the King's gold and the country's colours. Through the carriage window I take in the bleak landscape of war-ravaged homes, smashed windows and military garrisons. A horrible sight, but preferable to the one sitting across from me.

'It is a waste. The war will beggar us all,' Will observes. It's his third attempt to engage me in conversation since we set off this morning and I answer it with a repeated murmur of acknowledgement.

His efforts to establish a familiarity surprise me. I had thought the witch-hunter, a retired one, would be more severe, burdened by the weight of his past service. Francis would have responded to Will's charm. But I was raised on Stephens's history. His hurts are mine and, even if I could, I have no wish to forget what sort of man Will is. I stare out the window, satisfied when he concedes the silence between us with a sigh.

A while later the carriage halts outside a dowdy-looking coaching inn in St Albans. Day has crept into night and the shrill winds rake through me until the innkeeper ushers us inside.

'We will eat first,' says Will, and a servant leads us to a quiet corner in the busy dining area.

'It's him,' I overhear the innkeeper tell a nearby patron. 'Him,' the patrons repeat, their whispers a reverent tide I warn off with a hunched spine. Will seems immune to their gossip and gulps down a generous helping of the innkeeper's stew. 'How is your Latin?' he asks, in between mouthfuls. Impatient for an answer, he raps his fingers on the wooden table.

'Sufficient,' I reply.

'Your father told me you have some understanding of the law? Middle Temple?'

A paused response. 'My father has overestimated me.' A rare mistake on his part. Aside from my time at Oxford, my education consisted of following Francis on his jaunts around town or going over my father's accounts.

Will gives up waiting for more words and busies himself with his correspondence. The interest of the surrounding patrons is a swarm, but Will remains untroubled. When you have power it is easy to deafen yourself to it.

'Parliament,' I blurt, observing the letter's seal.

'Curiosity is Pandora's jar,' he remarks, but regards the letter anew. 'A request.'

I have been drawn out, but despite the danger do not hold back. 'A repeated one?'

He nods. 'Parliament desires my aid in remobilising the commission for witch-hunters.'

Am I supposed to be in awe or afear of you? I wonder in the face of his scrutiny. My life has forever been a performance. The versions of myself cultivated to my father's wishes. *You must give me the lines or else I am lost.* But his countenance remains guarded and in want of a hint my response is bland. 'The King himself declared years ago there were no more witches in England.'

'Parliament does not respect the King's words,' he answers. 'War is a costly endeavour and they'd be foolish to ignore the revenue to be raised from selling off witch-hunting licences.'

I shift in my seat, aware of the patrons' prying stares. 'Foolish or not. The King's wishes should be respected. He is still the King,' I insist.

He puts down his ale. 'King or not, he has been bewitched by his wife Queen Henrietta Maria.'

Catholics have always been depicted as the allies of witches, their prayers likened to spells. A slander made true after Guy Fawkes enlisted a witch to help blow up Parliament. The discord between King and Parliament was hastened by their refusal to give the King control of the army to address the massacre of English Protestants by Irish Catholics four years ago. At the time it was rumoured that King Charles had consented to the atrocities. A baseless rumour, but difficult to dismiss due to the dominating presence of his Catholic queen.

Not a subordinate, I decide at Will's wry expression, an equal or at least the pretence of being so.

'Broken then,' he concedes when I snort in disbelief, 'by his wife and the Catholic supporters that surround him. That is what Parliament says. And it is what the people will believe.' He passes me the letter and a quill pen from his satchel. 'You will not be idle in your apprenticeship.'

I read the short missive. 'How should I answer it?'

'With my most sincere refusal,' he instructs, and signals for more ale. 'The supernatural is a menace, but I will leave them for the Roundheads who are more adept than I ever was at spying them from treetops,' he quips, referring to the witch found dancing upon the River of Newbury until a cascade of Roundhead bullets ended her merriment.

He scans my response. 'You have a strong hand,' he assesses.

'Parliament's requests will see it worn down. They will think your refusal a negotiation tactic.'

He nods. 'They believe a turn on the Northern circuit, and letters from those in need of my services, will break me.'

'Will you break, sir?' But the sudden appearance of a tavern maid serves as an arras behind which his thoughts hide.

The town of Doncaster is an opaque glare. Will and I take shelter inside the Golden Fleece, a brick-built, alabaster-columned guest-house. Our journey to York has been broken up by restless stays in inns and marked by the hostile reception of the town's watch and a waiting letter from Parliament which we are never able to outrace. A two-day downpour keeps us stranded and the inn's over-occupancy forces our seclusion in this private room. Will sits at the table and pores over Parliament's latest dispatch, which greeted us upon our arrival. He has not yet passed it over to me to decline. Perhaps he is pretending that this will be the last.

For want of anything better to do, I study the passers-by through the window as they shiver and jolt in and out of the shadow cast by the crumbling walls of Conisbrough Castle. Orange-sashed soldiers trudge down the main street, which is rain-slick and worn thin by carriage wheels and the kick of horses' hooves. I note down all I see in my diary. I'd realised that first night that Stephens had salvaged what was left of the scattered pages from the fireplace. The diary was Francis's gift to me, one I had filled with my plays. It is the one thing of my own I carry, apart from Francis's last letter and the memento of a failed spell which hangs like a noose around my neck. A cord to my past self that even at this great distance I find myself reluctant to sever. With a snap I close the book and turn to Will.

'Do you miss it?' I say, only realising I'd spoken my thoughts aloud when he raises his head. 'Witch-hunting?'

'Sometimes,' he answers, but Parliament's letter steals his interest.

'I wonder how someone becomes a witch-hunter.'

He leans back in his chair. 'Usually because someone tells you you'd be good at it.'

I join him at the table. 'A past ambition to be a playwright,' I explain when he murmurs my name etched across the green spine of my diary. 'My brother told me I would be good at it,' I add when he raises his grey eyes in surprise. 'He gifted me it to aid in my endeavours.' My words see the mood darken. Francis's praise was an anchor and I wonder if I encouraged him to his fate so that I might breathe.

'When we get to the assizes,' says Will lightly, 'you will hear tales more fantastical than any you have heard before. The accusers are the playwright. The jury is the audience.'

'And the judge?' I lean closer and catch the silver glints of his witch charm.

'Master of the Revels.'

'My father has chosen the wrong profession for me.'

'The wrong choice is the one you let others make for you.' He pauses. 'The merchant king will summon his princeling home. From what I know of him, he would not want his son to waste his life clerking on the assizes.'

'That place was never a home,' I confess. It's a court where I have spent my life hovering unsteadily on the edges. Even now, at its centre, I cannot find my balance. A push and I will falter. 'I have no intention of returning,' I finish, forgetting for a moment I am not free to make my own decisions. Nor am I free to show him too much of myself.

'And here I thought one of us would be saved from a slow march into obscurity on the Northern circuit.' Will's voice is without pity, and I like him more for it. He nudges a glass of wine towards me. 'Drink,' he presses and tosses Parliament's letter into the fire.

'Thank you,' I mutter, but his eyes are drawn to the flames. My finger presses the outline of Francis's knot against my chest and with a lightness that isn't my own I make a toast: 'To obscurity.'

My triumph is marked by his smile and the bitter liquid that slides down my throat.

Chapter Four

'The country looks like something is trying to push forth from underneath,' I observe of the Yorkshire landscape surrounding our carriage. Will and I had set off for York this morning. The rains of yesterday had eased off, leaving the cold weather to turn the muddy roads to ice.

'It is all the dead bodies trying to escape,' he drawls and the tension in my stomach coils. 'Though I have spent a lifetime trying to forget everything about these parts.'

'You grew up here?'

He grimaces at his slip and tilts his head to the window. 'Many of Fairfax's men were stricken with typhus before the siege's end. Their bodies are buried in mass graves outside York's city walls. Apparently, at night you can hear their ghosts screaming.'

'A childish dare,' I mutter, and tuck my hand inside my cloak when I notice him eyeing my scar.

His attention is taken by the outdoors as our driver outpaces the other carriages uphill to Micklegate Bar with a stream of curses. York's walls have stood since ancient times and still stand, despite Prince Rupert's past bombardment. It is now a garrison city that glitters from the chains surrounding it. As we approach the heavy stone gates, dozens of soldiers supervise the activities of sinewy-boned labourers who strengthen the city's defences. The carriage soon comes to a sharp halt, and we barely have time to adjust ourselves when an iron-breasted soldier approaches.

'State your business,' he orders, his fingers resting on the cudgel at his side. Travel, since the war began, is rare and soldiers are suspicious of enemy spies sneaking through. Will's relaxed demeanour is gone. His expression hardens into that of a man used to getting what he wants. The shift is a subtle reminder of my changed status and I sit tall and adopt his rigid posture.

He hands the soldier our travelling passes. 'I am Judge Percival. The Lord Mayor is expecting us.'

The soldier lowers his helmet in deference and announces our presence to the overhead sentry boxes. We pass through the dark archways where the crowded mass of people and horses reduce the final stretch of our journey to a snail's crawl. The outside din is smothered by the vibration of the cathedral bells. I stare at the Roundheads marching by twos under a grey sky drawn tight like a blanket. The city is marked by several ruined buildings and dents to the city walls from Fairfax's cannonballs.

'You enjoyed that,' I discern once the carriage comes to a halt.

'Power is intoxicating,' he concedes, before instructing the carriage driver to unload our valises.

His eyes gleam when he looks over his shoulder, no doubt expecting a witty response, but the only thing I have to offer is the truth: 'Power is not something I have ever possessed.'

'Steal it,' Will urges. 'Just as I have had to.' He presses on before coming to a stop with a short whistle. 'I was told to expect a rationing of the usual luxuries.'

His attention turns towards a crowd of passers-by who, as if on cue, part to reveal our lodgings.

'A rationing?' I repeat. The judge's inn is an incongruous sight in an otherwise quiet row of smart townhouses. Our lodgings are a delicate skeleton: its flesh a puddle of rocks, glass and rotting timber.

'Is there an inn nearby?' Will asks the driver.

His response is muted by the appearance of a thick-bodied, sombrely dressed man who makes a breathless introduction. 'My apologies for my lateness. I am Lord Mayor Hale. The repairs to your residence have unfortunately been delayed.'

Before the war, the arrival of the King's judges would have been heralded by a grand reception with trumpets, bells and music. The Lord Mayor makes no acknowledgement of our poor welcome and Will is bemused by the absence of the customary pomp.

'I would be honoured if you would reside in my home for the duration of your stay,' Hale insists. We are given no time to refuse as he instructs our driver to deliver our luggage to his residence. 'I will give you a tour of the city,' he proceeds and saunters off, leaving us to follow.

The city is a spoilt landscape of slighted towers. Hale is at pains to divert our attention away from the ramshackle buildings and bruised spirit of the city's people. 'York Minster.' Hale points out the sand-coloured proportions of the cathedral that dwarfs the city.

We sidestep a channel that runs wet with offal and blood. The Shambles, as termed by Hale, is a sprung jaw of houses that jut out at each other from a great height. The homes are perched upon timber storefront perches, the nearest of which is bedecked with strung-up carcasses. The stench of meat fades into the smells of the surrounding tanneries and is buried under smoke as we approach a blacksmith's forge.

Hale is not so new to his post as to go unrecognised by the city-dwellers, many of whom acknowledge him with a crisp formality. The abundance of orange-sashed soldiers who litter the streets like lanterns does little to erase the memory of Sir John Scrope's surrender of Bolton Castle, which followed only after they'd devoured the last of their horses. The Battle of Marston Moor last year established Parliament's tenacious grip over the North. York is now occupied, an intolerable situation that the army demands payment for. It had been the same in Oxford. Many of the residents had complained of the forcible billeting of soldiers in their homes. Worse still were the accounts of soldiers, in want of pay, pillaging civilians. York keeps its resentments and the King's colours close to its chest. They are defeated but not broken, not while the King continues to muster his forces. I brace myself for a fight.

A few people look curiously at me, and more so at Will. 'The witch-hunter,' a stranger whispers, his voice betraying a mixture of fear and nervous excitement which is shared amongst the onlookers.

'You must be relieved to see your old profession so in favour again.' Hale draws our attention to a shop advertising the services of a witch-hunter.

'I do not believe the sentiment unanimous,' Will says plainly.

'That Grey business from years ago is long forgotten – and it's not as though you had anything to do with it,' Hale avows.

Will smiles tightly. The end of witch-hunting was heralded by a scandal like no other. Joseph Grey was a child who claimed to have been kidnapped by witches. His case was taken up by a local witch-hunter who took the boy from village to village to point out his captors. Hangings followed in their wake, until Grey's accusations were unpicked after King James personally investigated the matter. Will had already left the profession by then, but the resulting outcry over the countless deaths of innocents marked its end, in England at least. However, Parliament's lack of sanctions and their claims of witches aiding Royalist soldiers are encouraging many to take up the profession. The North has always been feared for popery and witchcraft, and there are many who seek to take advantage of that.

'The people here have been much distracted lately. Some are quick to seek solace in old methods,' Hale confides.

Will stops. 'Those that do will find my arrival a disappointment.'

Hale quietens and I hide my relief at Will's words.

'Shall we seek shelter from the cold?' Hale suggests once he's recovered.

'Yes,' I accept on my master's behalf and tug at my cloak as though it's a shield.

The stone-carved fruit above the grey door to Hale's townhouse adds a whimsical dash to the sombre-looking homes along his street. The bricked exteriors are punctuated by expansive windows, and I catch a glimpse of bright russet curls from the second floor before Hale bustles us inside.

The interior is dominated by heavy wooden panels and a narrow staircase that twists and branches off across the storied home. The darkness of the mahogany furnishings is lightened by the cream-coloured walls and a tapestry across the hallway. My nose wrinkles at a strange odour, but before I can name it, I am distracted by a pair of deft hands that relieve Will and me of our cloaks. A servant shows us to our chambers so that we might change out of our travelling clothes before dinner.

Will is led to a chamber further down the hall while I am directed to a small guest room which overlooks the street. The room is plain except for a young woman whose attention is taken by a hanging wall tapestry.

'Lovely.' She turns, her silhouette framed by the ill-fated romance of Pyramus and Thisbe in threaded strands of gold, brown, blue, silver and red. Her face reddens at my scrutiny and her red hair is hurriedly veiled by a white servant's cap. 'A belated wedding gift,' she says of the tapestry. She is around my age, with a high forehead and skin rendered almost translucent by the light that streams through the window.

'A strange gift for a bride,' I remark.

She smooths down her apron and her dark eyes flit up and down my person. 'You do not resemble a witch-hunter.'

'What should one look like?' I ask. She is tall, almost my height, but shifts at my approach.

'Not so young,' she answers and to ease the tension I laugh and step back. I am used to eyes passing over me in search of my father or Francis, and something inside me unspools from her direct regard.

'I am not a witch-hunter,' I explain, 'and neither is my master. He is retired.'

'A witch-hunter never retires,' she admonishes, and I colour under her frank assessment. 'The people are excited by the news of Judge Percival's arrival. Though they have warned each other from making ill-favoured faces, cursing their neighbours in anger and spelling cattle lest they find themselves accused of witchcraft.'

Her smile banishes the serious set to her speech. 'You have forgotten divining the future,' I tease, pleased by her continued attention.

Her expression turns thoughtful. 'It was not always a crime. Scribes, before they became witch-hunters, would read the stars and tell monarchs their fates.'

Witches and scribes were once branches of the same tree, though the former's betrayal has seen to it they are destined never to touch. 'They were wrong to do so. All magic is a gift from the Devil. King James wrote so in his *Daemonologie*,' I say. The book was one of many tools King James used to encourage the belief that witchcraft was the Devil's progeny.

'And yet his predecessor Queen Elizabeth sought the aid of a witch to blow the invading Spanish Armada off course,' she counters. 'Nor did the monarchs preceding her shy away from making use of witches' spells.'

Her eyes hold me as though she is weighing me up. 'Did your master set you to question me?' I ask once I've gathered myself.

'My master?' Amusement flits across her face and she tugs at her apron. 'I am under his authority, but he does not marshal my thoughts.'

Will startles us both with his quiet approach. 'You have not changed,' he observes, in his suit of brown velvet. With a quick curtsy, the young woman is gone, while I beg a moment to change into my black doublet and silently curse the ease with which I stepped into Hale's trap.

'This is my wife, Sarah,' Hale introduces us once we join him downstairs a while later.

We are shepherded into the dining room, where servants rush to ready the fire and laden the table with food. Mrs Hale stands near the table. She is a rigid line of black fabric, crowned with a white-coloured coif. The look she shares with her husband is a subtle balm to her glacial poise.

The young woman I spoke with earlier slips into the room with a curtsy to excuse her lateness. She has replaced her servant's garb with rich blue silks and places herself near the bass viol in the corner.

'This is my daughter, Althamia.' Hale beams affectionately.

Althamia's cheeks are a pink flush and her eyes light with amusement as she studies both Will and me.

Will raises his hat with a courtier's flourish and nudges me into making a similar show. Althamia eclipses her mother's demure greeting with an elaborate curtsy. Mrs Hale frowns and leads us to the dining table, a passing look in my direction. At the hesitant look on her face, I want to assure Mrs Hale that I am not a flirt. I am not in the habit of collecting hearts nor breaking them from a lack of care. To ease her mind, I incline my head to show I've taken heed of her unaired concerns and, to prevent either lady's pride from being ruffled, I grimace as though it has cost me something.

Althamia and I are seated towards the end of the table near the fireplace, close enough to slip in and out of our elders' conversations who converse beneath the golden glow of the chandelier and dripping tallow candles. I keep my eyes from hers. I am not of the temperament for games.

A single servant remains to dance attendance upon us, and my plate is soon loaded with a Lenten fare of pickled herring and vegetables. I wonder how many helpings of fish I must suffer through before I can make a start on the biscuits that smell deliciously of aniseed and mace but have been placed just out of reach at the centre of the table. A glass of wine does nothing to wash away my longing.

'If you had not lingered in Doncaster, you would have glimpsed Jack-o'-Lent paraded around the city,' Althamia says, digging into the pickled herring with delight.

I am not sorry to have missed it and try to hide my relief. Every year the straw effigy is toured through the city only to be pelted with stones and hurled with abuse on Ash Wednesday until its torment is ended in a bonfire on Palm Sunday.

Althamia rests her palms over the white linen tablecloth and continues to fling out her words like a fisherman's net. I refuse to be caught. I am smarting from her earlier trick and to her dismay I busy myself with a second helping of the main course.

The conversation at the table's upper end is punctuated by the clinking of glass, scraping of cutlery and Mrs Hale's brittle silences. Will, in search of a respite, leans towards us and, in reference to Althamia's earlier words, apologises, 'It is to our sincere regrets the weather delayed us.'

'The merriment was set out below my window like a play. Although, when the King and Queen resided in town, I was allowed out to see it.' The slight tension in Althamia's voice belies her playful tone, and Mrs Hale sets down her knife.

'The situation here is delicate,' Hale says, quickly defusing his daughter's remarks, 'especially with soldiers in the mix. My work limits my ability to act as a chaperone.'

'It is safer for women to be kept at home,' adds Mrs Hale.

Althamia disregards her mother's refrain. 'If you stay until Easter, perhaps we can all see the townspeople set fire to poor Jack.'

'I am not one for amusements,' I say, but I struggle to hold on to my annoyance. She reminds me of the ladies in Oxford, trapped by war, yet determined to seek pleasure where they can.

Althamia's smile widens when her father voices no objection.

'It is a pagan practice,' complains Mrs Hale. 'And I am sure Judge Percival and his . . . apprentice will have moved on by then.'

I try not to be discomfited by her emphasis on my lack of title.

'I will certainly, but Nicholas will probably have abandoned me to pursue a new career as a playwright,' Will teases. 'He is quite the talent.'

His opinion holds firm despite the scepticism of the elder Hales. While I'm alert to the danger of Will's attention, I allow a small part of myself to believe him.

'You write?' Althamia asks.

'With much less success than I read,' I reply.

'Nevertheless I would like to read your work,' she says.

'You would not find it cheering. My stories usually end in tragedy.'

'I do not mind,' she insists, and her earnestness forces my refusal to rest clumsily on my tongue.

Mrs Hale turns to Will. 'I am surprised a man with your history would be amused by his ambitions.'

Before its dissolution by Parliament five years ago, the Star Chamber was used with great efficiency to suppress domestic news and opposition to King Charles's policies. They made special enemies of dissenters, poets and playwrights. William Prynne's criticism of Queen Henrietta Maria's participation in court masques was punished by the removal of both ears and a brand on each cheek – something Will must have helped approve.

Will eases the tension with a flash of teeth. 'Nicholas is an uncommon and brave man. He disappointed the mercantile ambitions his father held for him with his desire to uphold the law and will now disappoint me with his notion to tell fables.'

'Your family is in trade?' probes Mrs Hale.

'His father is the merchant Francis Pearce Senior,' Will elaborates at my reluctant nod. 'His mother, the Honourable Sophie Pearce, is a scion of the Raynalde family.' Their names are greeted with approval by the Hales.

'I suppose with such a family you are at liberty to choose a profession,' says Mrs Hale, but the softening of her features is of no comfort. Nor is the smooth way she enquires after my age.

'Seventeen,' she repeats, and I imagine Francis's mocking retort, *Of age to be married and of a profession unlikely to see her daughter readily widowed.*

Will observes the proceedings with a smirk.

'The Honourable Sophie Pearce is my stepmother,' I clarify, unwilling to be claimed as her kin.

Hale frowns. 'I had not realised your father was previously widowed.'

A flicker of Francis's wildness courses through me. 'My father has only been married the once. My mother is dead.' There's a familiar comfort in the silence that descends as the Hales rush to drink away their distaste at my illegitimacy.

'I am sorry,' Althamia continues in the face of her parent's disapproval, 'for your mother's passing.'

The directness of her admission unsettles me. No one had ever attached any importance to my mother's memory before.

'Thank you,' I murmur.

The older Hales exchange a look before Mr Hale steers the conversation back to the assizes. 'Judge Percival, there will be a witch trial for you to oversee.'

Mrs Hale glowers at her husband and, at her silent instruction, the servant pokes at the fire. Sweat dampens my brow as the flames lick at my back.

'Parliament made no mention of the case when I accepted this posting.' Will's expression is bland, but his hand tightens around his wineglass.

'Lady Katherine Teversham was only recently accused,' Hale explains.

'A rushed decision,' says Mrs Hale, and is about to say more when her husband shakes his head.

In the face of her parent's stalemate, Althamia turns to Will and me: 'Lady Teversham is determined to prove her daughter-in-law a witch. She has convinced herself and the justices that her former maid, Lady Katherine, used a love knot to coerce her son, Lord Gilbert, into marriage.'

Elizabeth Woodville used the same methods on King Edward IV, a bewitchment which led to her coronation. Despite the turmoil that followed their union, Lady Katherine must have thought it worth the risk.

'Lady Teversham also claims her daughter-in-law spelled her husband to death. He is said to have been more opposed to the misalliance than his wife,' Hale adds.

Will finishes his drink. 'Was any thread discovered on her person? Knotted or unravelled?'

'Neither knotted or unravelled, but even so, undoing a thread would have hurt Lady Katherine and she looked no worse for wear,' says Althamia, reciting common knowledge that a spell's potency could be negated by unravelling the knots, even though such actions could be fatal to the witch.

Hale balks at his daughter's knowledge but Will ignores it, plodding on, 'Were any other instruments found? A charm pouch hidden among her husband's possessions?'

'She is no Anne Boleyn,' Althamia answers, her words recalling the rumour that the Queen had turned Henry VIII's head with such a charm, only to lose hers when it wore off. Unlike knots, charms and curses wear off quickly. Lord Gilbert's bewitchment, if he is indeed so afflicted, should already be showing signs of wear. If Lady Katherine had used a threaded knot, his passion would be much more difficult to undo.

'Althamia,' Hale reprimands his daughter, 'what Lady Katherine has done should not be made light of.'

'Husband, she has not yet been found guilty,' reminds Mrs Hale.

'Has she any relatives?' Will asks. The hairs on the back of my neck rise at his smooth enquiry. A witch is many things, but they are never alone. Entire bloodlines have been ended by a single allegation.

Althamia breaks through the sudden quiet. 'None living.'

To forestall further enquiries, Mrs Hale adds, 'And no close acquaintances either. It is a tiresome business. Lady Teversham is determined to undo the union and has exhausted her complaints in the church courts and at the quarter sessions and will now wear down the justices at the assizes. She is making a spectacle with her unchecked behaviour. The misalliance was to be expected with a son such as hers, but to delve up such old methods and taffle herself to a supposed expert—'

'Enough!' Hale interrupts. 'The grand jury found sufficient merit in the case for it to proceed to trial.'

At this, the women fall silent.

'It sounds like the subject of a play,' Will remarks. 'There is witchcraft enough in a smile.' The quip is a worn platitude, but Will loses himself to a memory.

'Is the lady at liberty until the sessions begin?' I probe when Will remains distracted.

Mrs Hale grimaces when her husband says, 'The young woman is being kept at Clifford's Tower until the trial.'

Will frowns. 'I would have expected Lord Gilbert to have used his influence to secure a more comfortable confinement for his wife.'

'The elder Lady Teversham's late husband was a former alderman,' Hale divulges.

'And people have not forgotten that Lady Katherine Teversham used to be so beneath them.'

'You are in a precarious position,' Will considers, 'unable to offend until you know which way things will fall.'

'We are for Parliament,' Mrs Hale answers for her husband and returns to the previous subject. 'I am sure it was easier in your time, when a man could condemn a woman for a witch with a single look.'

Althamia stirs in her chair while Mr Hale rushes to smooth over his wife's words.

'Your turn of speech, you are from Pendle?' Will asks. The shade of the Pendle Witch Trials casts itself over dinner even though it occurred more than thirty years ago.

'Nearabout,' Mrs Hale admits.

Her short concession affords a glimpse of the dead, whether innocents or true witches, in her past. Were they her neighbours, friends, relatives?

'Terrible mistakes were made by the witch-hunters in those parts. King Charles was right to place the responsibility of prosecuting witches in the hands of the assizes,' Will states.

Mrs Hale goes straight for his neck. 'You speak as though you do not count yourself among them.'

I press against my old wound and ground my back to my chair as though to lean into the blaze behind me.

'Madam, the matter in Pendle was rather before my time.'

'Yet you are still of those times,' she maintains, and I almost nod in agreement. Stephens's stories are forever in my mind.

Will ignores Hale's coughed interruption. 'I carry those women with me. Every single one of them. You have my assurances I have not forgotten, I cannot.'

He resumes eating and Mrs Hale's knuckles blanch around her knife at his retreat. Will retains his easy countenance, and a few tense moments pass until Mrs Hale excuses herself and her daughter with a measured look in her husband's direction.

Hale waits for their footsteps to subside before apologising. 'My wife lives in the past. It makes her overly cautious. A virtue she tries to instil in me.'

'Then I can learn from her,' Will jests, 'and determine how to regain my favour with Parliament.'

His admission elicits a laugh from Hale, who forgets his wife's lesson. 'You would be better served wishing for patience, for many of the townspeople here are convinced the King will prevail and put an end to the country's unhappy divisions.'

'Impossible,' Will banters. 'The King's allies have fallen away or are at least plotting to following his defeat in the North. The King overestimates his abilities, and his ruined reputation is the result.'

Hale reaches for more wine. 'Ruined or not, defeated or victorious, he will always be the King. I wonder at Parliament's wisdom in refusing to come to terms with him.'

'I would argue the reverse,' I say when Hale gulps down his drink. Their surprise at my uninvited admission forces me to elaborate: 'Parliament controls London and the seas, their number revived with fresh recruits from Scotland. From what I have heard, the King is hard-pressed to garner reinforcements from Ireland, supplies and even loans from the Continent. The Royalists lack the means to resolve the matter entirely to their satisfaction, yet persist in negotiating from a perceived position of strength.'

Will smiles appreciatively, but Hale's expression stops me from mentioning Fairfax's new army. I've seen that look before: the narrowing of the eyes and faint curl of distaste around the mouth. His familiarity with my father's name doesn't erase my illegitimacy. By myself I am not enough, his stern countenance reminds me. Though to his regret, it is not a look that can bruise.

'There is someone you should meet,' says Hale once the servants have cleared the table. He puts down his pipe and Will gestures for me to follow them.

The pungent scent I encountered upon first entering Hale's home strengthens as we cross the length of the hallway. It is a smell I am familiar with, smothered as it is under the scent of vinegar and rosemary. It reminds me of Francis and the memory of him makes me unsteady.

Hale's pace slows and he addresses Will over his shoulder. 'Lady Teversham had her husband exhumed when we first heard of your appointment.'

'I will be sure to thank Lady Teversham for her diligence,' says Will with a backwards look. 'Dark arts always leave a mark.' They descend to the basement and I pause and then force myself to follow where Hale stands with his palm resting on a coffin laid across the wooden workbench.

Will, standing next to Hale, acknowledges me with a grimace before pressing a handkerchief to his nose. Their conversation descends into wordless interplay as I take in the dead Lord Teversham from the room's outskirts. He is covered by the half-open lid and draped in the darkness of the room, save for the candles. With a squint, I make out a man far past his youth with a waxy greenish tint to his skin. His blind eyes bulge towards me until Hale wrinkles his nose and closes the coffin, leaving the top part of his face exposed. His actions fail to exorcise the smell and I try not to gag. I step backwards and bump into the corner table. My clumsiness draws no attention. Hale chuckles at Will's remark and raps his knuckles against the coffin. The sound is muffled and I lean back on the table cluttered with basins, sponges, a stack of medical texts and a small glass containing a stuffed mouse. The creature is decked in Cavalier colours and a white ruff. The sight does not ease me. When I was younger, the dead and those close to them would sing. They still do, for all my attempts to suppress them to lulls. His Lordship's withered remains are all but drained of song, but a stray lingering note of what was once a symphony lingers to invade my thoughts.

My decline is a subtle illness, a golden net I cannot cast aside. I play dead. And—

The voices of the dead are almost musical, their refrain pulls at my insides as though I am unplied yarn. A familiar feeling that I am helpless to ward off.

I flinch from the sensation of being pulled apart and clutch at my chest.

. . . slip from underneath. It changes shapes, its hawk talons a knot around my neck that flash gold.

I am always surprised by how sudden it is. A note and the world recedes from me until I am no more than a spectator.

Will and Hale have turned their attention to the case bundles spread across the coffin. I press on my scar as the rising tempo drains the light. When I was a child, the dead were a roar in my head. Listening to them was akin to trying to breathe under water. I drowned many times until I learned to smother them in turn. I increase the pressure, but still cannot drown Lord Teversham out. My fingers dig into my flesh, the pain a sharp embrace I lean into until his lento pace devolves.

I blink to see Will and Hale looking at me. I am no witch, not in accordance with King James's *Daemeonologie*. I have not sold my soul to the Devil for powers. What I am has never openly been whispered of, yet it is enough that people would hang for it.

I turn to Hale. 'Do you make a habit of keeping dead bodies in your home, sir, where your wife and daughter sleep?' The breathless address echoes as though I am on a stage. Sounds are louder, colours brighter once the dead have finished making their address. For myself, I feel deflated and must make myself bigger to fill up the space.

Hale sobers under my rebuke. 'I kept him here to protect Lady Teversham from making a spectacle of her husband's memory. I will ensure he is reburied with the respect his station warrants once the trial is over.'

'My apprentice is young,' Will says by way of apology, but our embarrassed host exits when I make no addition to my master's polished excuse. I am relieved. I would rather be thought ungracious than a witch.

Will's silent chastisement is welcome, as is his motion to sit with a dead corpse between us. Will passes me half of the case bundles, the weight enough to steady me. I stare at the mark on my hand. Stephens and I have never spoken of what I am. Though his suspicions were such that he marked my hand with a heated candle snuffle so that I would remember the kiss of the flames and take heed of it. Had he not placed himself before me like a rough shield, I would have slipped years ago. His love was a knot, one I unthreaded because I feared his protection had made me small.

Will looks up from his paperwork. 'If you harbour any hopes of winning fair Althamia's hand I would refrain from riling her father. The girl has much to offer. Or rather, her uncle does. He is a respected patron of the arts.'

'I will leave you to vie for her hand. I have no interest in marriage,' I reply.

He waves off my dismissal. 'I am much too used to my own company to suit a wife. In any case, I have frittered away too much of my fortune and have no hope of winning it back, given the Puritans' aversion to dice. But you on the other hand are young, rich and handsome.'

'The Hales' good graces hold no appeal to me, neither does their daughter or her uncle,' I snap, and his scoff smothers the flutter of movement from the doorway.

I lower my head, but the words before me are a sea of ink. It is not in my power to revive the dead, only to listen to them. I would have brought Francis back if I could. Lord Teversham is a lull in the background and I rifle through the court papers to quieten him. The songs of the dead are dandelions in the wind, and to stop myself from reaching out I turn to Will. 'The news of the witch case surprised you.'

Will sobers instantly. 'I should have hidden my emotions better.'

Holding up the case bundles, I continue, 'They seemed to have fixated upon Lady Katherine's guilt from the beginning.'

'You think she is innocent?' says Will and reaches for the paper-work.

'I think . . .' but my words trail off. Lord Teversham sang of his grievances. But lest I risk myself, I can do nothing for him.

'I am too bold.'

'An admirable quality,' Will replies.

'Not in an apprentice.' Or a witch. Reaching inside my pocket, I silence the corpse with a coin over his mouth.

'An obol for Charon,' Will remarks.

A bribe for the dead's silence, and now my own.

Chapter Five

My bedchamber is light and airy with a window that overlooks the street. It is still a cage, one I spent last night and most of the morning pacing as I remembered the stories Stephens filled my head with as a child. Of small rooms and the witches pressed into them by men like Will, emerging only once a confession and the names of their accomplices had been extracted. An outcome engineered by a lack of sleep, loss of blood and in most cases the maiming of limbs.

My pacing is interrupted by a knock and a servant who departs with a reminder of breakfast and a press of paper in my hands. My mouth twists to see the letter 'M' written in my father's strong hand. My mother's name began with a 'G'.

Father has made my life a puzzle. Though I should count myself fortunate he did not attempt to trade it away. I was born with my mother's cord tied around my neck. Babies born in such a manner are considered unnatural, a manifestation of knot magic made flesh. Had Father been there, he would not have intervened when the midwife moved to smother me. Stephens, with a mixture of threats and a heavy purse, saved me and kept the circumstances of my birth secret.

My mother could have tried to forestall her death from childbirth by trading my life for hers, or trying to save me. Whatever her intentions, it was a failed endeavour which has rendered me a purgatory for the ill at rest, now at the mercy of a witch-hunter. My father, were I to confess to him my true nature, would revile me for it. Or worse, fashion me into his blade. The dead do not rest easy, and I am full of their secrets.

I pull out Francis's knot from inside my shirt, his light strands threading my skin with gold. I bring it to my ear as though Francis's song has made a seashell of the thread. The soft, soaring texture of his aria belies its strength. Even without a knot, I would have carried echoes of his song with me.

I am a vision of white squares, a formation with an infantry at its centre and the calvary on either side. I shift in and out it, from the field hospital to home, and back again to a shrunken arrangement. The fevered cries of my friends are fired artillery over my head as I am shuttled to its centre. Our losses marked by a succession of stripped beds. My absences grow longer, though I pray for a return. My mother's prayers and Father's looks pin me in place until I grow smaller and slip free.

The pressure leaves me as his aria, a bright hymn, draws to an end. For all his youth, my brother met his death with a steadiness that surprises me. My failure to revive him haunts me, as does my relief. Only a witch can revive the dead. Even the immortal Pollux was almost dragged into the underworld alongside his brother until he cut the strands between them. I do not fear being pulled down. My mother's curse has seen to it that I am more for the dead than the living. Besides, I cannot let my brother die twice. His song is a memory and I will not let time blunt its edge.

I slip the knot inside my shirt and Father's letter in a hidden compartment of my valise. I depart my cage for a smaller one, the dining room where a look from Will over breakfast is enough to condemn me. But I will survive to place myself in an even smaller one until I can discover my mother's name and undo what I am.

The merchant prince enters the stage to be greeted by a look of admonishment from his hosts, a nod from his master and a smile from Althamia. I sit next to her and watch Will listen patiently to Hale's prattle. A timed pause, at which the servant who handed me my post earlier enters.

'Ah,' Hale exclaims and motions him forward as though he is a stagehand and they a prop. 'Word has just arrived from my brother-in-law, Lord George Carew,' he relays.

Not a stagehand, a fool, I decide at Will's schooled expression.

Althamia shifts uncomfortably in her gown of green silk, her eyes moving from her father to Will.

'I did not know you were related to Lord Carew. You must give him my regards,' Will offers.

Mrs Hale talks over her husband. 'We will, though we see him rarely.'

'The present situation is to be blamed for many delayed family reunions,' Will observes, while Althamia wraps her fingers around her knife.

Hale rushes the scene to its conclusion. 'The letter is for you, Judge Percival.'

Will finishes his bread before taking the letter from Hale's outstretched hand. He does not seem to mind my prying as I steal a look.

Dear Judge Percival,

In absence of a response, I must assume my previous letter to you was waylaid. I write again to offer you employment. My home parish of Rawton, Lancaster, is beset by accusations of witchcraft. I require a man of your experience to investigate. You will be well compensated for your time. I have enclosed a map and would be pleased if you could begin your journey here in haste.

Lord George Carew

'It is an invitation to join him in Rawton,' Will shares, his fingers stiff around the paper. 'He believes his parish to be beset by witches.'

Mrs Hale and Althamia are subdued while Hale waits expectantly for an answer. My fingers choke the glass's spine in the growing silence. We are puppets, yet must pretend we cannot see the strings. I set down the glass when Althamia notices it strangled in my grip.

Refuse him, I pray. Until Father calls me home, I must make myself so amenable that Will has no need to look too closely at me. I will not survive if I am forced to witness what kind of man he is.

'I could write to convey your regrets,' I blurt as all eyes turn to me. 'You are busy and I have the stamina to bear such requests.'

'You are hasty,' Hale blusters.

'But prescient,' Will interjects. 'I did receive a letter from Lord Carew weeks ago and my response must have been waylaid. You will write to repeat what I told him then — I am too removed from past experiences to be of any use.'

Hale's forehead turns shiny. 'But—' he protests.

'My present duties keep me occupied,' Will finishes and wipes his hands clean.

'Once the Lent is over you will be at liberty until the midsummer assizes,' Hale entreats. 'It would not be too onerous to travel to Rawton. I am sure your apprentice would value the chance to visit Lancaster.'

I stare down at my plate and offer no response.

'Husband,' complains Mrs Hale. 'You are badgering our guests.

These worries will pass with the war.' She turns to Will. 'I am sure my brother regrets sending the invitation. He will be relieved by your refusal. I will write to him of it myself.'

She and Will exchange a measured look while her husband visibly deflates.

'The aldermen of the town would like to meet you,' Hale says, changing the subject.

Will puts down his knife. 'I will not be so ungrateful as to say no twice this morning. Is it to discuss the assizes?'

'Among other matters,' says Hale, his face averted.

'Then we shall set off at once,' says Will with a nod in my direction.

'The invitation did not extend to your apprentice,' Hale blusters.

'I do not mind,' I interrupt to Hale's visible pleasure.

'You shall enjoy what remains of your liberty before our work begins,' Will remarks and then whispers under his breath, 'while I shall enjoy hell.'

Althamia and I bite down our amusement.

'Mr Pearce? Mr Pearce!'

Althamia repeats my name twice more, her voice a siren's call. I hover below her window, embarrassed. I had half expected Francis to appear beside me and answer.

'Wait for me. I will join you on your walk,' she calls from the first-floor window. Before I can object, she's gone, no more than a blurred figure behind the glass. I had plotted my escape soon after Will and Hale's departure. I was desperate to put some distance between the strain of inhabiting a dead man's skin and the discomfort of staying in a house that reminds me of death.

The front door opens and Althamia, wrapped up in a fur-lined cloak and velvet hood, hurries towards me unperturbed by skies that foretell rain. Her servant Agnes, a young girl of fourteen with a heart-shaped face and a guarded expression, dutifully follows behind her.

Mrs Hale watches us warily from the doorway. 'The Apothecary then home,' she reminds Althamia, looking ill at ease at her departure.

Althamia hurries off and I struggle to match her pace. York is on a grander scale to Doncaster, perhaps even Oxford, and the sense of history in each stone presses upon me and slows our march through the bustle of people. Althamia circumvents the crowd like she's been caught up by the wind. I trail behind her, trying to suppress my growing unease. For all the North's reputation for being full of the supernatural, I am at odds here. Althamia's attention is diverted by a man standing atop a gleaming pulpit in the city square. The halo of rosemary sprigs about his hat adds a dash of colour to the sky's blanket grey.

'The Earth is a common treasury for all, but King Charles and his papish wife have corrupted it! His French whore has made the Devil welcome and induced the King into using witchcraft to enact a false peace!' the speaker cries above the crowd. The Queen and the foreign consorts preceding her have always been plagued by allegations of magic. Witchcraft was always thought to be embedded in the female line, and it is only now people speak openly of the male line being spoiled by it. 'The Devil and his kin are among us! We will have no rest until their knots are unthreaded!' A rousing recruitment speech, but I am too well practised to flinch from the crowd's speculative stares. England is a country of unfolding dynasties, from the Plantagenets to the Tudors, and now the Stuarts. If King Charles cannot regain his influence, who will follow? It is between Parliament, the papists and the Devil.

The gospeler, having drawn the attention of loitering soldiers, jumps down and hands out pamphlets. One is pressed into Althamia's hands, and she mouths the signs used to identify a witch: deformed bones, threaded knots secreted about their person, a witch's mark – proof that their familiar, gifted to them by the Devil, has fed upon them. She laughs until a nudge from Agnes restores her composure. The pamphlet is crushed under her heel once we are out of sight of the crowd. Althamia is mindful to look at everything but me, and she surveys the scene and the city as though she's a stranger to it.

'It seems different somehow,' she murmurs to Agnes, who nods in agreement, and I wonder how often they are released from the confines of home. Althamia's nervous energy echoes that of mine in the days after Francis's funeral. I had kept to my rooms while Father had smoothed over the inconvenience of my succession. The brief joy I felt at being released was tempered by my deliverance into the hands of a witch-hunter.

I dismiss my earlier appraisal of Althamia as she hands her muff to Agnes, who shivers in the bitter early spring weather. 'You treat people's clothes like costumes,' I say, and offer my own in turn. An awkward reminder of our first encounter, but one I am proud of it until Agnes, half framed by Althamia, raises her brow. I did not mean to rebuke Althamia for her kindness and curse myself inwardly.

'It is cold and Agnes feels it more than I,' she replies, but accepts my offer and studies her hands encased in my brown leather gloves. 'Though it is fun to dress up.' She runs off with Agnes at her heels, her red curls falling free from her hood.

Without thinking, I run after her. York is all sly corners with streets that widen and squeeze like an unwanted embrace. My pursuit of them is a flash of colours as I sidestep the soldiers and the people of York, many of whom are dishevelled and patch-worn in what was once their Sabbath best. The stench of mud from the earthworks that surrounds the city almost drowns the market traders hawking their wares of fruits, meats, fabrics and news-books.

My chase ends at Stonegate Street. Althamia's cheeks flush pink and she adjusts her hood and grasps Agnes's hand before slipping into a well-lit bookshop. I wait a moment to catch my breath before entering. The shop is practically empty apart from half a dozen customers who circle the stacks and the shopkeeper, who peers up from his station in the corner to murmur a quick greeting. A mischievous smile tugs at Agnes's features and she disappears between the stacks with the air of someone resigned to a long visit. She gestures to the left and I catch a fleeting glimpse of Althamia's green hood between the shelves.

'*The Poor-man's Plaster-box.*'

I stop halfway down the aisles packed with household books. Althamia lowers the book from her face. I study her profile through the narrow gap in the shelves.

'This would make a welcome addition to my library,' she whispers as a patron walks past.

'The books in your father's basement are yours?' I ask, remembering the thick volume of Thomas Brugis's *Vade Mecum* and other medical textbooks in her father's study.

She nods with a rueful smile and takes off her gloves.

'Do you harbour ambitions of being a physician?' I tease gently.

'No more than I long to be someone's wife,' she remarks, and I blush even as I recall her mother's interested smile. I have nothing to offer a wife besides my father's begrudging inheritance sealed by my brother's death. Nor can I offer myself, unless I'm willing to wager my life on a woman's acceptance of what I am.

Althamia brushes over my mumbled apology and subconsciously touches the black ribbon around her sleeve. 'The books were a bequest from my late uncle, Oliver Hale. He was a surgeon and tended to Lord-General Thomas Fairfax's wounds during the siege and with less success to his brother.' Her voice softens at the mention of the Parliamentarian commander's younger brother, Charles Fairfax, and I stop myself from asking how closely she knew him. He was only a few years older than me when he died, and a decorated Roundhead at that.

'My uncle's passing has not lessened the general's favour towards us,' she shares, and sinks to the floor, her skirts a sea of green fabric around her feet. A patron wanders over to rifle through the adjoining shelves and she makes a show of burying her face in her book.

'It is your hair. Puritans wear it short,' she whispers when the stranger tuts at me in distaste. The Puritans, for all their usefulness, are a thorn in Parliament's side. Archbishop Laud, with the King's approval, pressed for the return of ceremonies, rituals and stained-glass windows in the English Church. Ornamentations the Puritans attributed to Catholicism. Laud was executed last month, Christmas celebrations have been deemed illegal, and Puritan soldiers across the country are seeing to the destruction of churches and religious regalia. Yet these victories have not gentled their sour disposition nor eased their paranoia of popery.

Althamia takes out the cross that she'd buried under her necker-chief, and places it proudly on display.

'There, now we are both a spectacle,' she declares and giggles when the stranger stalks away. I crouch to peer at her through the lower shelf as she confides, 'My uncle swore the eyes of the dead revealed their secrets.'

The serious set to her face makes me fear she's guessed at my pretence until she dismisses the ridiculousness of this claim with a smile. She stares at me expectantly and I wonder what her reaction would be if I said she was right to dismiss her uncle. The dead sing their grievances, making those who hear them no more than a conduit.

Her fingers trace the words on the book spine nearest to her. I beckon her close and she dips her head towards me.

'*When, in disgrace with fortune and men's eyes . . . I all alone beweep my outcast state . . . Haply I think on thee—and then my state . . . That then I scorn to change my state with kings.*'

'It is beautiful,' she murmurs.

'But misplaced,' I explain and point out the title of the book beside her. 'Shakespeare's book of sonnets. I can recite most of them by heart. When we were younger, my brother and I would collect words like kickshaws.'

'A sedate hobby for a child,' she remarks, and hands me the book.

'The one pastime I forced him into.' Remembrances of Francis come unbidden, and I wonder if this is a consequence of living at such close quarters with the dead, surprised at how clear the memory is.

'A far-sighted one for a playwright.'

'A natural one for the son of a Flemish actress,' a truth my step-mother let slip during an overheard argument with my father. I wait, but if she is shocked by my history, her eyes do not betray it.

'Is your mother why you became a writer?' she says, after a pause.

I rifle through the book. My mother's songs were the first kick-shaws I collected. The ones Stephens burnt me for when I let some of her words slip. It wasn't until my first visit to the playhouse that I realised her songs were pilfered from plays. The memory of her song is a slow stir in my blood. She still comes to me in my dreams sometimes, but save for murmurous silences, she leaves nothing of herself. Nor will she leave me alone. All I want of her now is her name.

I close the book with a snap. 'I am not a playwright. I enjoy watching them too much to attempt to better them.'

Her mouth opens as though to voice an objection, only to pause and then ask me about my favourite writers.

'Ben Jonson, George Wither, Euripides and John Taylor, the water poet.'

She leans towards me. 'The water poet?'

'He wrote an amusing dialogue between Prince Rupert's dog Boye and a Roundhead cur called Pepper.' She laughs, and I add, 'If I had the choice, I would like to disappear into an adventure, just like him.'

The yearning in my voice catches us both off guard. 'Were you close to your uncle?' I say to break the awkwardness of my reverie.

'No.' Her resolute response forces me to look up. 'He used to delight in confounding me about the many ways to determine a cause of death, only to grow sullen when I grew older and stopped relying on him for the answers. It made me see him differently. Or rather I realised how he saw me, and I did not like it.' The colour in her cheeks rises at revealing herself so openly. 'Do you miss home?'

'No,' I confess, and lean close enough to see the dark lashes that frame her eyes. 'I miss Oxford more.'

I draw back and remember the sense of freedom I felt in being more than just a rich man's by-blow. I had been surrounded by men convinced they would make their mark upon the world. For a moment I had counted myself among them, like an actor waiting backstage for my cue. But then the King had arrived, flanked by his court of increasingly impoverished nobles. The daily entertainments of cards, tennis and plays had done little to hide the throng of soldiers and mercenaries.

Althamia's lips part, but I'm saved from having to elaborate by the appearance of two wide boots which stop in front of her. The man's breeches are dotted with ink and the set to his face is enquiring when I hasten to her side.

'Mr Broad,' Althamia smooths the wrinkles in her skirt, 'this is Mr Pearce, clerk to Judge Percival.'

The suspicious set to Mr Broad's mouth lessens and I incline my head in acknowledgement as Althamia finishes the introductions. 'Mr Pearce is a writer.'

Broad's condescending smile puts me in mind of my father. I colour slightly at his derision.

Althamia must be blind to it, for she goes on: 'Perhaps you might find his talent worthy of print.' Turning to me, she adds, 'Mr Broad operates a print shop upstairs.'

'Our printing schedule is full,' says Broad.

Althamia is not so quick to accept defeat. 'My father, the Lord Mayor, would be grateful if you considered Mr Pearce's work. Lord-General Fairfax, I am certain, would also approve.'

Mr Broad isn't so skilled at masking his emotions, for he addresses me as though I'm the only one present. 'You keep company with the witch-hunter.'

'I am clerk to a *judge*, the esteemed William Percival.'

'What a shame,' he says, and draws our attention to a pamphlet stand in the corner.

'These are the words of Mr John Rush. He's a leading witch-hunter in these parts. He has been commissioned by Parliament and I have *twice* reprinted his last pamphlet.'

'I have neither read nor heard of him,' I admit.

'In the last one, he wrote of a confrontation he had with an imposter near Lancaster. He tied up the false witch-hunter by his toes and thumbs and threw him into the river. The man floated and ran for his life.'

'Did Mr Rush use the same method to verify his reputation?' Althamia asks, brow raised.

'I cannot keep up with public demand for his stories,' Broad divulges to me, ignoring Althamia's remark.

'I would pay for an account of the witch-hunter Judge Percival in his own words or those of his apprentice. Handsomely,' he finishes, with a considered look at the cut of my clothes.

My pulse quickens as I weigh up his offer. I'd be risking Will's displeasure by trading on his infamy, my father's too, though I suspect my choice to disobey would be met with a grudging respect. Despite his disdain for my literary talents, he wouldn't hesitate to come to terms with Broad. He had not reached his position by placing loyalty above self-interest. I am in no position to accept, nor do I wish to mould myself to Father's likeness.

'I am not a witch-hunter nor is my master. Not anymore,' I impart and take pleasure in watching Broad's face fall.

'Well, sir, if you're no witch-hunter or poet, then what are you?'

I stumble for an answer, unsure of who I am anymore. 'I like plays.' Regret lingers in my mouth the moment I finish speaking.

'I'm not in the market for plays, but I would consider any summaries you write of the assizes. I'm sure the ladies of York would be interested in reading about a witch from a witch-hunter's apprentice.'

I rub my neck and blurt, 'Lady Katherine's guilt has not yet been decided.'

The point is conceded with a nod. 'I look forward to reading your account of the trial in any case.'

'Thank you,' I murmur, more for Althamia's benefit. She forces his acknowledgement by handing him back his book and then heads outside with Agnes quick on her heels. I realise I am holding the book of sonnets in my hand and pass Broad some coins before hurrying out.

Althamia is agitated and she sends Agnes in to purchase the items on her mother's list when we near the apothecary. Once the young maid is out of earshot, Althamia reveals, 'My mother will be relieved by your master's lack of interest in witch-hunting. The senior aldermen hope to persuade your master to investigate a few local cases, and my father is determined for him to accept my uncle Lord Carew's invitation. My uncle's request has unseated him. He has never asked anything of us before.'

'And yourself? Are you pleased or fearful of witches running amok?'

'I do not believe in witches.' A bold statement. She flushes and regards me as though I am a pitfall she has stumbled into.

'A blunt admission. I will not censure you for it,' I say and hold her stare long enough to convince her of my sincerity. King James's *Daemonologie* warned that those who deny the power of the Devil also deny the power of God. Women have always been believed to be more susceptible to the Devil's temptations.

Lord Teversham is a remembered lull in my head. 'Do you believe Lady Katherine is innocent?' I press.

She pauses at the approach of passers-by. 'Yes. There were rumours,' she whispers, 'that Lord Gilbert had a hand in his father's death. He is a Royalist, though his father blocked his attempts to pledge himself to the King's cause. His mother had the whispers squashed and her husband's death blamed on a witch's curse.'

'Why did you not speak of this yesterday?'

'Because I am a woman and easily silenced,' she replies, and I colour from her look that seems to say, *Will you not speak up?* 'I apologise,' she says after a moment. Her chastised expression confuses me until I remember the rules guarding women's behaviour are more stringent than the ones for men, even those wearing a dead man's clothes.

'Do not do that. I do not want you to . . .' I flush, recalling the ease with which her father dominated her and her mother's talk last night.

For most of my life I have been voiceless, my wants put forth through an intermediary, only to lose all meaning in translation. Each ask had cost me and I am ashamed for, until now, I had convinced myself I was the only one. Althamia watches me, hesitant. I want her anger, not her apologies. But I lack the words to express this, especially to a woman I barely know. I move closer, only to remember myself and hold myself back. 'There is no need to apologise.' A formal response, but something in her stare convinces me she's heard everything I'm unable to say.

Chapter Six

'You have lingered,' Mrs Hale tuts at Althamia once we return. Her eyes miss nothing, and Althamia is quick to press my gloves into my hands. Our fingers meet, but the moment is curtailed when Mrs Hale snaps, 'You are wanted,' and motions me upstairs. My eyes linger on Althamia who loiters in the hallway.

'Mr Hale has given me the use of his study for the rest of our stay,' Will calls. The door to Hale's study is half ajar and I close it behind me. Will is seated behind a large wooden desk cluttered with stacks of parchment. The room is lit with candles though the dark wainscotted walls absorb much of its light.

I settle into the seat opposite him. 'How was your visit with the aldermen of York?'

'Worse than hell,' he mutters with a pointed look at the papers before him. 'They are inundated with allegations of witchcraft and requested that I investigate.'

Dear Sir,

I am in desperate need of your aid. My neighbour Margaret Sherwood is a witch. She has sent her familiar to lame my cattle. My servant attempted to undo her curse by scratching her forehead. His effort drew blood, but my cattle are still lame.

and the witch has sent her imps to torment my man's sleep and afflict him with fevers . . .

Dear Sirs,
My family is plagued by Mr and Mrs Bretton. They have bewitched my child to death and my eldest is stricken with palsy in her legs . . .

. . . Mrs McCafferty has sent her imps to spoil our crops and secreted curse charms about my house. Her spells have left my wife barren . . .

The Emmett family are a brood of witches. They have denied their baptism and regularly invite innocents to partake in the black sabbath . . .

Letter after letter land on my lap and pull at my self-control. The stories feel familiar, a passed-down tale lent an embellishment by time and circumstance. Each letter I imagine to be my own denouncement. The accusations fill my head like a song, until Will brings it to a halt. 'The charges all follow a similar vein, though only a handful will result in a formal charge,' he adds as I read through the rest of the accusations.

My expression sours. 'Formal charge or not, these accusations will forever be a noose around their necks.'

'The wise ones will take care not to drop,' he says with a paused touch of his collarbone. 'Or request a certificate to cite their innocence.'

To be certified by the same people who spoke out against them. My eyes darken as he passes me another letter.

'I am rarely surprised, although this came close,' he remarks once I am done. 'This gentleman terms his parish a *swullocking* nest of witchcraft and claims to have found a book compiled by the Devil that lists all the witches in England.'

'Do you believe him?' I ask with a stolen calm.

'The man is a fraud. Though in my youth I might have been tempted to enquire further. Anyway, it is a few years out of date,' he answers.

'Here is my response,' I say, and toss the letter into the fire. The pressure in my chest eases as we watch it burn.

'It is a shame I cannot answer them all in the same manner,' he remarks.

'Why not?' His attention swivels away from the fire and I am almost burned by his intensity.

'Parliament believes the upcoming witch trial will whet my appetite,' he says as though I had not spoken.

It is a murder trial, I want to protest, but hold myself back in time. I cannot afford to stir his suspicions or dislike. I must keep quiet even though it shames me to do so.

'Hale has admitted as much, although he said he will voice my reservation to the aldermen.' He sighs.

'That is kind of him,' I mutter.

He rolls his eyes ironically. 'He wishes to make me indebted to him so that I take up his brother-in-law's suit.'

'Mrs Hale will not be pleased.' Nor I, if he accepts. I'd sent off Will's refusal to Lord Carew last night. The words deployed were knife-sharp and I hope Lord Carew will retreat from the blow.

'It is his brother-in-law's pleasure that concerns him. He married above himself and without the permission of his wife's family,' he relays to my surprise.

I would have thought Hale too ingratiating for such action, but then I recall how Mrs Hale's vividness, shared by her daughter, coloured her interactions with Will over dinner. I cannot blame Hale for being transfixed by it.

'It is a game he cannot win,' he says with a shake of his head. 'Hale will forever be a debtor to his brother's interest, not an equal. Besides, I would never break my retirement on such a case. I would rather search for witches amongst Parliament's enemies than country beggars.'

'Surely, as the Mayor of York, Hale can find someone else for the task?' I say and cast my mind back to Mr Broad's words about the witch-hunter named Mr Rush. 'If witch-hunting is back in fashion, then there will be others willing to volunteer themselves.'

'The new witch-hunters lack my expertise and the men from my time are tainted by scandals.' I almost wince at this reference to his corrupt contemporaries. 'My reputation is unblemished and for that I am wanted by Parliament, Hale, Lord Carew and others with cause to make use of me,' he mutters with a look at the papers before him. 'The aldermen have asked that I reply to the accusers. I cannot answer them all in this manner' – his eyes fix on the letter dancing on the coals – 'so how am I to proceed?'

His manner turns sharp, and I answer in kind and explain my understanding of how to proceed in a witch case. Firstly, the accuser would present their suspicions to either a witch-hunter, constable or justice of the peace, who would then question the alleged witch before deciding whether to proceed to trial.

I relay as much to Will, and he nods. His approval does not relieve me. Witch-hunters of the past had a smooth time extracting confessions. *He* had it easy. Witches, both real and imagined, were betrayed by the very men meant to preserve their history. The royal scribes, now witch-hunters, felled witches with a witch's bridle that bit at their tongues to prevent them from enchanting knots, thumbscrews that drew blood and lamed hands, or by having their thumbs and toes tied together and then throwing them in a river. The accused either drowned in their innocence or floated and proved their guilt.

Yet I made no reference to this in my answer. I have sanitised his history. My omission has made him and his methods respectable. I curse myself for it, but I am forced to make it simple for him. I do not have the luxury of being forthright like Mrs Hale. I have too much to hide.

He pushes the stack of papers towards me. 'Temper the rest of your responses with ink not fire.'

I gather up the accusations. 'What made you leave the profession?'

'I had the foresight to realise it was becoming a relic of the past. King Charles saw us as no more than a reminder of his father, a bored monarch whose obsession with the supernatural soon turned to deer hunting. I saw the writing on the wall then, just as clearly as I see it now. King James set me to hunt witches and his son put me on the Star Chamber to root out dissenters. I am not a witch-hunter. I am a persecutor of men, and I am well-bred for the work.'

A villain's speech, one I would have flavoured with more malice.

'Can you not look at me?' he presses.

He is the monster in the shadows I was warned of, but in this moment I forget my caution and return his scrutiny. 'I am looking beyond you.' He stiffens. 'At the ones behind you, pulling your strings.'

'You are looking too close.' And I will look back, the warning conveyed by the dark flash of his eyes. One I heed with a swift exit.

Chapter Seven

The beginning of any entertainment is always preceded by a brief hush. The audience holds their breath, waiting for the show to begin, and the assizes are no different.

The courtroom is a tight square of narrow windows. Raife, the court clerk, sits beside me while the judge's bench is across from us. The gallery, filled with spectators, stretches behind my back and along the sides of the room until they converge into the dock and witness box on opposing ends. The hushed silence is broken by the audience, who discuss the day's proceedings as though reading from a playbill.

'Lady Katherine is sure to hang,' says someone at my back. A popular sentiment, I gather, from the chorused agreements. If anyone thinks kindly of Lady Katherine, they keep their thoughts hidden. The people of York are minded for a tragedy and Lady Katherine is spoken of with much resentment. She has placed herself above her neighbours and they will use rope to pull her down. The rumour of Lord Gilbert is a discarded plot, one I had spent last night uselessly trying to piece together. Lord Teversham's song has faded, all hints of his murderer an unintelligible lull.

Their voices press upon me until I catch sight of Althamia, a bright figure in the upper galleries. The weight in my chest is dislodged when she smiles, but she turns before I have a chance to return the greeting. All whispers die when Will sweeps into the judge's bench. His arrival is accompanied by a procession made up of the jury and the prosecutor, Mr Hym.

Will taps his desk and the show begins with a dull prelude to the witch case. To warm up the crowd, there is a hearing against Miss Hayes, a slight, nervous young woman of nineteen years who stands accused of theft. Following the testimony of both herself and her former employer, the jury form a closed circle in the corner of the courtroom. The jury foreman claps his hands across the backs of some of the more excitable jurors, a sound that echoes across the court. Miss Hayes's guilt is announced after a brief deliberation. Will's judgement spares her a second stay in the castle's dungeon, and she is ordered to repay the money she stole, along with an additional fine, within the next six months. A fettered curtsy and she is gone. I scan the charges before me. The witch case is next, and a flood of people enter to witness the case the city is buzzing about.

'I will take a short break,' Will announces and disappears through the door behind him. The noise of the crowd dips until the arrival of Lady Elizabeth Teversham and her son Lord Gilbert prompts a resurgence. Lady Teversham's natural colour is lost in her mourning blacks and her mouth is drawn tight as though death has stolen both her spouse and her appetite for merriment. Lord Gilbert wears the possibility of his wife's death easily. They take their seats in the front row with only the former's lady's maid separating them.

'A Royalist,' Raife the court clerk whispers contemptuously. He had caught my appraisal of the stag embroidered across the front of Lord Gilbert's grey velvet doublet, the King's sigil. 'Though his mother Lady Teversham keeps faith with Parliament. Her late husband's will leaves her in control of the family pot until Lord Gilbert reaches his majority. He will not have the funds to raise a regiment or bribe witnesses to abandon the charges against his wife.'

A measured look passes between Lady Teversham and the foreman of the jury. 'Mr Edmunds, her steward,' Raife explains.

Lord Gilbert, having caught the earlier exchange, favours the man with a look of his own.

'Is it fair for a servant to judge his mistress?' I ask.

Raife snorts. 'The same mistress who was subservient to him before her marriage? Though, he should have excused himself. Even if Lady Katherine is acquitted, Lord Gilbert won't forget him humouring his mother's fancies. He is master, after all.'

'There is hope then,' I murmur, suppressing my annoyance at his complacent shrug.

Amidst the impatient whispers, Lord Gilbert adjusts the white pearl buttons on his yellow hunting gloves.

'He hunts every morning,' says Raife. 'Even the potential loss of his wife will not put him off.'

Lord Gilbert's eyes flash when he catches us observing him. His forehead crinkles when I don't look away.

Raife draws me back. 'Do you think the judge will hang her?' His question lacks curiosity. Lady Katherine's trial is a play where we all know the ending. The excitement is all to do with how well the roles are played. I rise at the vision of a noose around her neck. 'I am sorry,' I mutter, unsure whether I'm apologising to Althamia, whose eyes bore into mine, or the seated judge and justices I sidle past. Closing the door behind me, I turn to face a spiral staircase that leads up to the tower's roof. The scent of the courtroom is eviscerated with each step I take. From the rooftop, the stone fortress of York Castle squats atop a silver-flecked motte and the city spreads like a tapestry beneath its feet. The flat parts of the stone keep, ditch bridge, walled courtyards and surrounding buildings crouch like tree shoots under the sharp proportions of York Minister. The water of the Ouse River ripples with the wind and the unspoiled landscape beyond the city walls holds firm to its beauty even in winter.

Will hovers near the roof's parapet that stops at his waist. He is a dark stain on the city's landscape. 'You are troubled,' he says when I shiver.

'I have read the court papers,' I begin, but then falter. I risk undermining everything Stephens did to keep me safe all these years. I cannot chance everything for a woman I do not know. For a woman who could be guilty or innocent. Lord Teversham did not identify his murderer. I close my eyes to an image of Althamia's face. 'Lord Gilbert is rumoured to have resented his father's influence. Enough to engineer his death.'

'A heavy charge,' says Will.

'One I can understand,' I say and return Will's look without shame. I have always wondered what my life would be like without my father in it. 'The evidence against Lady Katherine is slight, yet the justices did little to investigate whether witchcraft was the cause of her father-in-law's death. Or any other possible suspects.'

A weary side glance. 'The rumours about Lord Gilbert? He is not on trial and I cannot act on mere gossip. The lady, if she had any suspicions, should not have kept silent.'

'Perhaps she did not think her death could be the result.' I smother the anger in my voice. Lady Katherine could well be guilty. But if she is, surely Lord Teversham would rest easy in his death?

'It would not have mattered if she had spoken up. Parliament are intent on fashioning witches from their enemies, and her mother-in-law is allied with them.'

'A witch is made by the Devil not people. You cannot countenance this.' My look is pleading. He is a judge. He of all men should be able to deliver justice.

He looks at me as though I'm a simpleton. 'I have done so countless times already. By the time I came of age, my master and his ilk were performing their duties too well and too quickly. If there are any witches left, then they have hidden themselves well. Necessity forces us to make more.'

'The people will never accept such a ruse.' My protest dies off as I recall the crowd's anticipation over Lady Katherine's fall and the bundles of witch denouncements in Will's possessions. The common people have already begun to follow Parliament's example of using fear and perpetuating lies to sow doubt and lead people astray. I close my eyes. There will always be witches so long as those who would grasp power need a means to hang their enemies. My father's threats are a song, one that could see me in Lady Katherine's place if he chooses to sing of them to his wife. Neither my gender nor my position would protect me.

'The trial is a grand distraction,' Will muses, his attention taken once more by the view. 'A jest, that people enjoy because they are not yet the target. Life is a wheel. Lady Katherine will not be the last to be grounded by it.'

'And yet you have been spared.' He doesn't flinch from the accusation, but his hands trace the outline of the witch talisman hidden under his robes.

He gestures to the court. 'The trial cannot be stopped. I will not risk losing my property and liberty in an attempt to do so.'

My lips part but nothing comes out. I have done my best for the Lady and the late Lord Teversham. Meagre protests, but to do more would kill me. But then I remember his speech yesterday and draw breath for a final appeal. 'You will lose yourself if you act against your better judgement. You lack the appetite for this.'

He turns his back to me, staring out over the castle's cemetery. 'My appetite is not so sated that I cannot stomach another meal.'

I would have believed his smooth words if it weren't for his white knuckles against the parapet.

The court deflates at my reappearance. They have caught the quarry's scent and my neck tingles from the crowd's mixture of excitement, nerves, and anger at being denied. The more vocal members of the audience grind their teeth, and I sit down before I am pelted with boos. I sense Althamia's eyes on me but keep my face forward.

'Are we keeping to London time?' Mr Hym, the prosecutor, places his palms on the table and inches his face close to mine. He resembles a Van Dyck portrait with his dark eyes and silken attire that makes the magistrates in their ceremonial black robes plain. 'Did I mishear when His Honour said a "short break"?'

Hym was quick to prosecute Lady Katherine at her mother-in-law's behest. He should have investigated the matter fully, rather than chase after easy fame. His eagerness makes me want to punch him, though he is saved when the people rise like a fast-moving tide at Will's reappearance.

A rifling of the papers sends Hym back to his domain and I rise slowly to read the charges. My gut twists and my mouth stiffens as though caught in a witch's bridle as I form the words: 'Lady Katherine Teversham stands accused of murdering her father-in-law, the late Lord James Teversham, with witchcraft and using the same arts to induce her husband, Lord Gilbert Teversham, to marry her.'

Will motions for me to remain standing. 'Mr Pearce. Please define what witchcraft is for the jury's benefit.'

The simple question provokes a ripple of laughter in the gallery.

I pause, caught unawares by my sudden participation, but recover swiftly. 'The Witchcraft Act of 1604 makes invoking evil spirits or communing with familiar spirits a crime punishable by death.'

'Thank you.' Will turns to the jury. 'It is criminal to use supernatural means to cause harm to others.' He repeats himself and his words pool inside the courtroom. The spectators quieten down and lean close as though connected by an invisible thread.

'Mr Pearce,' Will calls upon me again. 'Is love a crime?'

Lady Teversham stares at Mr Edmunds in concern and he returns her concern with growing bafflement.

A smile tugs at my lips. 'No, it is not, Your Honour.' Nor is it a hanging offence.

'Love is not a crime. However, murder is. I instruct everyone to be mindful of the evidence and not to be swayed by rumour or undue pressure.' Will locks eyes with the jury, Lady Teversham and her son in turn.

Not everyone is amused by Will's attempt to change the playbill. They came to witness a tragedy after all. The confused mutterings in the gallery are curtailed with a snap of Mr Hym's fingers as he calls Mr Jarret, the petty constable, into the witness box.

'Mr Jarret, please tell the court what you saw last August?' prompts Mr Hym.

The white falling band around Mr Jarret's neck is the only bit of colour to his brown Puritanical attire. Throughout his testimony, he fiddles with it as though it's a handkerchief.

'Last August,' Jarret tells the jury, 'Lady Katherine was in a clearing near the Teversham estate. She was talking to her familiar. A white cat with reddish eyes. Two days later I was summoned to the Teversham estate where His Lordship had been found dead in his chamber. I spied Lady Katherine's familiar outside his chamber window.'

His testimony is smooth from constant retellings, his performance credible enough to elicit satisfied grumblings in the court.

Mr Hym surveys this with satisfaction and strolls slowly back to his seat, ready for the next witness.

Yet Mr Jarret's exit is stopped by Will's raised hand. 'What time did this occur?'

'Lord Teversham, the late Lord Teversham,' Mr Jarret answers, with a shamefaced look in Lady Teversham's direction, 'died in the late afternoon.'

'I meant what time did you observe Lady Katherine conversing with her familiar?' Will corrects.

Mr Jarret pauses, then stammers, 'Around noon.' His exit is halted by another question.

'What is your occupation?' Will presses.

'Your Honour, I do not see what bearing—' Hym's question is lost in the reverberating knock of Will's gavel.

'I am a shopkeeper,' Jarret answers.

'And your role as a petty constable is unpaid?'

'Yes, Your Honour.'

'You must be very diligent in your duties to neglect your shop during peak trading hours.'

A simple trap, but one he willingly steps into. Unlike the spectators, I am unamused by his misstep. He has reduced Lady Katherine to an object, one that he would sacrifice for favour.

It is easy for women to be reduced so, as Althamia's tense expression confirms.

Jarret balks. 'Well—'

'Think very carefully before you answer,' Will advises sharply.

Jarret stalls and dabs at the sweat on his brow with his collar. 'I . . . I . . . I wasn't there, but I have it on good authority that the woman is a witch!'

'Whose authority?'

Jarret casts an anxious look at Lady Teversham, whose impassive demeanour provides no immediate solution.

Name her, I urge, but his silence persists until Will loses patience.

'This man's testimony is dismissed!' Will declares.

Murmurs bubble about the room and Lady Teversham, much to her son's amusement, stiffens with anger.

Mr Hym approaches the judge's bench and hisses something at Will.

'He is dismissed,' Will orders, loud enough that the prosecutor stumbles backwards.

Hym reddens at the accompanying laughter and regains his composure with a deep breath.

Jarret leaves the dock and stomps from the room, only to halt at the courtroom doors and declare for all to hear, 'Lord Teversham died with the witch's name on his lips. His final words were that she lay heavy upon him. She tied a knot and spelled him to death and bewitched his son out of his senses!'

In a playhouse, this speech would have elicited gasps of condemnation for Lady Katherine. However, the court is now Will's domain and Jarrett slinks away in embarrassment when Will says, 'Lady Katherine could not have used knot magic to murder one man and make another fall in love with her. As written in *Daemonologie*, a thread witch uses their powers to cultivate a single talent.'

'Unless she bargained with the Devil for more tricks,' Hym mutters, his retort lost amidst the crowd's laughter and Will's loud call for the next witness.

It is an odd thing to witness the famed witch-hunter so determined to unmake himself. Lady Teversham marks her awareness of the situation with a reddish flush, while the jury's attention strays from Will to the bewildered justices.

I grasp my hand tight across my quill to stop it from shaking. Will manages to observe the entire court without settling his attention on a particular person. Is this real, or is he simply teasing an alternative ending?

Mr Hym makes a better show of masking his emotions, but his repeated dabbing at the shine on his forehead betrays his fear of this case slipping through his grasp. He is determined to rally and the tension in his bearing lessens when he calls Mrs Sayer, a midwife, to the stand.

'Mrs Sayer, could I confirm that it was you who led the search of Lady Katherine Teversham as instructed by the magistrates?' Mr Hym begins.

'Yes, sir,' she answers confidently. She stands upright, and carefully considers each question.

'Were you able to determine signs of a witch's mark?'

'From the little I was able to examine, I couldn't perceive signs of the unnatural,' replies Mrs Sayer.

'Mrs Sayer, is it true that your examination of Lady Katherine was interrupted by her husband?'

'During the search Lady Katherine began to protest when I and my attendant attempted to search between her legs. Her husband, who was waiting outside, burst in and her ladyship allowed herself to be swept away.'

In the midst of this telling, I look up at Althamia. Her hands dance uneasily below her throat until she notices my searching look.

'Hardly the actions of an innocent.' Mr Hym's remark draws my attention, and he smiles when Lord Gilbert curses loudly under his breath.

The midwife nods. 'The witch's mark is often hidden in a woman's secret place.'

At this Will intervenes. 'How many women have you identified in this manner?'

His attention makes her bashful until a click from Mr Hym's fingers reminds her to stay the course.

'None, Your Honour, but I have read the work of your late master Lord James Howard and know his methods.'

Mrs Sayer squares her shoulders and makes a show of using her fingers to count down the different methods. 'A witch can be identified by their ill-favoured looks, their inability to weep, swimming, corpses that bleed upon their touch—'

Her relish assumes Lady Katherine's guilt. Each of her words is a knot for the lady to hang from. And a rope for Mrs Sayer to climb upon. I straighten up and observe them all – Mrs Sayer, the jury, the crowd and Will – with a chilly resolve. I will not be reduced to a rope.

Mrs Sayer's shoulders droop when Will makes a merciful interruption: 'And yet your readings do not make you an expert. Nor do you possess a certificate to confirm the presence of Satan's mark on the accused.'

Will doesn't need a knife to silence her. She is made mute-like by his disregard that sees her depart from the dock with a clenched jaw. Will winks at the jury, who, finding themselves on familiar ground, laugh. The sound spreads to the gallery. Althamia, I note, does not join in. She frowns and it takes me a moment to discern she is upset by the ease with which Mrs Sayer's learning is rendered baseless.

Mr Hym wipes the shine on his face and calls the next witness, Miss Emma Thorne, a young woman plain in her grey dress and coif save for the strands of gold that escape it.

'You were a friend of the witch?' Mr Hym begins.

'The defendant's name is Lady Katherine and she has not yet been convicted of the charge she stands accused of,' Will points out.

His point is conceded with an insincere bow. 'You were a friend of Lady Katherine?' asks Mr Hym.

'Yes,' confirms Miss Thorne, 'I have known her ever since she entered her ladyship's household six years prior.'

'Can you tell His Honour exactly what you confessed to the magistrates?'

'She confessed to being a witch,' Miss Thorne tells Will.

Mr Hym is triumphant as the gallery and jury erupt in loud whispers.

Will cuts through the noise with his gavel. 'Were those her exact words? Please recount exactly how she made this confession unto you.'

Mr Hym grimaces at this question, but Miss Thorne rushes to speak before he can interject.

'It was two summers ago. Lord Gilbert, who was then still the young master, kept staring back at us during church. When his attention turned, she whispered to me that she would have him. I told her that his parents would never allow the match, but then . . .'

'Please continue,' encourages Mr Hym.

'She looked at me in a way that chilled my blood and said, "I will have him anyway."'

'You did not raise your concerns at the time?' Will probes.

'No, sir, I did not think it was her the master was staring at.' Her words betray a moment's sourness and she turns to Lord Gilbert. A pause and I wait for him to stand up and accuse her of jealousy. He flushes and with a steadfast look places his honour above his wife's life.

'And when they married, did your mind immediately suspect witchcraft?'

'No,' she says with a quick look at Lady Teversham. She raises her chin and adds, 'But then I found a waxed doll made in Lord Gilbert's likeness hidden under their marriage bed!'

Lady Teversham nods in satisfaction, while her son loudly protests until a look from Will sees him silenced.

Miss Thorne, but not her testimony, is dismissed and she hurries from the court.

Mr Hym allows himself a moment's smugness. 'Shall I call Lady Katherine to the dock?'

Will hesitates and then states, 'I shall speak to Lord Gilbert first.'

Lord Gilbert does not have the look of the bewitched, yet Will is obliged to ask him anyway.

'Are you bewitched?' Will enquires.

'No,' Lord Gilbert confirms. He stands proud in the witness box and repeats himself to the jury. His certainty does not reassure them, nor his insistence that his wife is not a witch. Throughout the trial their eyes have darted from Will to Mr Hym and Lady Teversham as though *they* rather than the witnesses are the answer as to which side the scales should fall.

Mr Hym secures Will's visible approval before approaching Lord Gilbert. 'Did your wife kill your father?'

Lord Gilbert stares over Mr Hym's head. 'No.'

Mr Hym smiles. For a man determined to ingratiate himself with his betters, Mr Hym then makes as much of a threat as he dares with Lady Teversham looking on. 'Well then, if your sire wasn't felled by witchcraft it must have been murder by another means. Did not the coroner originally suspect your sire of being poisoned?'

He falls silent and the connection between Althamia and I is broken when Lady Teversham jumps to her feet.

'My husband was killed by a witch's curse.'

'My father had been in ill-health in the months preceding his death. His passing was entirely natural and not brought about by witchcraft or poison,' her son adds.

My jaw clenches at the easy way in which Lord Gilbert is dismissed. Rather than press Lord Gilbert further, Mr Hym allows a moment's gloat before instructing Master Sheriff to bring in Lady Katherine.

Lady Teversham's displeasure deepens at her daughter-in-law's unchained ankles, her healthy countenance and petticoat laced with gold and silver. Apart from the shadows under her eyes, Lady Katherine betrays no obvious signs of her recent residence. The excited look on a nearby spectator's face vanishes. The war between King and Parliament has seen to it that anyone can be brought low. She imagines herself in this young woman's place and is discomforted by the thought of falling from such a great height. Yet, she, I am sure, will force herself to forget her fear, while I must do everything I can to remember.

Lady Katherine is poised, though her eyes remind me of a fox trapped in a badger's sett, let free only to be thrown to the hounds. Lord Gilbert's expression is one of tight encouragement, and she strides to the dock, seemingly deaf to the whispers of *witch* and *guilty*.

'My name is Lady Katherine Teversham née Maier,' she declares and faces the jury, whom she outranks by marriage. 'And I am no witch.'

Her voice is amplified by the sounding board above her head and the mirror reflector above the dock that echoes her sincere expression to the spectators in the back rows.

Lady Katherine stares at the crowd, while I take in her gold hair and wonder if it is the net that Lord Teversham was caught up in.

Mr Hym tuts away her denial. 'You have engineered your rise with a Devil's pact.' The Devil courts a potential witch with favours until she signs away her soul. The receipt of such gifts is enough to condemn a witch, regardless of how far she takes these encounters. Mr Hym isn't slighted when Lady Katherine's firm *No* denies him an easy victory. 'You learnt your foul arts from the Devil,' he insists, 'and deployed them to inveigle your way into the Teversham household where you compassed to marry Lord Teversham. When his father objected, you had your familiar bring about his death.'

'I am innocent,' she insists.

'Then why did your father-in-law die with your name on his lips?' Mr Hym demands.

She falters as though caught by a trap. Will is losing the crowd and the hounds prepare to tear their prey to a bloody pulp. An ending Mr Edmunds acknowledges with a reassuring look in Lady Teversham's direction.

Hym strides to his seat and picks up an object wrapped in a black cloth.

'Mr Hym,' Will warns.

The prosecutor places the prop in front of Lady Katherine, where it sits like a discarded cannonball.

'If you please, Lady Katherine.' Mr Hym gestures for her to pick it up.

Her fingers tremble as she hesitantly unwraps his gift.

'Hold it up,' he orders.

'No.' She recoils, a response mirrored by the court.

Mr Hym circles round and parades a moulded figure of white grey in his right hand for all to see. The poppet has eyes, a nose, a mouth, hands, and legs. For such an instrument of malice it looks peaceful, as though sleeping. Low-level witches' curses and spells are always of a temporary nature. A disadvantage they circumvent through the use of poppets. They seek to weaken their victims in stages by placing the poppet somewhere warm or driving a pin in the places they wish to cause harm. The unending succession of ailments will eventually lead to their victim's demise. Mr Hym points out the poppet's melted side and Lord Gilbert's name etched across its forehead. Lord Gilbert recoils from the sight of his miniature while Lady Teversham looks straight ahead.

'Mr Hym, I have no patience for theatrics,' says Will, though his response is lost amidst hisses of *witch* that travel through the gallery like a tide.

Mr Hym draws out the moment and then places the object back on his desk before resuming his attack. 'Miss Emma Thorne found that object hidden under your marriage bed.'

Lady Katherine's reticence only secures the noose that Hym envisions around her neck. I press my hands together to stop myself from scratching at the exposed flesh at my collar.

Will addresses Lady Katherine from the bench. 'If there was ever a time to speak freely it is now.'

Lady Katherine turns to the great Judge Percival as though realising for the first time that he's the only one with the power to save her.

'Miss Thorne was my friend when we were both in service to my now mother-in-law,' she answers, while Lady Teversham bristles at this bold display of kinship. 'Our friendship ended when I married my husband. She was jealous and has engineered the poppet to punish me.'

I almost rise up at the way in which Hym rolls his eyes at her excuse. Many alleged witches have been framed so, but the scene does not call for doubt.

Will had leaned forward during Lady Katherine's telling. He settles back and asks, 'How do you answer the charge that Lord Teversham died with your name on his lips?'

Lady Katherine, with a paused look at her husband, says, 'My father-in-law was most fond of my mother, who used to be Lady Teversham's maid until she died two years ago. I share her name.'

Lady Teversham visibly shrinks from the shame, while her son smiles broadly at his wife.

'How convenient.' Mr Hym rises from his seat. 'But I simply do not believe you. You are a witch and you have used your arts to murder Lord Teversham and marry his heir.'

At this Lord Gilbert also stands. 'My wife is not a witch, and I am not someone to be so easily unmanned by witchcraft.'

The crowd laughs and Mr Hym seems intent on pressing his point until Will draws the proceedings to a close. 'You know my reputation. I ask you to reflect on the evidence, which in this instance is highly lacking, and acquit Lady Katherine of all charges.'

Lady Katherine remains in the dock as the jury huddles in the corner to debate her fate. Even if I were a playwright, I would struggle to pen a happy ending. Will has done his best for her, but her fate is out of his hands now. In this moment he is as powerless as I.

Mr Edmunds rises and the reassuring nod he shares with Lady Teversham diminishes my hopes.

'We the jury find Lady Katherine – guilty.'

Mr Hym curses in relief, while Lady Katherine stands in stunned silence. Lady Teversham smiles, but the gallery's mood is subdued. She is innocent, a sentiment shared by some of the audience who murmur their doubts at the ruling amidst the general cheers. I glare at the cheering mob. They are treating this farce as a play, as though Lady Katherine will be resurrected between performances.

'Lady Katherine,' says Will. He coughs and the regret in his voice is cleared away. 'You have been found guilty of murder and bewitchment. Under the laws of the land, I have no choice but to sentence you to death.'

I resist the urge to huddle inwards. The Master Sheriff allows Lady Katherine and Lord Gilbert a brief moment. If I were further away, I would think Lord Gilbert was comforting his wife. His gold-yellow gloves are a net around her shoulders. The closing of it sees her desperate pleas smothered. Master Sheriff pulls her away and she stares after her husband in disbelief. The tension in Lord Gilbert's neck eases once she is gone. Whatever her knowledge, she will not denounce him. His mother comes up behind him. She knows the truth, but in favour of justice, exacts a like-for-like punishment.

'Pity,' Raife tuts when the Tevershams have gone. 'I was almost convinced that this would be a maiden season.' He points at a pair of white gloves amidst the stack of papers, a symbolic reward for judges who refrain from passing a hanging sentence.

My thumb traces my scar. 'She might yet be spared. My master could stay her execution.'

'Not indefinitely. Judge Percival did what he could for her. He would be a fool to do more. She is a witch. The jury's verdict has made it so,' he finishes and busies himself with the paperwork for the next case.

An innocent woman has been condemned by other people's lies. The lack of power made her easy quarry and I almost waver from the precariousness of my situation. With a raise of my head, I catch sight of Althamia. A moment's look that lasts long enough for me to regain my balance in the steadiness of her regard.

Chapter Eight

'There is hope yet that I will not be stained by another death,' says Will as we ride away from York Castle. The path ahead to the city centre is made sparse by the ending of the assizes an hour before. The resolution of the witch trial had ebbed at the spectators' excitement. To Mr Hym's relief, Will had made no further attempts to steer the proceedings. The rest of the session was a blur of guilty, not guilty, and partial verdicts that the jury handed out after mere minutes' worth of huddled deliberations.

My thoughts turn to Lady Katherine, her stunned silence, her wordless pleas, and her execution set for two weeks from now. A small mercy on Will's part that provides Lord Gilbert time to either confess, appeal or request his wife's sentence be commuted to life imprisonment. Whatever his decision, Lady Katherine's death will be a drawn-out thing. Even if the verdict is overturned, she will spend the rest of her life under a cloud of suspicion, while mine will be spent regretting my cowardice.

Conscious that Will is watching me, I resist to urge to remind him of his power to overturn the jury's verdict. Instead, I mutter, 'Lord Gilbert would need to appeal your ruling.'

'He will. He loves her,' Will remarks.

I slow my horse. If he loved her, he would confess. 'He spent this morning hunting. Whether he loves her or not, he will forget her.'

'He will try to,' Will replies. 'The effort will haunt him.' He straightens up in the saddle and reaches inside his cloak. 'I received a letter from your stepmother this morning.'

I reach for it only to almost be unseated when my horse jerks.

Dear Judge Percival, writes my stepmother in an urgent hand. *The memory of my son's death is fading. The gossips have found fresh carrion and my husband is set to summon my late son's replacement home. Yours, Mrs Sophie Pearce née Raynalde*

Her terse disdain – I cannot outrun it and almost crush her note in my fist. A plot? A plea, I wonder with a side-look at Will as I re-read it. She can't know about my role in Francis's death. I've not given Father cause to break his word. 'My stepmother and I have never been close,' I say. He waits, but I remain silent save for the sound of the reins being squished between my fingers. I have seen his way with words, and I have no intention of letting myself be disarmed.

'My arrangement was with your father and I act on his instructions. Until he sends word, we will wait out the present here. Hale has invited us to linger for a few weeks,' he adds.

The noose around my neck doesn't slacken. This extra time is a reprieve, not an escape. 'I will have to return home eventually.' I glower, remembering my promises while aching for more letters in my mother's name.

He nudges me with his horse. 'And embrace your destiny as a merchant prince.'

'I have no interest in trade.'

'You could write.'

I look away, the memory of Father's actions an unhealed wound.

'You should choose your destiny while you are still young and foolish enough not to be daunted.' Will slows his horse to a gentle trot. We have shared something today and I sense that if we continue along this path, he'll unburden himself and oblige me to do the same.

'Did you choose when you were young?' I ask, shielding my eyes against the rain.

'I was never young.'

The silence between us thickens, but the arrival of a rough-looking man stops me from wading through it. The stranger steps into the road and falls in line with us on foot. Will greets him with a reluctant familiarity and slows his horse to allow the stranger to match our pace.

'The years have been kind to you, William Percival!' the man observes. There's a trace of the Continent in his speech and he walks with a soldier's gait but not their colours. He turns his face towards us and Will takes in his right eye, a blinded cloudy blue. 'Blown out by powder in Newbury two years ago. The battle marked the end of a life spent soldiering,' he says with a smirk at his misfortune.

We dismount once we near the city centre and Will hands me his reins. The stranger's regard is equally dismissive when Will informs him, 'This is my clerk.'

'A pleasing-looking youth,' the man mutters.

'One that was pressed into my company,' Will complains. 'His father has paid me well to see him kept from trouble.'

They march ahead, leaving me to trail their shadows and wonder at the history between them.

'The army pensioned me off,' he confides when we reach the city's centre.

'And so you decided to seek me out in your retirement,' Will surmises.

'Why not?' says the stranger. 'I am still of use. I was at the courthouse. Your behaviour during the witch case was a surprise.'

'Hardly. Lady Katherine was always going to hang,' Will states with a certainty I almost trip upon. 'Regardless of Parliament's enthusiasm for witch-hunting, they have no wish to see the witch laws deployed amongst their own.'

'Lady Katherine was not one of them,' the stranger retorts.

'Regardless,' says Will, 'the people of York will take a warning from my behaviour and focus on routing out Parliament's enemies.' He shrugs off the man's amusement. 'Parliament is fickle, but I am in want of allies. Most of my friends are either dead or exiled.'

Will is playing a role, I tell myself at his careless tone, the thought edged by another. He is a persecutor of men. It is the only role that is true to him.

'You will win their favour,' the stranger reassures him with a slap on his back a lesser man would buckle from.

Will returns his grin while I tether the horses outside the tavern. The man commandeers a table inside.

'Run along,' Will orders, his short tone a reminder that I am an inconvenience, one that he was paid to shoulder. I wait long enough to determine that I am indeed dismissed from his company. I stare after him until an influx of patrons jostles me onto the street. I ride aimlessly through the darkening city, unable to reconcile the man I have come to know with the man I have just met. Will's 'Run along' taunts me until I'm brought back to my senses by a turn onto Stonegate Street and the smell of printing-press ink.

'So, the witch will hang.' Broad appears from between stacks of books and parchment. The bookshop is empty apart from a young man standing behind the counter.

I reach inside my knapsack and hand over the court summaries.

'I'd have thought you'd be drinking off the excitement.' He searches my face and grunts at what he finds there. With a jerk of his head, I follow him past the counter and up the narrow staircase to his workshop. On the first floor, pamphlets dangle from the ceiling like lanterns as they're left to dry.

Two boys sitting at their desks look up, a brief interlude ended by a sharp glare from Broad. The middle of the room is dominated by a small printing press operated by two apprentices, one of whom presses down on the long handle while the other replaces the paper underneath the wooden plates. The corners of the room are stacked with paper tied up in bundles.

Broad sits at his desk that faces out to the busy street below. His impatient fingers make his words rustle. 'I can pay you for a small circulation. I'd have paid you more were Judge Percival not so reluctant to talk about his past, unlike this one.' He passes me a book from his desk. *The Wonderful Discovery of Witches in the County of Lancaster* by Thomas Potts. Thomas Potts's account of the Pendle Witch Trials, and the people found guilty and hanged, met with the King's approval and public acclaim. I press the weight of the ten souls who sang their songs in Pendle back into Broad's greedy hands.

'My father printed the first edition. The print run bought this shop, and Potts the keepership of Skalme Park.' Broad takes my silence as disinterest and his words turn cloying as though laced with honey. 'The favour Potts found is not to be sniffed at, though a man of your background would of course merit a grander reward.'

He surveys his workshop, the desire for more evident in the hard lines of his face. 'Readers are starved for tales of witchcraft. I'll not be a fool and sate them with one volume but prolong their hunger with a succession of pamphlets. Help me and I'll reward you with a fair share of the profits.'

'Witches have never been my genre,' I tell him, even as I reflect on the promise of a regular income and a chance to free myself from my father's influence.

'Prove your worth and I'll let you pen your own stories in time,'
he promises.

I appraise the books in his workshop and imagine my words
counted among them. Lies, but plenty of men have built their fortunes
upon them. My father did, as have I. Another lie and I can build an
empire of my choosing.

'I will bring you something upon the week,' I decide.

Broad gestures to his apprentices. 'Now, or I'll have one of them
do it.'

This is said with enough force that I believe him. While the King
and Queen pawn the crown jewels to protect their dignity, ordinary
men rise amidst the chaos. The disagreement between King and
country has turned England upside down and Broad seeks to count
himself among the new order emerging to right the world. There is
nothing so precious that it can't be sacrificed for an advantage during
these times. Not even one's honour.

'*The life of Judge William Percival as related by Mr Nicholas Pearce*,' Broad
suggests.

'A pseudonym,' I protest. It is a Devil's bargain, sealed with
a handshake and my signature.

Will must have regarded his actions in court today as his duty
or perhaps a way to cultivate more influence in Parliament. He has
fulfilled his obligations and yet all I can think about is his cold disregard of Lady Katherine's fate. He let me believe that Lady Katherine
could be saved and I'm angry at how quick I was to forget who he
truly was. He has spent his life slipping in and out of different roles,
but history will only remember him for the one my words create:
The Butcherer of Witches.

I take Broad's seat, but even with a page before me, a quill shoved
in my hand and ink dripping from its tip – my mind is empty. I have

read so many witch pamphlets that I find it a subject devoid of magic. The chair digs into my sides and the back of my neck burns from the heat of Broad's breath as he looms over me.

'Will you not retreat from this position?' I request, but he scoffs and steps closer.

My fingers tighten against the quill. He doubts my capabilities. I should leave and save myself from the risk of Father and Will ever finding out. For all Father has promised me, I cannot help but reach for more. My mother's name, once earned, might still be a hopeless comfort. If I cannot undo what I am, I must make myself like Stephens, fruitless and alone. Writing eases the burden. The only time I have ever felt enough was when I let my thoughts pool unfiltered on a page. It was also the only time I ever felt close to fathoming my mother and in this moment I am unwilling to give it up.

'Spare the sermon,' says Broad when I begin with a preface. 'Hardly anyone pays attention to it and, besides, church is where people are taught to avoid the Devil's temptations.'

I cross out the line and begin anew with the main story.

'We have heard that one,' Broad interrupts when I am but two lines in. Despite Will's reputation, many of his exploits have been merged with his companions' histories. The tale I am writing is a familiar one. A witch whose soul leaves her body at night and plagues her neighbours' dreams until Will kills her.

The lines are crossed out and I start again with a tale of a witch sending her imps to kill her enemies' cattle.

'That is not new either.'

I drop the quill and twist my neck towards Broad. 'The stories are never new. The accusations are drawn from the same ink.'

His patience wears thin. 'You are talking yourself out of my employ,' he threatens with a meaningful nod at his apprentices.

'There is a witch,' I say quickly, flavouring King James's lies with truths, 'who has a talent for all things dead.' Broad draws closer. 'She is full of the dead's secrets,' I confide even as Francis's song warms my blood against it. 'They fill her like water.'

'Write it down,' Broad directs me.

'She is from Bagby,' I decide, giving life to a false woman so the dead's secrets, my secrets, may live again. 'A small hamlet. It is nearby but in Royalist hands. It is remote yet close still to draw alarm.'

'What does she do. This witch? How does she work her malice?'

'She torments the living. She uses the dead's secrets to seduce or scare people into signing away their soul,' I say.

He frowns. 'There has to be more.'

'She is a thread witch,' I remind him, 'and limited by a single malice.'

He throws up his hands. 'Then write her as a cunning witch!' When I protest, he insists, 'Readers do not want truth, they want *terror*.'

I nod and let the story unfold before me. My fingers are stained from the ink and smell of copper sulphate, oak galls and gum.

'Her looks,' he muses. 'She is a crone, haggard by sin with a witch's mark on her breast.'

It is my turn to frown. 'An ugly witch is not new.'

'Evil shows itself on a person's face. A cunning witch's face is marked by the charms they mix, while a thread witch's bones are broken by the threads they knot. King Richard III's spine was twisted by such arts,' he asserts of the King whose deformity was attributed to his quiet murder of those two princes in the tower, his own nephews. It is rumoured he used a death knot to engineer their removal from the line of succession. 'We may change some of the details,' Broad goes on, 'but the story must still fit convention. My readers expect to be frightened by an ugly witch and then saved by a handsome witch-hunter.'

Once I am finished, he handles the parchment with care. 'This will do.'

The story is a farce, but the people's amusement will lessen any suspicions my stepmother chooses to stir.

'I have more,' I volunteer, reflecting on the songs I have heard. I do not carry their songs as I do Francis, but traces of them are bruised on my skin.

Broad departs and the sting of winter cools my cheeks. You could not better me, I gloat at the royal scribes and witch-hunters who butchered the witches' history for their own ambitions. Shame creeps in as I twist the songs of the dead on the pages before me into something fearful. Something like myself.

Chapter Nine

My business with Broad drags long past supper. When I return to the Hale residence, a servant motions me to the parlour and whispers the Hales were waiting on my return to dine. From the threshold, I pause to study Althamia. She is flanked by her parents, her silhouette framed by uneaten food and candles half worn to their stubs.

Hale's tone is teasing. 'The boy gave a good account of himself, though Althamia was in a better position to observe.'

'The boy,' replies Althamia. 'Ah you mean Mr Pearce . . . yes, he conducted himself well throughout the proceedings. Though I would have wished for a better outcome.'

'You are jesting,' he mumbles, 'Lady Katherine was guilty and I am glad the jury saw past Judge Percival's tricks to indict her. Your brother,' he adds, to his wife's displeasure, 'has written again to request his aid.'

Mrs Hale closes her eyes. 'You will write back to refuse him. Remind him that he is a magistrate and well placed to investigate the matter himself.'

His eyes flash. 'It is not my place to refuse him. Though anyone can see that Percival has no interest in his pleas. Perhaps he will settle for an apprentice.' His eyes turn to Althamia. 'Address your attentions to the boy.'

Mrs Hale slams her palm on the table. 'You should not encourage him,' she warns, but her husband misreads its direction.

'You only say it because he is illegitimate.' Her scoff emboldens him. 'His father is richer than even Lord Carew and he has made the boy his heir. He's a far better prospect for our daughter than any other man in York.'

Hale wants me for my wealth and the promised upper hand my illegitimacy would provide him. I am no more than a pawn to him and I bristle at the conditions that have made it so that I can never push back. I study Althamia and wonder at how she sees me.

'I would not be a tempting prize,' says Althamia, her expression lost to the dimming light. 'Besides, I doubt he has any interest in myself or being your intermediary.'

It is as though she had not spoken, for Mrs Hale finishes, 'I say it because he is a witch-hunter.' My ink-stained fingers curtail my anger at how easily she paints me as the villain.

'He is a writer,' Althamia protests. Her parents look at her in surprise as if they'd forgotten she was present.

Mrs Hale lowers her voice. 'It is more than that. You know you would never be safe with him.'

'He would not be safe with me either,' she avows with a steadiness that grounds me. Her lips part to say more, but my presence is betrayed by a creak in the floorboards.

'Mr Hale,' I answer when he calls out. 'Mrs Hale, Miss Hale. I am sorry for my lateness.'

Hale is too tipsy to be embarrassed, Mrs Hale too composed, while Althamia looks away.

'Judge Percival is delayed by an old companion,' I explain in answer to Hale's searching look.

'Never mind,' says Mrs Hale, her tone brisk. 'We shall make a start on supper. Lest it resurrects from the wait.'

I make a start on the sea bream on my plate, while Mrs Hale wades through the thick silence.

'I hope you have enjoyed your time in York. Surely your master is eager to move on now that the assizes are over?'

Hale interrupts before I can speak.

Avoiding his wife's stare, he says, 'I invited Judge Percival and Mr Pearce to stay a while longer. The people of York are troubled by the allegations of witchcraft. Judge Percival's presence will have a calming effect.'

Had I not overheard their conversation, Althamia's smile would have lifted me. As it is, it twists my insides like a song. Her smiles I want for her own sake, not at her father's behest.

Mrs Hale presses her lips together. 'You are welcome, though I must admit your presence inspires my jealousy. I have a longing to travel. I hope someday to return home to Rawton for a visit.'

Hale's knife clangs against his plate and the couple exchange a wordless glare.

'I have only been home once since I married and that was for a funeral,' she persists in the face of her husband's silence.

'My father rescued her from being sent to a Spanish convent,' says Althamia.

Hale's face reddens. 'It wasn't as dramatic as that,' he protests to his wife's subtle amusement.

'Father worked for the Northern Commission for compounding,' Althamia explains, 'Mother accompanied her father when he was summoned to the commission to answer for unpaid recusancy fines.'

She pauses to let her words sink in. English Catholics are enemies in plain sight, long suspected of wanting to return England to the church of Rome. The late John Pym once suggested they be distinguished by a different set of clothing. In the face of his dismissed proposal, Pym's contemporaries settled for increased raids, fines and imprisonment for the recusants who refused to attend church. Mrs Hale's family history explains Lord Carew's reluctance to personally engage with the witch allegations. Too many witches have been fashioned from their numbers.

'My parents met and married within a week. My grandfather was not pleased. A bride of Christ demands a lesser dowry.' This she delivers with a flat tone and a direct look that dares me to turn away. I don't. My illegitimacy, regardless of my recent elevation, would be considered a barrier by many families. So would her recusant past. Mrs Hale's fingers twitch as though to snatch back her daughter's confession. Instead, she bites down loudly on a piece of roasted fruit. To her regret, she has made her daughter accessible, and I cannot help but reach for her.

Hale smiles, his merriment a stark contrast to his wife. 'Althamia, you shall play for us.' Althamia acquiesces to her father's request with a beckoned smile that strains at the edges. She retrieves her bass viol and her brightness returns as she conjures a melancholy piece. I fall into its moderate pace. 'Well?' Hale urges, once Althamia brings her performance to an end with a drawn-out note.

'You play for yourself,' I answer. Hale grimaces while Althamia grips her bow. He is after bland compliments, but the role of a suitor is an awkward fit. The tension in Mrs Hale's neck eases while Althamia puts her instrument away. 'I am tired,' she says, though her father delays her escape.

'Mr Pearce will escort you upstairs,' he says with a look that tells me he is giving me another chance.

'I will not be far behind,' warns Mrs Hale after us.

'If this were a play it would be drawn to a close with a kiss,' I say once we reach the landing. Althamia inhales, and stares over my shoulders to her mother, who hovers near the bottom of the stairs.

'Are we performers?' she says, a teasing transformation that robs her of her fire.

I stop myself. I do not want her practised smiles or blushes beckoned only by her father's commands. Althamia is a song and I cannot help but open to her, but not like this. 'I am tired of pretences,' I say loud enough for Mrs Hale to pause her approach. Her slow ascent is marked by the gathering of candlelight that pools around our feet.

You are saved, I convey with a look at Althamia. Perhaps Hale will withdraw his schemes once he hears his wife report of my coldness.

Her outstretched hand delays my departure. Her brief touch holds a promise and she whispers, 'I am not pretending.'

I have always been in two parts. As though half of me is standing behind the curtains watching to see how my other half plays before the crowd. I am still in two parts, but it is as though Althamia has caught sight of us both and rather than recoil, she steps closer.

She is about to speak, but falters at Mrs Hale's increasing nearness. Her back is towards me by the time I think of something to break the silence.

'You could have just said I was good,' she tells me with a look I almost melt into. Mrs Hale retreats by a few steps.

'A worn plaudit,' I retort, 'I wanted to convey something more substantial. I did not think my praise a disservice. I like things that stand on their own and do not try to charm.'

Althamia half turns and whispers in parting with a quiet pride, 'I have been playing since I was five.'

Chapter Ten

York, March 1645

Dear Lord Carew,
I write in response to your letter. I am humbled by the esteem in
which you hold my reputation. However, I must again decline.
I have no intention of returning to a profession from which I have
so long retired. I advise you to use your authority as Justice of
the Peace and your Christian conscience to investigate the matter.

Your servant,
Judge Percival

I review my letter to Althamia's uncle Lord Carew on Will's behalf.
He had asked me to make his refusal clear but respectful. A gentle
balance, one I had spent most of the morning labouring over. I lower
my pen and observe Althamia from my seat in the basement as she
leans over the table and carefully fills the white mouse's insides with
wool. At the far end of the table lie her past projects, including
a stuffed robin she has yet to name. My nose wrinkles from the scent
of rosemary and vinegar. The basement air is thick with it. The
preservatives prevent small creatures from invading any crack and
crevice in the specimen's body.

Lady Katherine's execution is today. Althamia's parents have forbidden her from attending the execution, despite her wish for Lady Katherine to see a face in the crowd that isn't eager for her death. She looks over at Lord Teversham. His coffin has been relegated to the corner and he is to be buried the day after next. According to local superstitions, a witch's victim often revives after their death, so Hale has nailed the coffin shut. The remains are a withered stench, his song a whisper, but from his place in the corner he is easy to ignore.

While Althamia distracts herself from today's events, I am hiding from it. Since the trial, Will has been much out of my company, his time taken by Hale and the aldermen. I spent my leisure busying myself with his correspondence and Althamia. Neither Will nor Hale had objected this morning when Althamia invited me to observe her practice. Hale is a determined matchmaker, but to his surprise we spend the time Mrs Hale allows us at work rather than stealing kisses. Will, I suspect, has quite forgotten me. His lack of regard saves me discovering whether I would proclaim Lady Katherine's innocence or simply watch her sway from the end of a noose.

Althamia and I work in silence, but there's an undercurrent that I find myself pushing against.

'Did you kill it yourself?' I ask Althamia.

A shallow distraction, but she looks up from her task, her white apron splotched with vinegar.

'We found it in the street,' says Althamia with a backward look at the door. A squeamish Agnes is gone, having slowly backpedalled away from her role as chaperone. 'You are in need of a diversion.' Althamia indicates the diary in my lap. Her interest in one of the unfinished plays had prompted my return to it. There is much I keep from her, but I take pleasure in the little I can reveal of myself.

'I am stuck,' I admit. 'My hero has been saved from death and must plot his revenge on the uncle who usurped him.' I shake my quill as though to force more words out.

'Who saved him?' queries Althamia.

'A mysterious maiden who disappears the moment he's recovered,' I answer. 'Do you think it a mistake?'

She bites her bottom lip. 'You should name your heroine. I find it strange convention in stories when a mysterious figure appears to help. The moment they have served their purpose they are gone as though they have been wished in and out of existence.'

'All characters are a fiction. You are right,' I admit when she apologises. 'Perhaps I should turn my mind to dialogues. They are all the fashion in Oxford.'

'They are not the fashion here,' she remarks. 'Dialogues are just people cutting each other with words. There is no poetry to it.'

'The times do not call for poetry.' She smiles as I note down her advice. Our eyes meet, one of many lingering glances we have shared over the past weeks. This time she is the first to look away.

'Perhaps I should take up weaving,' I say after a pause, pointing to the small table loom tucked away in the corner.

She starts and says dismissively, 'A family heirloom . . . an abandoned practice.' She motions for me to take a closer look at her specimen.

'It is quiet,' I observe.

'It is dead,' she says, her eyes soft.

Would she regard me with understanding or horror if I told her that animals in their deaths are quiet, they have no voices to rattle around in their flesh until they subside to a murmur?

'Is Mr Broad still considering your work?' she asks.

'No,' I reply, far too quickly to be believed. I have visited Broad's shop five times over the past two weeks. On each occasion, his assistant said he was out and would call on me once he returned. He has not called, nor has he responded to the three letters I've sent requesting he burn the pamphlet I wrote. Will and his ilk have made a fiction out of my kind's history, and I bitterly regret joining their ranks.

Althamia disregards my answer and focuses on making the mouse whole again with even stitches across its belly. I help with the last few, savouring the sensation of her touch.

'You must find something to occupy your time in between writing. Judge Percival will not have much need of you now that the assizes are over.' There's a questioning look to her face.

I have spoken vaguely of my impending departure, the colours dimming each day as I wait for my father's summons. Althamia is my only respite. She brings the sun even in this dark cellar and I say, almost desperately, 'I can be your assistant.' I've barely finished speaking before she places the specimen in my hands.

'You have to massage it,' she instructs, 'to help him keep his shape.'

The creature is cold and soft and leaves traces of its smell on my skin. I'm determined to suffer through the task, but Althamia loses patience and takes over.

'Did your uncle encourage your interest in taxidermy?'

'Not directly. I would watch him practise his surgical skills on small animals. When he sensed my interest, he insisted on teaching me a little of what he knew. I learnt the rest from books.'

She dresses the mouse in a soldier's uniform, complete with a red sash. 'It is a morbid practice to open up what was once a living thing. My uncle was sure I would faint. I did not, although at first my hands shook. The siege gave me time to master my emotions, and my resolve was bolstered with thoughts of my cousin Grace . . . I wanted to horrify her.'

'Did you?' I ask.

'She is much too worldly to be horrified. Our uncle, Lord Carew, has raised her since childhood. Her mother died giving birth to her and her father passed away from illness a few years later. She was a lady in waiting to the Countess of Derby and kept vigil with her when Lathom House was besieged by Parliament soldiers last year,' she relates of the four-month siege that ended in the Countess's favour. 'Uncle Carew sent another letter a week ago.'

'I can barely keep up,' I say with a nod at my penned reply.

'It was addressed to my mother,' she answers. 'She hid it before my father could see. He is desperate to please him.'

'Your mother less so?'

'My uncle is nearly a decade older than her and they are almost strangers to each other. He is a magistrate and well placed to investigate the matter himself. My mother worries his position is threatened by our family's recusant past. Fear may compel him to do something he later regrets.'

'I will write again and strip Will's refusal of all courtesy.'

'Do not trouble yourself,' but her fingers stray to her throat.

'I do not mind it. I feel emboldened in sending out plain refusals,' I say and rip up the old letter.

'I am jealous,' she confesses with a smile, 'A woman's refusals must always be draped in apologies. Though I do not envy your task. My uncle is stubborn. The rare times I visited he never failed to express his disapproval of my father. He shared my grandfather's distaste over my parents' marriage.'

'I am glad.' She looks up and I hurry to add, 'That your parents met. Otherwise, you would not be here.'

She smiles and returns to the subject at hand. 'Grace seemed impressed that I had made a pastime of putting others on display. It is not easy to impress her. She is married now.'

'I know what it is like to be put on display,' I muse as she puts the golden ruff on the mouse.

'The gossip from London,' she hesitates, 'has reached York. Your stepmother's kin claim you have grasped at your brother's inheritance. I do not believe them.'

I did it to save myself, but she would shrink from such a confession. 'It is true,' I admit and gesture to my attire, all cut for another's likeness. 'Everything I have is his.'

'I still do not believe it,' she persists.

'Your mother believes me to be a danger.'

'I do not,' she answers, and I cannot bring myself to contradict her. My father's wealth could persuade the Hales to overlook the circumstances of my birth. Although the Hales are respected, the recusancy in Mrs Hale's family would be looked upon as a risk. One that would only be heightened by my pursuit. My future is still uncertain, even if I survive my time with Will. Whatever my feelings, I will not have Althamia come to harm.

'Let me make myself useful,' I say quickly. Our hands meet over the stiff material of the ruff. I pull away, but she places her hand over mine.

I grasp her hand at the rush of footsteps towards us. Mrs Hale appears at the door and surveys us as though we are a painting. I reluctantly let Althamia's fingers fall away. Mrs Hale breaks the scene to hand me a note.

'I am wanted,' I disclose, after scanning Will's command to join him at the hanging.

'You should leave now,' Mrs Hale tuts. To her daughter she says, 'I will have you be my secretary today.' Althamia's look is regretful, but she carefully packs away her tools and then leaves to do her mother's bidding.

Whatever warmth I felt is gone and yet I do not begrudge the loss for it has never been mine. A dissolving touch, one that leaves me the moment I near the town centre.

Chapter Eleven

In York's hands, death is a spectacle, its arrival heralded by the presence of the master of revels. The crowd is a scrum of people who press me close when Will and Hale ascend the gallows' steps. The wooden gallows cut my breath when I scale it with my eyes. Will is solemn in his court robes, black velvet trimmed with miniver. Against the clear sky, he and Hale are dark blots.

My presence is a formality, but Will still finds a use for me. I've been instructed to write up a suitable account of the proceedings for Parliament. Lady Katherine will not be the first hanging I have witnessed. In London, I have passed the dead of Blackwall Point, waxed dolls left to swing and rot long after their execution, many a time. But this is the first hanging I've been to where I am certain of the person's innocence. The crowd jostles and crushes me with their impatience, but I lean into the sensation to swallow down my fears.

Hale comes forward. 'I am Lord Mayor Hale.' He pauses, a false start the people crow at. Their veneer of impatience is ready to boil over into dislike. Hale has given the people of York their sport, but he is Parliament's man and therefore resented. 'Katherine Maier,' he rallies, denying Lady Katherine both her title and married name, 'is a witch who spelled her father-in-law Lord Teversham to death.' A succession of heckles causes his talk to descend into mumbles, until it's brought short by Will's welcomed interruption.

'Lady Katherine Teversham,' he begins with an almost theatrical flourish as the crowd clears a small path for Lady Katherine's approach, 'stands before you.' The horse-drawn carriage has made short work of her journey from the castle dungeon. She passes me, a brief flash of white linen. She is perched on a brown coffin, with a minister at her side and the castle guards stationed at her front and back. I move to catch up to her, only to stop. I have no wish to take her place on the scaffold. 'You, the people of York, have judged her of murder and found her innocence wanting. There have been no petitions for mercy, no plea to commute Lady Katherine's sentence to life imprisonment.' There is a considered pause between each line that my mouth opens as though to fill it. 'You, the people of York, have demanded a like-for-like justice and I stand here before you now to deliver it.'

The cart stops and Lady Katherine, her arms tied in front of her, is helped down by a soldier. Her earlier stop at the tavern, a customary mercy for the condemned, makes her short progress to the gallows unsteady. Or perhaps it is Lord Gilbert's absence, which she discerns with an anxious look. Lady Teversham has also absented herself from today's proceedings.

The crowd is merciless. Their jeers threaten to envelop the poor woman. I retreat until Will, Hale and Lady Katherine are mere props on a stage. A cheer erupts at the executioner's arrival. The hangman, borrowed from the local garrison, does not hide himself away. To the crowd's delight, this young man preens for their attention and the promise of Lady Katherine's death is turned into theatre. Children, eager for a closer look, clamber onto their parents' shoulders, and vendors renew their hawking of ale, food and Lady Katherine's dying speech – a premature fake.

At Will's restraining touch, the hangman's theatrics stop. The crowd's excitement heightens. They are here for death and cheers erupt when Will holds up the warrant authorising Lady Katherine's execution. He then presents the hangman's protection from charges of murder. The latter's smile strains at Will's reluctance to relinquish it. *She is innocent!* I almost shout in the ensuing silence, only to stop myself. A plea on my part would see me in her place. There's a look on Will's face and for a moment I imagine he will pull back and allow Lady Katherine to keep her life. A futile wish, ended when Will hands the hangman the death warrant. Lady Katherine flinches at the burst of laughter that accompanies the jest.

As though by a conjurer's trick, Lady Katherine is suddenly centre stage. From this distance, she is a slivered outline. The chill in my bones is a slow fire that does not settle. Her lips part, but her dying speech is taken by the wind and renewed heckles. She stops and I'm reluctantly dragged ahead by people intent on committing her form to memory. With a stiff back and an enigmatic expression, she bears our scrutiny.

My life has been a rehearsal for such a day, and I imagine myself in her place. But what does she see? From her height she looks down on us. The planes of our hats point into arched spears, and she squints as though hurt by the sight. Perhaps she wonders at her choices, her hopes, what might have been. The hangman's shadow looms over her. The rope becomes a crown above her head. She closes her eyes, and the rope is now a necklace against her delicate throat. It settles, but she does not see it. She has removed herself from us, from the husband who has stayed away, perhaps to hunt.

The lady falls. I flinch.

A sharp crack – a shuddered moment – and it's over.

'The lady will not dance this day,' says Will to those disappointed at being deprived of the chance to pull upon Lady Katherine's legs or watch them flail.

With a look at the dead body, only seconds ago brimming with life, he addresses the spectators with a closing speech. 'There you have it. A young woman – no, a witch,' he corrects himself, 'is dead. A death you demanded and one I have made so. A harsh justice but justice nevertheless.' I turn to the people around me. Lord Gilbert's deed has cast a net over the town. The people stir but do not discard it. 'I pray you will be satisfied by it,' he finishes and steps back amidst a brittle round of applause.

He whispers in the hangman's ear and passes him a heavy purse to ensure a decent burial. Lady Katherine's remains, despite her husband's absence, will not be sold to a surgeon for dissection, nor will she be left to sway and rot for weeks. She is cut down. The hangman's sourness at being deprived of profit disappears once the severed rope falls into his hands. He pockets it, no doubt to cut it up and sell as tokens.

The guards place Lady Katherine on the cart. Her eyes have already lost their lustre and her face is swollen. It is too early for her to sing, but something of her rakes across my skin, the beginning of a screamed lament that steals all my warmth. The people crowd her body and Hale hurries down the stairs to lead the small procession that will follow the body to the cemetery. Until she is safely buried, Lady Katherine will have no rest from these stragglers. There is a trade in extracting liquids from dead witches and selling it as mummy, a substance believed to heal wounds. Queen Elizabeth herself, after her looks were marred by a bout of smallpox, would bathe in it. I glare at the stragglers and then squint when I see Broad amongst them. I start after him, but Will sidesteps me.

'Drink?' he suggests.

Broad is almost a hidden speck in the throng, but my throat dries at the shiny cast to his face. Not trusting myself to speak, I nod and let Will lead the way.

✱

'She died well,' Will surmises. A worn sentiment, but in want of others, I toast to it. The glass in my hand trembles. The inn is dim, but even from our secluded table in the corner, I'm aware of the patrons' furtive stares. My throat remains dry after I make short work of my drink. I still at Will's considered look. 'Today's events will fade from the remembering of it,' he says.

'It will not,' I retort. Lady Katherine will be given to the embraces of the buried dead, her song a sharp timbre. Each note a plea, but what can I do for her? I close my eyes to a flash of Lady Katherine's face before me. Will straightens at my sharp tone. 'I am sorry.'

He brushes it aside and signals for more ale. 'The words were a foolish comfort, passed down by my master.'

'How do you bear it?' I whisper. Everything I am is a pretence. Lady Katherine's death reminds me I will never be free of it. Why would a free man choose an employ which leads to so much death?

He opens his mouth, his answer curtailed by the maid with our drinks. 'I do not,' he admits, once we're alone. 'Like most, I mend after each break . . . badly.'

I turn away, unwilling to trick myself into believing there is more to him than his courtier charm.

'Judge Percival,' interrupts a man behind me. The loud register of his voice draws the patrons' attention and his arrival leaves me draped in shadows.

I crane my neck at the stranger Will ran into after the assizes. He wears a plain brown cassock fastened with frayed silk black buttons.

'Clements.' A resigned acknowledgement.

'Boy,' Clements drawls and rests a hand on my shoulder so that I feel every ounce of his solid build. He laughs when I straighten up into the pressure.

'My name is Nicholas Pearce,' I correct him, and brace myself for Will's dismissal but it doesn't come.

'Clements is an old acquaintance of mine. We were both in the witch-hunting profession,' says Will. Clements tips his hat in introduction. Will's expression strains when Clements commandeers a seat at the table's head. He sprawls out and his keen scrutiny makes me feel every strand of Francis's knot against my chest. My brother's song pulls me down, but I won't cut the rope.

More drinks arrive and I inhale the ale, a bitter perfume I down while Will sits in an uneasy quiet.

'Where did Will find you?' asks Clements.

'London,' I impart and try to guess who this man is to the judge.

The flex of Clements's knuckles across the table invites additional information. 'Born in the purple, eh?' he remarks at the mention of my father's name. He appraises me as though I'm a trinket.

'More like the woad,' I retort, but Will's glare warns me against elaboration.

'A bastard,' Clements guesses, and clicks his fingers for another round of ale. The cuffs of his shirt ride up and my attention is drawn to his wrists. The half-healed marks of handcuffs are still visible across broken flesh. He drinks fast and Will and I keep up with him in silence.

'The Will I knew preferred to keep his own company,' Clements muses.

'You never knew me well,' says Will as I drink to steady my nerves.

'True,' Clements concedes. 'My master did not move in the same circles as Will or Lord Howard. Nor did I have Will's advantages – I did not possess the looks of the King's favourite, Sir Michael Hobart.' His left finger strays to his nose bridge, unevenly set after a bad break. A slight mar to his fine bone structure, one he roughs with a coarse exterior.

Will drains the rest of his drink and places it down firmly. 'My relation to my cousin gave me no advantage.'

'It put you in sight of the King,' Clements argues. 'You served in his bedchamber during the brief detente between Hobart, Carr, the First Earl of Somerset, and George Villiers, Duke of Buckingham.'

I overheard my stepmother gossiping about the late King's favourites with her friends once. Hobart's rise was attributed to his charming grin and then, after his fall from the King's graces, a love charm. I had not realised Will was related to him. Not that I am surprised. Father had once sneered that King James kept a kaleidoscope of beautiful young men around him. Villiers, Hobart and Carr, the King's primary favourites, were lavished with public offices and noble titles. These favourites, in Father's opinion, were insubstantial, grasping and somewhat sordid.

'He exaggerates,' dismisses Will, and signals for another drink. 'My cousin was never a rival to Villiers or Carr. He was a passing favourite. A bright star soon extinguished.'

'One of the many you orbited,' Clements recollects. 'I remember you had a friend who was always at your side.' Clements clicks his fingers. 'Though his name escapes me.'

Will gathers himself as Clements spreads his arm across the table. 'It is of no matter. He is dead.'

'I disagree,' says Clements. 'I find the dead a fascinating subject. Though perhaps we should speak of a more exalted figure. The late King James. I barely caught a glimpse of him those rare times I was at court. What was he like?'

'A majestic figure,' Will offers reluctantly.

'I heard he was always leaning on his favourites for support,' says

Clements. He places his hand on Will's shoulder, an unwelcome touch he bears. He tilts his head towards me.

'Weak legs, like his son. He was not fond of washing, the old King.'

'He was not,' Will confirms, and his pupils darken despite the abundance of candlelight.

'He would remain enmeshed in his clothes until they moulted.'

This is a death that hasn't been sung off. It is a suppressed cry from dark corners, yet Clements forces its display.

Clements spreads his arms across the small table, his approach conceded by our narrowed elbows. 'He had a curious scent,' he muses, and sniffs in remembrance.

'Deer blood,' says Will, and I cannot look away. 'The old man was feted with it. He thought he could strengthen his legs by submerging them in the belly of a slaughtered deer. At night, I and the other grooms would pile up like puppies near the foot of his bed and awaken to the sight of the King emerging from it like an afterbirth from the creature's flesh.'

Will turns quiet. I stare at Clements and wonder if he's a spell. Clements returns my scrutiny and I drink to stop myself from fidgeting. The ale blunts the hard edges of my composure.

'Your host's girl is a pretty piece.'

The memory of Althamia's touch is a slow fire in my blood. Clements's lewd smirk sees it extinguished. I put down my drink as the cold settles in my flesh.

'Nicholas.' Will has come back to himself, but I am drunk enough to take the bait.

'She is more than that.' I square my shoulders.

His eyes widen. 'Oh?' he remarks, and I resist the urge to hit him.

'She is clever and unique and plays the bass viol with great skill. She is an accomplished taxidermist. She has a collection of mice, birds . . .'

To his amusement, my words trail off. I sound like a lovesick fool and Althamia no more than a list of accomplishments. I reach for my drink while Will slams his tankard down the table with such force that the people around us turn silent. My thoughts clear to reveal the heart of my feelings. Whenever I am with her I feel chosen, enough to dream of her acceptance were I ever to risk unveiling my truest self.

Clements waits for the volume to creep up before speaking.

'I always thought taxidermy was akin to knot magic. You are, after all, threading knots in dead creatures.' His casual manner chills my blood.

'You are mistaken,' I correct him, but my fear slips through.

He grins. 'I advise against giving her a lock of your hair as a keepsake. She might use it in a charm against you.'

'Taxidermy is a *science*.' The chatter around us dips when I pound my fist on the table.

Clements gives up with a shrug, but I am not so foolish to think the matter forgotten, nor do I forgive myself for letting my guard down.

'I prefer to see the world as it is,' I say when the barmaid approaches with more ale. Alcohol can only soften the world's hard edges. It doesn't remove it.

'The boy of yours is a fast learner,' says Clements, and I notice he's barely touched his own drink.

Will leans forwards. 'You have sought me out for a reason. Get to it.'

Clements clasps his hands. 'We should work together. There is a need for our services once again. Before your arrival, I advised Lady Teversham of the best methods to see her son legally widowed.' Under the table, my hands curl into a fist. His smug demeanour has no need for mending. 'I did not displease her.'

Will shakes his head in refusal. 'I am retired.'

Clements scoffs. 'I do not believe you.' He pulls a book from his knapsack. It is cardinal red with gold-trimmed edges. *The Lesser Key of Solomon*. One of the scribes' banned texts. They believed the sigils would help them to summon demons. 'Your master,' he boasts, 'would ride into towns and convince people that the demons from this book were running amok. People pay a lot to rid themselves of the Devil, they'll pay even more when it comes to his spawn.'

'I thought witch-hunters took their instructions from the *Daemonologie*?' I ask. Francis's song is a low undertone to the conversation and a tremble in my knees.

'We did,' Will answers, his eyes dark.

'Though King James encouraged us to use our wits against the Devil,' Clements adds.

I lift my drink to hide my disgust. How can anyone be certain of a witch's nature, if King James himself encouraged such distortions? Clements's giddy expression brings me up short. I have made things up for my own gain and enjoyment. I have dirtied my own people's history. Never matter that no one really believes it. My words are an added rope and I grasp the table to stop myself from running to recall them from Broad.

I hand the book back to Clements, who adds, 'Even my master was convinced. He believed witches were demon spawn and thought this book with its seals and invocations could give him dominion over them.'

'Was he right?' I ask.

He shrugs. 'A witch he had in his possession almost made him believe it so. She was just a desperate woman content to live like a dog if it spared her from the gallows. But my master was never inclined to mercy.'

'Your master's habits sound like witchcraft.'

'Only if you're a woman or a papist,' he smirks.

Will interjects, 'We are straying too far from present matters.'

Clements's face turns serious. 'I have met with the aldermen. They are eager for our services though I balk at their mean terms. I have received a better offer.' He leans closer to Will, and I crane my neck for fragments of his plea. Enough to know that Clements's employment depends upon Will's involvement. 'My employer and his parish will pay us well for our efforts. This is just the beginning. Men with our experience will be much in demand once Parliament re-establishes witch-hunting. It would be foolish to compete with one another as we did before. We should team up and leave the dredge cases to lesser men.'

I stare briefly at his worn jerkin. He is not humbled by my inspection. Like a beggar, he shows off his vulnerability in hopes of charity.

Clements raises his glass. 'To our partnership,' he toasts.

A clink of contact, ended by Will's 'To my retirement.' He rises, but Clements is quick to block him.

'I cannot let you refuse,' he says, but Will's cold look forces his withdrawal. His eyes glitter at our swift departure.

Chapter Twelve

'I will leave you to make the most of daylight,' says Will, once we are a safe distance from the tavern.

'He will not give up,' I tell him. Will stops and I study the sharp angles of his face.

'Clements was never of my calibre. He made a small living hunting witches in villages and hamlets until King Charles deprived him of it. But it's true, he will not give up,' he agrees. 'Witch-hunting allows men from mean beginnings to forget what they have always been – unloved, unseen and unwanted.'

'Are you beginning to remember?'

His face turns defensive. 'I am a judge now.'

'Still,' I say to his turned back, 'should I fear or pity such a man?'

'Both.' He is taken up by the crowd before I can ask more.

To the alarm of passers-by, I break into a run towards Mr Broad's shop. My deal with him was a mistake, one that witch-hunters will use to stir people's fear of the supernatural. I will not leave until my words are recalled.

'I must speak with Mr Broad,' I demand of the apprentice behind the counter.

'He is not available,' he says. The man is slightly older than me and his thinness gives him a pinched look. He has made the same excuses on the past four occasions I have visited and now he lies without blushing. 'I am sorry, sir,' he apologises, but the hint of a smile on his lips shows his pleasure in refusing me. He must doff his hat to me and call me sir because I am a gentleman. Between us, we have both taken Broad's coin and it must rankle that this does nothing to bridge the distance between us. I will get nowhere trying to reason with him. Ignoring his protests, I slip behind the counter and up the stairs. The commotion draws the attention of Broad from behind his desk.

'He just ran past me, sir!' The apprentice pushes me aside to plead his case.

'Who is minding the shop?' Broad asks at the man's stammered sighs. 'That is not an answer.' A surly look in my direction, followed by a succession of departing steps.

Broad's attention is taken by his work, but he mutters, 'I have received your letters requesting I pull your work from printing.'

I force his acknowledgement with a step towards him. 'Yet you have not replied.'

'My answer would not please you.'

'I have made a mistake,' I tell him, but there is no sympathy in his expression. 'My words are a knot,' I say with a flinched thought of Lady Katherine's fall. 'I will not have myself or anyone else trapped by them. I will compensate you for the loss.'

He chuckles. 'I am not interested in your money. Your words are what interested me. They are now in my keeping.'

'And I am asking for them back.'

He stands. 'A man must own his triumphs and his mistakes.'

I resist his firm attempts to shuffle me out of the workroom. 'This is more than a mistake.'

'Yet it is one you must stand by. Goodbye, Mr Pearce,' he says and turns his back to me.

I shall wait you out. But the rigid line of his spine offers no hope of surrender. 'You are printing lies,' I say, my voice raised. 'Ones witch-hunters proudly peddle.'

At last, he relents and faces me. 'Is this your master's confession?' He wets his lips. 'If so, I will pay you a King's ransom for it.'

He repeats his offer and, furious, I tear from the printshop and into the street. The day has grown dark during my short encounter with Mr Broad, but perhaps it is more to do with my mood. It has been coloured black by Lady Katherine's death, Clements's talk of witches and my actions in mocking their history for profit. People will not be able to feel the disdain in my words, my subtle mockery. They will take it as truth and use my words as rope.

I wander back into the heart of the city. York has deflated upon itself. In the aftermath of Lady Katherine's trial and execution people go about their business with a languor. The sensation seeps into my bones and slows my footsteps.

I stop. 'Althamia,' I murmur. She and Agnes face the now bare gallows with their backs towards me. The noose is gone, but my drunken boasts to Clements ring in my head, and framed as she is by the gallows' arches, I easily imagine the rope around her neck. The women crouch down and lace the gallows steps with a bouquet of lilies and hydrangeas.

Agnes notices me from the corner of her eye and nudges Althamia. 'Mr Pearce,' she says, her cheeks a dash of colour as she half rushes towards me once her task is finished. Agnes hovers at her side, while she balances a basket on the other.

'You are here,' I say.

Althamia looks behind her, face troubled. 'My father forbade me attending Lady Katherine's execution. He did not forbid me the aftermath. What was it like? Terrible?' she guesses with a look.

'Let us go,' I say and then balk at my harsh tone. 'Forgive me, I am not myself and I do not want to picture you here.' She regards me for a moment but then obliges. I am conscious of the scent of ale that clings to me as we cut a quick path through town. She does not speak of the hanging. Instead, Althamia lets me carry her basket and then relays the latest happenings of the siege of Scarborough.

The Parliamentarians besieged the castle over two weeks ago to cement their control over the North. Its Royalist master, Sir Hugh Cholmley, of wavering sympathies, shows no sign of surrendering despite the presence of his wife and the heavy bombardment of cannonballs and arrows raining fire. 'The recent news has caused an outbreak of migraines and my mother sent me to deliver headache plasters to our neighbours.' We reach our destination, a small fountain on the edge of the city centre. From the fountain steps Althamia tosses a coin to Agnes, who closes her eyes and flicks it in the water.

'Are you for King or Parliament?' Althamia asks. An abrupt question, but my raised hand stops her from recalling it.

My occasional sightings of King Charles in Oxford did little to endear me to his cause. The country has splintered into warring factions, but the King's obstinate resistance made him, in my eyes, a ridiculous figure in a city slowly starving amidst the Roundhead's siege. But Parliament's hatred of my kind is such that I could never declare myself for them either.

'My loyalty is to the dead,' I answer after a long pause. Althamia does not greet my answer with horror. Instead, her hand strays an inch closer to mine. This kind of talk is dangerous. If we were overheard, we'd risk being accused of disloyalty.

With a quick look to confirm we are alone, save for Agnes, she whispers, 'I used to be for Parliament. Now I am for the people.

Regardless of the victor, we will have paid a heavy price. Some of us have paid already.' Her fingers trail across her throat.

'When did you declare for them?' I ask.

'The Grand Remonstrance,' she admits, in regard to the list of grievances Parliament presented to the King before the war. Chief of Parliament's concerns was the King's Catholic Queen and his alliance with Spain.

'I did not agree with all of Parliament's arguments. People obey because it's what's expected of them. The war has changed things. I am changed.'

'I am not a soldier,' I say, 'but I support Parliament's grievances against the King. The country is coming apart at the seams and King Charles is not of the temperament to mend it.'

'You speak as though the King is a tailor,' Althamia jests.

'All monarchs are tailors. Though we only notice the bad ones.'

'By your reasoning, I am a soldier,' she says. 'My mother has charged me with disposing of my uncle's letters. Father has become suspicious of the ashes in the fireplace.' She pulls out a piece of parchment with a white ribbon around it from her basket. 'This arrived just after you left, though it is written in my cousin's hand. My uncle must have instructed her to beguile Judge Percival.'

'Is your cousin a writer?' I say. She pulls back when I reach for the letter.

'No. But there is magic to her words. I was afraid to open it. I have never been able to refuse her.'

'You *are* beguiled by her,' I tease, but she frowns.

'Perhaps I am,' she considers. 'Though I content myself that I am not the only one. Her husband is a Royalist soldier, and her estates were sequestered when her home parish fell into Parliament's hands. She persuaded the judge to waive her fine.'

'How?' I ask in surprise. Royalists whose estates have been sequestered must pay a fine to Parliament to recover them. Families have
been beggared by the huge sums demanded, and my father feared he
would be one of them when Francis ran away.

'She lied to the judge that she was a widow,' she relays with a fading
smile. 'Her ruse was discovered, and she has since resided with our
uncle.'

'Will you falter in your duty?' I ask as she studies the letter.

'No,' she answers, and she folds the letter into a paper boat before
throwing it into the fountain water. 'This is for you, from home.'

I accept the note reluctantly. 'Stephens,' I exclaim at his careful
handwriting on the folded page. 'My father's valet.'

'You are close to him?' she asks.

'He is more a father to me than my own.' And one I abandoned
the moment I placed myself in Will's company. Under Althamia's
inspection, I break the seal and slowly unfold the letter.

'*Dear friend,*' starts a hand different to Stephens's. I scroll to the
bottom of the page to Dodmore's scrawling signature, where he signs
off from the Royalist court in France.

*I have received your plays, of which two are suitable for stag-
ing. However, I would rather you send yourself as we agreed
when we last saw each other. Your man Stephens wrote me an
accompanying letter and has provided me with a brief insight
into what has transpired. People in our profession are apt for
long speeches, but I shall be short in this case. I have never
received payment from your father, nor have I ever corresponded
with him. I have complete sympathy for the responsibilities you
now find yourself assuming. But my original offer, made in
full sincerity and without any obligation of patronage, remains.*

My father lied to me, and yet I believed him without question. I press the letter to my chest. Stephens, despite not a word from me, has given me a way out.

'It is a letter from Dodmore, a friend from Oxford. He has offered me work as a playwright at the Royalist court in France,' I tell Althamia.

'It arrived two days ago,' she admits. 'The delay has made me a thief. A bad one,' she jests.

'I am not angry,' I repeat until she looks at me.

'Judge Percival mentioned that you are awaiting your father's summons to return home.' She studies the paper boat, drowning in the fountain ripples. 'You are changing things. I fear things would return to how they were if you left.'

'A worry I share,' I confess. 'My father lied that he paid Dodmore to humour my ambitions. He needed an heir,' I explain, seeing her surprise.

'You are humble to have believed him,' she says. 'You will be even farther away now.'

'I have not made up my mind. I have obligations to my father, to—'

'You cannot live for the dead,' she says gently.

'A part of me is dead already.' A truth she blinks at. 'Dioscuri.'

'More than one,' she translates.

'A childish nickname my brother and I adopted,' I explain. 'Father blames me for his death. Francis wanted to be a soldier, an ambition I encouraged. I did not think where it would lead.'

To my relief she does not turn away from me. 'It is not your fault.'

Her eyes hold mine. 'I know,' I murmur, and realise to my surprise I mean it. Francis would have enlisted anyway, whatever my words. He had no more desire to follow Father's plan than I did. I stare at Dodmore's letter again. 'But how can I leave when I feel as though my happiness must always be clouded by his loss?'

To this she says nothing, but draws closer. My thoughts turn to court entertainments in Oxford and the sense of I belonging I felt, standing as I was even on the crowd's fringes. Althamia interlaces her fingers with mine and I stare down at her head, a bright flame. My past will forever be a mystery if I leave. A part of me would have it remain so, were she only to look up and ask me to stay.

Chapter Thirteen

I secluded myself in my chambers after Althamia and I returned. Sleep, when it came, had been plagued by thoughts of Dodmore's offer and Althamia. I do not know what to choose. Perhaps it is why I was so quick to believe Father's lies. It is easier to let yourself be trapped by another's version of you. As I told Francis, I have never known myself enough to choose anything.

Since I am more for the dead than the living, to purge my thoughts I crept down to the basement to seek out familiar company.

Murder makes a fiction out of men and binds the perpetrators to myths. Youth lacks patience. All I am he coveted for himself and now possesses. A natural order, quickened with medicines laced with poison and an embrace that left me cold. My son. My son's hands.

From my stool, I listen to Lord Teversham's song. Still fresh from his forced exhumation and surrounded by candles at this late hour, he is entangled with tree roots that snake in and out of his wooden confines. His son's guilt is the faded strum of a violin and for a moment I comfort myself that it is enough that I have heard it. I finish transcribing the death chant. Lady Katherine's face is a flicker in the dark and I blink. Had I listened earlier, Lady Katherine would be a maligned daughter-in-law, not a dead one. Instead I had deafened myself to the truth in favour of doubt.

Too afraid to risk swinging from the gallows by bringing Lord Teversham's truth to light.

'I was drawn by the flicker of candles from the hallway.'

With a darted look at the doorway, I close my diary. Will leans against the door and my pulse quickens as I wonder how long he's been standing there. 'York is restored by Lady Katherine's death,' he says with a sniff at the smell of dried earth and decay. 'I predict the next assizes will be swamped with cries of the supernatural.' He pulls out a letter from his doublet. 'Perhaps you might find yourself amongst the accused.'

'The dangers,' Stephens warned years ago, 'are from the searching looks. If you let it, it will unseat you. You will not recover from the fall.' My breathing speeds up and I grip the edges of my stool to steady myself.

'Your stepmother is a determined correspondent.' His silhouette blocks out the surrounding light and he hands me the letter. 'The first few I dismissed as the ramblings of a grief-stricken woman. But the latest accuses you of seeking the aid of a witch, a servant named Stephens, to bring about your brother's death.'

I flinch at how smoothly Stephens's name falls from his lips.

'She was no Nun of Kent,' Stephens said years ago of Elizabeth Barton, the witch-nun renowned for prophecies until she fell afoul of Henry VIII, who had her hanged at Tyburn tree. Prophecy is a rare gift for witches and those favoured with it are often too broken by the experience to truly cultivate it. Stephens's mother was an exception. 'She could see the unfolding present,' Stephens had recalled. 'They were patched visions, but our neighbours sought comfort in them.' His expression darkened. 'The day King James's witch-hunters came for her, my mother heard the stomp of their boots but did not realise she would soon be crushed by them. *Those men,*' he spat, 'accused her of being the Devil's instrument. She did not confess. Not even when they tore off her fingernails and thrust needles into what was left. She did not survive.'

I am no prophet, but in that moment I have a half vision of my unfolding present and stay my tongue in search of the right words to save me from it.

'She is right,' I admit with a nod at my stepmother's scrawled accusations. Patient denunciations that get more desperate with each correspondence. *A changeling . . . a player prince who has taken my son's place . . . his creature, Stephens, whose own mother was hanged for witchcraft. My stepson is seeped in his knots.* Will straightens in surprise.

'My brother wrote to me of his plans to become a Cavalier. I did not discourage him. Had I known his death would be the result, my words would have been different. But my stepmother's accusations of witchcraft are lies. She has always hated me. There is nothing of her in me to temper her disgust, which extends to anyone who has ever shown me kindness.' Stephens has protected me my whole life, I would not have him suffer for it.

Will returns my look with an intensity I struggle to break away from. The stench of Lord Teversham's decay and my sweat make the air heavy. I smell like death. To avoid his stare would make it a reality.

'Shall we play a game of knots?' he asks.

I start. Childish games are made of whispering petty curses through looped thread. Francis and I had played it the day after our sister's death. 'You are lying,' he'd accused when I told him she was singing, and he'd pulled a rust-coloured thread from his breeches. The loop trembled as we murmured our sister's name and then sealed it with a knot. My stomach had loosened as though it was made of water. She did not awaken, and Stephens had interrupted us before we could try again. Francis soon forgot the incident, though Stephens saw to it I never did.

Will's frame is softened by the glow of candlelight from beyond the basement. I resist the urge to run even as I feel each of his accusations pressing me into the dark. Francis's song is a murmured lull. He faced his death with dignity and I lean into the sensation to calm myself. *This will not be the last room I see. Your face will not be the last thing I see*, I promise when Will reaches inside his cloak for his dagger and shears off a strip of fabric from his cloak.

A game one that would claim my life were I to decline. His suspicions are a noose around my neck and he wishes to see how snug the fit. He has no evidence, I tell myself as I reach for the proffered thread. Death, for all the years it's been by my side, has never been a welcomed companion, but my hands do not shake as I loop it. Each loop an escape, but I force myself to step lightly so that he cannot sense me running.

Stop me, I pray, as my actions begin to stir Lord Teversham's song.

'Enough,' a command that sees the unknotted thread fall to the ground.

He grabs Sophie's letter and hovers it over the candle. 'I will write back and warn her of the dangers of misplaced allegations.'

I sit down. 'Francis's death has made her fearless,' I say once I trust myself to speak.

'Then I will write to her family. They are obliged to me,' he explains. 'And at my command they will see her bridled.' He sits and at my look adds, 'With far gentler means than your father would care to deploy.'

His words reassure me. For Francis's sake, I would not have her harmed.

Will sighs at Sophie's words, now gossamers at our feet. 'False truths, but her condemnation would have been enough to make you my quarry. You need to take care.'

'From you? You are retired, are you not?'

He looks up at me, but the dimming light and my backward gait takes much of his expression.

Chapter Fourteen

I have lived with a noose around my neck too long to have ever breathed easily. Nevertheless, I make a good show of contentment to the Hales, Althamia and Will over breakfast the next morning.

'I have news,' I say and rush to fill in the subsequent pause. 'I will return home next week. I have written to my father to express my eagerness to learn the family business.'

'A wise decision,' says Mrs Hale, a sentiment dully echoed by her husband. Althamia spares me a quick look but to my relief murmurs her mother's sentiment. A word from her is a temptation and I cannot rely on the permanence of Will's grace. I had written to Dodmore this morning to accept his offer. In the meantime I will return home and warn Stephens of my stepmother's plots. Will, despite his assurances, cannot completely deprive her of speech. As soon as my travelling papers arrive, I will board a ship to France and ask Stephens to join me.

'Will you have time to prepare yourself?' says Will. I nod and the concern slips from his face. I hope to be gone before he has time to dwell on Sophie's suspicions or find out about my deal with Broad.

'You have been abandoned,' says Hale, and uses my announcement to assure Will of the abundance of young men willing to take my place. 'York is too full of witches.'

'They will find him a disappointing master. Will is a judge now,' I snap to Will's subtle amusement. I flush and finish eating the bread and leftover cold meats on my plate.

Will rises. 'More business with the men of York,' he tells me. 'Enjoy your liberty,' he says when I rise after him. Hale departs in his wake while Mrs Hale gives Althamia a pointed look before leaving us to linger at the cleared table.

'Judge Percival is well acquainted with my stepmother's family,' I explain with a cautious look at the half-open door. 'I dare not confide my true intentions.'

'I will keep your secret,' she promises.

'A thank-you present. I meant to give it to you earlier, but could never find the right moment,' I say, and hand her the book of Shakespeare's sonnets I bought from Broad's shop.

Her fingers caress the book. 'Thank you. I am pleased for you. You have chosen happiness.'

I have chosen escape, I almost confess. 'What would you choose if you had the choice?' I ask.

'In London, I am told that a small number of female surgeons have been granted permission by the Royal College of Physicians to practise medicine. Though any such ambition on my part would be smothered before it could take shape. We women must be patient Penelopes.'

'There is fame perhaps in the wait.' A petty consolation she frowns at. 'I am sorry. It is a weary burden and not one to make light of.'

'But for the right person . . . I would wait,' she murmurs.

The pause is broken by Mrs Hale's summons.

'I must be her scribe this morning,' she explains. 'We are transcribing the petitions of war widows who wish to claim a pension from the upcoming quarter sessions.'

I stand after her. 'What about this afternoon? A walk? I will hold you to it,' I say, and she smiles to accept.

✿

The light from my bedchamber window stabs at the parchment.

I have spent the morning and much of the afternoon trying to finish my play. Despite my intentions, my past creations shift into something new, with touches of Althamia in my heroines. She has trapped me like a knot.

'Will,' I say, when he strides into my bedchamber. A cascade of loose sheets fly from his hands and fall at my feet. I reach out, only to be greeted by the dark bold letters of the news-book. *William Percival and the Witch of Bagby, in his own words.* My words are accompanied by an illustration of a crone-faced hag. 'A fictional account,' Broad had said when I'd taken him up on his offer. Yet he has betrayed me. *As transcribed by Mr Nicholas Pearce.* I stare at my name at the bottom as opposed to the pseudonym we'd agreed on.

The Devil kissed her, I read. *The act enough for the witch to forfeit her soul in exchange for his petty gifts. I purified her with fire.* Broad has made additions to my account. *King Charles made the witch-hunters redundant, a past relic. It was a mistake. Evil never stops and by that measure neither will I.*

'You wrote this?' Will snaps, his eyes darkening when I don't refute him.

He snatches the paper and grinds it in his fist.

'By the day's end, everyone in York will have read it.'

My apology is caught in my throat. I had hoped that my desperate missives to Broad would have persuaded him against printing. In truth, I had hoped I would be away by the time Will found out.

'Why?' he asks, and I force myself to meet his glare.

'Because someone told me I would be good at it,' I confess.

His hurt, conveyed with a deep inhale, twists my insides. He leaves and I wait for the guards who don't come. He has kept his word despite everything I have done to turn him from it. I grab my cloak and chase after him.

'Our walk,' says Althamia when I almost bump into her on the staircase. 'I'll explain later,' I say when she follows me out and hurry after Will.

'I will fix this,' I splutter once I've caught up to him. 'I wrote it after the assizes when you met Clements. I was angry.'

He doesn't look at me. 'You were angry because I treated you like a clerk, so you took it as a licence to be selfish.'

'I am shamed with regret,' I tell him. 'Where are you going?'

He regards me and presses on. 'To seek out the printer and have this retracted.'

'I am sorry,' I repeat. 'Mr Broad has betrayed me too. I tried to stop this, and he printed the words against my will. Let me help, we can face him together.'

The crowd swirls around us as he considers my peace offering. He opens his mouth, but Clements emerges, jabbing a rolled-up news-book at Will's chest like a cudgel. 'I thought you said you were retired! I guess a dog never truly forgets old tricks.'

The gesture is without malice, but Will seizes up as though he's been attacked, 'This is not my work. And you will remove yourself from my presence. I have no desire to resume old habits.'

His face is puzzled. 'Oh come on. You know this is all we are fit for.'

But Will has no interest. He is off, but Clements, in an aggressive pursuit, grabs his arm from behind and snarls, 'I will not content myself with your scraps as I did in the past. I have made you a fair offer. You have no choice but to accept it.'

Will wrenches himself free. 'You are not my master nor are you my equal. Try my patience again and I will have you arrested.'

'You will regret this,' Clements curses, but Will strides away.

Our disregard is a mistake, I realise when Clements grimaces after us, but I race after Will as he cuts through the crowd into Broad's shop and storms past the apprentice to the upstairs workshop. By the time I've caught up, Will is scowling at my pamphlets that are piled up in thick stacks around the room. The apprentices busy themselves with their tasks, shirking Will's cold scrutiny.

'His apprentices say Broad has left York on family business,' says Will when he notices my arrival.

'They are lying.' I glower and cast a sceptical look in the corner in case Broad is hiding himself away.

'I do not doubt them. Broad is wise to keep away. I will need a court writ to undo this.'

'The first print run is halfway sold,' says an apprentice as he hangs wet copies of my pamphlet to dry.

'You are a success,' Will tells me. 'Forgive me if I do not congratulate you.'

He leaves and I reach out and touch the pamphlet that dangles from the ceiling. The ink is wet and seeps into my skin.

Outside, Will leans against the wall facing Broad's shop. 'I could burn it down,' I offer. 'I am serious.'

His eyes don't leave the shop. 'Your words are an unattended flame. One I am trapped by.'

'Parliament could not force you to re-establish the English witch-hunters. You are free to refuse . . .' My words trail off at his look.

'You think I am too fearful to say no? Amidst the decades-long conflict on the Continent, men like Clements and I hunted witches. Your story has reminded me of the possibilities. I warned you that I am still the same man. I hunted down witches to please my superiors, no matter how slight the evidence.' I resist the urge to shrink back as he looms over me. 'I am sorry for my past. In part because of their suffering, but mostly because their screams plague my dreams. I wish to sleep. But your words may have again bound me to the man I was. You would fear to face me.' He nods, content to see his words have sunk in. His attention turns to the flow of patrons who enter and leave Broad's shop with my pamphlet spread between their fingers. An hour passes in this manner, a forbearing torment as I resist the urge to snatch my words away.

Our vigil is ended when a figure flings herself at us. 'Agnes?' I say.

Her face is red, and she struggles to get her words out. 'I couldn't think of what to do but to find you. The master is out, and they are holding the mistress back.' She motions for us both to hurry. Will looks again at Broad's shop but then trails after us. 'Please, sir,' she begs at my slow pace. 'We decided to look for you when you ran out, but then he pulled her from the streets as though she was sport. The witch-hunter,' she explains, and at that I break into a run.

Chapter Fifteen

We come upon a crowd, with Mrs Hale standing frantic on its outskirts. I make out Clements at its centre. The people of York have formed a semicircle around him and Althamia, who struggles to free herself from his grasp. 'Let her go,' I shout, and try to push past the spectators. Agnes uses her small size to slip through the crowd, but Clements presses her back into the huddle of bodies.

'I will find the constable, sir,' Agnes cries as I battle my way to the centre. Her stance is determined, despite the bruise flowering on her cheek, and she fades into the crowd, her outstretched arm the last to be swallowed up.

'This girl keeps dead familiars about her. She is the demon Barbatos made flesh, a duchess of hell who uses animals to work her malevolence.' Clements's words draw the crowd in further and I struggle to stop myself from being forced to the sidelines. Their interest emboldens him and Althamia squirms against his tight grip. She stares at the people around her, who return her scrutiny. They are her friends and neighbours who have sought out her family's aid. But they do not see her in turn. All they see is the richly dressed daughter of a resented Roundhead sympathiser. The crowd tug at their mean apparel and believe this is justice. They do not know she has suffered, they do not care to know.

Althamia straightens, her bearing making it clear that she is alone.

I am sorry, I try to communicate, but her eyes go through me.

Clements's smile widens when he catches sight of Will and me. His fingers are fetters across Althamia's lips. 'She has the Devil's temper,' he says, and laughs off her bite. He grabs her hair to stop her from escaping and her coif falls from her head to the ground where it is trampled by onlookers. 'You should bridle her.' The anonymous suggestion finds favour. A horse bridle soon flies over the crowd and into Clements's hands. Clements stares at Will and raises the bridle like a challenge. He will not stop until Will gives in, and for a moment my master poises himself as though he means to accept. He steps forward, his attention torn among Althamia, the crowd and Clements.

'Will?' I press, but he is deaf to my pleas. In this moment, Althamia is indistinguishable from the many people he has seen condemned. It is as natural for him to step back as it is for me to slink into the shadows. Her death will not haunt him. Clements, enraged by Will's inaction, lets the bridle rest at his side and circles with Althamia in his grip. A surge of movement when Clements drags himself and Althamia back until they are framed by the gallows' wooden arches. The press of people blurs my vision, but I push ahead and squint at Clements's hands. A makeshift rope coils around Althamia's neck. Mrs Hale has gathered herself, but the wall of people keeps her on the mob's outskirts.

Clements stops, his mouth a leer. 'I grow ahead of myself. Fetch me a midwife to examine the girl for a witch's mark. Or perhaps I should do it myself. I have had enough practice.' The onlookers' laughter is an assault but I wade through it. Clements's hands drift from Althamia's mouth to her throat and then lower. The noise of the crowd is deafening, but a gentle strumming worms its way into my ears. There is sickness here, a creeping death I latch onto. I fling myself into the crowd but a hand wrenches me back.

'You will be fed to the flame if you reveal yourself,' Will hisses. He knows, I realise as he grasps my hand, clutch full of ripped thread from my cloak. 'Both of you,' he adds with a warning look at Althamia.

'I will not let him hurt her,' I say, disregarding my dread, but he doesn't let go until the thread falls from my fingers.

'Unhand her!' I shout once I've broken through. I pull my dagger and advance on Clements.

He presses Althamia hard against him. 'I have no wish to be run through.'

I hesitate until Althamia raises her eyes to meet mine.

Will steps in between us and Clements's grip loosens in surprise. He reaches out to restrain her, but he curses and then stumbles from a slice of my dagger. Althamia takes advantage of the confusion to stomp on his foot and claw at his face, her expression feral. She escapes and runs to her mother, who drags her to safety.

I launch myself at Clements. By the time Will separates us, my right eye is swollen. The crowd, devoid of its entertainment, begins to thin.

Clements spits blood and staggers to his feet. 'In my time, the girl would've been dangling within the hour from the end of a rope.'

Will's embrace restrains me from hurling myself at him again.

Clements notices Will's protective grip.

'You've deprived me of a witch. I will settle for her accomplice,' he threatens.

'He is not a witch,' says Will. 'He is a lovestruck fool, but one who falls under my protection nevertheless,' he warns.

'I do not need your protection,' I say and try to wrench myself free as he drags me home amidst Clements's repeated accusations against Althamia. She will be ruined by this. Her father is despised and they will use the accusations against Althamia to bring about his ruin. Even if I were to run Clements through, the accusations would follow her. Still I struggle against Will's grip.

'You are trying my patience,' Clements shouts after us. 'I have you on my leash now, though I promise not to be as demanding as your past masters.'

Chapter Sixteen

My bedchamber's modest dimensions grow smaller at Will's entrance. Day has bled into night and the empty hallway behind him is drenched in darkness until it's hidden by the creaking door. After being dragged back to the Hales, Will had explained to Mr Hale what had happened. Althamia and Mrs Hale had shut themselves away in their chambers while Hale and Will had ridden off to see the justices. In the meantime the doors were locked in fear of a mob descending to finish Clements's work. Will had instructed me to wait in my bedchamber and my first instinct was to begin packing. I stopped once I realised I had nowhere to run to, and nor did I want to. What happened to Althamia is my fault. For a moment I had wished I was a witch. I would have used it to kill Clements with a single knot. As it is, I can only store the songs of the dead with knots.

'I come unaccompanied and unarmed,' says Will. He tugs Francis's knot free from my shirt and studies it as though it's a specimen under glass. Where am I in all of this? I am hiding, shrinking as he turns the same look on me.

'A moment was all that was needed for you to become something I would hunt.'

I tense. I am not afraid of the strike but the waiting. The in-between moment that keeps me locked in place.

'The choice was made for me,' I confess. 'I have never resurrected the dead nor killed the living. The dead sing to me, but I can do no more than listen. No one else knows. I was born with my mother's cord around my neck. Her death made me a spell.' I pause and swallow down my anger at my mother's selfishness and how powerless it has left me. 'One I intend to undo.'

There is a patience to Will's listening. He has listened like this before. The speakers' pleas did not save them. Nor will mine.

His look is almost pitying. 'The dead sing. A burden for one so young.'

'I was never young,' I say, and he jerks to hear the words he once spoke repeated back to him.

'Where are you going?'

His hand pauses on the doorknob. 'To bed,' he answers as though it should be obvious. It cannot be so simple. Even if Will is no longer a witch-hunter, he is still a persecutor of men. 'You are safe,' he says, an assurance I shake off.

Witch-hunters have no use for distinctions. If they say you are a witch, you are a witch. I have made it easy for him by confessing. What comes now is a call for the constable, a quick trial and a hanging.

'I am marked,' I spit, and I remember Clements's words. 'As is Althamia. You are the protégé of Lord Howard.'

'My master did what he could to save your kind.' They are not my kind, but I smother the interruption. 'A tradition I am late to honour. Lord Howard made it so that both witches and humans were all affected by King James's paranoia. The concept of a coven and a covenant with the Devil in exchange for powers – a fabrication he confessed to King Charles. The late king gave him no choice,' he says at my look of disbelief.

'He chose himself,' I say, remembering Stephens's stories. 'Your master and the other scribes turned on the witches out of jealousy. They were threatened by the royal patronage shown to them.' Queen

Elizabeth, during her reign, recruited many witches into her household. She was impressed by their herbal remedies and unrivalled Venetian ceruse and hair-dye mixtures. 'The scribes thought they could oust them with King James's support and then persuade him to accept the right kind of magic – theirs.'

'You are wrong about my master,' he argues. 'The petty rivalries between scribes and witches would have remained so had King James not made them an offer. Repent, retire or become witches.'

'He chose the former.'

'He did not want to fade into obscurity. The decision broke him.'

'But his protégé stands, still.' I press my hand against the door. 'Why spare me?'

His eyes meet mine. 'I have had enough killing.'

'That is not the reason,' I argue.

'You were willing to sacrifice yourself for Miss Hale,' a slow admission.

'She would have been worth the loss. The person from your past that I remind you of?' I ask.

'You have the look of them,' he mutters. 'The memory of them is a shadow. Helping you this once,' he warns, 'is but a small mercy to ease it.'

We are besieged by Clements. These past few days he has been a scab over a seeping wound. One we refrain from touching for fear of making things worse. At present, he is stationed a few doors away from the Hales' residence, where I glare at him from my bedchamber window.

The family has been marked by Clements's assault and Hale lacks the support of his superiors to remedy the situation. The justices brushed aside his complaints. Clements enjoys the protection of Lady

Teversham, and Lord Gilbert hasn't forgotten Hale's reluctance to curb his mother's actions from the outset.

Robbed of support, Hale has sequestered himself and his family indoors. He is not one for confinement and spends much of his time ranting at Will. He and Mrs Hale alternate between anger at our presence and panic at what will happen once we are gone.

'He is your apprentice,' Mrs Hale told Will after I confessed my involvement with Broad. 'He has walked the path set by men such as yourself.' Will had accepted the blame without complaint and busied himself with planning our departure and warning Broad off reprinting further editions.

Broad has made enough profit to oblige him. We awoke this morning to find the streets papered with my words. A taunt on Clements's part to rile Will. Copies have even found their way into the Mayor's home. Hale had ranted when he caught one of his servants reading it. Will was right. My words are an unattended flame. Everyone in York has been singed by it.

Will has not publicly blamed me for what's happened. His feigned indifference, his mercy, is stifling and I have kept to my rooms to escape it. Until now. I pace outside Althamia's room, summoning the courage to knock. Hale has kept her confined since the attack. The house carries a musky scent. Rowan wood is meant to ward off witchcraft and, under Mrs Hale's instructions, the house is steeped in it, overwhelming my senses.

'Nicholas?' Althamia calls.

With a cautious look around me, I enter her dim room with its closed curtains and smells of rosemary and vinegar. Her fiery hair is a beacon in the candlelit room, and she hovers near the fireplace. She brushes her hair away from her face and I wince at the bluish-green stain around her temple.

'An easy guess, your pacing betrayed your presence. My mother has only sighs for me, while my father can only shout. So, these must be food for the fire.' She indicates the taxidermy projects gathered around her feet. 'Mother worries an official complaint will be made. People must see we are fearful and not to be feared.' She unconsciously touches her scalp, still tender from Clements's rough handling.

'This is my fault. I spoke of your hobby to that man when Will and I met him.' I sit down beside her. 'I drank too much, and I wanted to show him that you were important . . . to me.' A pause before a choked confession, 'The situation was wrought by the pamphlet I wrote. Clements saw it and thought that Will meant to resume witch-hunting without him.'

She looks away. 'It is not your fault. I encouraged you.' She brushes away my protest. 'You are leaving,' she says, and at my pained nod withdraws her outstretched hand.

I will return to London and wait for the arrival of my travelling pass for France. Though the memory of Clements's hands around Althamia's throat make my plan seem an undeserved reward.

'I will be alone,' she whispers to herself.

'She has left,' Hale had told me when I asked after Agnes's absence. During the fray she had gone to fetch the constable, who denies having seen her. Hale suspects that fear has caused Agnes to abandon her position. The quick departure of three household servants has served to embolden his suspicions. A suspected witch is never alone and the fleeing servants probably feared their names being tallied alongside Althamia's.

'Perhaps Agnes will return,' I suggest, remembering her small hands disappearing into the mob as my attention was fixed on Althamia.

'She would not have left without her possessions or even a goodbye.

My father locked me in my room overnight when I said I would go and look for her. He blames me for what happened.'

'You are not to blame,' I stress. 'I will search for Agnes on your behalf.'

'Thank you,' she murmurs. She hovers her stuffed robin over the fire.

'Don't,' I plead, but immediately regret it. It rests on the ground, a temporary reprieve.

Her fingers trail across the creature's feathers. 'Father is writing to his sister in Kent on my behalf to arrange a prolonged stay. I will ask Agnes to accompany me when she is back.'

'You will not have to go anywhere. Clements will lose interest once we are gone.'

She motions for me to pick up one of her taxidermy projects from the unlit pyre. 'Please, a keepsake to remember me by.'

I stir in my seat but stop myself. 'I cannot. It will get lost in my travels.'

Her shoulders slump and she studies the fire. 'Before, I was some-thing to be protected. Now I am something to be shunted away. Yet I am what I always was: an object to be manoeuvred.'

'You are more than that.' I take out my dagger and hand it to her. With a ginger touch she traces the jewels around the handle until I help her adjust her grip.

'And if I wish to draw blood?' she asks, and stabs the dagger in the air.

'Never stab. You cut to or across your opponent.' I catch her hand gently with my own. 'Relax your wrist,' I say, feigning a swipe at her. 'That is called a grapple. You use it to manipulate your enemy into a better position to strike them. You are quick,' I observe when she mirrors the trick.

She smiles and springs to her feet to grab something from her side table. She returns with a cross fashioned from the twigs of the Rowan tree. The bark is a purplish-grey colour. She cuts off a strand of her hair and binds the talisman with it. The colour red is also believed to ward off witchcraft.

'Now you are doubly protected,' she whispers and presses it into my hands.

I hand it back. 'I do not deserve protection. I must go,' I say, but she grasps my wrist, her eyes registering the mark on my palm.

'You have been hurt.'

'A lesson in caution,' I mutter.

She traces the damage. Her touch is kind, but I am unused to the heat. 'Your left hand shows the fortune you are born with. Your right hand shows what you will make of it.' In the pause that follows, our palms kiss. I reach up and caress the falling strands of her hair.

'Althamia,' I say, a breathless question she leans into. My arms find my way around hers. She whispers my name as I draw her close. Her breath quickens and she tilts her face towards mine, but a loud banging pulls us apart like string.

'Stay here,' I warn when the knock is accompanied by Hale's raised voice and a piercing scream. I race downstairs. Despite my warning, Althamia is close behind me.

'Mother,' cries Althamia and rushes to Mrs Hale, an almost collapsed figure on the floor. Althamia almost loses her footing and she leans on her mother to steady herself as she takes in the sight of Will, her father and a labourer who cradles a wrapped body in his arms.

I have been numbed. I have been petted but I have never been regarded by all but one. A small unseen thing with a mouth heavy from the taste of iron.

142

The dead figure's song jolts me to my knees. The aria digs in my bones and takes my sight. I clasp my hands to numb the sensation and listen for the rest of the labourer's explanation.

'We found her outside the tavern last night. A passer-by recognised the girl as being in your service.' He gently places the body down and departs with a coin from Will. Will hesitates at the open door. From the staircase, I look out to the street, where Clements stands at a distance until he is shut out with a thud and a curse.

Althamia kneels over the supine figure and pulls the covering from the crown of the girl's head. Her brown hair is wet and stringy from the trough she was drowned in. Althamia's cheeks are wet with tears, and she looks up from the body that she cradles in her arm. 'Agnes has returned.'

Chapter Seventeen

'We are in his web,' says Mrs Hale. She swallows the tremble in her voice and finishes embroidering a hare with slow stabs. Hale, Will and I absorb her words in a grim silence.

Agnes's remains wait in the basement for her burial. The coroner swiftly ruled her death a misadventure. Hale has forbidden any outward displays of mourning. The unveiled windows and mirrors leave Agnes's spirit free to linger. Her song is a dull ache in my bones, but I do not fight it. Her death is my fault. I should have looked for her the moment she went missing. She has died a hundred times already and will do so again whenever I catch a shadow of her likeness.

'He will tire of his games,' offers Will, a shallow reassurance. Clements has stationed himself at a distance from the Hales' residence. There is nothing to tie him to Agnes's death. He is at liberty while we remain indoors like trapped prey.

Mrs Hale sets down her embroidery. 'Yet you are set to leave long before your words can be proven true.' Clements is hell-bent on revenge. He has taken part of it already, and Will's refusal to engage only emboldens him. Will is determined we both must leave, and even my father has sent another letter to hasten my return. I cannot go, not when our departure will only endanger Althamia.

'I have spoken to the aldermen about procuring a certificate to confirm Althamia's innocence,' says Will.

'No one would sign it,' Mrs Hale snaps.

She grasps her husband's hand when he rises from his chair and sends his drink flying. 'I am minded to call him out,' Hale blusters. Will blocks the tottering man's path to the door until he reluctantly sits back down.

'He is not here for you.' Will's words do little to ease his wounded pride.

'You should face him,' Hale shouts, 'instead of skulking away and leaving us to it! Ah! You blame me for this,' he accuses in the face of Will's silence. 'I made his kind welcome.' He looks away. 'I did not think Althamia would be hurt by it. I am one man, but I am forced to shoulder the weight of an entire city. I do not have an old family name or abundance of allies, and to remedy the lack I must make concessions.' Hale grasps his wife's hand. 'I am drowning,' he murmurs.

Will turns to me. It is the first time he's regarded me in full since this all unfolded. We are trespassing, he conveys with a discreet look. He sighs and his footsteps fade as he retreats to his bedchamber.

'My master is helpless,' I say, but only Mrs Hale returns my look. In any other situation, I am certain she would respect Will's resolve not to agree to Clements's demands. But then in an alternative situation Althamia would not be so at risk. Her eyes usher me away. 'I am sorry,' I murmur.

Upstairs, I knock on Althamia's door. The floor creaks and the door flutters but she does not open it. 'Althamia,' I whisper and press my hand to the door, but with a soft inhale she retreats. She has not spoken, not since her mother pulled her away from Agnes's body. She has kept to her room since then and the stench of her burning taxidermy collection had filtered from underneath her door the same day Agnes was returned. She is shrinking into herself and letting her flesh harden into armour.

'Mrs Hale,' I mumble when I notice Mrs Hale standing near the top of the staircase. Her beckoning hand draws me close.

'Lord Gilbert is already shopping for a new wife. Women like Lady Katherine are fodder for the crowd, I do not wish my daughter to be among them.' She fiddles with the thread of her tie-on pockets that sit about her waist like reddish wounds. 'I was raised under Pendle's shadow,' she whispers, 'I thought it a spell. How else could people be so quick to turn on each other? Experience has made me wise. Of all my would-be suiters who told me I was charming and beautiful, it was my husband who won me with promises of safety. His failure has broken him. Althamia is broken too.' She doesn't have to blame me. The weight of her gaze is enough. 'Althamia thinks the two of you are a pair.' Her hand trembles as though she would prise back the letter that she presses towards me. 'She is not wrong – but you are *not* for her.'

'I am not for anyone.'

Her fingers twitch as though she would touch my face, but she releases me instead and I return to my chamber. Behind closed doors, I clutch my chest. I do not know how much time passes in this manner. I am shaken. The letter she pressed in my hands shakes as I dare read its crumpled words.

Dear Judge Percival,

I have been made a persistent suitor in the face of your refusal. Your pamphlet has reached here and I hope to wear you down with this final entreaty. My parish has changed hands between Cavaliers and Roundheads with such regularity that at first, we paid no mind to our new occupier. Our attention was diverted by the dead taken by the war. By the time we took note, it was too late. The Devil has set his familiars to work their malice and we are steeped in it. Our town is depleted of men, many of whom are either dead or fighting for Parliament. We lack the manpower to fight, and I humbly beg your aid.

By the hand of Lord Carew

His words are a tight scrawl, the ink smudged from being shoved into a messenger's waiting hands. The sight of Dodmore's letter on my desk does little to anchor me. Mrs Hale will bear the costs of her actions like a secret hurt if I do as she wishes. Althamia will not forgive me once she realises I am the cause of it. I flinch at the memory of Clements's hands on her. People care for convenience, not the truth, and Althamia has been publicly condemned. My absence will not save her. Agnes's song rattles in my head, demanding more than my regrets. The words I wrote for Broad are a song I must silence. With that, I stride out the door.

Clements is leaning against a wall mere houses away from the Hales' residence. His casual demeanour makes me want to run him through, but instead through gritted teeth I say, 'I am here to bargain.'

He folds his arms across his chest. 'Your terms?'

'We have received an invitation to investigate witches in Lancaster. The payment offered is substantial. You will join us and will leave Althamia, her parents and her household alone.'

I shove the letter at his chest. He seizes up in mock pain as though I've pierced him with a blade. His eyes pass through me to Will, who makes a silent approach, his face accusing. I've betrayed him again, but I do not apologise. I raise my chin. I have done what is necessary.

Clements unfolds the letter. 'It appears we have the same master. I too am in Lord Carew's employ.'

'You lie!'

He shrugs. 'My employment with Carew was conditional on your master's involvement.'

'Carew will not want you after he hears what you have done,' I tell him. 'Althamia is Lord Carew's niece.'

Clements steps towards me. 'Then Lord Carew's dismissal will leave me at liberty to pursue her.'

It's as though his hands are around my throat. 'We will set out to meet Lord Carew by the week's end,' I concede. 'Our involvement is conditional upon you staying away from both the Hales and York.'

Clements turns his attention to Will. 'Are we in agreement?'

Turn on me if you will, I beg, *but only after our business in Rawton is done.*

Will answers my silent plea with a slight incline of the head. Victorious, Clements saunters away.

Will's eyes are flat. 'I could hand you over to him. He would be satisfied by it.'

'You would not.' An inhaled bluff. 'I remind you of someone you loved once.'

His response is cutting. 'My love is a danger. They were not spared by it.'

'Clements has a hold on you.' He looks away. 'Althamia has been marked by Clements's accusations. Our leaving wouldn't lessen the burden or our guilt or the threat Clements poses.'

'He is just one man,' Will counters.

'And yet the crowd did nothing but watch while he grabbed her off the street. Althamia's father is despised and his enemies will use this as a tool to undermine him. Must Althamia spend the rest of her life taking care not to drop?'

He returns the hurt: 'She is not your redemption.' I recoil at the memory of Agnes and Lady Katherine his words invoke. 'Clements can be drawn away but he will not be leashed.'

'He does not need to be. A thorough investigation will convince Lord Carew that his parish is not beset by witches.'

'And after?' Will probes.

'Our association will end. You will return to your work on the Northern circuit, Clements will keep to his word and stay away from Althamia and York, and I will return home.'

'A clear plan,' he says and I turn at his nod of acceptance.

'What did they sing of? Lady Katherine and Lord Teversham?'

The question pulls me back. 'Lord Teversham, his murder by his son. The lady, had I stayed to listen, would have sang of her innocence.'

He marks my guilt with a knowing look. 'Your silence weighs on you. Mr Pearce, you forget that this is not a hunt that can be hindered and I will not save you if you try.'

'I do not need to be saved. I betrayed the only father I've ever known by placing myself in your company. I have kept quiet when the dead sing. I have betrayed Althamia, myself and even you the great witch-hunter. It will not be a hardship to fool Clements,' I tell him with a direct look he returns.

'No, it will not be a hardship,' he says, weighing me up. 'I have set a fine path. Let us see how well you follow.'

Chapter Eighteen

Six bells were rung for Agnes earlier this morning and an additional fourteen for each year she lived. Hale, keen for this whole business to be forgotten, arranged for Agnes to be buried at night. He, Will and I wait in the parlour for the arrival of the torchbearers and undertakers who will carry Agnes's body to the local graveyard. Tomorrow, we depart for Rawton. I have written stalling missives to Father and Dodmore and hope it will hold until this business is done and Althamia is safe.

Will and I had immediately informed the Hales of our decision to go to Rawton, and of Clements's connection to Lord Carew. Mrs Hale had said nothing; only her pained strikes at her embroidery betrayed her. Hale opened his mouth to blame us, or so I assumed until his jaw ground so loudly I thought it would break. None of this would have happened if we'd accepted the invite on the first request. 'They are in partnership?' he seethed, furious at Clements's victory and how it had lessened him in his brother-in-law's eyes. Agnes lies dead, Althamia remains in jeopardy, but Hale's pride was his first concern. I cannot forgive him for it, nor will Mrs Hale.

When the undertakers arrive, I quickly volunteer to inform the women. I walk the mournful stairs to the basement where Agnes's melody plays.

'Turn around,' Althamia commands at my presence. 'She is not to be looked at.'

Agnes lies shrouded on the table, layered with rosemary, with Althamia's muffs resting on her stomach. Obeying the instruction, I turn while Althamia and her mother finish preparing her friend. Agnes has been well served by her mistress's familiarity with death. Preservatives have kept her remains from decay and her song rings starling sharp. It chisels at my bones.

I have been numbed. I have been petted but I have never been regarded by all but one. A small unseen thing with a mouth heavy from the taste of iron. I'd rather be a mistress with a silk bit between my lips. Quarry no matter my station. I am caught. The water keeps his eyes murky shadows while his grasp turns me into a mermaid. One with a stinging blindness to my sight and a whisper of air in my lungs that robs me of my siren's call.

The last thing Agnes saw and heard was the eyes of the man who drowned her and the cheers of the people who watched. She was powerless throughout her life, a state even death could not lift. I will deliver justice for her. I will give her a voice.

'It is time,' I announce.

Mrs Hale sighs at my back, longing for this dreadful day to be over.

'I cannot do this—' Althamia's voice breaks, but the nearness of Mrs Hale stops me from turning.

I make a silent plea.

'I will stall for time,' Mrs Hale concedes, her footsteps a slow march.

Althamia stares at Agnes. 'You will meet my cousin Grace,' had been her muted response to the news of Will's and my departure. Her expression had given away nothing to indicate her feelings about me placing myself in the company of the man who attacked her and murdered her friend. Nevertheless, the lack had shamed me more than her expected condemnation.

She raises her head. 'Agnes was an orphan. I regarded her as a friend and sister. She hovered on the edge of my world, but I knew nothing of hers. She was young and vulnerable, and I let her come to harm.'

'You cannot blame yourself,' I console her, but my thoughts turn to Francis. I did not let him see me as I was, but that did not diminish what was between us.

'Can I not? I went out to search for you that day, leaving Agnes with no choice but to follow me.'

'Her death was an accident.' My lie is overshadowed by her pained laugh.

'My father said I should content myself that the coroner did not pass a suicide verdict. They have blinded themselves to the bruises around her neck. No one will listen to me anymore! Perhaps I am cursed like Cassandra of Troy.'

'You are not cursed.'

'Then why I am not believed?' she demands. 'Why do my parents deny Agnes justice, why do they deny me, choosing instead to ply me with bitter almonds for green-sickness?'

I turn my head, but she is bent over Agnes's body and does not look to me for an answer.

Will harboured suspicions about Clements's involvement in Agnes's death, but the protection the witch-hunter enjoys meant the magistrates lack any real appetite to question him. Agnes was a servant and Althamia, though the Mayor's daughter, is a mere woman. Her opinion holds no weight. Mine would, were I to tell them of what Agnes sang of. My admission would be a noble sacrifice, had I not already added Agnes to the dead people around my neck.

All of a sudden, Althamia is upon me with her hands raised. I stumble when she pushes me, but as I ready myself for another blow she backs away.

'When that man put his hands on me, I was so afraid I could hardly breathe. Now I want to kill him. I want him spread across my table, his insides laid bare for my inspection.' She turns away. 'You have chosen *him*. You will be in his company. You will breathe his air as though he did not kill Agnes, as though he did not put his hands on me.' She moves to push me again but stops. 'Why?'

'You know why.'

'Yes,' she acknowledges, 'but does it have to be you? You were always out of reach, but now . . .'

She holds out her hands to me and for a moment I am tempted to take them in mine. Agnes hums, a reminder that I am too full of the dead to make room for the living. Because of me, Althamia is stained by rumours of witchcraft. I will not endanger her further. I let her hands dangle in the cold, dead air, killing whatever she thought was between us.

She smooths the tears off her face and steadies herself for the evening ahead. With her back towards me, she surmises, 'You will forget me. You do not dwell on things that pain you.'

I lessen the distance between us and reach for her hand, tempted to take her away from all this. My hand drops and she is gone before I have time to regret the moment. I face Agnes. If I hadn't known the truth, her calm demeanour would have convinced me she was sleeping.

'I am sorry,' and she sings in response.

Chapter Nineteen

I finish writing a letter to Stephens, a brief warning one padded with a ring for him to hawk just in case he wishes to flee or join me in France once my work is done. Its brevity will meet his approval, but the sentiment? I ask myself as I re-read it.

Dear Stephens,

You were more my family than anyone else and still I turned from you. I am sorry for it. I have written to Father and my friend to inform them of my intended return once I have finished assisting Judge Percival. I hope neither you nor Sophie will be disappointed by the delay. It warms me to know that she now turns to you in memory of me.

Yours,
Nicholas

In place of adding more lines, I murmur a brief prayer over it and then leave it on my desk with a coin for Hale's servant to deliver. 'It is not too late for regret.' Will enters my bedchamber, valise in hand. In his black morning suit, Will looks as though he is dressed for a funeral rather than half a day's travel to Rawton.

'I am set upon this course,' I say, and finish packing.

He hands me an anti-witch talisman. 'It will not burn you. A harmless token, one that the people of Rawton will expect you to wear.'

'Another lie,' I remark at the pendant's cool touch. In the dark it will be a slither of moonlight around my neck.

'One you will wear easily,' he replies and is gone before I can apologise.

When I finish packing, I find Mrs Hale standing guard outside Althamia's bedchamber. Her apron hangs about her as though fashioned from steel. Where she was tentative before, she is now resolute. Her eyes remain fixed on my silver talisman as I thank her for her hospitality.

The door opens. 'Goodbye, Nicholas,' Althamia murmurs, a salutation I return. We exchange a wordless look that neither of us is willing to break. The planes of her face dance in and out of the shadows as Mrs Hale closes the door. This is how she will appear to me in my dreams. Mrs Hale breathes a sigh of relief once I am out of sight. Will and I are leaving, and her daughter is safe.

'Your master is waiting,' snaps Hale from the entrance.

'Goodbye,' I murmur. My mouth opens to say more, but he turns his back and a servant is quick to shut me out.

I climb into the carriage and find not one but two people waiting. Will is sitting beside Clements.

'Don't be so surprised,' Clements smirks. 'A soldier's pension only stretches so far.'

The last time I saw him was through Agnes's eyes and I half flinch from the reminder. I sit as far away from him as possible in the cramped space. It would be unreasonable to expect him to travel separately.

'To our partnership,' says Clements.

'To our partnership,' I echo, but there is no warmth to it. In fear of being cut we are all sharp corners with each other. The carriage door closes and mutual distrusts and resentment make us silent.

'I can be of use,' I offer when Will grimaces at his correspondence. Clements takes in his brusque dismissal and then myself. His steady interest is a maelstrom, one that would crush me were Will to let go. I turn my gaze outwards and slow my breathing. In London, you have only to open your window and the world comes rushing in. It has been tamed by men who build over land and rivers. Here there is a vast silence and I write down the details of a masterless landscape that arches and rounds itself like a spine.

'Is our partnership to be coloured by brooding silences?' I look up, but Clements's question is for Will. 'You are starting to resemble the man I knew,' he jibes.

'While you have never changed,' Will retorts. Their exchange, peppered with past anecdotes, leaves me with no doubt of my place in it. They have been friends, rivals, enemies but in the ensuing silence they become a mixture of all three. They are a shared history and I am no more to Will than an obligation, one he can shrug off or hand over to Clements.

I rub my neck, stiff from nerves, as the carriage comes to a temporary halt near a small town. Clements steps down from the carriage with an inviting look I choose to ignore. He shrugs and the slammed door seals Will and me in from the cold. Will closes his eyes, while in the quiet I muse on his invitation. There is an emptiness in Clements that I recognise in myself. But whereas the dead rush to fill me in, he feeds on the living. He would feed on me unless I can find a weakness to leash him with.

'Are you in want of a new path?' says Will when I reach for the carriage door.

'We three are an uneasy party and will split at the seams unless I uncover some secret of his to bind us.'

He closes the door and pulls me back. 'He will suspect you.'

'He suspects everyone. There is no trust here, only hatred. The only advantage I have is that he hates me a little less.'

His face is grave. 'You will have to reveal something of yourself in turn.'

'I know, but how else am I to see him leashed? Or get justice for Agnes, Althamia and all the other people he has hurt?' The bile rises in my throat. I do not fear for my safety. I am fearful I will lose Althamia completely by placing myself even closer to Clements. 'He has a hold on you. I have no claim on your secrets, but you will have my aid nonetheless.' My father had no use for love or friendship. Until now, I would not have likened myself to him. I have used people – Will, Althamia, even Francis and poor Agnes. I have led him here and I am now honour bound to free us both.

'Your aid will not save me. Parliament will see that I have said yes in this matter and will expect me to say yes again. I was a fool to believe I ever had a choice. Besides, it is not only for my sake you seek an advantage.'

'I have no real standing in this partnership,' I confess. 'I am alone and exposed with not even my secrets to call my own.' I exhale when he draws back.

'Nicholas,' he says when I open the door, 'your secrets are yours. I'll not leverage them against you.' His promise feels a more tangible link than the nostalgia and obligation that has tied us together so far.

I step out to a drab collection of shops along the main street. A noisy flock of starlings hurtles above me. Their plumages are silver flecks in the sky. I walk until I find Clements standing in the middle of the town square.

A quick acknowledgement. 'The North is a rebellious place,' he says of the two men who dangle from the makeshift gallows. They have been stripped down to their undershirts and breeches, their bodies covered with tallow and fat. The signs around their necks denounce them as Royalist spies.

The stray notes of their forlorn duet betray their regrets. Those who die badly are filled with them and I swoon into their rhythm.

Our hands were fettered from behind. The crowd stares, a sight we swayed in and out of as our eyes bulged and our faces swelled.

Their staccato song tears at my limbs. The men had taken the Cavaliers' food to feed their families in exchange for showing them the area's terrain. They begged, they pleaded, they cried even as the noose was secured around their throats. Their song clings to me and I grind my feet to stop myself being swept up by it.

'A waste of rope,' says Clements, and I catch my breath in the interruption. 'In Scotland we would strangle the witches who didn't recant. A mercy before burning.'

'You do not strike me as a merciful,' I say.

'I am not,' he says and mimes squeezing an invisible rope. 'I hated being a soldier. Much of my time was spent marching over muddied roads trying not to be killed by the enemy who leapt out at us from hedges. Or else fighting under a sky of sparks and smoke. I fought in continental armies and for the King, where I lost an eye. And when I dared protest about our treatment and lack of pay, they strung me up and made me stand on tiptoe for a day.' He rolls up his sleeves to show me the marks around his wrists. 'I should not complain. I am lucky not to have perished from exposure or camp fever as most of my regiment did. I fight for myself now.'

'I imagine the women you have condemned would have gladly stood on tiptoe rather than flail from the gallows for lack of grounding,' I retort sharply. It is impossible to pity him. Agnes, Althamia and all the other women he's hurt or killed are seared wounds on my brain. For a moment, I worry I have overplayed my hand, but he does nothing but roll down his sleeves.

'You are staring,' I observe after a while.

'I am making a study of you. Do you seek Lord Carew's favour?' he asks. 'Religion? No, that doesn't drive you. Bloodlust?' Clements shakes his head. 'The girl. You are in *love*.'

'She was a passing distraction,' I lie, and his head tilts at my callous tone. 'I am here to make my fortune.'

'You have enough of that.' He motions to my ivory pearled doublet.

'I will make my own,' I say, and his knowing look convinces me he has heard something of my family history.

'I fear you will be disappointed. Your master lacks the ambition of his youth.'

I do not take the bait. He would suspect me if I showed myself too eager. Instead, I make a show of hiding my disappointment. My breathing steadies as he moves out of sight with a grunted refrain not to tarry.

Chapter Twenty

The rough halt of the carriage pulls Will from his gentle slumber and Clements's eyes from mine. His scrutiny throughout our journey made me feel like a portrait. Now his attention is drawn to Lord Carew's estate. A three-storey red-brick manor house, flanked by acres of green at its front and a forest at its back. A hungry whistle escapes his lips.

'We have business with Lord Carew,' Will informs the gatehouse porter, who waves us through. Clements strides through the manor entrance, but Will and I pause to observe a couple stationed near the gatehouse. The woman is near thirty with fair colouring and holds herself like a flower turned in on itself. She is all thorns, and her male companion keeps himself apart as though fearful of being pricked. The materials of their clothes are rich, though the man's garments hang loose enough that he shrinks into the excess. They are as unmoveable as stone and our approach is guarded.

'We are here to plead our case to Lord Carew. Mrs Ingram and my husband, Mr Ingram,' she says, giving her sullen introduction.

'His Lordship refuses to see us.' Mr Ingram's voice is rougher than his wife's cultured vowels.

Will gives his title but is not inclined to linger. 'Your accusations have not gone unheard. I am here to assist Lord Carew with the investigation.'

Mrs Ingram blocks his path, her voice desperate. 'Ann Greer killed my son. She used magic to murder him in his sleep.'

'You are certain your child's death was by supernatural means?' Will asks.

Her nostrils flare. 'You do not believe me. His Lordship was the same. He ordered me to marshal my doubts.'

Will inclines his head respectfully. 'I am sorry for your loss,' a departing platitude she sneers at.

'We will investigate fully,' I promise. 'If Ann Greer is guilty, she will not be able to hide it from us.'

'Thank you,' says Mr Ingram. But his wife is not content and scowls at the word *if*.

'Sir,' she says, in a tone that makes me feel all the years of my youth, 'Ann Greer is a jealous creature who took my son to punish me for my wealth, my land and my husband.' When Mr Ingram steers her back towards their carriage, she shouts, 'Mr John Rush, the witch-hunter, will speak on our behalf!'

Mr Rush. That name is familiar, but I dismiss it from thought and follow Will into the extravagant manor house. The flooring is paved with black and white marble, and we are led up a staircase of carved oak leaves. Lord Carew's wealth is displayed to its full advantage in the long gallery, which is decorated with tapestries, Persian rugs and portraits of Lord Carew's ancestors. My father would no doubt feel like a beggar in comparison. The gold plates and silverware on display put Father's own collection to shame. Whatever Lord Carew's concerns, he has weathered the war well. Many great houses, under Royal or Parliamentarian directives, have had to melt their gold to make bullets for the reigning armies of their counties.

Ahead of us, Clements paces in the great hall, a luxuriously vast room though it is let down by its bare display of arms. Lord Carew's weapons were probably ransacked by the reigning army at the time. Our host, as Hale grudgingly confided before we left York, is a leading landowner in these parts, and like Thomas Howard, Earl of Arundel, a collector of Greek sculptures. Will looks appreciatively at the statues that line the chamber, while Clements cranes his neck at the marbled head of a vestal virgin. His eyes flicker from the vast, glazed windows to the elaborate plaster ceiling, which depicts Orpheus's descent into the underworld to rescue Eurydice, Hade's kidnap of Persephone, and Phaeton's ill-fated chariot ride. Through narrowed eyes he absorbs the wealth of Lord Carew's home and I imagine, whatever they have paid him, he is cursing himself for not demanding more.

'We will seek him out ourselves,' Clements snaps when a servant imparts that a hunt delays our host's appearance. Will and I trail behind Clements as he strides past the protesting servant towards the woodlands.

'He thinks I am past my prime,' Will mutters under his breath after I recount my earlier conversation with Clements.

'I will encourage his delusions and earn his trust until I have gained sufficient leverage to force his retirement.'

Will shakes his head. 'You are too ambitious. At best you can prevent him from returning to York. If you hope for more, you will have to kill him.'

'Then I will kill him,' I declare.

A light mist borders the Carew estates, a few strides and we are lost to it. Lord Carew stands in a gown of green velvet in a large clearing to the back of his estate. Neither he nor his female companion is dressed for a hunt. He is tall and carries himself with ease despite his solid build. He is much older than Mrs Hale, his temple lined with grey and his face haggard from lack of sleep. The attending servant rushes ahead of us, while Clements sets himself apart and removes his right glove to acknowledge our host's superior position. His mouth thins when our host doesn't acknowledge our presence, and his jaw tightens when Will and I incline our heads respectfully in His Lordship's direction.

Our impatience has annoyed our host, though he is too polite to show it. As punishment he makes us wait in the cold, his attention focused on a young woman, only a few years older than myself. I study her profile. This must be Althamia's cousin, Grace. Her hair is brownish-gold, and her cheeks want colour, though her kinship to Althamia is marked by her long neck, jaw and eyes. It's a fragile resemblance and on closer inspection I break.

Lord Carew assesses us. 'You have received my letter,' he says needlessly. Will nods and his eyes settle on the witch talisman around his neck. 'Do you hawk, Judge Percival?'

'Occasionally,' Will answers.

'It is a dying art,' he reflects.

'I prefer guns,' Clements chimes in.

Grace takes no notice of our exchange. Her attention is focused on a goshawk perched on her gauntleted fist. Grace slips the hood from its face to reveal a stripe of pale grey across a brown head. On her command, the falconer releases a heron. She eyes the creature and releases the goshawk once its prey reaches its stride. The birds are a flash of colour in the afternoon sky. I step closer towards her. She is not what I expected, and I remember what Althamia told me of her ruse to reclaim her estates by pretending to be a widow. I had thought she would possess some of Althamia's vivacity, but she is too controlled. A premature assessment dismissed by how impatiently she toys with the black ribbons of her bodice.

Her eyes turn upwards, searching for the creature that has soared out of sight into the mist. The goshawk, visible once more, circles above the heron and then swoops in for a killing strike. At her mistress's command, the bird returns and perches on her fist. I move towards her and note the flesh caught in the goshawk's claw and the smell of the woodlands now spiced with blood. The predator, ever alert, catches me observing it. I hurriedly look away. They do not like to be stared at.

'You hawk,' Grace states after observing the interaction.

'I had a merlin when I was boy.' Her scorn brings a flush of embarrassed anger to my cheeks. Father only allowed Francis a hawk. They are costly creatures favoured by the nobility and even then Father made it clear he saw nothing in me to justify the expense. 'Does she have a name?'

'Beatrice,' she answers and uses her thumb to rub at the speckles of blood on her exposed hand. 'It whitens the skin,' she says, and I swallow my distaste as she dabs the blood across her neck.

The creature's grey wings, yellow eyes and talons are covered in blood. The bird snaps at the meat Grace feeds it from her pouch. 'I manned her myself,' she preens, but her mouth drops in disappointment when her accomplishment goes unremarked. Her reaction probably would have been the same had I complimented her feat. 'Birds are very easy to tame,' she shares. 'The process is similar to how you man a witch. Deprive them of sleep or come at them with the hood. If you are firm, they will become accustomed to it and will do anything to retreat to it.'

Her words are a chill I cannot shake off. For a moment I imagine myself a hawk, hooded to prevent me from taking fright.

'Grace, we are going inside,' her uncle announces.

Grace jingles her pouch at him. It is half full of meat. She tilts her head to Beatrice. 'She is not yet—'

'I am done.' Carew's tone brooks no argument.

'I will take her with me then,' she snaps at the falconer and hoods the goshawk.

Lord Carew sets a measured pace for the procession and we pretend to admire his home anew. Grace and I walk in step while Will and Clements match Lord Carew's leisurely pace.

'The winter room,' she points out when we pass an elegant parlour. The goshawk on her fist flutters and I flinch from the brush of its feathers on my face. 'My uncle's domain is the sun-room near the end,' she says as we near Lord Carew's parlour. A large marble table dominates the room's core. A blaze rages in the corner fireplace, and the family's coat of arms hangs proudly above it. Lord Carew sits down on his day bed. It's of an identical fabric to his gown and his slow recline makes him look disembodied. He picks up a book beside him, while Grace ties her goshawk to a perch in the corner and sits near it, opposite her uncle. She is framed by the creature, which spreads its grey wings to reveal the expanse of ivory underneath. It's a similar colour to the pearls around the seams of Grace's dress and the ones at her neck.

At our host's invitation, we sit on the elaborately carved open-back chairs. Grace's attention is taken by a coin she holds in her hand. The glow of the nearby fire makes it seem as though she is twirling flames.

'My Lord—' I start, but our host pays me no mind.

'I hope you are not too disheartened by your demotion from the Star Chamber,' he remarks.

Will inclines his head. 'My employments since have done much to lessen my distress.'

I still at Lord Carew's arched brow. 'I am acquainted with your stepmother's family. I met your brother on a few occasions. A charming youth.'

Will and I exchange a passing look at his rehearsed set-downs. We have answered his summons, yet he resents having to beg our acquiescence. He will slacken the reins once we have taken the bit, a sentiment Will acknowledges with a tight smile.

Still, I will not make it easy for him. 'I am his replacement,' I respond, with an edge to my words that forces his reassessment.

'Uncle, Althamia has written to me of Mr Pearce's talents,' says Grace, retrieving the pamphlet I wrote from a pile on the corner desk. 'These were all the copies we were able to round up.' Will's mouth thins and I wince at the knowledge of how far my words have travelled. The words are a song and for a moment I doubt my ability to silence it.

'The people of Rawton were quite taken with it,' Lord Carew remarks.

'My uncle is a collector of men such as yourself,' says Grace.

'And the abandoned,' finishes Lord Carew.

I clench my teeth only to realise from Grace's stark reaction that I am not Carew's target. The coin slips from her fingers and rolls across the floor. A waiting servant rushes to retrieve it for her.

Nodding at the pamphlets, I say, 'I have a playwright's touch. One I will apply to this present situation.' Lord Carew regards me anew and exchanges a look with his niece. At his gesture a servant leaves and then returns with a bundle of papers. He hands them to me and I spread across my lap the venomous accusations of witchcraft that have beset their town. My fellow witch-hunters join me in scanning the pages; some of the accusations concern our hosts. Grace and Lord Carew are accused of being church papists, their manor a sanctuary for foreign priests – an accusation that Lord Carew could hang for.

Will's and my eyes meet over Clements's head. Lord Carew's authority has been lessened by suspicions of his recusancy. He has exposed his weakness and we will need to bind Clements before he has a chance to exploit it.

'There is no truth to any of it,' says Lord Carew.

'They have taken his pledge,' says Grace of the Protestation Oath men signed to confirm their allegiance to the King and Church of England. Those who refused were taken to be Catholics.

'Freely,' Lord Carew adds.

'Are you not able to use your influence as magistrate to intervene in the investigations?' says Clements, a probing blow.

Lord Carew grinds his teeth. 'My influence is resented. War, bitter weather and an outbreak of smallpox last year have left people unsettled. In normal times I could dismiss these accusations with a harsh word. That was until the stranger arrived.'

'What stranger?' I ask. He made no mention of this in his letter to Will.

Lord Carew sinks even lower into his day bed. 'He calls himself John Rush and has been riding up and down the county encouraging people to plague the magistrates with complaints of witchcraft. At first, he was run out of town until the people . . .'

'They began to listen,' Grace finishes.

'I have heard of him,' I interject, and tell Will and Clements of Mr Broad's pamphlet.

'He has papered the town with his exploits,' relays Lord Carew. 'He calls himself Witchfinder General and claims he has been appointed by Parliament, though my friends have yet to confirm if this is true.'

'Perhaps he flew here,' Grace murmurs.

'Witchfinder General,' says Clements, 'he has given himself a title.' There is envy in his voice, a regret that he had not thought to do the same in his prime.

'A pretend one,' Will reminds him.

'One that places him above you,' says Clements.

'A title he demands payment for,' complains Lord Carew. 'An

extortionate sum, one I will be blamed for when the cost of his investigation is recouped through parish taxes. He is rumoured to have hanged at least fifty witches. He had a hand in putting an end to the Slaidburn witches,' he adds, referring to a coven found guilty of making the revived dead – including the deceased gentry – their servants. 'Some claim he is the reason for the King's defeat in the North. I mean Parliament's victory,' he corrects himself. 'He is said to have stopped a coven near Sawley from sending imps to aid Prince Rupert during the Battle of Marston Moor.' Clements snorts. 'He has exposed witches hiding under the garb of ministers and even witch-hunters,' he adds, a detail that brings Clements's amusement to an abrupt end. 'He is fearless when it comes to the hunt and pays no mind to a person's position or rank.'

'He will find himself in like company,' says Clements.

'He is as all men,' Grace drawls, 'intent on turning himself into myth.'

'Myth or not, he has set my own people against me. The minister himself has welcomed him as if he were Christ come again, and the people are at my gates every day,' he snaps.

Will and I share another look. How are we to bridle Rush and Clements if the town is as eager for a witch-hunt as the witch-hunter?

'The Ingrams,' remembers Will to Lord Carew's displeasure.

'Grief has made them wild since their son died two years ago,' says Grace. 'They blame his death on a witch's curse, and since Mr Ingram is a church warden he is believed.'

Lord Carew's jaw tightens. 'I want the man gone. He is pressing me to take the people's depositions.'

'You have not done so already?' I ask.

Lord Carew colours. As magistrate, he should have taken the testimonies of the accusers and accused before deciding whether to dismiss the charges or proceed to trial. He is either a fool or ill-advised to have so ignored the people's grievances. Or frightened of his neighbours turning against him. Whatever his reasoning, he is wrong to believe that doing nothing will be enough to save him.

He turns to Will. 'People respect your reputation, Judge Percival. If you were to investigate and find everything in order, they would believe you over Mr Rush.' It is as much a cajole as Lord Carew dares and completely unnecessary. Had Lord Carew been more transparent from the outset, Will would have been less inclined to refuse his original invitation.

Clements's jaw drops. 'My Lord. That is not what you wrote when you offered me employment.'

'Then you have misunderstood. You were employed to bring Judge Percival here,' Grace reminds him. She motions to a servant who approaches Clements with a heavy purse.

Will reaches his hand to stop me when I half rise. Clements will ride straight back to Yorkshire, to Althamia, if we allow him to be dismissed. At the increased pressure on my arm, I reluctantly sit down.

'I am here, despite my reluctance, because of Clements's efforts. He is vital to our investigation,' Will stresses and does not blink at the long look Grace favours him with. 'He is experienced in identifying witches.'

At her nod, the servant retreats, only to be stopped when Clements snatches the purse.

'I have fulfilled the first part of my contract and will take this as early compensation,' says Clements.

Grace makes no reaction, though Lord Carew wrinkles his nose. Clements's greed offends Carew even though the witch-hunter is only seeking what he is owed. I survey the surrounding luxury. It is easy to be offended when you have all this.

Clements uncrosses his legs. 'Are we to hunt witches or Mr Rush?'

Lord Carew rises. 'Rawton is entirely lacking witches. You are to rid this town of Mr Rush. My niece shall handle this matter on my behalf.'

'We are pleased to serve you.' Clements grins once Lord Carew has left.

'Althamia wrote to me of you,' Grace says, and Clements bristles at the nonchalant way she rests her hands on the arms of her chair. A woman's chair is supposed to be armless to allow them to sit and sew at their leisure. She has put herself in a man's place. Flattery will not pull her from it. Clements's eyes move from the low cut of her gown to her face. 'I am not here to please, but to command. There is a town meeting in two days. Mr Rush will be there. It would be the ideal moment to make your entrance.'

Will nods our acceptance. 'Will your uncle be present?'

She shakes her head. 'He is worried his attendance will embolden the people. He is the only magistrate. The others fled once the town was secured for Parliament.'

'His absence will anger them,' I explain. 'For this to succeed he will need to play his part. We will make a show of investigating, but he must pretend to listen.'

Will's look is appraising. He is as surprised as I am by how easily I slip into the role of a witch-hunter.

'I will persuade him,' says Grace. 'You will be paid six pounds in exchange for securing a satisfactory result.' Her smile slips when she addresses Clements. 'Our space is limited. I assume you will not mind making your bed in the garret. Bannister will lead you.'

Clements rankles at the slight, but he duly departs.

'I shall escort you both your chambers.' Grace pauses at the staircase near a portrait hidden behind a purple taffeta curtain. 'My aunt, the late Lady Carew,' she says and unveils it for our inspection.

The young woman or rather girl in the portrait is made lifelike by her brown eyes that almost follow our movements and the hand that cups her swelling stomach. A portrait to the left is of Lord Carew. He has just come into his youth and faces his young wife. 'My uncle found favour with the late King who rewarded him an heiress. She died in childbirth, along with his heir.' Something about her directness reminds me of Althamia, though she lacks her softness.

'I was not yet born when she passed,' she says of Will's murmured condolences. She stops on the second flight of stairs. 'Judge Percival, your room is at the end of the hall to the right.'

'Our mothers, Lord Carew's sisters, were twins,' she relays once Will is out of sight, drawing my attention to another family portrait once Will is in his room. I recognise Lord Carew as a boy in the centre between his parents. Two young girls complete the tableau on each end. They wear black gowns trimmed with gold and clutch identical handkerchiefs edged with pansies and a white ermine in the centre. Grace stands a finger length from the portrait. 'My mother had meant to accompany my grandfather to York, but he took my aunt – Althamia's mother – instead after she did something to put him in a rage.' I assume she is musing aloud until she turns to me. 'If he had not, my mother would have met Althamia's father and I would be in York and she would be here in my place, neither wife nor widow, but a halfway between a waiting-woman and a steward.'

'Althamia has not had an easy time of it.'

She takes my words as a rebuke and her tone is sharp. 'Yes, she made it plain to me in her letters. It was my uncle who secured Clements's service. He promised to deliver Judge Percival to us. My uncle regrets that Althamia was hurt, but she will be stronger for it. I harbour no ill will towards my cousin. It is natural to imagine yourself in someone else's place.'

Her eyes scan the length of my person, a discomforting scrutiny brought to an end when she strides off towards my bedchamber. 'I had the servants prepare this room for you.'

The room is dominated by a wooden framed bed in the middle and the valance of yellow silk that forms a canopy over it. The fire is at a low blaze and in the corner is a dark oak cupboard, marble dresser, small table, two armchairs and a looking glass.

Grace hovers near the door and arches the heel of her shoe near the thick rugs that line the floor. 'You are different from your letters. I assume your master's replies to my uncle came from your hand.' At my nod, she adds, 'I wrote to your master under my uncle's instructions.' Her eyes narrow at my lack of surprise at her admission. She points towards the window. 'Pendle Hill. We live in its shadow.' I walk up to the casement windows and make out the hill, clouded by mist in the distance.

'I did not know it was so near,' I remark, but the door closes, and I am left alone with the hills in my sight. A bleak mass, one that drapes me like a shadow when I turn my back to it.

Chapter Twenty-One

'You do not belong here,' remarks the tavern maid, her tone curious. She is a year or so younger than me, and places a jug of ale on the table. I sip and study the backdrop of Pendle Hill through the slight window in front of me. I am at liberty until we meet with the townspeople tomorrow. Last night I dreamt of Agnes, and of Pendle Hill, a gothic landmark, one that haunts the peripheral of my vision. I'd had enough and this morning over breakfast had decided to ride out to Pendle to cool my unease. I had stalked the hill's skyline across bogs, breaking my journey with a small stop at a tavern in Barley.

'Sir.' The maid curtsies when she remembers her manners. She is small and dark-haired.

'I am in the area on business, and have ventured here to see the hill,' I divulge, and when she shows no interest in resuming her duties, I add: 'I am from London.' I peer again in the direction of the hill, until the girl shifts and blocks it from sight. I am grateful, as it shields me from the other patrons' curious stares. I am plainly dressed but feel out of place in this worn-looking tavern frequented by the villagers.

'London,' she whispers to herself. 'I have seen it in my dreams.'

'I would not waste your time dreaming of it. It will steal your breath. It is too full and dirty.'

She frowns. 'I had thought the only thing London would take from me is my purse. I did not think it would begrudge me the very air I breathe. I will dream of York instead. My father,' she says of the innkeeper who keeps a subtle watch over us, 'has family there.'

I smile. 'I have just come from York. It far surpasses London.'

'The place, or the people?' she teases.

It is as though she can read my thoughts of Althamia on my face, and I flush and mutter, 'Both.'

'Are you lodging nearby?' she asks.

'I am a guest of Lord Carew.'

'You are the witch-hunter!' She says with a flinched look at the talisman at my neck.

'My master is,' I correct.

She backs away with a quick curtsy and hurries to whisper in her father's ear before busying herself with attending to the customers on the opposite side of the tavern.

The flat top of the hill is again blotted out, this time by the innkeeper, who places himself in front of me.

'My daughter tells me you are from London. I am Mr Wren, the owner.'

I incline my head and accept the tankard of ale he offers me.

'It must be exciting to have lived near the King and Parliament's men.'

'I have seen the King, but at a distance. Though I regret the closest I have come to Fairfax or Cromwell is through the news-books.'

He nods and muses, 'It is strange, but I feel as if I know these men. They have touched our lives, but it is doubtful men such as myself will ever touch theirs.'

'We are pawns to be manoeuvred,' I reflect.

'You are not here to listen to me prattle,' he says, but his tone is only slightly apologetic. He looks back at the hill. 'If you ride straight ahead you will reach Faugh's quarry within a few miles. Old Demdike, the matriarch of one of the two families who perished in the Pendle Witch Trials, is rumoured to have met the Devil here. She is said to have sold her soul in exchange for a wish from the Devil who took the shape of a boy named Tibb.'

'And if I wish to ascend it?'

'It is easy to find it from there. You will not get lost.'

'Thank you. The hill is beautiful from a distance. I wish to admire it up close.'

He turns to leave but then stops. 'It's a striking but harsh legacy and it's always within sight. Be careful with your horse. The land is boggy. You should put it on the leading rein when you get close.'

I finish my drink and rise to leave.

Wren stops me. 'Sir, my home is no stranger to your sort. Young, old, rich, poor. It makes no difference what disguise you don, you are always the same man. I do not mean to be insulting. But you are not welcome here. We have been pillaged of names and will give no more.'

The tavern grows quiet as people listen our exchange.

I should tell them that I am not that man, and I am here to help, but I can't. Francis, Agnes, Lady Katherine; I have had a hand in all their deaths.

'I take no offence,' I answer, and tip my hat in goodbye. I am that man and can't claim to be anything less until I remove Clements and Rush without any casualties.

Faugh's quarry is a stony pit. From its rocks protrudes the face of a wizard carved with a moustache, beard and eyes that remain visible despite the green that covers it. If the Devil stalks these parts, he is not minded to appear. I am somewhat relieved that I will not have to test my resolve to exchange my soul to undo my mistakes.

The closer I get to the hill, the bleaker the landscape around me becomes. It is lined with mosses and purple moor grass, and the ground oozes water with each step. The limestone cottages become sparse and disappear from view as I proceed. The sounds of grazing cattle are lost and the trees with their splintered trunks and skinned bark look as though they are in retreat.

At one point I am startled by a flutter of cloak-textured feathers. A short-eared owl, I surmise, from the accompanying curt yowls. The creature is gone, and I am once more alone. The narrowness of the path threatens to strangle me in places. Branches snatch at my cloak and tree roots dog my steps. The Pendle witches walked the same path and, had I not done so much to engineer this situation, I would think it fate. The thunder of hooves makes me jump as Clements rides out of the surrounding mist.

'Were you expecting the Devil?' he jests.

'He is in view.' The easy retort hides my surprise. He has followed me here and I place my hand in reach of my dagger.

He chuckles and keeps the pace on horseback beside me.

'I have been thinking,' he broods.

That is a surprise. But I force myself to soften. His truth will not be won with thorns, nor should I be quick to underestimate him.

He dismounts and puts his horse on the lead. Together we navigate the steep path. He times his footsteps with mine and stands close enough for me to hear his breathing.

'Lord Carew is misguided in his hope that Mr Rush can be scared off. The servants tell me our host lacks the respect of the people. The little authority he has left is worn down by that niece of his. She eloped without her uncle's permission, a Royalist union that has seen her estates sequestered. Lord Carew had to bribe Parliament with his weapons to forgive the charges against her. They do not trust him. He is a reluctant ally, but the Royalists will not have him back.' He pauses. 'Lord Carew promised me free rein to hunt as many witches as possible yet has changed the terms of my employment without warning. Unlike your master, I have no wish to undo my reputation. So, *you* should seduce Grace,' he concludes, a suggestion I almost choke on. 'I do not think it will take much effort. She is foolish and wanton and inclined to spite. She was spitting fire at her uncle all afternoon. She wants him to pay her fines.' He chortles at the memory.

'I doubt the lady will be so easily won, not when she paid so heavy a price the first time.' Nor am I keen to play the lover to Althamia's cousin. Regardless of the connection between them, something about her leaves me cold.

'You are handsome enough,' he says, ignoring my gentle demurring. 'A kiss or two will encourage her to push her uncle to your favour.' A kiss will remove me from Althamia's regard. But Clements's conspiratorial smile banishes my reservations. My reluctance to let go leaves me vulnerable.

'My master would not approve of us acting against Lord Carew's wishes,' I counter, with enough doubt in my voice to encourage him. Again, that appraising stare greets me in response.

'I can give you power. Enough so that when you walk in a room people will give way to you. Judge Percival is too full of regret to be of any use. To him, power is akin to curdled milk.'

Clements is a child. A feral child who confuses violence with affection. He is in want of understanding, but he is no fool.

I make a show of considering him. 'You are not to be trusted.'

A gentle objection he brushes aside. 'No one is. Anyone who tells you otherwise is lying. I used to be as well-regarded as your master. I will reach those heights again. I will make this place my base.'

'As will I.' I hold out my hand, but he favours a more familiar greeting. He embraces me and then pulls back to study my expression.

Satisfied, he sets his terms. 'I want you to report to me on your master's intentions. I fear he will persuade Lord Carew to abandon the investigation altogether before you've had time to tumble his niece.'

'You have my loyalty,' I promise.

He mounts his horse. 'The little it is worth. You are a mystery to me, but I have untangled enough to know you will not make the ascent. You are not ready.' He digs his heels into the horse's side and disappears under a bruised sky.

Clements has taken my measure and has not been left wanting by it. After he rides off, I stand at the bottom of Pendle Hill, urging myself to step forward only to remain rooted to the spot by the image of Agnes's outstretched hand. I am too fearful of what awaits me at the top. After a while I return to the quarry and ride back to the manor.

Upon my arrival, a servant agrees with good grace to procure some hot water. In the privacy of my bedchamber, I rub the cloth roughly across my skin as though to remove today's events from memory. A flash of feathers draws me to the window. Beatrice, Grace's goshawk, soars upwards into the sky and is lost to the thickening mist that borders the estate. Grace waits in the garden below, a bright figure in her yellow cloak. Her profile is slashed by the bars on the window. She stands a breath apart from a man and places a gauntleted hand on his and another near her bodice. Suspicion draws my attention. There is no mistaking that familiar purple cloak belonging to Will. Will has played so many roles that I shouldn't be surprised to see him play the lover. My lips curve into a smile as I imagine Clements anger at how quickly Will has placed himself in the role intended for me. I examine the couple. I had not sensed an attraction between them in our short encounter. A temporary pleasure, I guess, with a thought of Grace's absent husband. I step back as she brings her face towards his.

A sudden swipe of his hand causes her to stumble, her fall cushioned by her full skirts. Will lingers long enough to ensure she is not hurt. Once Will is out of sight Grace starts to convulse. I make to reach for my cloak until I realise she has been taken by a fit of laughter. As though sensing my presence, her pleasure eases and she tilts her head towards me. Her face is lined with annoyance and her unblinking look prompts my retreat into the shadows.

Chapter Twenty-Two

'I sometimes imagine myself akin to one of Althamia's projects. Stuffed with wool and held together with pins and preservatives. Even in death we are pricked at and swaddled tight. I wish to breathe.' Grace enters my bedchamber, showing no embarrassment at the sight of me undressed.

With a snap of her finger, she dismisses the attending servant. Taking note of my concern she says, 'He sees and hears only what I tell him to.' Her demeanour is cool, as though daring me to look away and forget what I saw yesterday. I cannot and finish getting dressed. I have no desire to be late for our meeting with the townspeople.

'This is too fine for church,' she determines when I reach for my green doublet on the dresser. Lord Carew had taken Will's advice to hold the town meeting at the church. 'Better a church than a court-house,' he'd cautioned. 'You have to win their trust, whereas I must content myself with making an impression,' Grace says, registering my doubtful glance at her gown of gold damask. She saunters over to my valise and pulls out my grey doublet.

It is surprising how quickly I have gotten used to someone dressing me when at Grace's urging, I lift my arms for her to put on my clothes. Unlike Stephens, our dance lacks poetry. At times she is close enough for me to smell the perfume on her skin and feel the gold set of her mourning ring against my flesh. Her touch raises goosebumps on my skin and I seize up like armour when she gets too close. She makes a show of being embarrassed at our nearness, but it happens too often for it to be a coincidence. Is she so eager to move on from her encounter with Will?

Her deliberate fumbles almost tie me in knots. With a demure look, she surveys my exposed flesh. For all of Clements's words yesterday, I do not mistake her inspection for interest. She is looking, I imagine, for a sign of weakness or a mark.

'Althamia wrote to tell me of your arrival in York. The letter was accompanied with an ordinance that I was not to let you fall in love with me if we were ever to meet. Most men do that, even my husband. Though the spell came undone once we married. The marriage knot is a heavy burden.' Her teasing leaves me cold, there is something too practised about her demeanour.

Still with Clements's words in my ears, I say lightly, 'My heart is my own.'

'You are wiser with it than I.' Her smile is a brittle thing. 'You stole your brother's place whereas, to my loss, I stole my marriage rather than face my uncle's refusal.' I stiffen, but she turns to stare out at Pendle Hill. A sharp wave beckons me close. 'The deer park,' she says, gesturing at the blanket of land before us. 'My uncle displaced the tenants and levelled their homes to make it so.'

I grimace. Many landowners have enclosed their land at the expense of the commoners who had ancient use of it. The practice has caused much resentment and Lord Carew is wary of allowing the townspeople an opportunity for revenge.

'My uncle has the authority to order Mr Rush out of town, but he is afraid to use his voice lest it comes out a squeak.'

'These are troubling times. He is right to be cautious.'

'He is guilty and fearful,' she says and I almost blink from her unwavering stare. 'Rumours of our faith spark the people's hatred.

Two of my relatives, priests, were butchered in the months following the Gunpowder Plot. The rest of my family were forced to take Communion lest they be accused and martyred.'

'My aunt had the sense to escape. This place makes you realise what it is to be afraid. They say I am a witch. Do you believe the accusations?'

She places her hand over mine and I recall her interactions with Will. Witch-hunters were rumoured to exact favours from desperate women. 'I do not think you are a witch,' I say and ease away from her touch.

'My child's death condemns me in my neighbours' eyes.' She falters slightly at this admission.

'I did not know,' I say in surprise. Althamia made no mention of her loss.

'You are obliged to our history.' Half veiled by the door, she whispers, 'I did not spend my tears for the child . . . I could not.'

'You are at risk of losing yourself,' Will warns when I later relay my agreement with Clements. We trot behind Lord Carew's carriage, where our host, Grace and Clements are comfortably ensconced. Pendle Hill is no less ominous despite being draped in the morning sun.

'I am lost already,' I say with a look at the witch talisman around my neck. His horse nickers and Will hunches in the saddle when Grace looks at us from the carriage window. 'Will,' I murmur, but he turns his attention to the surrounding fields peppered with snow for the remainder of the journey.

We arrive at the church, medieval in style with a bell tower. A fair distance away is a huddled winter piece of men, women and children veiled by the encroaching mist.

'The condemned,' Clements whistles, though a look from Will prods his departure.

Lord Carew and Grace saunter past, and Will's lips narrow at the fleeting look Grace favours me with. 'Have you commenced your careless romance?' he asks drily.

'It is not in my temperament. Nor is it in hers . . . My bedchamber overlooks the garden.'

'So it does,' he replies, and his horse paws under him, making his legs tremble. He quickly dismounts.

'I saw you with her,' I say, unwilling to drop the matter, but I fall silent when an older woman approaches.

Will inclines his head towards her with a slight inhale of relief.

'Mrs Ann Greer,' she introduces herself, though she remains a safe distance from us and the church. She does not resemble the Ingrams' depiction of her as a cold-blooded murderer of children. She is a striking-looking matron with a determined tilt to her head. 'You have heard of me.' A young woman calls her name. She turns, the cold wind has turned them to paper, but with their joined hands a knot, they do not shake.

'You should enter,' Will advises her with a gesture to the church. 'Those with petty resentments will be less inclined to speak against you.'

She gestures to the horseshoe nailed to the church door. 'They would not let a suspected witch cross the threshold. Anything I say in my defence will be thrown back at me and I will be helpless to defend myself, for a witch is never allowed the last word.'

'Then why are you here?' asks Will as, to distract myself from her scrutiny, I tie up the horses.

With a direct look she makes her address. 'So you can see us as we are. Before they embellish us with riches we have never possessed nor asked for.' She turns her back to us and at her return the group splinter into the white background.

We enter the church to a craning of necks beneath a ceiling panel of flowers, birds and male dyads playing pipes. Archbishop Laud's reforms ushered in ceremony and glass-stained windows. Parliament's grip of the North had seen them smashed out. The church's windows have been replaced with cheap glass. The church's spoilt beauty is still in evidence through the wall panels and a pulpit that's decorated with twisting vines and wood animals, alongside evidence of the soldiers' iconoclasm. The door separating the clergy from the congregation has been ripped away.

Grace and Lord Carew take their family pew. He holds himself stiff in his ivory ruff as though caught on the executioner's block. The candles stretched across the nave on wires are a faded crown about his head. Grace keeps her head high and observes the people around her. It reminds me of Althamia's intense concentration. She is, in her mind's eye, realigning their bones and massaging them into place.

The townspeople crowd the remaining pews, the Ingrams at the very front. The minister sits before us. Beside him, a clean-shaven young man of around twenty-six years dressed in dark brown, who holds a soft look about him. His youth is belied by a keen look that misses nothing. Grace catches my attention and, with a nod in the young man's direction, mouths, 'Mr John Rush.'

Rush rises and Will introduces himself. 'I am Judge Percival. I am here under His Lordship's instructions to listen to your complaints.'

At Will's approach, the minister offers him his seat. Will's face dutifully softens at Rush's whispered welcome.

With my master's warning in my head, I sit beside Grace for a side view of the congregation. Clements wishes to be seated alongside Will but is afraid to make an approach. He scowls and then settles next to the minister. He scans the crowd for me. I have erred. I should have sat next to him and offered my unvoiced support.

'We are grateful to His Lordship for bringing you here,' says Rush with a respectful nod in Lord Carew's direction. 'Between the two of us, we will bring an end to the disturbances.'

Will nods and the townspeople murmur their approval. Rush does not appear discomforted by Will's presence. The people regard both witch-hunters equally, despite the latter's youth. Yet no one rises to voice their suspicions.

'My time is yours,' Will says.

At this a small-boned man faces the assembled crowd. 'My name is Mr Wilson. I am the coroner and have been much disturbed by the spate of deaths these past years.'

Rush stirs and murmurs encouragingly, 'Please.'

'The death of Henry Ingram,' he begins, with a look in Mr and Mrs Ingram's direction. 'Two years ago he sickened and died and there is no medical cause to explain it.'

'The witch Ann Greer sent her imp to steal him from us!' accuses Mrs Ingram. Her husband grasps at her hand to quieten her.

'Mr Gibbon's wife was also struck down without cause. As was Mr Cross. An autopsy revealed him to be full of Devil's balm,' says Mr Wilson.

'Their relatives believe a Jane Foley sent her familiars after them,' Rush tells Will.

'I will have the people tell me so directly,' he replies.

Rush smiles away the rebuke as the townspeople take their turn in dredging up generations' worth of complaints and resentments.

'Mrs Greer also set her imps on Mr James Wells!' Mrs Ingram cries.

Mr Wells, a middle-aged labourer, rises at this introduction. He is situated near the back and his speech is hesitant. 'It is true. Ever since I argued with her, I have been stricken with the falling sickness. It has cost me my livelihood and I have pressed money in her hand to undo the curse, but she would not take it.'

The people closest to him cast discreet look at the patches on his clothes.

Mr Ingram looks troubled, even guilty at Wells's denouncement. His wife catches his unease with a smile.

'What did you argue about?' asks Will.

Mr Wells coughs. 'A bill. My son took ill. Mrs Greer provided some herbs. I paid her for her services, but she claimed otherwise.'

Will raises his brow. 'Mrs Greer is a healer?'

'A witch,' corrects Mr Wells.

A young woman rises. She is plainly dressed, and she blushes from the scrutiny she finds herself under. 'Mrs Greer is a healer and has served many of us during our illness. She cured Mr Wells's son and many more besides.'

Mr Wells is sour, but he does not dispute her claim.

'*A suspected witch will carry herself like a saint on earth,*' quotes Rush, but amidst a chorus of agreement the woman remains standing.

'She is a healer.'

Rush's mouth thins at her insistence, and he readies himself to argue until Will intervenes. 'We will handle the investigation with due care.'

It would be tedious if it wasn't so frightening. I keep my hands folded in front of me lest people see my scar and think it a witch's mark. The townspeople accuse their neighbours of sending familiars to spoil their crops, sicken their children, lame their animals and harm whatever else they hold dear. No one laughs at the accusations.

186

The legacy of the Pendle witches is not a story to them. There is no room to doubt that everyone speaks the truth.

I am not the only one to stiffen when someone stands to make an accusation. We are waiting, with bated breath, to be told that we are not one of them. That we are witches.

I watch Rush as he listens to the townspeople telling of their suffering. Their words do not ruffle his silken composure.

'It would make her a papist,' Grace whispers when a man accuses a suspected witch of muttering foreign words within his hearing. I snort, more from nerves than anything. The sound attracts a few disapproving looks and to compose myself I stare out the window. I blink as I catch a glimpse of brown eyes staring back at me through the glass, but the figure is gone when I open my eyes.

My attention is once again taken by the congregation, where a woman big with child is helped to her feet. 'My name is Mrs Blake. I have been cursed by Bess Heath.' Her hands rest under the swell of her stomach. 'Her spells stop my child from being brought to term.'

'Who is Bess Heath?' asks Will with a brief look at me. I shake my head slightly. Mrs Blake carries death in her stomach, a tumour no doubt. Her song is but a murmur, one that will rise in pitch once death takes her. The tragedy of it is a tobacco taste in my mouth. I bite the inside of my cheeks until the flavour is diluted by the metallic tang of blood.

Mrs Blake is exhausted, and Mrs Ingram is quick to stand in her place. 'A vagabond. And her father Eli Heath is no better. He used to be a husbandman but took to drink when he lost his living.'

Lord Carew blinds himself to the renewed attention. I guess the Heaths owe their mean circumstances to his deer park.

A man rises. He is too far behind for me to make him out, but his clothes and the way his neighbours regard him confirms he is a man of influence. Mr Keller, as he introduces himself, freely condemns both Bess and her father. 'They are both witches. I oversee the parish relief and against my better judgement, I offered them work and a room in my barn. They failed to pay rent and were slovenly at their tasks. When I rebuked them, they cursed my son.' He points at a fair-haired child next to him. 'My son recovered, but my herd of cattle went lame. When Bess turned her malice to my wife, I realised she was a witch and searched her. The poor and lazy are easily swayed by dark arts.'

'You searched her yourself?' I interrupt.

The man pauses and turns to face me. He is affronted at being questioned.

'My wife attempted to search her but she ran off and her father soon followed with a barrel of my ale,' he answers.

Rush is quick to reassure him. 'Any marks she had may well be gone. Witches are quick to cut them off when they fear discovery.'

Mr Keller prods at his wife. The wealth apparent in her clothing does nothing to disguise the lines of fatigue around her eyes and mouth. 'She has set her imps on me. They steal my sleep.'

Her words encourage a wave of accusations against the Heaths, and by the time everyone has said their piece there is a wealth of names for us to investigate.

Rush calls for volunteers. 'My landlady has agreed to search the accused for the Devil's mark, but I will need watching men.' The position to help interrogate the witches by subduing them and watching to see if their imps appear, elicits an enthusiastic response. Rush does a quick sift of men who are eager to turn on their neighbours. His recruits are drawn from the labouring class. Is it the pay that motivates them, or do they truly believe that witches are amongst us?

Disgusted, I turn my attention to Grace who rolls a gold coin between her fingers. She does not stop even though her uncle's lips thin from her play. He rests his hand on her arm, but Grace refuses to relent her play even when her uncle's fingers redden.

I jump to my feet, and at the accompanying stares murmur, 'You look overly warm. I will escort you out for some fresh air.' Lord Carew releases his grip when I hold out my arm to her. Clements's eyes are approving while Will's turn pensive as I take Grace outside.

Grace rubs her arm and, without looking at me, asks, 'Has anyone told you you'd make a fine soldier?'

'No.'

'Good. You are too full of hesitations . . . and regrets. Do not think yourself unmanned. My husband is of a similar countenance. As is the Countess of Derby, despite all the talk of how she wears her husband's breeches.'

'I am gladdened by your reassurance,' I say. Nor am I easily ruffled, I convey with a look.

She stares out at the surrounding fields. 'I was in the Countess's company during the siege of Lathom.'

'Althamia told me of it.'

'She does not know all that occurred,' she retorts. 'The castle foundations threatened to fall about us like snow. The news-books talk about how the Countess led her council of war and faced Fairfax's subordinate Rigby, yet they make no mention of how she would shake when she thought herself alone or safe in my presence. I gave her guidance despite my fears. My face was splattered with blood when a stray bullet pierced my bedchamber window and lodged itself in my maid's brain. I would have borne the brunt, had she not moved to dress me. There were other losses.' Her hand briefly rests on her stomach. 'When I thought I could bear no more, it was over; Prince Rupert graced us with his presence and called us fierce Amazons, as though we had not lived like soldiers for all those three months.'

'You are brave.'

'I am powerless. I thought marriage would change my state, yet here I am. My husband's estates are sequestered, but I am not without power. My uncle has made me his heir.' She colours and her attention shifts to the ground. It is Lord Carew who should feel shame. 'I am not in need of rescuing,' she bites, but I bite back.

'I am not a rescuer.' The truce holds and the townspeople begin to file out of the church.

Grace inclines her head towards the retreating Ingrams flocked by their neighbours. 'Mrs Greer and Mr Ingram were childhood sweethearts, though Mrs Ingram was a better match. Her family is the local gentry, and her husband took her family's name upon marriage. His liaison with Ann Greer is rumoured to have persisted long after he said his vows. Mrs Ingram holds Mr Rush in high regard. And the women of the town think highly of her in turn.' There, her look conveys, your discretion has been rewarded.

Lord Carew approaches. 'Your master is speaking with your rival.' He looms over me to hasten my departure. I square my shoulders and he backs away from the look in my eyes.

'We are leaving,' he tells Grace and then enters his carriage.

'He blames me for this. He thinks I can stop it.'

'He is unjust to believe that.'

She tilts her head. 'Is he?' she teases.

I stare after her. Whatever her fears of being targeted, she is enjoying the present situation too much to apportion out her knowledge as though it's a reward. Her motives are a spiral and, in fear of getting lost, I turn my thoughts from her. Alone in the crowd, I feel the want of Althamia's presence and direct speech even more.

✳

I return to the warmth of the church where Will and Clements have formed an intimate tableau with Rush.

'I heard you killed fifty witches,' Clements half accuses.

His hostility pleases Rush, who responds with a sinuous smile. 'A gross inflation. I do well enough, though it pales in comparison to your reputation.' The latter words are addressed to Will as Rush rests his hand over the ivory-studded head of his staff.

At my approach, Rush makes a gentlemanly greeting with a slight touch to his hat.

'Mr Pearce. I much enjoyed your account of your master's past. I hope you will find your time here inspiring.' There is a caution to how he spends his words. I doubt it is from shyness from the frank way he assesses us. His accent is neutral though his vowels are flavoured with a touch of the North.

'I have had much to inspire me already.' My retort is sharper than necessary. The reminder of dealings with Broad cuts me to the bone.

Still Rush does not retreat from it. 'Good,' he says. 'You shall not take offence when I voice my hope for your master to write his memoirs.'

'What I am is not for posterity.' The finality in Will's tone prompts Clements to direct the conversation to something more to his liking. 'They say you are a general. What battles have you fought in? Edgehill, Oxford?'

'Nowhere as far afield as that,' Rush deflects. 'This corner of England is my battlefield. It is a bed of knots. There can be no peace until they are weeded out.'

'So, you are a gardener.'

Clements grins appreciatively at my put-down while Will's eyes narrow. I shrug off his warning. There will never be peace. Witch-hunters will always be preceded by some war, some crisis that they will blame on innocents. *Men like myself*, I add, when my talisman glitters before me.

Rush's fingers are tight around his staff, but his manner is affable. 'In a manner of speaking, you are right,' he answers, 'though I go by another title . . . Witchfinder General.'

Chapter Twenty-Three

Francis's hands rope around my neck. His touch steals my breath, but guilt makes me slow to resist. The sensation pulls me from sleep and I sit up gasping and then blink, my attention caught by a dark figure. His mouth is an open cavern as though he means to devour me. He steps back, blocking the moon's silhouette through the window.

'You were thrashing about in your sleep as though the Devil was after you. Or perhaps it was me. Come. I have work for you,' Will says, and throws me my cloak before I can mumble a refusal.

The candles in my chamber are worn stubs and I rely on the light that filters through the windows to find my way outside. Will is flanked by two horses who whinny at my approach. The manor is a dark shadow, apart from a flicker of light in the far window. My attention sees it snuffed out.

Will urges his mount on and I ride after him into the night. The darkness robs him of expression, leaving nothing for me to latch on to. Here in the dark we are distilled to the essence of what we are: a witch-hunter and a witch. Will dismounts near a graveyard. I tense at the silver glint of the shovel he loosens from the horse's side.

I look around but neither Clements nor Rush appear to be lying in wait. The Witchfinder General had invited Will, Clements and me to call upon him three days from now. Will had accepted, though I could tell he was troubled by the young man's resolve. It would be a simple matter for him to liberate himself from this business by handing me over to them.

Whatever his attentions, my dagger is within reach, and fully alert I follow him past the gates. The mist makes this world a dream and us the nightmares on its edges. The ground crunches beneath our feet and I sniff at the cloying scent of mud and rain. There is no rest to be found here. A graveyard is no more than a chamber of dead things and their songs rush to chisel at my flesh. It gets worse when we pass from the old graves to the new. Some are badly kept, overrun with bracken and bramble.

He stops, his eyes bright. 'We have walked into this scene blind. Grace is a witch,' he says.

'She would not have sent for us if she were,' I say and try to laugh off my unease. It is a bitter sound that grates. I would have sensed her nature. Unless I *have*, as I think back to my discomfort in her presence. A feeling I'd dismissed to her soft likeness to Althamia.

'She worms her way into people's thoughts.' He is telling the truth. It frightens me more so when he says, 'She is in mine.'

'That day in the garden?'

He blanches at the memory. 'I could not hold. A whisper and I was hers long enough to tell her what you are. I could not help it.'

'She is accustomed to being hurt.' I tell him of Lord Carew's heavy handling of her and their dispute over her sequestered estates. 'She wishes to unseat her uncle. She is desperate to free herself and her estates, and will risk death to do so. Still, she cannot force us to do her bidding. Whatever Grace is about, her spells are not particularly strong.'

Will cuffs my collar. 'Have you not asked yourself why? The lady has overspent herself.' A dawning realisation pricks at me like thorns. 'She tried to persuade me to abandon Rawton to Mr Rush.

She is either behind the town's flood of accusations or at the very least eager to profit from them. Perhaps she wishes to scare her uncle into abandoning his estates for her. However much her endeavours might have weakened her, she is still dangerous. I am half ruined by her tricks . . . we both are.'

I shake off his despair. 'Why are we here?'

'To salvage the situation. You had not counted on Rush when you made me a hostage to your plan. The people's accusations are lies, but Grace's meddling has emboldened the situation. Neither Rush nor the accusers can be reasoned with.'

'So you mean to use blackmail instead?' I hazard, seeing him survey the graves.

'We need leverage, and the ones who would give it freely reside here. Rush and Clements are only as powerful as their accusers. We will force the townspeople to drop their claims.' His fists unclench to reveal a thick strand of red silk.

I step back. 'I am not a witch.' If I were, I would have hoarded more of Francis than just his death rattles, his laboured refrains. 'My mother's death—'

'Has no bearing on what you are.' My jaw clenches at the certainty in his voice. He has made my kind a minced history and I cannot bury the resentment I feel. He thrusts the threads towards me. 'Leave,' he says when I refuse to take it. 'You are no use to me as you are.'

My eyes flash. After the church meeting, I'd returned to find a letter from my father ordering me to conclude my business with Will by the week's end or face the withdrawal of his promise. I'd fed his missive to the flames. I have given up too much – Althamia, my mother's name, Stephen's regard, Dodmore's offer – to leave now. And to ensure Althamia's safety, I will give up more, even my life if necessary.

'I will see this through to the end. I do not need those to unthread the dead's secrets,' I say and dismiss the silken threads. Nor will I carry them with me like Francis.

He gestures to the well-kept grave of Henry Ingram beside him. A child's song is different, a gentle pulse in your bones, a tiny hand that slips from yours. The graveyard is a necropolis of buried songs, but the whisper of young Ingram makes itself heard.

Mother: the same hands that shape dough make me a soldier. 'A game' and at her command I slip into Father's tracks. A small clearing. A jumble of shapes that my eyes strain to decipher. A shout. A fall. A crack. A mass of broken pieces that my mother can't reshape.

Henry Ingram's song ends, but the image is clear in my mind. He ran after coming across his father with another woman. He tripped, the fall enough to pull him into a slumber that never broke. This, of course, is not the story Mr Ingram told his wife.

'A witch's curse is often easier than the truth,' Will says when I relay Henry's song. 'Though Mrs Ingram is too grief-stricken to be swayed by reason or threats.'

He points to the neighbouring grave. 'Malcolm King,' I read aloud, but his deathless song is soon overtaken by the rushed tempo of his buried companions. A tangle of voices that I cannot unpick. I stumble as I'm rocked by a pulling sensation.

'The dead are too loud,' I wheeze. 'I cannot control them.'

He reaches for Francis's knot around my neck and sighs when I pull it free from his touch.

'This is my brother's knot,' I protest.

'Those with a talent for death used knot magic to preserve what remained for a brief time. The best parts of them, for their relatives to take comfort in. A service reserved for royals until King James put a stop to it. This gift of yours, this prolonged goodbye, was never meant to be of a permanent nature. The knot robs you of your self-control. You have spent your life suppressing your powers. You are not strong enough to carry it, not if you wish to save Rawton. If we are to succeed you must undo it.'

I step back. 'You are not a scribe.'

'No, but my master was.' He takes another look at the knot before I hide it beneath my shirt. 'It is an open wound.'

I stand firm. 'But one I'll carry.'

His voice softens. 'A lonely burden that will weigh you down. One that blunts your edge.'

'Then time will see it sharpened,' I snap, and to my relief he relents.

'A privilege we lack,' he says. 'Still, we will make do with what we have. In the meantime, we'll assist Rush with the witch-hunts. A show of loyalty to minimise their influence.' He steps back and motions me to resume my efforts. I will master myself, I promise as the dead clamour for my attention. I have no other choice.

Chapter Twenty-Four

'We are to be foot soldiers,' I tell Clements, my expression dark as we trail behind Will and Rush. We had ridden out early this morning to visit Rush's lodgings. Rush had been waiting for us on the town's outskirts. He'd stepped out of the descending mist as though he was part of it and was quick to commandeer Will's attention during the walk to town.

I have spent the last two nights at the graveyard with Will looking on. For all my efforts, I cannot separate the songs of the dead; the secrets I've amassed so far have been petty thefts and harmless slanders. I bring my hand to my neck, now bare of Francis's knot. Having sensed Will's growing impatience, I'd hidden it this morning. Will thinks it's an easy matter to accept his words as truth. He has no knowledge of the anger that slithered inside me the moment I realised what I was. Take it away and what is left to me is loss. I cannot extinguish it. Nor can I risk discarding all that remains of Francis on his word alone. Either way, my brother's knot weighs on me. He is Castor pulling me down, a descent I would submit to were it not for Althamia, who is tied to me.

'I will not let us fall out of step,' says Clements, and for a moment he nudges me along as though to place us in step with the two men. The mist softens both his envy and faltering advance. Despite my distaste of his person, I find something to admire in his ambition. In my father's home, I had been content to recline into the shadows.

Sometimes I imagine I am still there, hiding in corners. The memory of those times shames me. I wish I had fought harder against the bridle rather than meekly take the bit.

To distract myself, I survey our surroundings. Rawton is a medieval layout of timber-framed houses with gables that overlook the streets. The town has passed between Cavaliers and Royalists, yet it wears the cost of its occupation lightly. It has not been overly pillaged, although I notice some shop windows are missing their glass windows. The palpable air of neglect makes the town seem almost abandoned, the passers-by drifting phantoms.

I lower my hat to guard against the scrutiny we are subjected to. The town is smaller than York and the people are quick to sense we do not belong. Rush's lodgings are near the end of the main street, and he uses the distance to his advantage. Clements's eyes darken when he notices the high regard Rush is held in by the townspeople, who curtsy or tip their hats at his presence. The only exception is a forlorn woman of sunken appearance who crosses the street with her children to avoid our approach.

'Have you any news?' Clements whispers.

'No. My master had me write down a summary of the town's denouncements but keeps his intentions secret.'

His displeasure gives way to lewdness. 'How close are you to a conquest?'

Since Will's admission, I have taken care to avoid Grace, apart from when we meet for breakfast and supper. Had Will not said anything, I would have dismissed my awareness of her due to her soft resemblance to Althamia. It's more than that and I remember how I'd shrunk when her eyes assailed me over breakfast this morning. I have no wish to be derailed by her knots.

'Midway,' I lie when Clements repeats his question.

He appraises me, but our arrival keeps him from saying more.

'Mrs Barnett.' Rush makes a short introduction to his widowed landlady. 'She is to be my searcher.' Mrs Barnett smiles. There's a suffocating scent of jasmine about her and I stare at her bulky apron pockets and wonder if it's filled with sweetly fragranced bags to ward off bad smells.

'My watchers,' a sparse introduction of the three young men in the parlour whom he had chosen from the eager volunteers yesterday. Their attention is taken by their task of stuffing brown bellarmine jugs with nails, pins and cloth, a bottled concoction of counter-magic hidden under fireplaces or beneath the floors to ward off witchcraft. 'I am keeping them busy making witch bottles which the townspeople are eager to purchase. Though I hope to win Lord Carew's approval to begin the investigation soon.'

He ushers us into his study on the ground floor. Rush apologetically explains that it used to be Mrs Barnett's still room. The stench of herbs clings to my clothes like sweat. The room is spartan in appearance with only chairs and a table which is crowned with a large map and a copy of King James's *Daemonologie*.

'You have been busy,' remarks Will once we are all seated. Rush smiles over the North of England, now a river of red dots.

A maid knocks on the door and fills our glasses with wine. She is diligent at her task, though her hands tremble slightly.

Clements waits for her to leave before speaking. 'I have heard you charge thirty shillings to clear a town of witches.' He smiles when Rush answers the question with a brief nod.

'That's more than a foot soldier's monthly salary,' I blurt.

He shrugs. 'I am a general in God's army. Besides, I must pay my searching men and watching women.'

A warning look from Will I disregard as I remember Lord Carew's complaint about Rush's fee. 'Your men are paid directly by the parish,' I argue.

'Yet I must bear the cost of their bed and board when our investigation takes us out of town,' says Rush.

'Where did you learn your craft?' Will interrupts.

'We had the same master,' Rush confides and stands to place a copy of *The Lesser Key of Solomon* on the table.

Rush is untroubled by Will's patronising smile.

'Lord Howard wrote that witches were demons in disguise. This text provides the means to hunt them,' reminds Rush.

I pick up the textbook and carefully go through it, counting each red dot next to the listed demon. I pass the book to Will. 'You have twenty-one more witches to identify,' I observe to Rush. 'You have killed fifty-one so far.'

'You have not counted their spawn,' he points out.

Will flicks through the pages, the tightening of his hands against the spine his only reaction.

Rush rests his palms against the table. 'The country is drenched in the Devil's malice. I will not let others be corrupted by it.'

The book falls to the table with a thud. 'These were never my master's teachings,' says Will.

Rush's tone is almost pitying. 'And your kind was made weaker for it.'

'Weak?' Clements argues, half rising.

Rush raises his hand. 'Forgive me. I am blunt with my words, but the men of your time were too insular. Like the King, they thought they were head of a state, only to prove impotent without its body.'

Will rests his eyes on the books between them. 'And your body?'

'This town,' Rush answers and gestures to the window. 'More than half of what I am paid for my services is spent before the coins reach my purse. I am generous to those who spread the news of my work and gather about myself a staff of searching women and male watchers.'

'You have built yourself an army,' I say, whereas the people he deems witches must keep to the shadows and wait to be picked off.

'There is the old guard and then there is me. But I have no wish to trade blows with you.' His smile is too glib to be believed. He is too mercenary to be a zealot. But if the former, surely Lord Carew's opposition would have prompted his departure. *Why are you here?* I wonder, but his guarded expression does not lend itself to easy discernment.

'Then retreat,' Clements barks, his jealousy stark amidst the room's brightness. He covets fame and power and resents Rush's possession of both, along with his youth.

'I understand that Lord Carew sent you here to block me, but I was called here by God, and I will not back down.'

Clements's hackles rise at his measured tone, but Will is quick to intervene.

'We find ourselves at a stalemate. Neither of us is willing to give way.' He closes his eyes, a brief deliberation. 'We will work together. I will help you overcome Lord Carew's objections.'

Rush considers him. 'That is a sensible solution. I will give you a share of the profits once I have concluded my investigations.'

Will shakes his head. 'There is further profit to be made once the witches are found guilty at the assizes. We will divide the suspects between us. I assume you have a list of names?'

For a moment Rush looks as though he'll refuse, but he inclines his head towards Will and turns his back on us to retrieve something from his drawers.

Will's expression is as inscrutable as the mist over Pendle Hill and I try to determine what his game is. We are meant to curb

Rush's approach, not encourage him. Perhaps he has already lost patience with me and has decided to disregard our plan for one of his own. My thoughts are interrupted when Rush covers the table with a collection of sketches.

'A pretty piece,' remarks Clements of a delicately drawn portrait of a young girl whom I recognise from the group outside the church.

'Evil often is at first glance,' Rush replies with a look in my direction.

I have stored the names of the accused in my head from the church meeting, but Rush's drawings make them flesh.

'Margaret Greer,' names Rush of the sketch in Clements's hand. 'She is Mrs Greer's niece but has not yet been formally accused.'

'Then you have no right to her image,' I tell him.

His amiable expression doesn't falter. 'It is only a matter of time. She is much in her aunt's company.'

'That alone shouldn't condemn her.' My argument is abandoned at Clements's annoyed grunt. There is too much at stake for me to needlessly incite suspicions.

'Why draw them?' Will queries.

'To identify a commonality of evil,' Rush answers.

Will holds up a drawing of a weathered-looking woman, whom Rush names as Jane Foley. It is a fair likeness of the sad little woman I glimpsed earlier who had seemed so fearful at our presence. During the church meeting, Jane and her natural children had been described as a plague upon their neighbours, selling charms and spitting curses whenever their wares are refused.

Clements holds up another sketch of a pockmarked old beggar. 'And this old man,' he says with a disdainful expression.

Rush looks over. 'Eli Heath.' He picks up a picture of a scowling young girl in rags. 'Bess Heath, his daughter. They are guilty of at least two deaths.' My eyes are drawn to the girl's dark eyes and then the tiny number in the corner.

Rush, noticing my curiosity, explains: 'It is how much they have cost the town in parish relief over the last year. My fee will be triple that, plus my expenses.'

To his disappointment I hold my tongue, while Clements rifles through the pages, counting up the numbers in his head. 'Who provided you with the figures?'

'Mr Elwick, the senior alderman,' says Rush. 'He handles the town's account and entrusts Mr Keller to administer the relief to the poor.'

'Are Lord Carew and his niece among the named?' I ask.

'There are stories of Lord Carew and Grace's manor being home to priest holes and black sabbaths, but the rumours hold no weight in my opinion.'

I lift my head. Grace, he calls her, not Mrs Rawle, but no one reacts to his slip.

'Divide up the names,' Clements orders.

Will hands over the drawing of Ann Greer. 'I will take Jane Foley.'

Rush keeps her image out of reach. 'She is of no value.'

'Then you will have no trouble in handing her over,' Will counters.

A maid interrupts with more ale. We witch-hunters suffocate the light, but Clements waves her off when she moves to light more candles.

'It is your turn to compromise,' says Rush once we are alone.

Will drinks from his glass and pauses as though searching for the right words. 'Jane Foley harbours a Jennet Device in her nest. I am not foolhardy or drunk enough to give her up.'

'You cannot use a child,' I object, even while recalling Jennet Device, the nine-year-old girl whose testimony ensured the death of her family during the Pendle Witch Trials.

Rush points to his book of *Daemonologie*. 'Ordinarily no, but exceptions are made for witch cases.'

Clements gulps down his drink and then slams his glass on the table. 'We shall play for her.'

'Noddy?' Rush suggests.

Will looks up from the sketches. 'I had not realised you were local to these parts.'

Rush tenses for a moment. 'I have spent enough time here to absorb the people's fondness for card games.'

'Anywhere in particular?' I probe.

'Nowhere of note,' a clipped response that wards off further queries.

'I have no luck in card games. Dice?' Will suggests.

Rush rises. 'I am sure my men will have some dice handy.' He returns with three dice made of silver, a board marked with diagonal lines and his three watchers eager to observe the entertainment.

'We shall raise the stakes by playing for them individually,' Will tells us.

'You shall keep score,' Rush instructs the more mature-looking of his men, who introduce themselves as Henry, Walter and Samuel. They are lean, spare men with hard eyes despite their youth. Henry perches himself in between Rush and Clements and rests the scorecard on his lap.

The maid arrives once again to refill our glasses and the air turns heavy from wine and sweat as Rush's man keeps tally as both men try to score close to thirty-one points. Will wins Jane Foley in the first round but loses Margaret Greer in the second.

They are content to play in silence, but Clements is suddenly minded for conversation. 'What are your methods?'

Rush fumbles a throw of the dice and barely suppresses a curse. 'Anything legal.' His words are undercut with a wink.

Clements laughs so hard that the wine spills from his hand and onto the rug. Rush's men laugh with him.

Clements turns to them, pleased to have found a more eager audience. 'My master was fond of swimming witches. Though I was more minded to take a turn with them about the room.' He slaps his hand across Will's shoulders. 'Do you remember your first?' Will nods, a faint smile tugs at his lips. 'I ran the witch up and down her tiny hovel so fast that I was sick before she was.' They laugh and I force a sound from my throat. If Althamia were here she would never forgive me. Nor would Stephens. His mother was made sport of by men like these. Men like me.

As Rush and Will play for witches, their cravats and speech grow looser and everyone overindulges in drink.

'I find pricking to be an adequate tool,' relates Will after a fortunate throw.

Rush's face is drawn tight in concentration as he rocks the dice in his hands. 'I tend to leave that task to my searching women. A man should not put his hands on women, even if they are witches.' Clements sinks slightly in his seat. Many witch-hunters, following the abolishment of their commission, were employed by the local justices as witch-prickers. 'Though the women I've employed are apt to panic at the sight of blood. It often takes a few pricks to find the bloodless mark of the Devil on their person. Mrs Barnett is a surgeon's widow. I am certain she has the stomach for the upcoming trials.'

'You should bridle her if she becomes hysterical,' suggests Clements. 'I bridled all the witches I came across. Their screams would have deafened me otherwise.'

Did you bridle Agnes? I wonder as a snippet of her song: *A small unseen thing with a mouth heavy from the taste of iron*, rushes through my head.

'Nicholas will step in if your woman flounders,' says Clements, the offer accompanied by a hand on my shoulder that leaves me cold. 'He is eager to prove himself.' His words are kindly meant, and I am forced to voice my eagerness over the protests of Rush's men, who hurry to volunteer themselves.

Will does not save me. His attention is taken by the game.

'I dare not accuse you of cheating,' Rush complains. 'Though I will say you are cursed with good luck.'

Will laughs off the accusation.

Clements's face darkens. 'It is true . . . I spent years travelling from parish to hamlet in search of a case that would make my name. Whilst you and your master used your court connections to your advantage.'

'It was not as simple as that,' Will argues.

Clements grunts. 'We did the same work, yet you were rewarded with the best cases because you were more polished to look upon.'

Will protests, but Clements's resentment has taken over. There is a hierarchy to witch-hunting, with the second sons of minor nobles at the top.

'Your friendships were why you were chosen over me to oversee the Bamberg Witch Trials,' he complains. After their practices were banned over here, many witch-hunters sought employment on the Continent. The Bamberg Witch Trials were the pinnacle of their achievement. Thirteen years on, the mass burnings of nearly a thousand suspected witches has yet to be rivalled.

Will fluffs his next roll. 'I merely consulted.'

Singed by his admission, I down the rest of my drink.

'You did more than that,' Clements crows. He turns to face us. 'He and the chosen few made a treasure hunt of pursuing witches. Your master had a knack for finding thread witches. He made them watch from the pyre while they unloosened their knots. Their spells weaken them, even more so when they are unthreaded,' he explains for the benefit of the other younger men present.

And you burnt them afterwards. I clench my fingers around my glass to stop them from shaking. Thread witches were rumoured to hide their threads and I imagine Will peeling apart Francis's knot like flailed skin. 'We will never see the like of it again,' Clements muses. 'Now there is only a whisper of them left.'

But still he hunts them. Witch-hunting is a game to them. A game they play because the victims have never been people.

'It is a new age,' says Will, a brusque consolation the men toast to.

'Let your apprentice take a turn,' says Clements to Will. 'If he wins, he will have sole charge of investigating a witch.'

Will obliges and tosses the dice towards me. I keep my eyes from his.

'You are also cursed,' Rush remarks when I win Ann Greer and he gifts me her image.

Clements grabs the dice from me. 'I will even the odds so that Mr Rush does not accuse both yourself and your master.' There is laughter again and the game carries on in earnest. I lean into the memory of Francis's death. His death rattle steals the men's conversation and accuses me in a way that shakes my soul.

'A moment,' I beg and rise on unsteady legs. They wave me off, too engrossed in their games to care. Outside, I lean again the wall and almost retch my insides away. I rest my head between my legs until I open my eyes to see I am under inspection. I turn and take in the young girl's tattered clothing. A beggar, but her proud stance stops me from reaching for my coins. 'I have seen you before,' I say, recalling those eyes that Rush committed to paper. The same eyes that spied me through the church window.

'You are the girl who stares through windows.'

'Bess Heath,' she says, her curtsy veiled by shadows.

The men's merriment pierces the night and I wince away the sound. 'You should not be here,' I warn.

From the corner window she steals a peek into the study. 'I have lost something,' she tells me, 'I thought a closer look would see it restored.' Her cultivated tone is at odds with her attire.

I pull her back. 'You must resign yourself to your loss. If the men see you here, they will accuse you of casting spells. You are in danger,' I insist when she scoffs. I press my case by listing the neighbours who have spoken out against her. At the mention of the Keller family, she flinches as though I've hit her. Still, she doesn't run, and if not for her appraising look I would think she was slow. Not slow but foolhardy, I realise when she says defensively, 'I had to see if it was the same man.'

'Judge Percival is a fair man, despite his reputation.'

She frowns. 'It was the other man I was speaking of. The one who calls himself Witchfinder General. But you are right. It is a danger to be here.'

'You know Mr Rush?' I begin, but the sound of back door opening sends her running.

'You are missed,' Clements tells me. His face is half-hidden by shadows, and I cannot tell what, if anything, he has overheard.

Chapter Twenty-Five

Dear Nicholas,

I lack a poet's sensibility or an inclination to waffle. I am too old to run. I will wait for the prodigal son's return. My son.

Yours
Stephens

I look out the window at Pendle Hill draped under falling clouds of white mist. Stephens's letter arrived this morning. I had feared the connection between us severed and re-read his note until I'd committed to memory. A prodigal son, but one he will wait for even if the cost is his life. If Stephens won't run, then neither will I. I will survive to see him again.

'You are early,' I remark to Will when he bursts into my chamber unannounced. I quickly slip Stephens's note inside my shirt.

In the days following the dice game, he has overseen my repeated attempts to wrestle secrets from Rawton's dead. A failed endeavour that we have yet to acknowledge.

'You are late. Mr John Rush is here,' he says, and I rise after him. 'Clements is with him. A coup,' he warns in the short distance to Carew's study.

Clements acknowledges our arrival with a grin. Will and I note his staff, of a similar make to the one Rush carries, that leans at his side. Rush nods, while Lord Carew, from behind his large desk, looks small and distant amid the heavily panelled room decorated with hanging pastoral tapestries.

'You are here,' says Lord Carew, interrupting Rush's apology for the impromptu visit.

Abandoning all pleasantries, Rush straightens up to make his address. 'The people look to me to root out the supernatural.'

He is cut short. 'My father turned a blind eye to the dangers of the Pendle Witch Trials,' says Lord Carew. 'His failure anchored him to his deathbed. You are a danger, and I will not repeat my father's mistake.'

Clements grinds his staff into the carpet. 'You are quick to judge.'

'We all have agreed to work together,' says Rush with a look at Clements, Will and me. 'Between us we will ensure there is no repeat of past mistakes.'

I turn from Lord Carew's entreating stare and look at Clements. He would kill Althamia were I to make myself an obstacle.

'My sister believed you had reason to repent your past,' he says at last to Will.

Will's face is blank. 'We cannot escape who we are.'

'Shall I take that as an apology?' asks Lord Carew.

Clements rises and places a document before him. 'Take it as you will. All we require from you is your signature.'

'It is a petition demanding the investigation of the Rawton witches,' Rush explains, with a forced smoothness.

The petition is a black sea of signatures. Our host lets it slip and rests his head in his hands. Clements places another document in front of Lord Carew.

With a look at Clements, Rush concludes: 'This is to confirm we have your sanctioned approval,' and points to where his signature is required.

The quill between our host's fingers is sliding across the table when Grace enters with a knock and a swish of silk. Her eyes take in the scene, and she goes to her uncle's side.

'I am betrayed,' he tells her.

She regards us. 'Are we accused?' she asks Will, but Rush intervenes.

'Complaints have been made, but I am not of a mind to investigate.' Rush's and Grace's eyes do not meet, a deliberate lack of regard that draws my suspicions. They are partners in this scheme, conveys Will with a brief look. I blink in agreement, though for Rush's part I cannot understand why. He is far too determined to be under anyone's spell, and as for Grace, surely with her powers she has no need of allies. But if this were true, she'd already have possession of her estates. Even so, why would she choose Rush of all men to ally herself with? She is everything he professes to hate. Then again, perhaps she is wondering the same of my partnership with Will. She straightens at our inspection.

'I cannot sign,' Carew whispers.

My velvet doublet sticks to me. I look to the closed windows. It is too hot. The thick tapestries choke the air and warm my blood. Such heat is reserved for the sick room or birthing chamber.

'Your resistance has been admirable, but would you have us martyred by it?' she says.

Carew dabs at the sweat above his brow. 'It will not come to that,' he replies.

'That is what Grandfather said, and yet your cousin still found herself called before the assizes, alongside Alice Nutter. She would have hanged if our friends had not intervened. Our family has always been disliked, but now we are friendless.'

Rush and Clements arch forward while she whispers condolences in her uncle's ears. It is as though we are midwives, helping to beckon something forth.

Grace wraps her uncle's finger around the quill.

'It must be by your own hand,' Will warns when she guides her uncle's hand to the paper. His look for Lord Carew is pitying. He knows what it is like to try to hold firm. Grace hesitates and then relinquishes her touch.

Lord Carew searches Rush's face for a sign that he will withdraw. 'This is how it begins,' he tells us. 'A signature, a search, a court case and a funeral.'

'You mean a hanging, Uncle. They hang witches.' She kneels beside her uncle, and with a considered look in my direction whispers, 'Better their deaths than our own.'

Clements, catching this, smiles at my assumed conquest. There is a game being played, but a look from Rush to Grace assures me I am very much in the dark.

Carew lets the quill rest. 'My signature will start the fire. I have the strength to withstand it. I have equipped myself well so far.'

'Uncle, the Ingrams harass us almost daily for justice. No doubt there will be more upon the week. If we do not give permission, they will take it and then we are lost,' says Grace. Her tone is fearful and, if I did not know the truth, I would not doubt her. Lord Carew begins to sign his initial, only to pause again.

Grace smiles her encouragement. 'Pontius Pilates kept his hands clean and his conscience clear.' As he signs, she locks eyes with Rush, a clandestine look not meant for me.

To the annoyance of Clements and Rush, Lord Carew passes the signed document to Will. 'You are in charge of overseeing the investigations.'

'We will take our leave,' Will answers, his face shuttered at being so singled out. We depart, but I steal a look at Grace who leans even closer to her uncle. The strands of her hair fall around his face as though he is a creature to be hooded.

'Come,' says Clements. 'Rush has promised us the use of his men and searching-woman. We are to seek out your prize, Mrs Ann Greer.' He slaps my shoulder and strides outside to where Rush, his men and searching-woman rush to ready themselves under a dark sky that holds a promise of rain.

Will hangs back and we study the searching party. We are long past those days when witches would proudly advertise their services from shop windows. Yet you would not think so from how proudly Rush sits upon his horse. He is off, his regiment close behind him to hunt witches or rather a whisper of them.

Will and I hang back as though we are the baggage train. 'I caught it,' Will confirms when I relay Rush's slip of Grace's name and my suspicions of them. He hands me a thin book from inside his doublet. 'I stole it from Rush when he and his men fell into a drunken sleep after our game of dice.'

I flick through it and raise my brow. 'A blessing book?' Something expectant mothers write to their children in the event they do not survive the birth. My mother's legacy, to my regret, is written in my blood.

'It belongs to Grace.' He points to her name written inside.

'It proves nothing,' he says when I make to return to Lord Carew. 'Rush could have bribed a servant to steal it,' he replies.

I tuck the book inside my saddle bag. 'You do not believe that.'

He shrugs. 'What I believe has no bearing on the situation.'

I say nothing and my impatient mount kicks at the ground as I wait for him to outline a plan.

'You did well last week,' says Will at last.

'I won a witch. I cannot,' I balk, when he nudges my horse forward.

'If Mrs Greer confesses, I will make sure she will suffer no more than being bound over to the midsummer assizes. We have not run out of time yet,' he assures me, and I flush at the memory of my failed attempts. 'Whatever happens today, you will learn to bear it.'

That is what I am afraid of. I have borne much already in my desire to survive. To bear more would see me become someone like him. A man capricious with both his mercies and his hates. Either way, there will be losses. Althamia if I falter and myself if I don't. 'It is the only choice left to us,' I say.

Chapter Twenty-Six

Ann Greer resides in a medium-sized limestone cottage. The house is neat with a small herb garden near the entrance, soon trampled by the horses of Rush and his men. The windows have been broken. The damage is not recent for the lattice is veiled with cloth. This does little to keep us out. Rush, Clements, Will and Mrs Barnett barge inside to begin the investigations, leaving myself and Rush's watchers, Henry, Walter and Samuel, to stand in wait lest Mrs Greer's familiars come to her aid.

'Have you ever seen a witch before?' Henry asks.

Every time I catch sight of my reflection.

'No.'

'We shall all see them by the night's end,' Henry brags, and then straightens up at Mrs Barnett's appearance. Her apron pocket is bulky from the sweet bags of jasmine and the coins that jingle with each step.

Walter helps her onto her horse. 'A witch's mark was found,' she volunteers.

'Where?' asks Samuel, but she is not inclined to linger and kicks her horse into a canter.

By itself the Devil's mark is not enough to secure a conviction. A confession is needed and I turn to see Clements stood on the door threshold. I do not wait for him to beckon me close and instead hurry inside to prepare to claim, by a lucky throw of the dice, my prize. Mrs Greer is sitting in the middle of the room, her limbs bound to the chair with ropes. She raises her head, and I am afforded her grudging recognition. My eyes linger on everything but her. The room has been cleared with most of the furniture pushed towards the corners. A cat mewls but keeps itself hidden.

Rush's watchers commandeer a place for themselves in the corner and Mrs Greer's feet grind into the floor in silent protest at the familiar way they handle her belongings. The men bask in her disapproval and scrape their mud-spattered boots on the rugs. Will and Rush are sitting next to each other in the corner, their expressions veiled by shadows.

'Nicholas is to lead,' Clements reminds Rush when he attempts to banish me to the reader's desk in the corner. The table is empty apart from an inkpot, quill and paper. I resist the urge to make it my shield.

'The circumstances call for experience,' says Rush.

'I am experienced. I have trained under Judge Percival,' I argue. To do anything less would arouse the witch-hunters' suspicions and see Althamia in Mrs Greer's place.

'I will guide him if he missteps,' says Will with a look of encouragement, while Clements finishes, 'He has earned this.'

Rush concedes and I soon find myself close enough to Mrs Greer to count the freckles spread across her nose and hear her rapid breathing.

'Are you a witch?' I ask, remembering the game Stephens had made of being questioned by a witch-hunter when I was a young boy. I step back into the memory and try not to shiver from its lost warmth.

'No, sir,' says Mrs Greer to the watchers' amusement.

I press on. 'Have you dabbled with curses?'

She raises her head and shakes off my attempt to embellish her with a firm refusal.

My stilted attempts test Clements's patience and he pulls me aside. 'Do you need me to write you a playbill? Tell her what she is accused of and question her until she breaks.' He confuses my resistance for nerves and whispers, 'It will get better after this. You will learn to enjoy it.'

I stare at him and Rush and wonder how one develops the stomach to do this, solicit the necessary answers to lead people straight to their graves.

I take in the fear and confusion on Mrs Greer's face. The more fixed my gaze, the more her features blur into the background and it is this that allows me to address her as though I'm performing to an empty audience with no concerns but my own.

'You have been accused of spelling your neighbours' child, Henry Ingram, to death,' I charge. 'How long have you been a witch?'

'I am innocent,' she pleads.

'What of your niece, Margaret Greer?'

Some of her defiance escapes and the coldness inside me spreads when her bearing sags. 'My niece is no witch, sir.'

'That was a good start,' Rush cuts in, but Clements stops him. I make myself a terror under their inspection. Her attention is fastened on me throughout the interrogation and I am glad, for it would be worse were she to see the creatures behind me.

'Your neighbour Michael Wren accuses you of laming his cattle. He says you and your niece lingered near his farm, your looks black when he ordered you away. You sent your imps to punish him.'

'Not I,' says Mrs Greer.

'In that case,' I announce, hating myself for how I preen to my small audience, 'your niece is condemned by your innocence.'

'I am no witch, nor is my niece,' she cries, but I prod her with the same questions. We are left exhausted by it. I have many words at my disposal and shuffle them like cards to catch her out. But Mrs Greer is not afforded the same freedom. There is only one way in which she can answer the charges set to her and her sole excuse is worn to dust. 'I am innocent.'

I am about to scream at the absurdity of it when a hand on my shoulder stops me.

'You have done well,' Clements congratulates me. At his urging, I sit behind the reader's desk. I search for the sun, which hides itself from view. A day has dragged by in this manner. More will follow until she confesses.

Rush and Clements take over while I sit and watch my words take shape on the parchment before me. I have read the transcriptions of Thomas Potts and his ilk detailing witch investigations. Each writer is at pains to elaborate on the witches' crimes and the investigators' bravery in holding them to account. But there is no bravery here. Just a bound woman and a group of men hoping to make their reputation at her expense. The writers make no mention of this, nor do they mention the silence as both sides wait for the other to falter and give way. At various moments I'm tempted to save Mrs Greer from their abuses, but the image of Althamia in her place forces me into stillness. And so I sit and watch, banishing thoughts of Althamia and the soft parts of myself until all that's left is my calm resolve.

Torture is illegal, but Rush's men make a show of going through their master's instruments. Mrs Greer's eyes widen at the thumbscrews and witch bridles they produce. She flinches when they prick themselves with the witch pricker. Rush puts an end to their sport. But his refrain is gentle. Their antics amuse him, unlike Mrs Greer, whose flesh has already felt the kiss of the needles. Mrs Greer, despite her fear, draws on her inner strength and Rush's voice turns hoarse from his questioning, which elicits monosyllabic answers.

By dawn's approach words are abandoned.

'Take her for a turn,' Rush instructs his watchers, who handle

Mrs Greer with a rough familiarity to disguise their fear. They have never done this before, but the opportunity of holding some form of power in their measly lives proved too intoxicating to refuse. Now, like me, they are trapped by it.

'Wait,' Clements interrupts. 'Nicholas will help. I am sure he does not want to start the day behind a desk.' This is a kindness. And if I were true in my intent to remake myself in his likeness I would be pleased. I turn to Will, who has spent most of the morning observing us as though we are a play, unable to decipher whether he is disgusted by the spectacle or merely bracing himself for more. His face gives nothing away and I gently take hold of Mrs Greer's arm and run her up and down the length of her home.

'Faster,' Rush commands, his voice a whip I answer to. Sweat pours down my face and dampens my vision so that all I'm aware of is the blurred scrutiny of the others and Mrs Greer's and Samuel's exhausted pants as we keep a hard pace. Samuel's grip is fetter tight and Mrs Greer's feet slap against the floor as he half drags her.

'This is not meant to be pleasurable,' he spits when I urge him to be gentle.

'We will break for a moment,' Rush announces, and Samuel releases Mrs Greer, who slips from my grip and falls straight to the floor. She looks up at us, at the boys she has seen grow up who now bait her worse than a trapped animal. Rush lays out the objects in his knapsack: a thumbscrew, bodkins and blades of various sizes. I help poor Mrs Greer to her feet and onto the chair.

As the men laugh, their eyes glinting at their newfound toys, I whisper into her ear, 'Madam, you must not falter.' She glares at me, hate mixed with hope which dies when Rush begins to rearrange his instruments. 'You must bear it,' I tell her. 'It will not get worse than this.'

Will intervenes to insist on my respite. Rush grudgingly agrees and I'm exiled to my desk. It affords a more distant view of the action and my gut twists from the comfort I take in it. Mrs Greer's feet scrape across the floor as the men run her up and down again and again.

'I heard the scuttle of mice. Perhaps it's her familiar!' Henry suggests. He pauses, half leaning on Mrs Greer, who struggles under his weight. He wipes the sweat off his face and looks around the room for support. Finding none, he tightens his grip on Mrs Greer's shoulder.

'You are tired,' says Rush, not unkindly. 'Her familiars will appear when their mistress calls for them.'

Clements and Rush are disinclined to keep at their run. They bind Mrs Greer to her chair. We wait in silence, the only sound made is when one of the men flicks Mrs Greer whenever her eyelids droop. The room turns dark; while Mrs Greer is sparsely lit by the candles surrounding her, the rest of us are rendered shadows. Tired though I am, I pinch myself to stay awake and bear witness to this. Will drops a piece of bread onto the desk. 'I am not hungry,' I say, and make it clear with a look that I will not eat – not while Mrs Greer is so denied in her own home.

'I will have it,' says Samuel.

I rub my ears. 'Give it to the cat,' I spit. 'If you won't feed the woman at least feed her pet. The creature is hungry.'

The bread is crushed in Will's hands, but it is Rush's smile that assures me I have made a mistake.

His staff clatters to the ground. 'Her imps are lurking. Search every crack and crevice.'

'She has no pet,' Will whispers to me, and there is fear in his eyes before he schools his expression. Grace. Whatever her partnership with Rush, she has relayed enough for him to be wary of me. The men, to Mrs Greer's distress, pull at the floorboards around her before heading to the rooms in the back.

'Stop it,' she cries, her protests a whimper drowned out by the sound of metal being ripped out. Rush, Clements and the watchers return to the room. They're covered in the ash of a dying fire and Clements cradles a swaddled bundle to his chest. The song does not pull at me. What remains of the dead child is a faint perfume, a sensation that slips through my fingers like silk.

Henry leaves the cottage, but his retching is still heard. The other watchers sit white-faced in the corner while Clements places the child at the woman's feet.

'Whose child is this?' Clements asks.

Mrs Greer shakes her head. The child is of Mrs Greer's flesh. Its death is mingled with her. The child and what remains of its song is slight, so slight that I cannot be certain whether the child was stillborn or had its life cut short.

Clements reaches for the softest weapon in arsenal and kneels beside Mrs Greer, his face almost tender. 'You bought your child clothes.' She turns her head from his and he shuffles towards her. 'You were not trying to conceal its birth. You will not be blamed for the child's death. My friend Judge Percival will tell you the same.' This approach is not kindness. Still, Mrs Greer, with a gape in Will's direction, clutches at it. Her chest is racked with sobs when he affirms Clements's words with a gentle look.

Rush rests his hand on Clements's shoulder and reluctantly steps back. 'We are not here for this,' he dismisses the child at his feet. 'Tragic though it is. When a witch bargains with the Devil, he takes what is most precious to them.'

'I am not a witch,' she says, but her refusal is devoid of fire.

'Think of your niece,' Rush threatens. 'She is of your flesh and has been seen keeping company with yourself and your familiar. You are both damned unless you tell the truth. When did you meet the Devil?'

Mrs Greer closes her eyes. She has been robbed of sleep this past day and a half. Her ordeal has taken from her, but I would lose Althamia and myself if I were to bolster her. I lose myself anyway when she squares her shoulders to do Rush's bidding. 'I met the Devil when I was a young girl.'

Will is impassive, but Rush arches his head at her confession, while Clements and the others let out a soft exhale.

'What happened when you met him?' Rush demands.

She looks down at her child. 'I met him in the forest. He was a boy of a well-formed appearance except for his cloven hooves. He promised me beauty and wealth if I renounced my baptism and signed my name in his book. I couldn't write my name, so he had me make my mark and stole my soul with a kiss. He gifted me a familiar. An owl named Snow.'

'What did he take from you in exchange for these gifts?' Rush presses.

'He took my child. He took everything,' she confides.

'What do you have your familiar do?' he asks.

'My familiar taught me how to make a doll of clay. I fashioned it in the shape of my late mistress and poked pins in it until she withered and died. I married her husband and five years later made another doll that I held over the fire. He died in agony.'

'The Ingram child?'

She shrinks, her eyes darkening. 'I sent Snow to steal his soul. His father took from me when I was a girl and then spurned me for his now-wife.'

'Do you fly?' asks one of the men.

She hesitates until Rush repeats the question. 'I fly at night,' she answers.

The watchers lean close despite themselves. 'What does it feel like?'

'Like I am a bird. The souls of the people I killed gather about me like wings.'

'Do you have anything else to confess?' Rush asks.

'This is all I am guilty of.'

Clements steps forward. 'And the others? What of your coven?'

Rush pulls out the drawings of the accused from his knapsack. 'Do you know these people?'

'I know them.' Her face turns eager at Rush's open encouragement. 'They are of my coven. On the black sabbath, we huddle together until we are of one flesh. Jane Foley, Bess Heath and her father Eli Heath, Mr Nelson and his wife Margaret Nelson.'

Rush inclines his head in thanks and looks to me to make certain that I have taken a thorough account of Mrs Greer's confession.

'Wait,' she cries, 'there is another.'

'Who?' Clements demands.

'Thomasine Ady,' she offers.

The watchers scoff, but Rush's face is measured. 'The Ingrams' maid.'

At his unsaid command, the men untie Mrs Greer.

'Take her to Lancaster Castle,' Rush instructs them.

'Please,' she begs, her bound hands stopping her from wiping away her tears. 'May I hold my son one last time?' Rush, to my surprise, obliges. What is left of the child's cries has subsided. I cannot hear him anymore.

'I did not look at him when he was born. I was afraid to commit him to memory,' Mrs Greer confesses and reaches to unravel the swaddling.

'That will cause you more harm than good,' warns Rush, a gentle admonishment, and Mrs Greer and her pleas are bustled away.

Rush snatches my transcript out of my hand. 'I wish to make a copy,' he explains when I protest. 'I will strike out the witch's claim regarding Mr Ingram and Thomasine. They are malicious accusations.'

'I agree,' says Will, to Clements's visible displeasure.

Is this mercy, I wonder, observing the flash of relief in Rush's face.

Then I realise: there is no mercy in this act. The Ingrams are the corner from which Rush has spun his web. He would not want his foundation picked apart by accusations of adultery and witchcraft.

Chapter Twenty-Seven

'There will be another investigation tomorrow,' says Will. After the investigation, Clements had accepted Rush's invitation to drink to their victory. Citing the late hour as an excuse, Will and I had ridden back to the Carew manor.

'I will steady myself for it,' I tell him as we head inside. 'I am not hungry,' I say when a servant approaches with an offer of supper. 'I will have a bath in its place.' To my relief, Will doesn't try to dissuade me and I hurry to my chamber to distance myself from the events of the past two days.

Someone has been in my room. The air is full of the spicy smell of the narcissus flower. The scent that belongs to Grace. Neither my sheets, my valise nor my diary have been spared her touch. She is trying to provoke a confrontation, perhaps to determine if I am more malleable than Will. I check the bookshelf where her blessing book and Francis's knot remain undiscovered inside a thick tome. I will not confront her with my suspicions . . . yet.

I am so busy searching for what is lost that I almost overlook the letter on my desk. The embroidered silk-floss is soon strewn about the floor as I open it to find the note bare, save for 'Althamia H' written in the top corner and the rowan sprig I'd refused of her in York packaged inside. I handle it between my fingers. I am not worthy of her regard and sink in the chair to pen a response.

Dear Althamia,

I have dreamt of you every night since I left York. The only other woman I've ever dreamt of is my mother. The loss of her has made an Orpheus of me. I walk through life unable to move forward as a part of me longs to look back . . . until you.

When I left York, I had the sensation that I'd abandoned the best part of myself to linger by your side. I would sink were you to look upon me now. You would not recognise what is left. My worst aspect, one people would shrink from, though you I imagine would cauterise it with a quick and steady hand.

I am writing to you in the midst of a witch investigation. Earlier, myself and the other witch-hunters invaded the home of Mrs Greer, tied her to a chair, ran her up and down the room and threatened torture. There would be no rest, we told her, unless it was preceded by a confession.

A witch is no more than the words a witch-hunter puts into her mouth. The same mouth that whispered poetry in your ears has also whispered spite in another's. I have filled her mouth with spells and malice. In the space of a few hours, I have become everything you would detest . . . everything I detest. Yet I will repeat these measures again and again.

I do not know why I am writing to you, except, even as I sit here, I feel your token beneath my heart, its touch enough that I will not abandon hope of an alternative ending, even though I have given up all hope of us.

Yours
Nicholas

A procession of servants arrive armed with hot water and I hand over the letter before I am tempted to interline it with excuses. Once I am alone, I submerge myself in the bath. The steam rises like the Pendle mist, thick enough that I imagine drowning in it.

Francis stares at me from within the bath water. The sight does not alarm me. The two weeks I have spent in Lancaster have numbed my senses. My guilt cannot be washed away. The events of the past two days will haunt me. I will dream of it. I will sing of it when I am dead. I half jerk when Francis's reflection is drowned out by a pool of blood. The reflection settles and I blink to see Clements staring up at me. I tilt my head. The sight of him is an unwelcome balm.

'You are performing your baptism,' he jests, and Grace's scent is soon over-powered by the stench of ale that clings to him.

'You should have knocked,' I complain, but the lack of bite to my words emboldens him to perch on the edge of the lead tub. He arches his head to take stock of the possessions in my bedchamber. My awe at Lord Carew's wealth has subsided but I do not allow myself to forget it. Such surroundings make it easy for a person to resign themselves to becoming a fixture. Clements takes in the room's furnishings and observes my wrinkled bed with a sly smile. 'I see now why you excused yourself from the festivities.' His attention turns to the view of Pendle Hill through the window. 'We are reduced in number. Henry, one of Rush's men, has abandoned us. A drink or two and he was overtaken with remorse.' He snorts. 'He will soon be replaced. My life has been a slow descent into poverty. My family borrowed from their neighbours to bind me into the witch-hunting profession. They did not have your master's foresight to see how it would be so quickly dismantled by King Charles. He always lacked his father's love for the hunt.' His face darkens at the memory. 'Has your master revealed his intentions to you yet?'

The water ripples at my touch. 'He has said nothing except to commend me for my questioning of Mrs Greer.'

'And rightly so. You impressed me, and Mr Rush too. He is full of plans to widen the scope of the investigation to neighbouring towns. He is sending out his men to scout for new businesses. Your master lacks the ambition of his youth. We are much behind.'

I wonder what else Rush has confided in him. I stretch out my arms along the rim of the tub and try to channel Francis's easy charm. 'My master is content to rest on past laurels. His long retirement has made him too merciful.' He leans close, his eyes lingering on my exposed skin. 'But mercy is a luxury denied to men like us. The world has treated us harshly. It is only natural that we use the same methods.'

'Us,' he repeats, savouring it. 'In my youth I was not so fearsome. King James and his court liked soft boys with elegant manners.' His reflection is a raw sight. 'I tried to rival them.' His expression slips when our eyes meet. He shrugs off the memory. '"The boys", they called us . . . we all have our stories.' He draws back and places his hands on his knees. 'I tortured a friend of your master years ago. Richard Knight, a young courtier. The boy made a powerful enemy, and my master and I were paid to find him guilty of witchcraft.'

The water around me trembles. 'What did he do to warrant such a punishment?'

He shrugs either because he cannot remember or doesn't care. The latter, judging by what comes next: 'The boy had a loose tongue. He claimed that a lord had made a forceful approach. Lies, of course, but young Will was implicated. The men were close companions and my master thought it an opportune moment to prune the competition.'

'You failed.'

He bristles. 'I wouldn't call it a failure. We used every instrument at our disposal.' He rests his hand on my exposed skin, lets his thumb trail across my collarbone. 'The boy was quick to confess to witchcraft, but couldn't be persuaded to implicate Will, not even when we promised to spare him.'

'A sorry tale,' I remark, and he draws his face close to mine as though to make a study of me. He digs his fingers into my shoulders when I attempt to shrug off his touch. 'Your master survived the scandal as he does everything else.'

'Judge Percival is not a witch,' I protest, and he digs his nails in deeper.

He pauses, a brief respite from his touch. 'It is not witchcraft I suspect him of,' he says with a quick look at my bed. 'He's a sodomite.'

My careful expression doesn't slip, despite my shock as I recall my guess at the woman Will loved but couldn't save. An assumed backstory on my part, one he has refrained from colouring with further details.

'It is true. I have whispered something of my knowledge to Rush. Not all,' he says when I tilt my head back. 'Otherwise he'd be quick to place one of his boys in Will's bed.'

I almost huddle inwards at his suspicion. 'Suspicions, not proof,' I correct him.

His eyes darken. 'You are right. Lord Carew would not believe me were I to voice them. But you are of his set. He would believe you if you told him Will had attempted to force his attentions.' The pressure on my shoulders increases until the water reaches my chin.

'A hanging accusation and a lie,' I reply.

'One he could easily shake off. It is his disgrace I seek, not his death. Either way, the result would place responsibility for the investigations in our hands.'

'And Rush?' I ask of Clements's reflection in the water as he leans hard against me. This is how Agnes last saw him. A shove and I would be submerged. The water blurs the panic in my eyes. I tell myself that, even if he suspected, he wouldn't dare harm me in Lord Carew's home.

'We will finish the investigation together and divide the neighbouring towns between us,' he announces, and I imagine all the people of Lancaster caught in their net. They will not escape, not if Rush and Clements succeed in removing Will from his post. This is not a plan I would ever oblige him in. But unless I can persuade the dead to sing, I will be a helpless bystander to their schemes.

'I will think on how to frame my concerns to Lord Carew,' I say, and he begins to draw back.

'A few words are all that is needed,' he presses.

'They are not just words. Time is needed to craft them to their best effect.'

A reluctant nod and he eases away from me. 'You are in danger of drowning,' he warns from the doorway, a departing remark I gasp at once I am alone.

Chapter Twenty-Eight

'The Devil came to me three times,' Eli Heath confesses.

The accused witch sits unbound in Rush's parlour in an ash-coloured attire of a shirt and breeches pieced together with patches. Will, Clements, Rush, his watchers and I face him in a loose semicircle. Eli regards us as though he is holding court. His manner makes it easy for us, or at least for me. I fashion him into a jester and myself a tolerant onlooker. Rush's watchers had arrested him and his daughter Bess yesterday. Rush had seen to it that they had been searched for a witch's mark before our arrival. Eli is the first to be interrogated, while his daughter Bess awaits her turn in the basement. Eli is hunched over from drink. Lord Carew's enclosure had seen his living forfeited. His bloated features are a testament to his new employment. He did not take long to break, even with the inducement of ale that Rush's men had pressed to his lips.

I ignore the weight of Will's concern. I have not told him about Clements's suspicions. Though he senses something is amiss from my inability to meet his eyes and the looks Rush and Clements exchange over his head. Sodomy is a hanging offence. The suggestion would ruin him. My efforts to steal secrets from the dead have failed. I would not blame him were he to abandon Rawton to the combined schemes of Clements, Rush and Grace. Althamia would not be endangered by his abandonment. But to give up hope of an alternative ending would ruin me. Especially when I have acted so much against my nature to aid it.

'On the first and second visit the Devil gifted me with revenge on the strangers who could spare a sermon but not a coin. With his aid, I have spoiled wells and maimed cattle.' Eli speaks with a thick accent and every so often Rush makes a point of looking to his men for a translation. His men think it a joke and do not see that they are making both Eli and themselves a spectacle.

'He sickened the Keller boy at my command. His father had me enslaved. He made me work and withheld the parish relief I was due and more. I have kept him and his family in silks. My daughter—'

Rush cuts him off. 'And on the third occasion?' He motions for me to strike Eli's last remark from my transcription.

'He offered me revenge on Mrs Cropley,' says Eli. 'She accused me of giving her a look and set her husband on me. The Devil said he would take her child, but it would cost me.'

Clements leans in close and grunts, 'The price?'

Eli stares at the jug of ale on the watcher's lap. 'My soul . . . Every time you say yes, a piece of your soul is taken.'

His words take something from me. I have said yes to everything that has been offered to me – Francis's life, Broad's offer of publication, Lord Carew's invite. I have bargained my soul away in pieces. Rush signals for one of his men to press a jug of ale to Eli's lips. 'Just a sip,' he admonishes. Eli eagerly slurps at it, and I wince at how he clings to the jug when it's pulled away.

'I know them,' says Eli excitedly when Rush waves a succession of sketches under his nose. His legs sprawl out and he boasts, his features lewd: 'They are part of my coven where I am master. I have had them all.'

'Does your daughter Bess share your guilt?' The men turn in surprise when Will speaks. For much of the night he has been a watchful shadow. He frowns when Rush's men again press more ale under Eli's nose. The old drunkard sniffs after it like a dog when it is withdrawn, then looks to Rush. 'It was she who enticed me to sell my soul to the Devil. When darkness falls, she flies into people's windows and induces them to sin. She is queen of the night.'

'Take him to the castle prison,' Rush orders once Eli, having exhausted his stories, begins to repeat himself.

'Wouldn't it be better to wait for Bess's confession? Else we will be travelling back and forth,' Samuel complains, his nose wrinkling with distaste as he helps Eli to his feet.

I put down my quill. 'Miss Heath has not yet confessed.'

Eli's laugh is more bitter than the ale he's imbued. 'My daughter is made of sterner stuff.'

Rush doesn't dispute this and calls for Mrs Barnett to ready the girl for our inspection. Bess Heath is dragged into the room by Mrs Barnett and tied to the chair. Her clothes are too bedraggled to be attributed to a day's confinement in the basement. She had not submitted meekly to the search and her ragged woollen skirt is stained red from Mrs Barnett's bodkins. Bess is halfway between girl and woman and her fierce expression does nothing to conceal that in a few years she will be striking. She makes no sign of recognition when our eyes meet. To acknowledge our former meeting would be to remember the warning I imparted and oblige her to gratitude. A wasted emotion. Courtesy will not save her, nor will I.

'Your father has confessed to being a witch,' Rush informs her, 'He claims that you are of his likeness and have signed your soul away to the Devil. You keep a familiar about yourself, a dog called Seer which you send out at night to spoil wells and plague your neighbours' sleep.'

She mumbles a response.

'Louder,' Rush snaps and steps closer, only for Bess to spit in his face. Rush's remaining two watchers rise to his defence.

Rush orders them to stand down. 'We do not put hands on women. Even one as foul as this.' He wipes his face clean and Bess hides behind a curtain of raven-black hair. 'Your former employer Mr Keller accuses you of cursing his son and laming his cattle. This you did in revenge when he rebuked you for your slovenly work. You have also sent your imps to plague Mrs Keller's sleep. You refused her attempt to search you.'

She lifts her chin and her green eyes flash. 'That is a lie.'

Will is more guarded with his emotion, but the others are slow to hide their surprise at her speech. It lacks her father's roughness and is in stark contrast to her beggared appearance.

'Then tell us the truth,' says Rush.

'I served the Keller family well. I was a diligent servant. I am no witch. I have no spells or tools to work any magic,' Bess answers.

'You have your tongue,' says Clements.

'And your eyes. Have you used them to take an image of your neighbours?' Rush asks, no doubt suspecting her of being too poor to read and write her own curses. Illiterate witches enact their curses with stolen images, whether from a look or their victim's looking glass.

She laughs, a bright sound amidst the men's guffaws. The sound is curtailed by Rush's hissed threat, 'I could put your eyes out to counter your malice.'

She flinches. 'I am innocent, though I doubt my denials will save me.'

'Who taught you to speak like that?' Rush demands.

'Like what, sir?' she replies, and Rush appears regretful at allowing his curiosity to give her an advantage.

'Probably another gift from the Devil,' Clements remarks. 'Pity he couldn't have gifted her a wardrobe to match.'

Bess cranes her neck towards him. 'I learnt the same way that most people do. I listened.'

A confession Rush jumps on. 'Where? Do you send your spirit to fly through windows at night?'

'My spirit is lodged here,' Bess answers and tilts her chin to her chest. 'I listen at windows and taverns frequented by both rich and poor. Or rather, I did. Now that I am older, people take heed of both my appearance and speech and find fault with it. They resent me for it, even though it is mine. Or perhaps because it is *mine*.'

'You have nothing except what you have stolen,' says Rush, but casts the accusation towards Will and me.

He knows, I realise with a thought to Grace's blessing book.

'You are angry now,' Rush concludes from her flushed appearance. 'Will you send your familiars after us as you did your neighbours?' His watchers are alarmed at this turn, yet Rush picks at his hat feather and twirls it between his fingers. He has asked this question too many times to truly fear the answer.

'Ill-thoughts are not curses. I haven't harmed anyone,' she states.

'What about Mrs Blake?' asks Clements.

At this, she falters. 'That was not my fault.'

'Mrs Blake accuses you of preventing her child from being born,' accuses Rush.

'A lie. She was never pregnant. I know the signs,' she protests and flushes at the men's knowing chuckles. 'Not from myself,' she clarifies, 'but when I served my mistress, Mrs Grace Rawle. She was ill when she was carrying and had cravings, all the things which Mrs Blake showed no signs of.'

'You know Mrs Rawle?' I interrupt.

She nods, her look brief. 'I was in her service for a time. Everyone doubted Mrs Blake, but I was the only one brave enough to air my suspicions. I should not be blamed that the only thing she carries in her stomach is her death.'

'So you are both a seer and a witch?' Rush taunts.

'Neither, sir.' She looks at him for a long while. 'But despite the lack I see through you.' Her nose wrinkles when Rush caresses her face with the feather. He steps back only to close the distance between them with a fist, the first to her mouth and a second to her eyes. I rush towards her as she falls backwards.

Will makes a seated objection. 'Any confessions obtained by such means are unlawful.'

'She flew,' Rush tells Mrs Barnett, who is drawn by Bess's cry. He smiles away her concern and wipes the blood from his knuckles. 'It is not broken, though my kerchief is spoiled,' he adds and tosses the spotted handkerchief to a backpedalling Mrs Barnett.

Clements finishes his ale and looks down at Bess where she lies sprawled at his feet. 'She flew,' he repeats, and the men laugh at his quip.

Bess's lip is split, the broken blood vessels under her eye a constellation of stars. Bess scowls when I hand her my handkerchief and I remember that she is bound.

'May I?' At her nod, I gently dab at the wound as she tries hard not to wince.

'I should have hidden better,' she mutters.

It is not your fault, I want to say, but I turn to Rush. 'You told me a man should never put his hands on a woman.' He pays me no mind.

'I see no men present,' Bess spits.

Clements half rises only to stop when I place myself between them. Rush grins. Her resistance excites him, and she plays into his hands with her anger.

'I see no woman. Only a witch and a whore,' Rush taunts.

'I do not know why you are so amused,' Clements remarks at her laughter.

'I am rejoicing at my good fortune. Yesterday I was an impudent beggar and today I am somewhat more substantial!' she taunts.

'You are nothing but a dog,' Rush spits.

'And yet you all have gathered to hear me bark.' She lets out a loud yelp.

'The hour grows late,' Rush complains and a wordless signal sees the door closed. 'I have not the patience to wear her out with words.' There is a quiet menace to him that makes us mute.

Rush turns to me. 'Hand me an instrument.'

'Mr Rush,' says Will. A gentle refrain that Rush scoffs at.

'An instrument,' Rush repeats and stands over me. 'You are in this room with us. You cannot hide behind your papers and pretend otherwise.' He nods towards the trestle board in the corner and the instruments atop it; the witch's bridle that will be placed around her head to ruin her tongue and force her silence, the pricking needle to search for the Devil's mark, the pincers that her fingers will be slid under as though they are flowers to be pressed.

He tuts when I reach for the pricking needle. My hands hover over the pincers, but I'm held fast by the memory of the songs of Francis and Agnes. It is a promise of something, I tell myself when Will approaches. A promise of escape. But then he grabs the weapon from under me and hands it to Rush. The voices of the dead get louder and send my thoughts scattering. Will sits down and Rush teases Bess by hovering the pincers under her nose. Her face turns white, but she doesn't cry out, not even when Rush hands the weapon to Clements and holds out her arm like a length of rope. Clements slides the thumbscrew over her fingers and presses his face close to her. The remembrance of Agnes's song is a jolt in my knees and

I swallow down the metallic taste of her remembered fear. 'Keep her steady,' says Rush, and he surveys us as though we are a scene he has conjured. A wicked smile tugs at his lips.

He likes this too much to ever stop. His men, this town, they have made it too easy for him. I have made it easy, stoking the fire within him every time we greet his abuses with laughter instead of scorn. Will's warning shake of the head slides over me. We have been holding on to a dream that disintegrates on closer scrutiny. Even if we were to force Rush out, he would persist with his work in the next town and the town after. I will end it here.

Clements smiles, ready to press down until I throw him off balance with a push. 'The girl,' he wheezes once he's regained his footing. Althamia. I am ruining things, but I cannot let another woman sing on Clements's behalf.

I've barely had a chance to respond when he's upon me. Will places himself between us but is pushed back by Clements's blows. Bess and the others witness the scuffle, their shock visible from the way they hang back.

'Her name is Althamia,' I shout when Clements tires. 'And Agnes Wright is the name of the young girl you attacked from behind and then drowned.'

His eyes widen in surprise. He is hurt, not by the accusation, but by the possibility of it all slipping away. He was too busy plotting his future to suspect I wasn't genuine in my professed disloyalty.

'I am no murderer,' he denies.

Agnes's song is a haunting lament.

I have been numbed. I have been petted but I have never been regarded by all but one. A small unseen thing with a mouth heavy from the taste of iron.

'Liar,' I spit.

He pauses and his lip curls. 'I have no regrets, except one. The maid . . . The whole thing lacked ceremony. It was over far too quickly to be entertaining.'

I almost choke from the rush of bile to my mouth.

Clements snorts at my reaction. 'Born in the woad,' he taunts. 'You have money and power and yet you think you are so hard done by because you are a bastard.'

'You know nothing of me!'

He takes in the careful stitches of my black velvet doublet and pearl buttons. 'I know enough to know that you have never had to demean yourself for anything. Not like your master.'

Will's face turns white.

'We have exhausted all legal methods,' I tell Rush. 'A witch's mark was not found on her. You will give Bess Heath her liberty.'

Rush watches the scene play out before him. He inclines his head and snaps his fingers at his men. 'I will leave the girl in your care,' he concedes, and departs to his study. His acquiescence offers no comfort. He is plotting his advantage.

I untie Bess and help her to her feet. She takes the handkerchief from me and holds it to her mouth.

'We must go,' I tell Will as Clements stands insensible. I do not want to leave him here to spew lies in Rush's ears, but we cannot stay and have it out with only a wall to block his accusations.

'Do you think yourself a hero?' Clements has followed us outside and I help Bess on my horse and climb up behind her.

'I am not of that opinion,' Bess retorts as I nudge my horse into a trot.

Will lingers as if caught in Clements's net and I circle my horse towards them.

'Richard Knight,' says Clements and the whites of his eyes are bright in the dark. 'My master and I tortured him for days, yet he did not say one word against you.'

Will makes a choking sound and looks around but the street is deserted. Clements grabs the reins of his horse to keep him close.

'A man can only withstand that amount of pain from fear of something worse – or love. You are unnatural. Ganymede. Sodomite,' he spits the last word.

'You are a liar,' I say when Will fails to deny the charge. He cannot speak, his face is stiff from shame.

Emboldened by his stillness, Clements turns to me. 'I always suspected something between you. But you are in love with a witch and your master loves a dead man. Richard Knight. Your lover whom I killed.' He smiles when Will flinches and turns to me. 'What ties you to him? Are you his catamite, his boy? Why give him your loyalty?' His look is piercing, and it is only when Bess's fingers brush across my sleeves that I remember to breathe. At my exhale his face twists into a grin. 'Witch.' A hurled accusation but my hesitancy gives him something to latch onto. He will never let go.

A vicious laugh escapes him as Will jerks the reins free from his grip. 'A witch and a sodomite. While the pair of you are swinging from the gallows I will go back to York for the girl,' he crows.

Will blocks my attempt to go after him. He shakes his head in warning as Clements saunters off whistling into the night.

Chapter Twenty-Nine

'He will tell Rush,' I warn as we ride off. 'He has primed him already with a tease of his suspicions.' I turn back, but the path to town is shrouded by mist. The rendered pools of darkness dissuade me from wading through it. 'He will return for Althamia once he is done with us.'

Will closes his eyes. 'The girl,' he reminds me, nodding at Bess sitting behind me.

'He will not want to share the glory or reward,' he murmurs as we widen the distance between ourselves and the town. 'He will drink to his good fortune and then plot his next move. We will plot ours.'

'Have you no family to take you in?' I ask Bess when we near a clearing in the forest. She had asked us to bring her here.

'Only my father,' she replies as I help her down.

I grimace. Eli Heath betrayed her for alcohol and the promise of meagre meals in prison until the assizes.

'I will do as the women in my place have done for generations. I will seek sanctuary from the storm.' *As should you*, she conveys with a careful look that I disregard. Her lips part, but she gulps down an invitation for me to join her. She is not a witch, yet a word from her neighbours is enough to make it so. We are the same, yet I have been in the witch-hunters' company. I have practised their methods, and this is not something that can be forgotten. Bess is wise not to forget.

'We can make arrangements to send you somewhere safe,' Will promises. He looks at Bess, who is small enough to be swallowed up by the vastness of the forest.

'I belong here,' she insists. 'My family owned a smallholding for generations until Lord Carew drove us away. I will reclaim it and will not be steered off course by a witch-hunter. He is just a man, and it is only our fear that makes him more so.'

'Have you met him before?' I ask, remembering Rush's violent reaction to her. She shakes her head too quickly for me to believe her, but the sight of her crimson mouth stops me from pressing further.

'I am not my father,' she says, refusing the cloak I offer her, 'I do not take charity.'

'It is not charity,' I argue. 'Besides, it is cold.' At that she reluctantly accepts it.

Will removes the leather pouch from his waist. It lands at her feet. 'For your discretion.'

A cheap gesture, but he is too desperate to be shamed by it.

Bess picks up his purse and hands it back to him.

'That is not necessary.' She heads towards the forest and with her face in profile addresses us from its edge before she's swallowed by the tawny velvet: 'Mr Keller offered my father and me work in exchange for food, shelter and the parish relief owed to us. It was a mean bargain but one I was grateful for. He is corrupt but his methods kept us fed and prevented my father from drinking away our parish relief.'

'What happened?' I ask, in spite of Will's glare.

'When Mr Keller asked for more of me, my father did nothing to dissuade him,' Bess whispers. 'My father was angered by my refusal and Mr Keller was sour when I fought him off loudly enough that his wife came running. My honour is not for sale, and I am a witch

243

because of it.' Her hurts she bears like a soldier, though she is still a child.

'Miss Heath,' I call, but she is gone, lost to the night.

'A common tale,' says Will.

'She was not lying,' I snap, until a look from him shames me. He too has suffered from such methods.

The details change, yet the girl never does; she is either wanton or a mercenary whore, but never the victim. My stomach turns at the thought of a man selling his child. And I grow angry when I remember Mr Keller's pompous demeanour. His life is without censure, and he will have Bess hanged for it to remain so.

Will nudges his horse to retrace our steps back to town. 'I will seek out Clements alone,' he says when I move to join him. 'The sight of you will enrage him. Your attention had flattered him into believing you a faithful follower.'

'And now he thinks me a witch.' And I did not deny it. I stare at the trees, their promised sanctuary lost to me. 'He confessed to Agnes's murder.'

Will's face is bleak. 'And who apart from us heard him? It is not too late for you to return home.'

'I have done too much to believe myself worthy of rescue,' I snap, but again his mount blocks mine. 'Clements told me he wanted either your death or disgrace. He will see now they are the same thing.'

The question of Richard Knight hangs between us. I reach for it first. 'Richard Knight?'

Will answers with a direct look. 'We grew up together at court. Two boys sent away by their families to make their fortune. His bravery made him powerful enemies. I could not save him.' He breaks off. 'He is the knot I carry. Do not ask me to unravel him with speeches.'

'A confrontation will not stop Clements,' I argue when he nudges his horse forwards. 'I will go to the cemetery and gather secrets enough to force both his and Rush's retreat.'

'We are robbed of time,' he says simply. 'I will reason with him instead.'

I snort. 'You mean beg! It will not work.'

'Then I will bribe him with my life's savings,' he says.

'Your plan is weak.'

The grim set to his face twists my insides. 'Yet one I will spare you the witnessing of.'

'Will,' I call after him, but he is gone before I can gather my words. I will not catch up. I believe myself robbed of time also. I forget the dagger, a flash of silver at his hip. I convince myself that he means what he says. I keep my hands white.

Chapter Thirty

'We are lessened,' says Lord Carew with a look at Clements's empty chair. A passing observation that comes four days late and my eyes dart to Will sat across the dining table.

'I could not find him,' said Will when he'd returned from his mission to reason with Clements. I did not question him further and he has kept himself apart in the days that have followed. If Clements is dead, he should trust me with the knowledge instead of leaving me wondering where Clements is and who he's spoken to. Yet I do not believe he is gone. Surely, if he were, Will would have abandoned our nightly visits to the cemetery in the vain hope of making allies of the dead. No, he is alive and he is waiting to have his revenge.

Grace finishes her breakfast and in the face of our silence Lord Carew cuts to the quick of the matter. 'I did not remark upon it earlier for I found the man's absence a respite, but Mr Rush writes to complain that his truancy has brought the investigation to a standstill,' he says, waving the letter a servant had carried in moments before.

'I will seek him out,' says Will.

'If only Mr Rush was the one to have disappeared,' says Lord Carew with a flash of impatience.

'We are proceeding with caution,' says Will.

Grace and I study the interplay between the two men as Lord Carew says, 'Then pray proceed.'

'My uncle lacks patience,' says Grace when he abandons breakfast with a sigh.

'He has not the stomach for a drawn-out strategy,' Will retorts, unable to hide his resentment. Whatever Clements's fate, our circumstances have not been altered by his disappearance. Grace is the reason for our presence here and, like Will, my composure strains from having to pretend otherwise.

Grace concedes his response with a raised brow before following her uncle out.

Will scowls at his plate, laden with fruit and bread, and heads outside. 'I will search for him alone,' he insists as the servant rushes to ready his horse.

He is off before I can brace myself to ask where he will search. I pace the grounds. The day is damp and overcast and in want of light my hand reaches for the rowan sprig Althamia sent me. I twirl it between my fingers and watch the red strands glimmer.

My thoughts turn to Grace. My time in Rawton is a fast-moving play and it seems Grace is the one writing the lines. I am not content to be a mere player. Whatever her terms with Rush, she cannot be satisfied. She'd have possession of her estates otherwise. Her restlessness might make her eager for a new partnership or at least chip away her caution.

I turn, only to bump into a servant. My apology goes over her head as she curtsies an invitation to join Grace. She leads me to the parlour where Grace is sat at the table in profile towards me. The backdrop of Pendle Hill adds a misty glow to her blue gown. What little sun there is this afternoon, she takes. 'A diversion,' she explains of the table loom before her and the pile of ribbons at her feet. As she weaves the silken red strands into fabric the deft movement of her hands casts a spell, one I must break. 'I wish to speak with you plainly.'

'Are you going to beg me to stop what I am doing?' she asks without breaking from her task.

I sit on the chair nearest to her. 'What *are* you doing?' My question is answered with a condescending smile.

'I knew someone like you: the dead spoke to them.'

My fingers are nails in the chair's upholstery. 'I am not a witch.'

'Oh yes, your master has spoken to me of your mother,' she says, and I am cut less by her words and more by the fact she doesn't say it to wound. 'A tale wrested against his will, of an apprentice more dead than living. Though I doubt Rush would delight in it.'

'And what of you?' I accuse. 'You are a thread witch. You dazzle people out of their senses.'

She does not shrink from the accusation, and her lack of surprise reduces me to no more than a player reluctantly spouting their lines. 'Good,' she says after a pause. 'For a moment I thought you had come here weaponless.' She resumes her weaving. 'I am a witch, not a thread witch. Though in want of Prometheus's fire, I forgive your ignorance. Witch-hunters were not completely mistaken in their distinction. Women of my class cultivate a single talent with knot magic. Those beneath try to master it all and badly. Who was your tutor? Surrounded as you are by the dead, someone must have taught you to control it. You would have been overwhelmed otherwise. You may keep your secrets,' she says at my silence. She stops to cast a critical eye over her handiwork. 'People lose themselves to my whispers. My uncle taught me to refine it, though he lacks power himself. I am one of the rare few magic chose to flower in. When I was a girl, he put me to use in binding his business partners to unfavourable terms. I have served him well, yet he will do nothing for me in my current state. I must settle for what is his.'

'You are too spent to force such a result,' I say, remembering her failed attempt to manipulate Will. 'Mr Rush?' She stiffens under the accusation. 'Whatever bargain you have struck, he will not stop here. He will kill innocent people and will comb the country for more once he is finished.'

'Innocent?' She scoffs. 'A knot was all it took to spark Mrs Ingram's hysteria. In truth, I have done nothing wrong. It is not my fault that men find devilry where they will. I merely show them what is in their hearts.' She twists in her seat and addresses me plainly. 'I am a woman, a recusant and a witch. The conditions force me to be either the hunter or hunted. Of course you have no care for my sufferings,' she says when I turn from her. 'Male witches have always been a small concern to witch-hunters.'

'I have been frightened my entire life, but I would never do what you have.'

'You have done worse,' she retorts, and I flush, wishing for a shadow to retreat to.

'You requested an audience.'

'Well?' she conveys with a raised brow. 'What have you to offer me?' Her laughter colours the silence. 'Whatever plan you and Will have concocted to stop me has failed. You are too unrefined. Still, I am minded to generosity. Pick a town of your choosing. Once my uncle's estates are in my possession, I will come and make it your stage.'

She has no wish to be reasoned away from Rush. Instead, it's as though she has reached inside of me and grasped at my most selfish parts. To my shame I am slow to shrink from the sensation. I can either lose myself to her knots or, with her aid, have Father tell me of my mother. A whisper from her would see any man who crosses me reduced to a puppet.

'And Rawton?' I ask.

'It will be safe in my hands.'

'You mean Mr Rush's hands.'

'You cannot refuse me,' she says, her composure tempered by her rapid breathing. I take in her flushed cheeks and the fatigue that clouds her face. Whatever power she has, she has squandered it on forcing Mrs Ingram and perhaps Rush to do her bidding. If she had more to spare, her uncle's estates would already be hers.

'You would not survive the effort,' I tell her plainly.

She reaches for the small bell beside her. 'I will outlast you,' she says, and a few rings later a visitor is ushered inside.

The swift closing of the door prompts him to step into the room's centre. I jerk in surprise to see Walter, one of Rush's men. In place of his usual smock, he wears a faded brown doublet that reaches his knees. His breeches are looped with orange ribbons at the waist that he is at pains not to fiddle with.

'Our guest comes with news,' says Grace brightly, and my unease grows at this orchestrated visit and Walter's reluctance to look upon me.

'I have seen Clements,' he says. At Grace's unvoiced encouragement, he adds, 'He was stumbling along the road three nights ago, drunk. I wanted to be on my way, but he promised me a fortune in return for my time. A merchant's fortune.'

My neck strains from the weight his words place upon it.

'What did he tell you?' Grace urges, the angles of her face shifting in and out of the shadows.

'He said that both Judge Percival and his man, Mr Pearce, are witches. He said more,' he adds with a sly look in my direction, 'but I dare not repeat it in front of you.'

'Have you told your master of this?' asks Grace, watching for my reaction.

She draws close to Walter, her fingers entwined with strands of red silk. 'You did well not to,' she says, and hands him three coins.

'I was promised a merchant's fortune,' he says, taking in the parlour decorated with gold-threaded tapestries and silverware.

'So you were,' she agrees, and motions him to sit. She turns to me. 'Shall I be merciful or drown him?' Her hands, drenched in red, keep the startled Walter in thrall.

A word from him and I die.

She shrugs off my silence and cups his chin. 'You will drown.' He squirms, but her grip holds him fast. 'Look at me,' she orders and stretches out the red thread between her fingers. 'You are mistaken in what you saw that night. You wandered home and encountered nothing but the shadow of Pendle Hill at your back and the drudgery of your life before you.'

Walter's face turns slack as Grace loops the thread into a knot. Even though I am not the target, her words are a song that digs deeper the more I try to remember myself. There will be no easement until I am hers.

'Now leave,' Grace orders Walter, and as she releases him I discover I can breathe again. Walter's hands fall to his pocket, full of the charity she gave to soften her refusal of his service. He stumbles out with a dazed expression. Grace closes the door behind him and presses her back to it. Her chest rises and falls, and she sits beside me until she's recovered.

I am too afraid to even look at her. 'Why not use your tricks on your uncle? Why sacrifice so many for your revenge?'

'The power in our blood makes him resistant to my spells. Do not pity him. He betrayed me first. His employment has made me small.' She looks down at the silken threads still taut in her fingers. 'I have offered you the world, but perhaps you wanted something smaller.'

When I make no reply, she leans closer. 'At my word, my uncle would praise your work.'

Still I say nothing, my eyes fixed to the floor.

'Althamia,' she whispers.

'I do not care for her,' I say, resisting the urge to look at her.

'The letter you sent her – I intercepted its flight. You are here for her sake . . .' The softness in her voice disappears. 'Nothing will come of it. Your father may be a merchant and a wealthy one at that, but my aunt would frown to see her daughter tied to a bastard. Though your stepmother's kin are a welcome polish.'

'A borrowed polish. And one I have no wish to claim.'

'Even if my aunt and uncle were to abandon their misgivings towards you, Althamia would not have you. The memory of you is an unwelcomed burden. She wishes to forget.' She stretches out the thread between her fingers before letting the offer dangle. I flinch from it. 'I would rather she forgot me. I have no wish to see her pulled apart.'

She tightens the threads again. 'You are easily riled. Once when I was in a rage, I used a knot to force my maid to thrust her hand into the fireplace.' Bile rises in my throat as she smiles at the memory. 'I thought it funny,' she goes on, but then her amusement stops. 'My husband was watching. A mere hint of what I was and he fled. But you would not flee,' she finishes, and I do not blink from the challenge in her eyes.

She is wearing Althamia's colour, and her hair is styled in a similar manner. 'Another temptation?' I ask.

'Has it found its mark?' She presses her lips to mine, a soft touch I allow to linger. The memory of the people I've hurt weighs me down. Grace is wild and uninhibited, and in a moment, I am dazzled by the freedom she offers. But she is not Althamia, and I pull away.

'No,' I tell her, but to my surprise her eyes are bright with amusement.

'Althamia,' she replies.

'No,' I insist, more firmly.

'Althamia!' She straightens up. Althamia is veiled by the half-opened door. A raking look and then she is gone, the door snapping shut behind her.

Grace reclines on her chair. 'She has seen a flicker of you.' Her taunts follow me as I flee.

I can smell her on me. I scrub off Grace's scent with my sleeves and hurry after the sounds of Althamia's footsteps to the kitchen. By the time I get there, she's gone, her presence marked by the bewildered reaction of the kitchen servants and a half-opened door to the garden. I'm doused with flour from a servant stacking it on the large overhead shelf. My attempted smile is more of a grimace as I rush to smooth over the woman's anxious apology.

'You have been crowned,' Althamia observes once I've caught up with her.

She is dressed in labourer's clothing and frees her hair from a rough-looking cap. She makes a show of studying her uncle's herb garden, a pattern of rosemary, thyme and other herbs bordered with hedges.

I pat myself free of the flour. 'It's not what it looked like.'

'You need not explain,' she insists, her expression shrouded by the Pendle mist. My mouth opens to protest but she cuts in, 'I received your letter.' I freeze, but the coldness leaves me when she doesn't flinch away. 'The very next day I traded a servant a dress for this attire and plotted my escape by coach. I arrived this morning. I covered myself with dirt to make myself look more like a boy. I fell from the carriage,' she adds, when my eyes fall to the mud caked upon her breaches.

'A dangerous risk,' I say.

She pulls the dagger from her cloak. 'I was not unaccompanied.'

At the sight of the shallow line of exposed flesh I reach for her hand. 'You are hurt,' I say.

She shrinks from my touch. 'It is nothing. I was overeager in my practice. Since you left, York has been flooded with accounts of witch-hunters from East Anglia to Lancaster hanging women. I know you are not like Clements. But your letter made me remember when he . . . took a hold of me. The people in the crowd who laughed and the others who watched.' She steels herself to face me. 'You wrote that you were like him. I had to see if it was true. If I had somehow made you up.'

I do not shield myself from her inspection.

She sighs. 'My mother told me what she asked of you.'

To my shame, I make a rushed confession. 'We needed to draw Clements away from you. You shouldn't have followed us. Clements could still charge you with witchcraft. It is not safe for you here.'

Her face darkens. 'It is not safe for anyone.' She shakes her head angrily when I open my mouth to protest. 'Your letter was a shrived confession, but I am not a saint. I am here now and mean to free the town from those men.'

'Men like myself,' I warn her, but she doesn't back down. I promise myself I will see her safely returned to York this evening, even while I inform her of our dealings with Mr Rush and our fractured alliance with Clements. She absorbs the brief account in silence.

Finally she says, 'I will not let Agnes's death go unpunished. I will tell the people her story and the kind of men they have welcomed. I will help you to drive them out.'

'I am at your service,' I promise.

She nods and averts her eyes. 'Grace is married. Do you care for her?'

'No.' To say anything more would endanger her, so I look her steadfastly in the eye until I am certain she believes me.

'I am not jealous,' she assures me.

'Charles Fairfax,' I counter. She starts in surprise. 'Did you care for him?'

'He was brave and dashing.' My jaw clenches when she softens at the memory. 'I was quick to believe myself in love, though he only ever treated me with a brother's courtesy. I was a child.'

'I am not jealous,' I say, echoing her words. 'My letter . . .' but her expression remains guarded, so I step back.

My breath gives the air movement, one she cuts through with deliberate steps.

She doesn't pull away when I reach for her hand, and for a moment I fool myself into believing I could tell her the truth of who I am and have no fear of my admission being met with revulsion.

'I have secrets,' I begin, but a cry stops short my confession.

'Nicholas!'

Althamia peers over my shoulder at Will, who stands on the kitchen steps.

'I have found Clements.' He draws close and my eyes drop to his hands. They are covered in a dark liquid that sings.

Chapter Thirty-One

We hunch under fallen clouds of white.

'I did not kill him,' Will repeats during our ride into town. We are to visit Mr Wilson, the town's coroner, in the hope he will prompt the jury to rule Clements's death a misadventure. While Will contrives to divert Wilson from other possibilities, I will listen to Clements's song to determine if his death has freed us.

'It was by chance,' Will had explained to Althamia, Lord Carew, Grace and me. His throat had dried during his account of how he found Clements's body. The servants had informed our hosts of Will's bloodstained appearance and Grace had appeared to usher us into the grand chamber. 'I had given up hope of finding him. I assumed he had sought alternative employment.'

'Where was he?' asked Grace. She placed herself beside the reader's desk to take down his account. I had flinched the one time our eyes had met. Her expression betrayed no anger at my refusal. Rather she had looked through me as though I was not there, as though I was dead.

'Near a brook,' Will replied. 'I spied his horse milling around and retraced his tracks. He had been thrown.'

Lord Carew had seemed troubled by Will's account, though Althamia's arrival was a gentle balm. 'You look like your grand-mother,' he'd murmured, a tender welcome that found acceptance. If Althamia had been relieved by the news of Clements's death, she did not show it. With her back towards us, she'd faced the window during Will's account.

'I believe you,' I tell Will, and as we ride into town and I relate my encounter with Grace and her act of bridling Walter. 'He came across Clements three nights ago – alive, drunk and determined to spill our secrets. Grace made him forget,' I say, and his flash of relief is overtaken with worry.

'His death was an accident,' I remind him.

'That is for the coroner to decide. Or the lady herself,' he mutters.

'We should take the matter to Lord Carew,' I tell him.

'If what she told you is true, he has been exploiting her magic since childhood. Lord Carew might not be a witch, but its power is in his blood. He cannot turn on her without condemning himself. You must be wary of the whole family.' His warning includes Althamia, and I turn from it. 'Grace's magic did not work on you?'

I shake my head.

'Good,' he says. 'She has spent herself with her foolish schemes. Whatever hold she has over Rush, he will turn on her soon enough.'

'He is a hypocrite,' I spit.

'Regardless, the man has a hold over me.' At my sharp look, he explains, 'Rush witnessed my argument with Clements. His death discredits me.'

'I will vouch for you,' I say, even as I recall the thinning deference of Carew's servants following Will's discovery. We are not ruined, but while Clements's death remains an unsolved mystery, we are in danger – as is Althamia, if Clements told Rush anything of her.

He dismounts and grimaces at the sight of Mr Wilson's home. 'Rush will use my diminished influence to his advantage.'

'I am getting stronger.' A lie, but one I don't stumble upon. 'There is still time to force the town to abandon Rush.'

'Nicholas—'

'Althamia,' I cut in before he can finish. 'I believe Grace is fond of her. Her arrival could persuade Grace to change course.'

His eyes glitter. 'She will be persuaded, or she will be stopped.'

Mr Wilson's home, a narrow two-storey building at one end of the main street, doubles as his office. On our arrival, Will immediately deploys his weapons; overblown compliments that leave the coroner red-faced and swooning.

'May we have a moment with the deceased?' Will presses, and Mr Wilson, still light-headed from Will's campaign, motions us through to the backroom.

Clements rests on a centre table, his remains wrapped in a white sheet. Like most, he is rendered vulnerable by death and the soft glow of daylight that illuminates his remains.

'He looks peaceful,' I remark, somewhat bitterly, even while I take in the table beneath him stained with blood from his head wound. After all he's done, surely peace should be denied to him. Still, I am glad he is gone. Althamia is safer for it and will be more so once she returns to York.

'They always do at the end,' says Will, warding off the metallic smell of blood with his handkerchief. 'What do you hear?'

Clements was never one for silence. Even in death, he drowns out the other bodies in the morgue. A murder, after all, I determine from the staccato rhythm. My limbs go numb as a slither of his song crawls inside me in search of a weakness to latch onto.

My body has never flinched from it. The smell of kindled wood. My excitement,
a tinder of brine on my skin, that leaves a witch's neck a stem of red dents.
My body, bruised by their looks, broken by their touches, reduced to carrion

by their disdain. My body, discarded and remade to break bones, drain blood and draw confessions. My body, felled by a blow to the head.

His song rattles around. I brace myself as if faced with a clenched fist, but then the rhythm subsides.

Felled by a flame in the dark . . . The pretty piece. The witch Althamia.

'The stench,' I mumble and wave off Will's concern. It was raining the morning Althamia arrived, though the mud she was quick to explain away was caked about her. The dirt too thick to be blamed on a day's travel. She has been in Rawton longer than she cares to admit. Long enough for Clements to scream her name in his death.

'He fell from his horse,' I say. 'Walter said he was drunk.'

'An accident then,' Will agrees. He looks at Clements. 'I would not have thought he could be felled by an accident. I imagined a struggle . . .'

'You imagined your revenge,' I finish for him.

'I have done too much to deserve it.'

Richard Knight is an unanswered question. I don't know how to address it. I have never been given the language for it. Men like Will have long been diminished by sneers and bawdy jokes. My silence makes him smaller, but his turned head forbids my broaching the subject.

Will is the first to break the silence. 'My cousin, after his looks were spoiled by his misuse of witches' charms, decided to remake himself in the mould of Thomas Overbury,' he says, recalling the courtier famed for cultivating Carr, Earl of Somerset, to King James's taste. 'We share a resemblance, and my cousin thought a daily reminder of himself might be enough to restore him to favour. He served me up to the court like Ganymede. The King's a spider, the court his web. He did not touch me. I never got close enough to reach the web's centre.'

But there were others, and his stillness confirms my suspicions.

'I never had a choice until I met Richard . . . I did not betray him, but I did nothing to save him when he tried to speak out against the abuses.' He closes his eyes. 'An accusation of witchcraft was used to silence him. Clements and his master were deployed to torture him to death.' He swallows. 'I did not speak up for him. I chose myself.'

Behind the closed door, a coughed interruption.

'Go,' says Will, with another look at Clements, 'I will remain to play the flatterer.'

I ride back to the manor, Clements's song a roar in my head. Althamia is not a murderer, I tell myself, even as I picture her slim fingers curled around a rock and aimed at the back of his head. His song was a lie – but then why sing of her? Unable to dismiss my suspicions, I return to the manor determined to seek her out and demand to know why she lied about her arrival. Inside, the sounds of tinkling glass and hushed whispers draw me to the sun parlour.

Althamia and Grace sit in profile near the fire. Althamia, I notice, has replaced her breeches with one of Grace's white gowns. Veiled by shadows, my resolve is abandoned. Whatever she has done, it changes nothing. I have done worse and would have done even more to protect her.

A flash of colour stops my departure. A basket of silk lies between them that they tie into ribbons. They are deft at their task, their hands sorting through a bed of knots. The thought clutches at me and I imagine myself strewn between them, my insides looped strings for them to practise upon.

Althamia picks up the silk and twists it into a ribbon, for her hair perhaps, or a dress. But then Grace does the same and their whispers drop to murmurs as they weave their knots. Mrs Hale's fingers were similarly deft, her hands fiddling with her pockets during her plea for Althamia's safety. I reach for the rowan sprig inside my shirt, the one Althamia knotted with her hair. 'An abandoned practice,' she'd said of the table loom in her family's basement. But a forgotten one? She is well-versed with knots and I close my eyes to the image of Althamia patiently spreading her creatures to bind them. Is my love for her a spell? If so, she is softer in her practice than Grace. Unless her need for revenge has hardened her.

As if sensing my presence, Grace cranes her neck until I draw back into the shadows.

Chapter Thirty-Two

'I wish to see the dead.' Althamia brushes past, her face bright from the morning sun that streams through my bedroom window. 'The coroner,' she says. 'I am no expert, but I will use what I know to determine Clements's cause of death.'

Clements's death offers little relief. As a mark of respect, the investigation has been suspended in the two days since Will's discovery. A temporary courtesy that Rush is already pressing to be waived. We are losing our influence.

'Mr Wilson was unwilling to share his thoughts as to how the coroner's jury might rule on Clements's death,' Will had revealed over dinner the previous night.

Lord Carew had taken a long sip of his wine. 'Procedure, I'm sure.'

Althamia's eyes had met mine. The jury take their direction from the coroner. No comfort can be found in Mr Wilson's discretion if there's a risk they will decide Clements's death was murder.

'Nevertheless,' Lord Carew went on, 'I will need your travelling pass, for propriety's sake.'

'Do you think my master is guilty?' I'd protested, holding Lord Carew's gaze until he looked away.

'Nicholas,' Will had warned, but Grace had intervened.

'The constable was here earlier. A witness has testified to seeing Justice Percival ride after Clements.' I'd peeked at Althamia from the corner of my eye as I wondered again at Clements's song. Our relationship has always been coloured by doubt, but her steady composure did not betray her.

'What witness?' Will asked.

'They have been granted anonymity for the time being,' Grace answered.

Bess, I surmised, and I grimace at the thought of her in Rush's hands. She would not escape him again.

'Until the jury comes to a decision, my uncle cannot afford to be seen as remiss in his duty.'

Lord Carew raised himself up in his chair. 'Your travelling pass, sir. My servants have retrieved your weapon from the chamber already,' he'd said, and for the first time I recalled noticing the heavy presence of male servants that night.

We should fight this, I conveyed with a look at Will. A look he'd ignored. Instead he'd reached inside his doublet for his travelling pass with a murmured apology to Lord Carew for the inconvenience. The exchange was completed by a servant and dinner had been concluded in an uneasy silence as though we were not stranded there, trapped and defenceless, while Rush and Grace prepared their advance.

Althamia interrupts my thoughts. 'The exhumed bodies of the witches' alleged victims – I will examine them too.'

'No. You would make yourself too visible an opponent,' I say, remembering Grace's smile over her victory last night. No doubt she'd imagined Will and I would slink away, but I will not abandon Will or this town to Grace and Rush. Instead I shall spend my nights in the graveyard in pursuit of the truth.

Althamia's eyes flash. 'Women are being tortured and killed

263

without reason. I will not render myself invisible, not while I have the means to help.'

'It is too dangerous,' I say, as I imagined the likelihood of Bess meeting the same fate as Lady Katherine.

'I will not give way,' she argues, 'unless you have a better plan. We should hurry,' she says, conceding my defeat with a smile. Her feet tap against the floorboard while I get dressed.

'Another lesson?' she asks, drawing close enough to trace her fingers across my scarred back.

'A punishment from when I was a boy,' I reply, remembering the sting of my father's whip. 'My father gave it to me.'

'Why?' she asks, and I cannot help but lean into her touch.

'He thought I was running away.' When I was ten, I'd tried to seek out the cemetery where my mother was buried. It was a foolish endeavour. I did not know her name and after the years that had passed, her song would have been no more than a whisper. Stephens had caught up with me when I was no more than two streets away. My father had whipped away at my courage.

'Let us go. Before we are caught.' I turn too quickly, for she stumbles into my arms. Her face tilts towards mine. 'I am caught,' she whispers, and I stop myself from leaning into her. My suspicions are a silent hurt I nurse, and I have not the words to ease the awkwardness that follows. I am saved by the sound of footsteps. The house is slowly waking up and we creep out before we can be missed. Her face is nestled against my back and her arms fast about me during our ride to town. I am tempted to keep riding to steal more of the sensation.

Mr Wilson's eyes are dulled by sleep, yet he is cheered by my unexpected presence. His greeting turns sombre when he notices Althamia behind me.

'Sir, I am here to offer my opinion,' she explains when he gestures to the waiting area. He looks from me to her and his beard bristles when I make no correction to her statement.

Clements is as he was before. Mr Wilson points him out for Althamia's benefit before introducing us to the rest of the dead. Her leather gloves stiffen as her eyes pass over Clements.

Mr Wilson points to a body in the corner. 'May Gibbons – she was found dead outside her house three months ago from no apparent cause. Her husband believes Jane Foley sent her familiar to spell her from this world.'

Althamia bites her tongue when he unveils the woman with a flourish. Mrs Gibbons is dressed in a white shroud that covers her like spider's silk.

Mrs Gibbons's aria intermingles with Mr Wilson's words.

A shout. A raised fist. A storm I could never shelter from. My husband until death do us part. A separation I prayed for. My shoulders forever slumped from the weight of him that robbed me of my youth. A weight I bore to keep my children light.

Children, she hums, her song an outstretched hand I must refuse. My business is blackmail and there is nothing in Mrs Gibbons's song that I can use on her behalf. Society condones such treatment with silence and turned heads. As I do now. The bitter accusations settle as I force my attention back to Mr Wilson.

'See this mark here,' says Mr Wilson. He gestures to the reddish discoloration around Mrs Gibbons's throat. 'It is where the Foley woman's familiar sucked the life from her.'

He shuffles aside to allow Althamia a closer look and winks at me over her head.

'I have seen this before,' Althamia tells him. 'The woman was struck by lightning.'

He laughs. 'You are mistaken.'

'The surgeon Thomas Brugis recounts a similar instance in his book *Vade Mecum*,' she insists.

'I have heard of him,' he mumbles, though his workshop is bare of textbooks.

'Then you are familiar with a similar case he encountered when he investigated the unexpected death of a young man. He discovered that the strike of lightning leaves a fern-like pattern on the skin,' says Althamia.

It occurs to me that my ability to hear the dead and her taxidermy make us both, in our own ways, preservers of the dead. In that moment I'm ashamed that I have not made more of it. I am no more than a hoarder of the dead's grievances; not once have I attempted to get justice for them. I start, surprised by the loose thread between my fingers, pulled free from my cloak. I tease it into a loop, but then let it fall to the ground as I think of my mother – who, if Will is right, I have unjustly maligned my entire life, chasing away remembrances of all she has left me. The loss is permanent, even if I should succeed in discovering her name.

'You are overly knowledgeable for a woman,' says Mr Wilson, a thinned-lip compliment.

'I am knowledgeable about death,' Althamia answers, and I have to hold myself back from stepping between them. She is too visible, but she ignores my warning look.

'My uncle was a surgeon. He taught me all he knew,' she says, and turns to inspect the other bodies that Mr Wilson claims belong to victims of witchcraft. 'They are very decayed,' observes Althamia of Mr Gair and Miss Burtt. Both died years before from a wasting sickness their families now blame on a witch's curse. She can neither confirm nor deny Mr Wilson's reasoning without insulting him, and their songs make no mention of witchcraft. Mr Wilson takes her caution as approval.

Mr Gair's song twists my insides like Clements's. But while he was all malice, Mr Gair is desperate hope.

> *Summer is a cruel mistress. So consumed by its delights I failed to notice fall's approach. Its presence marked by the want of colour in my cheeks, the looseness of my flesh. I fade into her grasp.*

I shift from the hunger I feel in each measure. Its rich tones sink into my warm places. I cannot bring him back and Mr Gair's need turns me cold and makes me a false promise.

Mrs Burtt does not sing of her death. She hums of the husband of her youth, the one whose kisses she remembered as she lay dying.

> *Our love was a dance. I counted your absences in measures after you left. Another step, another husband. A lifetime. A whole dance spent counting down to the measures until I fell back in step with you.*

I look at Althamia. *I am out of step with you.* A tragedy I will spend my life regretting.

'Perhaps more candles,' Althamia suggests when she notices me blinking.

I clasp my hands together and when I look up Mr Wilson has circled back to Clements. Althamia braces herself and with a deep breath unveils him. His skin is rubbery and there's an unpleasant stench to him, as though he's been fed upon by maggots.

'It is well that the jury has been convened,' he remarks, trying not to gag. 'He has started to rot.'

Althamia lifts Clements from the waist with far more gentleness than I would ever think to deploy. She inspects the hole in the back of his head where the white of his skull shows through.

Clements's face is inches from mine. His lips are unmoving, but I am lost again to the song he sang the last time I was here. Althamia's name is a screech in my ears.

'You are unwell.' Althamia looks at me in concern.

'It is the smell,' I explain and breathe into my handkerchief.

She is not convinced but lowers Clements back to the table.

'I was one of the first to see the body when Judge Percival raised the alarm,' Mr Wilson informs us.

'Did you assume it was murder?' Althamia asks, reluctantly drawing her attention away from me.

Mr Wilson directs his answer to me. 'Not at the time. It appeared he had fallen and hit his head on the rocks nearby.'

'Was there a lot of blood found at the scene?' Althamia asks.

'I did not personally attend, but the constable described it no more than a smatter across the rocks.'

'The wound could have been inflicted post-mortem. That could explain the lack of blood. Here,' says Althamia, and the coroner joins her in examining Clements's head. 'The wound is messy, as though he had been struck more than once.'

'I suspected that,' he mutters, and turns away at my sharp look.

'How was he positioned when you found him?' she asks.

'As you see him,' he replies.

Clements's arms are folded across his chest with his hands resting on his shoulders.

'An old-fashioned burial position,' she observes. 'It is the custom to cross the hands on the pelvis or the side of the thighs.'

'I thought he had clasped himself in prayer before he died. I would be out of a job if you were looking for employ.'

Althamia opens her mouth as though to apologise but then straightens up. 'A woman such as myself could never rival you,' she says. A woman's accomplishments cannot withstand comparison to those of men. I redden when I recall teasing her on account of her desire to be a surgeon. Her sex forces her to make patients of the dead.

Mr Wilson concedes her point with a bitter smile. He readjusts Clements's hands so that they rest on his thigh, his look daring Althamia to stop him.

'The jury expects to see him as he was,' I point out.

'I will describe it to them. He should be laid to rest in the proper custom,' he insists, but then concedes, 'I was minded to direct the jury to a verdict of misadventure until I noticed this.' Mr Wilson rolls up Clements's sleeves and gestures to the stab wound on his upper arm.

'He would have bled out quickly,' he tells us, while my eyes rake over the wound stuffed with wool. He smiles when Althamia doesn't contradict him. 'Mr Rush has convinced most of the town that Judge Percival is a murderer. I am sorry that my findings will not clear him.'

There is little reason to linger after Mr Wilson's assessment. Althamia and I hover a distance from the coroner's office. If she is guilty, she shows little discomfort at Will being blamed for her crime. For a moment, I allow myself to believe I dreamt Clements's song and try to forget the image of Althamia's fingers clasping a rock and the rage that propels her to bring it down on Clements's head again and again. The illusion saves me from wondering how far I will let this go. Then I picture the noose around her neck. I will not condemn her.

It is not cold, but Althamia shivers and wraps her cloak tight around herself. I study her as though she is a stranger and spy the dagger I gave her, its shape visible through her cloak.

'Mr Rush,' I exclaim. He steps out from the mist and for a moment I fancy my hands would go right through him were I to touch him.

She sidesteps me to introduce herself, 'Miss Althamia Hale,' and he tips his hat in response.

'He is a witch-hunter,' I tell Althamia.

'And in good company,' he adds.

'I doubt it,' she replies in a frosty tone.

His pleasure at her disdain is short-lived, and he turns to me. 'I saw you enter the coroner's office.' His eyes narrow when I draw nearer to Althamia. 'A terrible business. I hope Judge Percival is not overly troubled by it.'

'Accusations have been made,' I confirm, and his forehead creases at my smile. 'But my master retains Lord Carew's support. He is at liberty and will remain so.'

He pauses. 'I am relieved, though I hope your master will forgive me.' I frown and he explains, 'Lord Carew has just permitted me to resume the investigation. You are welcome to join me. I need a scribe and my men lack your talent with words.'

'No.'

'I take no offence,' he says. 'My watchers are good men, though they are too coarse for me to enjoy the same closeness you and Judge Percival share.' I stiffen at the barb. 'We ride out tomorrow for Jane Foley and her brood.' My eyelids flicker in distaste at his excitement. 'The youngest of them, a leveret, is said to have frightened the neighbouring children with tales of Mother lying down at night with the Devil. She says he donned the guise of a frog on his last visit.'

'You cannot believe that,' Althamia interrupts.

'The girl confessed,' says Rush, but she refuses to look away.

'She is a child,' she cries and Rush's fingers twitch as I step beside her.

'She is,' he agrees. 'But witchcraft is the Devil's net which nothing Christian can pierce through. I will not shrink from tearing it apart.'

'Even at the expense of mercy?' she argues.

'My maker did not instil that virtue within me,' he confides.

'Wait for me by my horse.' Please, I beg her silently.

'She speaks her mind. I can see why Grace is fond of her,' he remarks after her.

'If you go near her . . .' I threaten.

'I would never,' he insists and hands me a pamphlet from his satchel.

'*A Wonderful Discovery of The Rawton Witches*,' I murmur with a look at the woodcut illustration of a witch with an exaggerated half-moon face and an owl-shaped familiar she cradles to her breast. My eyes skim to the additions made to my transcription of Mrs Greer's interrogation. Rush has embellished it with overblown descriptions of her misdeeds and the added viewpoints of Mr and Mrs Ingram, who relay their sufferings. *The Rawton Witches* also includes the confessions of Eli Heath and Jane Foley and her children, whom Rush likens to the Devil's spawn. They are rendered monsters and we witch-hunters God's heroes. The whole thing is a trick, bolstered by a smug confidence that readers will ignore the set-up in exchange for the promised gore. I am unable to tear my eyes away from it and I trail my fingers across what my words have wrought.

'My men are busy distributing them in the neighbouring towns.'

'You are too forward. The accused have yet to be proved guilty,' I say, a pointed reminder that pamphlets are normally published after a guilty verdict is rendered.

'A foregone conclusion.' His confidence renders me speechless. The people he's condemned are nothing beyond the words put in their mouths. 'I will ensure you are credited in the next print run,' he adds.

'I have no desire to be so honoured,' I say and crush the pamphlet underfoot.

'No?' he says with a paused look at the ground. 'I envy you. I wish I was a simple man with meagre wants.' He inclines his head, but halts in his departure. 'Women are like knots. The act of separation unravels us.'

A threat, I wonder, when he eyes Althamia. Though his distant expression lessens my fear.

'Have you lost the lady's favour?' I ask, careful to keep the disbelief from my voice. I doubt magic is what ties Rush and Grace together. Nevertheless, there is a snag in their partnership. I wonder why else would Grace try to bribe my complicity?

He turns. 'It is of no matter. I will not be lessened by it. Give my regards to Judge Percival. I regret our partnership should end in these circumstances.'

'The loss does not diminish us,' I shout after him.

Chapter Thirty-Three

'We make a fine pairing,' says Grace, comparing her sage coat to my green doublet. Under a dark sky that threatens to overspill, she places herself between Althamia and me. It is not a day to be out and yet we slip into a leisurely pace, the town and its people no more than grey shadows.

'Our uncle is magnanimous,' Grace had commented when Althamia revealed early this morning that Lord Carew had written to her parents and secured her extended stay. She has been sharp with Althamia since her arrival, as though afraid of softening. Althamia's presence annoys her, though not as much as having Will and me around. The investigation into Clements's death keeps us tied here and she fears being thwarted. Will presses me to leave, ignoring my resolve to stay until Rawton is rid of the Witchfinder General.

'We should dance. Barley Break,' Grace had suggested in the parlour after breakfast.

'We lack the numbers,' I replied quickly. The dance is performed by six couples, the rules of which see the last pair confined to hell.

'You are sour this morning. No matter,' she complained and turned her spite to Althamia. 'I doubt my cousin knows the steps. You are supposed to let a man catch you when they shout "Break".'

'What say you to Box About instead?' Althamia retorted, and I'd winced in remembrance. The game requires you to hit someone as hard as you can. I'd ended up with a bloody nose the one time I'd played it with Francis, and he received a swollen eye in return.

Althamia stood and the threads between them tightened and then eased when she moved to study the stuffed jackdaw on the corner wall. Its sleek black feathers were pinned in flight and its irises retained something of the moon's light. She turned to Grace and exclaimed, 'I cannot believe you have kept it. I am glad to see it. I have had to rid myself of my collection.'

'You gave it to me,' Grace replied. 'That makes it worthy of saving. If my son had lived, I had hoped you would have taught him the practice.'

Althamia reached out and squeezed her hand. Grace's brow had knitted together at this brokered peace.

'I am going to town for some air,' Althamia said before the calm could be broken. She was amused when we both stood.

'We will accompany you,' Grace conceded. Her watchfulness isn't just for propriety's sake. She is afraid to leave us alone and I take a small pleasure in it as it assuages my doubts that Althamia is involved in her schemes. Grace's fears are a wasted emotion. If I told Althamia, she would ask and I would not be able to deny that for a moment I was tempted to say yes. As though she were an object to be passed around.

'Produce from my estate,' says Grace now, drawing our attention to a stallholder selling rye. 'Usually it is hoarded over the winter.'

'Why?' The question slips from my lips too quick to be recalled. We are enemies yet I am forced to greet her like a friend when we happen upon each other. I must return her looks over supper and hope she will not use knots to inveigle her way into my thoughts.

Her face is mocking and Althamia explains, 'Mr Pearce's father is a merchant.'

'Then I shall use merchant terms. My uncle waits for the farmers to sell off their produce. He then sells ours at a higher price. He has sold his early. Last year's harvest was poor and the grain from the other stallholders is already depleted.'

'You disapprove,' I gather as she surveys the townspeople around the stall.

'My uncle should have waited,' she replies.

'And let the town starve?' I demand.

'People pay more when they are hungry.'

Althamia places herself between us. 'Mr Pearce has no head for farming. Cousin, I wish to learn more about the produce we sell. Mr Pearce, perhaps you should seek out inspiration in the meantime.'

Althamia leads Grace closer to the stall before she can refuse. When Grace's attention is occupied, she turns and tilts her head. From the corner of my eyes, I spot something akin to the flutter of birds and follow it to a narrow alleyway.

Bess Heath is draped in the tawny cloak I gave her. She steps forwards, her fingers encased in gloves of knitted white wool. Her lips and eye have begun to heal, and she is clean and bright-eyed.

I doff my hat with a flourish. 'Mistress, I scarcely know you.' Her pleasure is short-lived when I add, 'I thought Rush had found you. I am glad you are safe.'

Her mouth tightens at the memory. 'He did not find me. I was betrayed by Jane Foley who led him to Margaret Greer and some others,' she explains. 'She thought she was protecting her children.'

'Whatever her belief, she has made Rush's work easier.' I tell her that Jane has been taken into custody, with her children set to testify against her. 'I have heard that you have spoken against my master.'

Her eyes do not shift from mine. 'Mr Rush promised me my

freedom in exchange for my testimony. I told him your master rode after Clements. I made no embellishment to the tale.'

'Judge Percival helped you.'

'You saved me,' she argues. 'Not him. Mr Rush gave me no choice. Either his name or Margaret and the others. Shall I have given them yours? He gave me my liberty in return for an account of what I saw.'

'A temporary pleasure,' I say. 'You are not safe, whatever he's promised you.' Neither am I. 'He will turn on you the moment he's secured my master's conviction.' It will be soon, I realise, and I resist the urge to rush back to the manor.

'Forgive me,' I say when Bess's expression falls. 'You sought me out.'

She starts and I turn to see Althamia behind me. 'Do not be frightened. This is Miss Althamia Hale,' I reassure her.

'Grace is in the haberdasher's. I took my leave amidst her fascination with the array of ribbons,' Althamia tells me.

'You know Mrs Rawle?' Bess frets.

'I am her cousin.' Her answer brings no comfort, for Bess steps back.

'Althamia,' I warn, but she places herself before me.

'I have heard of you. You were in my cousin's service for a time.'

'I was employed as a maid of all work until your cousin took notice of me. On her instructions, I would listen at the windows in the town and gather secrets like a magpie. I accompanied her when she eloped and stayed with her when the Roundheads besieged Lathom Castle.' Her eyes close at the memory. 'I almost died. A cannonball struck the castle foundations and a man pushed me out of the way while the walls crumbled about me like sand. He was badly wounded. He was moon-kissed before the accident and people said it would be a kindness if he perished. Grace tended to us both, though we left before it was certain whether he would live.'

'My cousin is kind,' says Althamia, her words almost a question.

Bess considers this for a moment. 'I thought so too, but kindness is easily given when you are content. I erred after she lost her child during the siege. I offered her sympathy, when a person like me should have nothing to offer.'

'Is that when she dismissed you?' Althamia presses, ignoring my warning look. She is stepping too close, and I do not trust Grace not to turn on her.

'It was Lord Carew. I stole his brooch. My father said I should have chosen something easier to miss.' Bess grimaces at the memory. 'Grace intervened so that I was only punished with the loss of my job and my good name, the little it was worth. I have lost my standing in your eyes.'

But Althamia shakes her head. 'I have done worse. I had a friend.' She stops and starts again. 'I had a servant named Agnes. She was killed and it was my fault. I used her when she was alive. Not cruelly, but I used her nevertheless. Even now I have made her death about myself. I did not truly see her, and I am angry because my disregard made her small.'

Bess places her hand on Althamia's arm, a welcomed gesture.

'If I am right, I suspect you have been used in turn?' Althamia tentatively suggests.

'I cannot even remember taking the brooch. All I remember is a dream I had and the telling of it to Grace.'

'A dream?' I ask.

'They become curses when spoken of. See what it has wrought,' she warns, but at my look says, 'I was in the birthing chamber with Grace.' She blinks at the memory. 'Grace . . . there was blood everywhere. I could not stop it. And then suddenly between her legs appeared a bed of knots. It started to grow, and I tried to claw at it to no avail.'

'What did Grace do?' asks Althamia.

Bess shifts on her feet. 'She just watched. She was steeped in the knots as though they were part of her. He and I both were caught up in them.'

'He?' I say with a start.

She closes her eyes. 'A man, the same one who saved me at Lathom Castle. Grace dismissed it as a silly dream when I told her. She pressed her head to mine and stroked my hair until it was entwined with hers.' Like a knot, I guess when her speech falters. 'All I remember afterwards was the brooch in my hands and Lord Carew's men at my heels.'

'Have you ever had a dream like that before?' asks Althamia, and Bess shakes her head and then nods. 'A vision . . . you are a witch.' Bess flinches but doesn't deny the accusation.

'A week after I was dismissed, the man who saved me showed up in Rawton. Though he was different from before.'

'Mr Rush,' I say, and she nods.

'Mr Rush,' I press, 'what name did he go by at Lathom Castle?'

She shakes her head. 'I cannot remember. Grace . . . somehow she took it from me.'

'You must take shelter,' Althamia urges, and I am surprised to see it is raining. Bess covers her hair with her cloak.

'Mr Rush is Grace's tool to reclaim her estates. He has not finished his hunt.' Her mouth opens to say more, but a sharp whistle sends her running. Althamia and I turn to find Grace standing a few yards away.

'Who was that?' Grace asks when we reach her. She flicks the rain away.

'A beggar looking for alms,' Althamia lies.

We still at the raking look she passes over us. 'You should not encourage them.'

Chapter Thirty-Four

Althamia and Grace sit on either side of me in the carriage. I am made a knot between them and have a sensation of being squeezed. The interlude with Bess signalled the end of our venture into town. The journey home is punctuated by Grace's steady breathing and Althamia's rigid silence.

What sort of creature are you? I wonder with a side glance at Grace. Not a creature, a false god who uses people for her purposes. Mr Rush, the same man who pushed a young girl to safety, now pushes women to the gallows. You have done that, I accuse. It is not natural. But then I remember how easily I persuaded Broad to conjure new truths with my words. Look at what I have wrought with the little power I possess.

When the carriage comes to a halt, Grace disembarks and makes her way purposefully into the manor. Instead of following, I close the carriage door behind her and turn to Althamia.

'You always knew what Grace was.' An accusation she does not flinch from. 'Will you not look at me?' I accuse when her eyes fall to her lap. 'She made Rush out of another man's flesh as though he were clay. Mr Rush will kill your uncle and Grace will have her freedom. But she has done too much to be satisfied by the result. You lied to me,' I persist when she refuses to look at me still. 'You were there when Clements died.'

She inhales, but again doesn't lift her head. 'Will you not look at me, or are there too many dead people between us for our eyes to truly meet?' I sink back. 'You have tied me in knots.'

'Another charge?' she says, her expression guarded.

'No.' Whatever is between us, I do not want to be free from it.

'The Grace I knew would not have done this. She is different now, but so am I. When Clements attacked me I wanted to become all he accused me of. I wanted to kill him in turn after Agnes's murder. I am all buried rage and I cannot breathe. I still can't.' Her anger is a flush of colour and she makes a breathless escape.

Will is waiting for me in my chamber. He sits at the mirror and I have the sensation as though I'm the one intruding when his eyes meet mine through the glass. He drops the quill in his hand and turns to face me. 'I was about to make an addition,' he says, and hands me an unopened letter from my father.

I rip off the seal to see a solitary 'S' written in bold in the top corner and a few lines below.

Dear Nicholas,

I write to warn you of the change you will find upon your return. Your stepmother's health has taken a turn and I have arranged for her to recover in the countryside. I do not know long her removal will be, but I expect your swift return.

Your father

I rip it up. 'A threat. Sophie has probably told him of her suspicions. Her regard was always a lingering hate.' His face darkens. 'Though it was tempered by Francis's presence. Now he is gone, she has nothing left. She must hold on to it or lose all sense of self.'

'That is no excuse,' says Will.

I shrug. 'I doubt Father believes her, though he'll use her threats as another string to bind me with. I was wrong about Grace,' I say before he can interrupt and relay all that Bess had told me. 'She cannot be reasoned with and only her command can stop Mr Rush. Lord Carew is her target and she does not care if the whole town must hang for it. I will search for her knot and try to undo her hold over Rush.'

'Her bond with Rush is strong, undoing it would probably kill them both.'

'Then they die,' I snap.

'You are not a killer,' he says. 'Miss Hale's regard of you would slip were you to become one.'

Unless she is one herself. 'You underestimate me. Without hatred I have nothing to drive me.'

'Was it hatred that drew you here?' he argues. 'Is hatred why you remain? Whatever spell Grace has worked will not be quenched by blood. The matter has grown beyond them both. The people Rush has arrested will hang at the next assizes and even with him gone, there would be plenty of men to replace him.'

'So are we to step back and play the roles Grace has assigned us? There are people here worth saving. You are the master of revels!'

'I am a suspected murderer and lack the influence to alter this course. Perhaps that was Rush's intention. He might be behind Clements's death. I have no intention of leaving,' he says when I begin to pack my valise.

'We will seek alternative lodgings in the next town. Rush will use Bess to have you convicted of Clements's murder. I am surprised they have not already arrested you. I will gather more secrets from the dead,' I say when he makes no attempt to move, 'and will write to the Countess of Derby to uncover Rush's real identity.' I reach for Francis's knot. 'I can . . .' but he shakes his head at the unsaid offering and turns to study his reflection.

'The people have no wish to look behind the mask. The Countess's word will not sway them.'

'We must try,' I insist.

'It was never a specific hatred,' Will murmurs. 'By the time Lord Howard took me into his services most of the witches had fled. In my mind those I hunted all wore *his* face.'

He turns, his look distant in the glass.

'You did not come here to sacrifice yourself,' I say.

'For the people I hunted this was the last thing they saw. My face. It was always me, even behind the mask, and I can no longer fool myself into thinking otherwise.' He regards his reflection with an intensity I almost turn away from. 'I have been a martlet, my entire life spent flying with never a moment to roost. I am tired and would like to see what the sky looks like from the ground.'

'The look will cost you,' I say, a warning he disregards by adjusting his talisman so that it sits squarely across his chest.

Slabs of beef are laden upon silver plates. Althamia, Will and I make a poor start on the fare, while Lord Carew's plate remains untouched. His attention is taken by the view of the woodlands through the windows. Grace is sitting at the end of the table. She had forgone dinner in favour of preserved plums and now savours each bite. The present company is burdened by secrets, and I stare at my companions through the reflective surfaces of the silverware in hopes of catching a glimpse of their elusive truths.

'What dull company we are,' complains Lord Carew of the listless conversation. He is suspicious, the more so because of the muted reaction to his declaration. He fidgets with the sleeves of his purple gown and snaps his fingers for more wine. I meet Althamia's eyes across the table. I have become my father and to my regret our shared look is laced with unsaid remonstrations. The contact holds until a servant blurs it with wine.

'We are tired by the present situation,' Grace drawls. She presses her hand to the ribbons along her bodice and stares at the knife in my hand. A tug of her ribbons and the knife would cut clean across my throat.

I let go of the weapon and arch my head towards her. 'I am not tired. The end is in sight, and I am invigorated by its promise.' I am not resigned to defeat, I convey with a considered look at Will.

Grace smiles and takes out her gold coin and rolls it between her fingers. I catch traces of the others in its round edges. Lord Carew savours his claret, his face flecked with gold.

'You are a child,' he seethes, but she does not stop. 'Stop.' The silverware rattles when he slams his fist on the table. The coin falls into a spin before lying flat.

'No,' she says, a hissed objection when her uncle motions for a servant to remove the coin.

'You need not be shamed by it. It was you who gave it to me.'

Lord Carew puts down his glass. 'I am not ashamed. I am tired. We are all tired.'

'Cousin,' says Althamia, her voice tight, but Grace pays her no mind. She faces her uncle down the long table with the rest of us resigned spectators.

Lord Carew pushes his plate away. 'I will not be blamed for your unhappiness. You have authored your fate.'

'You betrayed me,' says Grace. 'You turned me in to Parliament.'

'Your pretence to be a widow would have come undone. Even in exile, your husband is not one to live quietly. I gave Parliament my word and my arms to secure your freedom. You betrayed me first and I betrayed my King to save you from prison.'

'I am in prison,' Grace cries, but Lord Carew brushes off her distress. 'You wanted to punish me. When I begged you to pay the fine on my estates, you gave me this.' She picks up the gold coin and throws it towards him. 'You are drowning in gold, yet you are content to have me live under your thumb like a poor relation.'

'You are free to leave. You removed yourself from my concern when you married without my permission!' shouts Lord Carew.

Grace's smile is bitter. 'While my property is occupied by Roundheads? I will not leave. This is my home. I am your heir.'

Lord Carew's eyes linger on Althamia. 'You are overly confident in your position.'

Grace is quick to puzzle it out. 'You have replaced me?'

'My father denied my sister her inheritance. Naming her daughter as my main heir will redress it.'

Althamia rises. 'I did not ask for this.'

Grace doesn't take her eyes off her uncle. 'That is why he has given it to you.'

'You have had too much of me already,' he replies.

Grace bares her teeth. 'I have been your creature since I was a girl. I could demand your soul in repayment and it would still not be enough.'

Lord Carew opens his mouth, but shame perhaps makes him think better of it.

'Uncle,' says Althamia.

'Say no more,' he snaps. 'I am tired of women and their speeches. You will learn what is it to be quiet.'

'I know what it is to be quiet. I have had lessons from men such as yourself.'

We are intruding, Will conveys with a look. But the presence of flustered servants delays our departure. And the arrival of Rush causes us to sink to our seats. Lord Carew is the only one surprised by his appearance and the swell of half a dozen of his men, who spill into the room. I exhale when they pass me by.

'I have a warrant for your arrest,' Rush tells Lord Carew. 'You have been charged with witchcraft.'

Althamia's hands are clenched around her knife while Will and I can only look on. Grace breaks the tableau by reaching for another plum.

'I am a magistrate,' Lord Carew splutters when he's roughly handled by Rush's men.

'You are still answerable to the laws of this land,' Rush reminds him. 'You will be bound over at Lancaster Castle until the midsummer assizes.' At his word, Lord Carew is pulled from the room. 'That will not be necessary.' My head turns to Will, who addresses Walter from his chair. 'Am I similarly accused?' he asks Rush.

'Of murder, not witchcraft,' he corrects him, his nostrils flaring at Will's nonchalant acceptance.

'You have no evidence,' I protest as Will prepares himself to be led away.

'I have a witness who will testify she saw Judge Percival ride after Clements with murderous intent,' Rush divulges.

'The same witness who will hang once her purpose is served?'

'Do not fight them,' says Will, but I cannot stop myself.

I do not back down at Rush's nearness.

'Did you aid your master in the murder?' he asks. 'You were much in Judge Percival's company.' He gestures to his remaining men while Althamia places herself before me.

'The witch,' says Rush. 'I am no Clements. I would have you examined more thoroughly for witchcraft.'

'You will not touch her,' I cry, while Althamia raises her knife at his threat.

'A love spell,' he says, and sneers when I step between them.

'You fraud,' I spit, while Althamia holds her knife steady.

'I fear I know you more in the light than I did in the dark,' she says with a considered look at Rush's staff.

His lips tighten. 'Arrest them,' Rush orders. His men spring at this crisp command. Will pushes his captors away and launches himself in front of me, while I push Althamia back and trade blows with the men.

'Mr Rush,' says Grace with a look that subdues but doesn't vanquish. She intertwines her fingers in the ribbed knots of her bodice, a silent threat he considers. Whatever hold she has over him is gone, I realise, when her hands eventually drop to her sides.

'Let them go,' says Rush, a small mercy Grace acknowledges with a nod. Will's falling band is a noose around his neck and the sleeves of his doublet tear as he is dragged away. I race outside to where Will is pushed into the waiting carriage alongside Lord Carew.

'You have no authority!' My protest is curtailed when one of Rush's men pushes me to the ground. I get up and run after them, but the darkness robs me of my sight. I return to the manor where Althamia is waiting alongside Grace and a servant who throws my valise at my feet.

'Whatever your scheme, it ends now,' I tell Grace as Althamia steps between us. 'You have got what you wanted with your uncle's arrest. You will order Rush to release Will and the others.' Althamia turns to Grace, who remains silent in the face of my tirade. 'You can't, can you? Are your reserves so depleted you can't even drive him off to another town?' Her eyes flash but still she says nothing. No, I realise. She will spend herself completely if she tries to undo him and he her. Neither of them is inclined to martyrdom.

'Come with me,' I beg Althamia, but the knot in my chest tightens when she slips free of my touch.

'My place is here,' she whispers and steps away. The shadows from the nearby shrubberies make it seem as though she is being enveloped by thorns. There is only loss between us now as she allows Grace to shepherd her away.

Chapter Thirty-Five

The landlord blocks my entry. This is the fourth inn I have tried this morning. I do not believe their dismissal solely due to the dirt I've collected from a night spent sleeping rough in the cemetery.

'A bed,' I demand to his amusement. The town's allegiance is to Rush and not even my abundance of coins will sway them. But the flash of gold around the landlord's finger reminds me that I possess a more valuable currency. Last night the dead had sung of stolen kisses, petty thefts and slanders. Meagre secrets that would be greeted with scorn if I attempted to leverage them for Will and the others' freedom. But valuable enough to secure me lodgings. The murmured lulls of the landlord's cousin are in my ear, a sly ode to their dreams of castled gold, funded by keepsakes pilfered from their guests.

'A bed,' I repeat and push past him. It's my first attempt at blackmail, but tiredness robs me of any guilt.

This is how it starts, I decide as my landlord leads me to my bedchamber, an arched garret with a thin pallet and a small table. An impatient want easily satisfied when you possess the upper hand. The same advantage you use to nudge people as though they are no more than pawns on a chessboard.

'The water is fresh,' says the landlord with a pointed glare at the basin and a water pitcher.

The cold presses into my skin like a kiss. I am almost defeated, yet, aside from the shadows under my eyes, my reflection shows little sign of it. I am running out of time and in my sleep had half begun to pull at the entwined knot that binds me to Francis. I'd held back and in the morning light had penned a letter to the Countess of Derby in the hope that she might be able to unveil Rush's identity.

My footsteps must carry as the landlord stands to attention near the bottom of the stairs. 'Leaving so soon?'

I pass him a letter and a coin. 'Please ensure it reaches its recipient unopened. And I wish for this to be displayed outside your door,' I say and hand him another letter. He scoffs as he reads it, though my expression brings him up short.

'The people will drive me out if I display such a thing.'

His pleas do little to move me. 'You are free to blame me for it. But I want that nailed to your front door. Oh,' I warn, 'my possessions are to remain unmolested.'

Lancaster Castle is formidable in its history. It is a dark shadow that even the sun cannot lighten. I almost balk but then urge my horse to the place where the Pendle witches met their fate. The sentries wave me through the gatehouse to the bricked tower.

'I am here to see Judge Percival,' I tell the castle keeper. His square face screws up at my tone, but he brings me to the dungeon in exchange for a few coins.

'Thirty feet deep,' the keeper sniffs as we descend the witch tower, a maze of ante-chambers, jagged walls and narrow staircases. The underground dungeon is near the wells and the echoes of our footstep mix with the gurgling of water. There are no windows, nor any light save for the little that spills from the top of the stairs.

It feels as though I have sunk underground. Rats scuttle across the floor and I brace myself at the stench of unwashed bodies and human waste.

Rush has been busy. In the corner I spy Mrs Greer, who stares at me with unseeing eyes. She rests her head on the lap of her niece Margaret, whose face is covered in bruises. The rest of the battered prisoners crowd the small cell. Jane Foley is surrounded by her children. She smiles at me. She would not do so if she knew that for a roll of the dice it could have been me running her up and down a room.

'Will,' I shout, but step back from the huddle of bodies that groan at my call. Lord Carew breaks free and launches himself at the thick metal bars.

'Mr Pearce,' he cries and grabs at my collar to pull me close. His breath is sour, his purple gown crumpled and stained.

His grip is choking. 'I am sorry,' he apologises and reluctantly loosens his hold.

'You must help me,' he begs. 'It is Grace. It has always been her.'

I prise his fingers from my collar.

'Lord Carew.' Will approaches. He looks well despite his attire being smeared with dirt and his eyes red-rimmed from lack of sleep.

'It is our blood. It makes demons of the women,' Lord Carew imparts, his eyes desperate, and again I recall Mrs Hale and the way her fingers had teased the loops of the side pockets as she pleaded with me to save Althamia. 'I will name them all in return for my freedom,' he finishes.

'We have had enough names,' I say, and he flinches at the look in my eyes.

Will rests a hand on his shoulders and Lord Carew deflates and places himself in the corner, using what's left of his authority to commandeer a small space for himself.

'He is ill,' says Will. 'And hungry. We all are. Evil cannot be fed and for that same reason neither can a witch, at least not in any significant quantities,' he explains.

'I will bring food on my next visit,' I promise.

'I have had to stop him tearing strips of his clothes to make knots,' says Will with a passing look at Lord Carew. He casts his eyes over my mud-flecked coat. 'You have been busy. Are you still at the manor?'

'Grace kicked me out. I have found lodgings in town,' I add at his concerned look.

'You should have taken Miss Hale and run.'

'She would not go with me,' I say.

'Then leave.'

I lean in close. 'And abandon the town to monsters? I have written to the Countess of Derby. She can vouch for Bess's claim about Rush.'

'Her words can only prove him a fraud. They will not prove my innocence. Besides, Grace could have used her arts on Althamia.'

'I must try. There is time until the midsummer assizes. Enough for the Countess's reply to arrive and for myself to undermine Rush's influence.'

'You have done what you can.' He steps back and my ears are filled with the sounds I've been ignoring since my arrival. There is a sickness here. The taste of it fills my mouth. I can hear it in the succession of coughs and the low stirrings of songs. The healthier prisoners will sing soon enough in the wait until summer. 'I release you from my service.'

'Will,' I beg.

'Out of all the people here, I am where I belong,' he whispers, and loses himself to the press of prisoners.

The sky has fallen, no more than swirls of white around a blue silhouette in the path ahead of me. I slow my horse and reach for my dagger. The rider lets down their hood at my approach.

'Althamia.'

Her face is wet from the afternoon dew. 'Your landlord pointed in this direction when I came to see you.' She unrolls the pamphlet in her hand and noting my anger says, 'He made no objection when I asked for a copy,' and then she begins to read its contents aloud:

Dear Reader,

A witch-hunting pamphlet often begins with a sermon on how to resist the temptation of witchcraft. I start with this: God has a hand in the fortune of men, not witches. A break in convention, I admit, though not a novel one. I speak in the tradition of Reginald Scot, whose treatise against witch-hunting in The Discoverie of Witchcraft was silenced upon the accession of King James.

The Bible makes no case for witch-hunting, yet witch-hunters, armed with a biblical turn of phrase, will ride into towns and convince you to turn against the neighbours you have lived side by side with all these years. Mr Rush and others of his ilk are motivated by power, money and the ease in which you part with both to settle past grievances. They are an unnatural cull of the poor, forlorn, infirmed and anyone else the majority deems undesirable and unwanted. The confessions of their victims are aided by the following tools: torture, threats and the complicit silence of the unmaligned.

Witch-hunts are no more than a revel. The price of admission your complacent disregard for the innocents you push into their paths. By my words you might wonder if Mr Rush himself is a witch. You are mistaken. He is no more than a man, a thing of flesh that we can push against. But we must all push back.

By the hand of Mr Nicholas Pearce

I have used words with a careless abandonment despite my love of them. My words didn't kill Francis, but my father holds them as leverage against me. My words emboldened Clements to threaten Althamia, and even now they encourage men to answer Rush's call. My words are an unattended flame, but they are the only weapon I have, one I now hope will press people to my cause.

'Why are you here?' I say when she finishes. 'I have been to see Will. I saw your uncle too. They are defeated. As am I. You came looking for me. Why?'

'To ask if you still wish to push back,' she explains. 'Grace has always had a way of making people do what she wanted. I never minded bending to her will. She was not as she is now. She has been forced by circumstances.'

'Forced?' I repeat.

'Yes. You have put yourself in Will's company and judged him to be a good man despite all he has done. Or is redemption only reserved for men?' she asks and I'm tormented by my determination to think myself a good man despite my silence at Lady Katherine's trial. 'Whatever power my cousin had over Rush is gone. She will expire if she attempts to undo it.'

My thoughts turn to her uncle's warning. 'And what of your power? And your mother's?' I accuse. 'You have lied to me.'

'I have no power,' she answers. 'My mother shares Grace's talent, but by the time she met my father she wanted none of it, nor her family's schemes. She has not used it in all these years.'

A fast she would have broken to protect Althamia. I cannot blame her for it. In this moment, I most keenly regret my uncertainty about my mother. But then I remember Stephens, who has dedicated his life to my safety, and Will, who is prepared to sacrifice himself to ensure it.

She faces me. 'Grace told me you are like her.'

Her steady demeanour remains so when I tell her, 'The dead sing.' I do not temper this announcement with excuses involving my mother. 'Do I frighten you?'

'No,' she answers steadily. 'We are all singing.' I do not know what to make of this, but she is not inclined to patience. 'I did not kill Clements. Though I did see him the night he died.' Her face tightens at the memory. 'It was dark, and I had been turned about on the path as I walked to the manor. A rider approached me from behind. When he stopped, I saw it was him. He was quick to see through my disguise.'

I line my horse alongside hers. 'Did he hurt you?'

'No,' she answers. 'He was drunk and began to talk about the searches. I was distressed and he liked it and would not let me pass. He was amused when I pulled out my dagger and then angry when I struck at him.' She scoffs. 'The only blood I drew was my own. The knife turned back on me when he deflected it . . . He laughed, even more, when I punched him in the chest. He called me a spirited piece and pushed me to the ground. I thought he would do more, but someone on horseback called out. I ran off and slept in the woods.'

'Rush?' I guess, and she nods.

'I did not know it then. All I could see in the darkness was the ivory-studded head of a stranger's staff in the dark. The same one Mr Rush carries.'

'Why did you not tell me?'

She looks up at me. 'I told you once I wanted Clements spread across a table, his insides laid bare for my inspection. You would have thought me guilty.'

'I would have believed you,' I insist. 'I do believe you.'

Her eyes close. 'I have forgotten what it like to be believed.' She nudges her horse into movement. 'I am going to the prison to tell them what I know.'

'No,' I warn her. 'Rush already has Bess as his witness to Clements's murder. He will accuse you if we speak out against him.' Before she can protest, I tell her of the letter I have written to the Countess of Derby. 'She will write back.'

'But when? If?' she whispers.

'Will and the others won't be tried until the midsummer assizes. I will use the pamphlets to gather support here and in the neighbouring towns against Rush. I will listen to the dead and use their secrets to blackmail the townspeople into withdrawing their claims. Rush's influence will be destroyed if the accusers admit they were lying. I used one to inveigle myself a room, despite Rush's attempt to blacklist me from town,' I add at her sceptical look.

'I will help,' she offers.

'Grace will not be pleased,' I say.

'No,' she agrees. 'But she will not harm me.'

'It is too dangerous. The dead's songs are a matted thread. I will not have you hurt by my failure.'

'I am already hurt,' she says. 'And I will not leave.' She grips my pamphlet in her hand like a baton. 'You have raised the standard and I have answered your call.'

'I am not a commander,' I argue.

'Yet still I am here,' and she looks around as though to say *I am the only one.*

Chapter Thirty-Six

'His words are poison.' Althamia leans towards Mr and Mrs Ingram. We are sitting in their parlour, where the grey interiors are lightened by the morning sun. Three days have passed since my first visit to Lancaster Prison. I have spent the past two nights in the cemetery whittling more verses from the dead. Yesterday Althamia sent me a note pressing me to begin our plans today. Rush and a group of his men have set out to scope the surrounding towns for more business. His time in Rawton has neared its end. His beginning was sparked by the Ingrams' bereavement – a word from them could see this matter ended.

'Mr Rush has no interest in witches,' says Althamia. 'He wishes to make his reputation and will sacrifice this town to do so.'

'You are mistaken.' Mrs Ingram bristles while her husband sits in a subdued silence.

'I am sorry for your son's death,' Althamia tells her.

I had told her the truth of Henry Ingram's death and have shared Will's scepticism that Mrs Ingram could be swayed by it. 'Then we lead with hope,' said Althamia. 'A witch-hunter has no use for it,' I replied. 'You are not a witch-hunter,' she said, and held fast until I conceded.

'But I do not believe witchcraft is to blame,' says Althamia. 'Mr Pearce has been to the castle dungeons. He has seen Mrs Greer and the others.'

I make a blunt interruption. 'There is nothing supernatural about them. They rot in an underground pit.'

'I do not pity them,' snaps Mrs Ingram. 'They condemned themselves when they sold their souls to the Devil.'

'Children are held there. Some younger than your son,' pleads Althamia.

Mrs Ingram doesn't flinch. Death is unreasonable and she must have someone to blame.

It is no use, I convey with a look at Althamia. The Ingrams are a knot. If they can't be unthreaded by reason, I will use shame instead.

'Mrs Greer did not summon a curse to kill your child. Henry came across your husband with her, then as he ran away, fell and hit his head. Your husband kept it from you,' I say when she stands. 'But you already knew. Your son was there on your instruction.' She flinches. 'I will keep your husband's secret if you withdraw your claim.'

'My son is dead. My husband's good name will not remedy the loss,' says Mrs Ingram. The parlour door slams behind her.

'Will you not speak up?' I say to Mr Ingram. 'Or is your good name worth fifteen lives?' He lets out a sunken murmur and recoils at my hard look until Althamia gently pulls me away.

'It was never going to be easy,' says Althamia once we are outside the Ingram house. She reaches for the pamphlets in my satchel and hands them out to passers-by.

'Rush and his ilk are like monuments. We need hammers,' I complain when the townspeople ignore our outstretched hands or discard the pamphlet once they've skimmed the contents.

'We are not William Dowsing,' she says of the Puritan soldier tasked by Parliament with destroying anything vaguely Catholic. 'There is magic to your words, enough to sway people to our side.'

'Any magic I have is spent,' I say but continue with my task. Her gaze is reassuring, but I wonder how long she'll look at me this way. Monuments cannot be destroyed with words. I have tried it her way and we must soon try mine.

'I sent a copy to Mr Broad. Perhaps he will be tempted to print it,' she says.

'He will not,' I say as the townspeople give us a wide berth.

'He will. There is profit to be made from sensation,' she argues, pointing to the drawing she added to the pamphlet. My mouth quirks at the image of Rush standing upright with a staff and a pair of horns on his head.

'We should go,' she says with a worried look at the watchers Rush left behind. They have been following us since the moment we rode into town. Rush's influence is a spider's web and wherever we turn we are in danger of getting caught in it.

Althamia holds me back when one of the men spits at our feet. Mr Dewhurst. Miss Sarah Davies sang of him from her grave last night. A callow youth who forgot his promises to her the moment she quickened:

He gave me daisies, the petals a trick to his constancy, one he remedied with a bouquet of mugwort. The taste of it ran bittersweet between my legs. An unwanted, misshapen mass. His shame, but one I must carry.

Althamia steers me to the apothecary with a swish of silk. The sole customer notes our arrival with a look of disdain and to Mr Elwick's regret storms out. Mr Elwick, the same man who shared with Rush the value of those dependent on the parish relief, surveys us from behind the counter. 'Miss Althamia Hale,' she says with a forward step. She wears one of Grace's dresses, lined with jewels at the bodice.

A skimmed inspection on his part followed by a rushed condolence. 'I am sorry for your uncle,' he says and passes her a bottled draught of almond milk mixed in with barley, violets and rosewater. 'For melancholy.'

She sniffs at the draught and passes it back. 'This concoction is generally prescribed for insomnia. My late uncle always recommended merry company as a cure for melancholy.'

His head jerks in surprise.

'You have accused Jane Foley of witchcraft,' I say.

He nods. 'A patient of mine, Miss Lockton, died due to her curse. The fault was not mine.'

'A wasting sickness,' I question as he fidgets. 'One her family did not think a curse until you spoke out at the town meeting.' The rows of brightly coloured medicinal bottles lend his skin a greenish tint.

'A lie,' says Althamia, and she sniffs at the scent of gin that lingers in the air like perfume.

'A lie,' I repeat at his bluster. One his late wife has sung of.

I was flighty. A butterfly until he caught me in his net. Trapped, but willingly so. I found a balance in his steadiness until his habit tipped him off-scale. I found my balance in this chaos. My hands over his righten the scales.

'You killed a child, no older than your own, through negligence.'

He squares up to me. 'Leave,' he orders.

'Not until I have your word you will withdraw your claim against Jane Foley.'

'Does Rush know you're here?' Our silence emboldens him, for he leans across the counter. 'Your master is a murderer and many are angry that you were not arrested alongside him.' He turns to Althamia. 'Your uncle is a witch. I have heard it whispered the affliction is a family trait.'

'Whispers,' I dismiss, and rest my hands on the scales between us, 'have never been something I have cared to deploy.' I pause to let the words sink in. 'Drink blunts your accuracy, yet you have cast the blame on Jane Foley to save yourself from the suspicions of your victim's parents. You will withdraw your accusation and persuade the aldermen to dismiss Rush.'

Fear makes him shake but I do not soften. A witch-hunter has no use for hope or mercy and neither do I.

'I am just one man,' he says.

'And soon you will be one of many,' I promise while Althamia pins the pamphlet on his door. It's as though my words are a song, for his head lowers in defeat. It is not enough. I will not stop until I have made a chorus of this town.

Rawton is a dull blur that Althamia and I cut through like a comet.

'We should pause to rest,' she says when I head to the next accuser.

'I am impatient,' I apologise. 'This is a dirty business. There is no need for you to stain yourself with it.' When I see she will not give way, I tell her, 'Mr Turner killed his daughter Alice. He is an alderman, so well placed to dismiss his daughter's death as an accident. To put an end to the rumours, he blamed it upon Margaret Greer's imp.'

Each word cuts me like glass. A kick, a shove, I near break from the force of it. A thing of glass. The smudges of his touch, a rainbow of bruises dressed by layers of fabric. Each wound a crack. A final one and I splinter.

Her song is ground glass across my skin, but I can do nothing for her. To Miss Alice Turner's rage, I have dredged up her lament only to bury it once I have gotten what I need from her father.

'My uncle was a surgeon,' Althamia reminds me. 'I have seen the dead and the dying. I have lost someone I loved.' *I can bear the weight*, she conveys with a direct look and sets off in the direction of Mr Turner's home.

He is slow to admit us. No doubt hoping we'll lose patience and spare him the discomfort of entertaining a murderer's apprentice and a witch's kin. A servant leads us into an elegantly furnished parlour where Mr Turner rises from his chair. His hair has been lightened with cyprus powder and flecks of it gather around the neck of his black doublet.

'Welcome,' he says, and had I not known what he was I'd be taken in by it. The quicksilver charm, the light prattle. I would have dismissed the quick look he flashes at his youngest daughter Jane Turner and the hurried way she scurries from the room.

He is a knot, one Althamia and I unravel with our silent regard. His smiles dims and I look at his hands, once scuffed by the deliberate attacks he unleashed on his eldest daughter.

'You will withdraw your accusation against Margaret Greer,' I say.

He splutters. 'Well,' he says and eases his legs.

'You killed your daughter. You hit her so hard she fell and broke her neck.'

His face pales at the ease with which I accuse him.

'You would not hit a man,' I say calmly when he looms over me. 'Your targets have only been those too weak to fight back.' I rise up and he stumbles in his haste to put distance between us. 'You will tell Rush that Margaret Greer is innocent and will keep your fists to yourself.'

'Althamia,' I press when she remains seated. I grab her arm. 'We cannot leave her,' she says when we pass his daughter. I am shamed by her quiet stance and helpless expression. I have treated the dead as though they are off-stage happenings that interrupt the main plot. The dead are not a subplot and my interferences push their stories out of orbit, but I cannot set it all right.

'I am sorry,' I murmur and lead Althamia away.

Chapter Thirty-Seven

'I have surprised you,' says Althamia. We are marooned on the hills, a few yards away from the farmhouse of the Kellers, Bess's former employers and accusers. The day is half veiled by mist and whispers of light from the winter sun.

'No,' I answer. Though I had hoped she would not appear. We paused for the day after our visit with Mr Turner last night and had agreed to meet in the late afternoon near the Keller residence to resume our plan. The meeting with Mr Turner was deflating. If our plan succeeds, then Will and the others will be free. But what of Alice Turner? I have dug up the victims' grievances, used them for my purposes, only for their murderers to walk free.

Has the horror set in? I wonder as Althamia's eyes scan the surroundings which have started to shed their winter colours. Finally her eyes meet mine. 'Did you hear Agnes after she died?' she asks. I nod, but she shakes her head. 'Even though she is gone, her secrets are still hers. I have no right to them.'

'*My love too full to be distilled into parts.* My mother's song,' I explain.

'It stands by itself,' she says, and my chest eases to hear my words repeated.

'I'd take something plainer in her own words. Her songs have been with me since birth, but they were all pilfered from plays. Only her silences are her own.' The wind softens the bitter edge to my speech.

She dismounts after me. 'I am sorry.'

'I was born with my mother's cord around my neck. I thought it a curse. Her song a knot pulling down like Castor.'

'Dioscuri,' she murmurs and re-wraps her cloak around herself.

'A prophetic nickname. Father promised he would tell me my mother's name if I apprenticed myself to Will. A promise he is threatening to withdraw unless I return. I thought to unpick her spell,' I explain.

'Your mother's name . . . you have given it up.' *For me*, a realisation she turns from.

Will's words are in my head. 'Now that I am here,' I say when she turns back, 'I am not sure I want to undo what I am. Or even if I can.' Despite my fear, I cannot look away and exhale when she closes the distance between us and places her hand in mine.

'You are not cursed,' she says, her warmth a reminder of the last time we touched in York. 'Your mother is not Castor dragging you down. You are raising her up. You raise all the dead up.'

'Sir.' We jump apart at the distant call of the Kellers' servant.

Althamia holds me back. 'There is meaning to my silences when I play the bass viol. Your mother's story . . . perhaps it is hidden there.'

The silences of Mr and Mrs Keller hold a story. Althamia and I try to work it out in the Kellers' well-appointed parlour.

'Are you enjoying Rawton?' Mr Keller asks Althamia. News of our activities must have travelled, for his eyes turn wary whenever they meet my own.

A trap? Althamia asks with a raise of her shoulders, before brightly prattling about her stay. *No*, I convey with a look of my own. They would not have opened their doors to us if they suspected me of being a witch. Whatever the Kellers' secrets, the dead have not sung of them. But I do not need them to. Bess's words are enough.

With gathered courage Mr Keller addresses me: 'You are here to talk about the witches? The Foleys turned to the Devil from laziness.'

At this Mrs Keller comes alive. 'My husband arranged an apprentice-ship for the oldest Foley boy. I said it was a mistake and I was proven right. The family's situation is hopeless. The children are all bastards,' she whispers.

'The boy disgraced himself?' I probe.

'The business failed,' she reports, making it clear she blames the boy for it. 'Since then, he has pestered the men of the town for odd jobs.'

'He sounds industrious despite his circumstances,' says Althamia.

'He is crafty,' Mrs Keller complains, 'like the rest of his family.'

'What was Bess Heath?' I ask Mr Keller.

'A liar and a witch,' he answers.

Mrs Keller nods and breathes into a pouch filled with aniseed. 'I am forced to bear it. My husband's role as parish overseer brings him into contact with such creatures. Bess Heath and even Jane Foley. I let them attend to my family as servants, yet they have scorned the example I have set. I am disgraced by this business.'

'When did you realise Bess was a witch?' I ask.

'Oh, quite quickly. My suspicions were proved right when our cattle died and my son sickened.'

Althamia catches my eye and I lean back.

'I admire your strength,' Althamia praises her. 'I do not know if I would be brave enough to search a witch.'

'My husband makes me brave,' says Mrs Keller with a preening smile at her husband. 'He knew what that girl was before I did. I assisted in the search.'

'You must have been frightened,' prompts Althamia.

'I was,' she admits. 'But my husband had already made a start in our bedchamber when I entered—'

'The barn,' her husband interrupts, and she colours from her mistake and then pales at his restraining touch.

'Please,' says Mr Keller when Althamia and I rise. Their pressed silence tells another story and we hurry out amidst their protests.

'Whatever Bess has told you is lies,' he shouts to our backs.

I stop to address him. 'You mean the claim that you have been pocketing parish relief? Or her claim that you tried to assault her? I believe them both.'

Mr Keller's curses shadow us. Flanked by his wife and servant he stares at us from the doorway as though he means to drag us back.

'I think it is time you return to York,' I say as I help Althamia to mount her horse. To my relief she doesn't argue and we ride back in silence. The Carew manor is only a mile away, its sprawling proportions diminished by the mist. We are deep in the heather and Althamia's back straightens at the forced stillness. I catch flashes of moving shadows amidst the copse.

A trap, I mouth to Althamia and gesture for her to ride ahead. Her flight is curtailed by the rustle of the nearby trees.

'Mr Pearce,' greets Rush. He and his men encircle us with their horses. They bring the evening with them, and I am startled at how dark it is and how alone Althamia and I are. The trees imprison us, wall-like.

He tuts and I reluctantly draw my hand away from my dagger.

He pulls out a copy of my pamphlet. 'You are stirring rebellion,' he admonishes, my words destroyed with a slow patience. The same patience deployed on Mrs Greer and Bess.

I turn to Althamia. *I'll cause a distraction*, I convey with a look, but her eyes glitter with resolve. She will not leave.

The circle tightens and I place myself in front of Althamia and fend off the men's clawed grasps.

'The few you sought to recruit have been drawn back to my side,' he boasts, and waves another letter in my face. The words I wrote to the Countess of Derby are soon crushed beneath the horses' hooves. 'You should have lodged out of town.'

I grab Althamia's reins. 'Fair advice. We will be on our way.' He blocks our path. 'You are a witch-hunter, not a constable.'

He scoffs and one his men kicks at my horse.

'You cannot fight them all,' Althamia whispers and I draw back.

'You will let us go,' I tell him.

'The girl,' he says to his men.

I move to shield her. 'Miss Hale has committed no crime.'

'Her uncle is a witch.'

'That is no reason to condemn her,' I argue.

'Well begged,' he says as I kick away his men's grasping hands.

I draw close and whisper in his ear. 'That same reasoning condemns Grace. But her harm would be your undoing. You will let us go.'

He nods and for a moment I think he will give way. The moment ends when he brings his fist to my face. Althamia screams and the ensuing scuffle sees us pinned in place by his men's hands around our arms.

'You are no more than a poppet,' I spit, hoping to draw his attention from Althamia. 'A blunted blade.'

'Stand him up,' Rush shouts, and I lock eyes with him.

'A murderer,' I taunt, even as Althamia shouts at me to stop. 'You killed Clements.'

His men chuckle at the accusation as Rush reaches for my neck.

'A love charm,' he says, and snatches Francis's knot from me.

'It is mine,' I say when his eyes pass over Althamia.

'Ah and a confession too,' he says, and his fist is a flash of movement, the blow hard enough to draw blood. Not a punch. Amidst the muted echo of Althamia's screams, I note the pool of blood that stains my shirt and the dagger in Rush's hands. I fall as the second blow fills my mouth with a sweet, coppery taste. I stagger to my feet and hold on to Rush's cloak. The seams rip and the grip in my hands tingles and then slackens as I am kicked to the ground. Althamia rushes towards me, but one of the men holds her fast. She hits and scratches at his exposed skin, but he makes no reaction. Rush studies his torn cloak and then my knot in his hand. My brother's rich texture dulls as Rush slowly unravels it. The loss of it is a jab in my side, a strip of flesh. My brother's song is taken by the wind once his task is finished.

'Althamia,' I shout, and try to pull myself up to reach her.

'I will not be undone,' says Rush, with a kick that sends me falling into the dark.

Chapter Thirty-Eight

'Be at ease.'

'Althamia . . .' I blink into the light, but her hair is too light and there's a weary cast to her eyes. 'Grace.'

I sit up and realise I've been returned to Lord Carew's manor. My fingers brush the stitches at the back of my head. I wince as the memory comes back to me. Rush and his men were on me like a pack of dogs, snarling, kicking, ripping and punching. It hurts to breathe, and there are bandages wrapped around me. There's lump on my side and a metallic taste in my mouth that I can't swallow away. 'Where is Althamia?'

'Beyond our reach. Rush did not take her to the dungeons. He knew I would deplete myself to free her.'

'I do not need your help,' I snarl, almost stumbling to the ground in my effort to brush away her hand. I lean on the bedpost for balance and wince at the yellow bruises that line my arms. He is gone, I realise when I reach for Francis's knot, only to grasp the air. All that's left of his song is a fistful of grain that time will let slip through my fingers.

'My belongings,' I bark, and Grace obliges by handing me my valise. I rifle through it, only stopping when I see Francis's letter still among my possessions.

'Althamia, Bess, Judge Percival and the others will be tried at the church two days from now,' says Grace, her eyes dark despite the abundance of candlelight.

'You are confused,' I tell her, my fingers digging into the wooden post. 'It is too early for the midsummer assizes.'

'Mr Rush has appointed himself judge and the town his jury. It is illegal of course, but his word here is law. I have made it so.'

'I will not stay here,' I say when she manoeuvres herself between me and the door. 'Your creature has Althamia.'

She flinches. 'You will not find her. You wish to strangle me,' she says with a look at my clenched fingers. 'I do not blame you, though I have restored you to health this past week. One of the watchers is a spy of mine. I sent my men to retrieve you when I got word of the attack. I found this in your possession.' The blessing book is cradled to her chest. It falls to the bed when I grasp her wrist.

'Were your schemes worth all this?' I say with a gesture to the room's possessions. 'No? Then why let this go so far? Rush has Althamia. If you care for her, you will help me to stop him.' She tugs and I let go of her. 'Who is he?' I ask.

'For all the midwife's attempts to ply me with dragon's blood – the resin of the dragon tree – my son was born too early to be saved. All I had of him was this,' she confides. She pulls out a lock of hair from the book, savouring the feel of it between her fingers. 'I feared I would not survive the delivery and filled the pages of this book with advice to my child. I wrote of how they could harness their powers, manage an estate, but nothing of kindness.' She stops, and I shudder despite the blazing heat from the fireplace. 'It was during the siege. After my loss, I was pressed to make myself of use tending to the wounded. Rush was among them. My son's death was regarded as a loss, a misfortune, but never a child. And there was Rush, both a hero and an empty vessel. The lock of my son's hair pressed against my skin, and I thought, *What if I could fill him, this empty man.*' She stops and my breath is caught in the pause. 'And then my thoughts became a knot. I wanted something that was *mine*.' It is not an excuse, nor an apology. 'You have done the same, in your own manner.'

'It was not the same,' I say softly, and her eyes lower. 'You have been scheming with Rush from the start.'

A murmured denial on her part. 'I thought my attempt unsuccessful, until he appeared one day with my legacy book in his possession to prove our kinship. I had buried it at Lathom, but he was able to sense its location. Rush is almost of my flesh, but I sent him away. I was frightened and wanted to forget. But then Bess, that cunning girl, dreamt of what I had done, and Rush fell in with witch-hunters soon after, I suppose to punish me. I made him what he was, but sentiment kept him tied to me for a while.' She caresses the knot. 'I reached out to him after my uncle refused to pay the fine on my estates. Rush has cultivated his own powerbase, but he wants more. He has no wish to return to those blank days.'

'And will destroy everything you care about to ensure it.'

She nods and hands me the knot. 'The connection between us robs me of my strength.'

'To undo it would kill you,' I say, even as I pick at the knot's centre. 'Your death will not change anything,' I say and hand it back. 'The town will blame Rush's death on the accused and find someone else to replace him.'

'You would kill him directly,' she assumes when I reach for my cloak and dagger. 'You are too weak.' She places herself before the door and dances her fingers around my stab wound until I gently move her aside.

'He will kill you,' she says to my back.

My hand traces the missing outline of Francis's knot. 'He has killed me already.'

Chapter Thirty-Nine

I ride away from the manor, a blurred silhouette amidst the liminal mist. Every breath deepens the break to my bones. I have two days to save Althamia, Will and the others, but their liberty will not be gained by seeking aid from a nearby town. It will be found here, amongst the dead. I slow my horse as we near the cemetery. With steady hands I pull out Francis's letter and break the seal.

Dear brother,

I am dying. I did not think this a possibility when I became a Cavalier. I am not our father. Even now his eyes are upon me. I am a loss to him, but I have no doubt he has schemed already to minimise the fallout. He will turn to you. The thought fills me with regret for I have no wish to see you submit yourself to his purposes. It is not an easy task and I fear you will lose yourself in the undertaking. We grew up side by side, but I regret that I never really knew you in full. Nicholas my brother, Nicholas the playwright, but never Nicholas the witch. Never the boy the dead would sing to. Never the heart of you. I am sorry for it. Fear of the consequences made us shy of each other, and it wasn't until I left that I resolved to redress it. A departing regret, but still I am comforted by the parts you chose to reveal of yourself.

Your loving brother,
F.P.

His loss is a dull ache in my heart that his words see mended. He knew yet did not revile me for it. The relief I feel is tempered by my shame at how much of myself I kept hidden from him. The years spent smothering my powers to a blunt edge because I was too afraid to trust in his regard. I have made myself small, a decision I regret, for it has put everyone I love at risk.

With the shovel I'd begged off the servant, I step into the cemetery grounds. The words of the dead are a serpent's hiss. I hiss back. They roar in my head until a hard thrust in the ground sees them silenced. Finally, it is done. I peer down at the four-foot hole now dotted red from my re-opened wounds. The stench of mud fills my nostrils as I fall back into the open grave.

The ground is buried in songs, but for the first time I do not fear being overwhelmed. Francis's knot sapped me of my control. While Rush's actions have lightened me, there is still a small weight pressing me down. A knot, one spun from my blood like silk. Her song is in the silences, Althamia told me, and I wait for it; a wordless libretto that spins a web.

I cultivated myself from threaded knots. What little magic I possessed was bartered away for secondary stage roles. Dutiful daughters, maligned queens until my heart was caught by a merchant. Mistress, another role, one I never knew I was playing, until it was over. A new part. A mother. A role that made the women in my family remote and distant figures.

I had no wished to be lessened. But then I had you. My love too full to
be distilled into parts.

I would have drowned had my mother not crowned me in her songs.
Her melody kept the dead muffled until I was strong enough to silence
them in turn. She threaded her history in my blood and waited all
these years for me to unravel it. A part of her will wait still.

My body is racked when the remaining dead clamour for my
attention. The dead sing to me, but Grace said they would speak if
I let them. I breathe in and invite them to make their address. Their
rush for my attention is a death of sorts but I do not lose myself to
it. I am myself despite the voices that sift in and out of me. Their
secrets are ropes, and I will use them to bind the people of Rawton.

Chapter Forty

I arrive with the breaking of light.

From the outside, the church door reverberates with the sounds of shuffled footsteps and raised voices. For a moment I hesitate, though not from fear. I am reconciling the two versions of myself: the one who keeps to the shadows and the one who now steps forward into the light.

I am at the back of the church. My clothes are caked in mud from having spent the last two nights in the cemetery. I am lightened, despite the effects of Rush's beating. A stranger studies me through narrowed eyes. He is trying to place me, but my bedraggled state puts him off.

They are drowning. The Rawton witches are penned behind a makeshift dock in the packed church. Their clothes are spoiled with brown marks, their faces drained of colour. They blink into the daylight and stoop under the townspeople's stares. A castle keeper stands nearby and the keys to their shackles hang about his waist. Will swipes away the dirt that clings to his shirt.

Bess has been recaptured. She holds her head high despite her tiredness, her pride causing the Kellers to stiffen. As does her father Eli Heath, who keeps himself apart from her. Mrs Greer looks unseeing into the crowd. Her niece Margaret places herself before her as though to protect her aunt from Mrs Ingram's loud censure. Jane Foley and her children make desperate entreaties to their neighbours. She holds

315

up her youngest child, a crying girl of two, but her neighbours are not moved by this display.

A sound draws me to Althamia, standing proud in the centre. It is pleading, confused and belligerent. A dying song but not hers. Lord Carew attempts to ward off his decline with a desperate look in Grace's direction. From the pews she stares back at him, her face resigned. Althamia bears visible signs of mistreatment and her eyes flash defiantly at Rush and Grace. She has not been broken and the knots in my chest ease despite the danger she is in.

There is no jury, only Rush, who places himself between the witches and the townspeople in the pews. I am late. The trial is already under way, and Althamia is next to be condemned.

At Rush's command, the coroner, Mr Wilson, takes the stage.

'This is a mockery,' Will cries, but he is silenced by Rush's watching men who brandish their cudgels and knives at their master's instruction.

'When did you suspect Miss Althamia Hale to be a witch?' Rush demands of Mr Wilson.

Mr Wilson hesitates. 'She came to my office with Mr Pearce. She tried to convince me that Mrs Gibbons died by alternative means.'

'How so?' Rush urges.

'She claims Mrs Gibbons had been struck by lightning,' he answers. He does not look at Althamia during his testimony. His attention is fixed on Rush and his men. The forced accusation pains him, but he will speak it to save himself.

Althamia holds herself still as the crowd jeers.

'The Foley women sent my familiars after her.' A man's voice cut through the uproar. He must be Mrs Gibbons's widower, for Jane Foley curses at him. A slap from Rush's watching men silences her. She staggers back and Althamia, Bess and another help to bear her weight.

'Miss Hale was insistent I believe her and, when she left, I noticed a blush of red around the dead woman's throat,' Mr Wilson imparts.

'The dead bleed from a witch's touch,' says Rush, and Mr Wilson reluctantly nods in agreement.

'She was struck by lightning,' Althamia interrupts. 'That is why there was a fern pattern pressed across her chest.'

'You helped Jane Foley summon it,' Rush accuses her.

'I am not a witch,' she insists. 'I was not even here when the woman died.' This she says to the widower, but he is too busy staring at Jane Foley.

'You flew,' says Rush.

Althamia laughs but then quietens when she sees his words taken as truth. 'Lightning is not caused by the supernatural—'

But Rush cuts short her explanation and turns to Will.

'You, sir, stand accused of the murder of Clements Lint. Will you say nothing in your defence?' Rush demands, his face reddening at Will's considered disdain.

'His guilt makes him mute,' suggests one of Rush's men and the townspeople murmur in agreement.

Will's eyes meet mine across the crowd. He takes in my bruised face and shakes his head in warning. I am condemned, either way, he conveys with a look. He will not legitimise Rush's authority by speaking or demean himself by begging.

'He is innocent of the charges levelled against him, as am I.' Althamia pushes herself to the front. 'I was there the night Clements died.'

'A witch and a murderess,' someone whispers.

'You killed him,' Althamia accuses Rush.

'You are mistaken,' he tells her.

Her voice rises at his patronising smile. 'Clements came across

317

me in the night. We had an altercation and I glimpsed you and your staff before I ran off into the woods. You were the last person to see him alive.'

'And yet you have stayed silent until now,' Rush mocks. 'Why?'

Don't, I urge her, but Althamia rises to his challenge.

'Because I did not want to be accused in turn. I drew my knife on him, although the only blood spilled was my own. He hurt me and killed my friend Agnes Wright.'

Rush turns his back on her. 'A diversion,' he reassures his audience, 'Judge Percival is acquainted with Miss Hale. They have conspired together in Mr Lint's death.'

'You are making this up as you go along,' says Will.

'See how he comes to her defence,' says Rush. His voice is laced with innuendo and Althamia blushes when the public look at her as if she is despoiled.

'You are nothing but spewed hate,' she tells him and then glares at the surrounding spectators. 'One you have sanctified.'

'You are a fraud.' My shout draws Rush's attention away from Althamia. As the crowd parts in front of me, I limp to the end of the nave and stand before Rush.

'Nicholas,' cries Althamia, but I motion for her to stay where she is.

Rush's face screws up in denial while his men circle us. They sport the same sneers they wore when they were kicking me to the ground.

I swallow my fear and point to Rush. 'This man grew up in Lathom. He was injured in the castle siege. Afterwards he took on the identity of John Rush and began to hunt witches illegally. His title is a fake.'

'Another diversion,' Rush argues. 'His loyalties are to his master and the witch.'

'He intercepted my letter to the Countess of Derby, and to stop our attempts to expose him, he had his men attack Althamia and me.' The people gasp when I raise my shirt.

'He is lying,' Rush insists.

'You are the liar – and a murder. I have sent off another letter to the Countess of Derby. You should not fear her answer if you are telling the truth.'

His fists clench. 'Seize him,' he orders, but his men's movement is stopped by Grace.

'Mr Pearce speaks the truth,' says Grace, finally coming to our aid. 'I tended Mr Rush's injuries during the siege.'

'You are lying,' he shouts, but the break in his voice gives his men pause.

'The Countess of Derby will speak for me on this matter,' she insists. Grace is a woman and resented, but her rank places her out of reach of ordinary men. Her words have sway, but she has no wish to witness Rush's unravelling. She angles herself away from Rush's accusing stare. Mrs Ingram hurries to Rush's side. 'Why should we believe her? She is a liar and her uncle stands accused. She wishes to save him. Mr Rush is a respected witch-hunter.'

Rush straightens under her regard while his men draw closer like dogs.

'I am sorry for your loss,' I tell Mrs Ingram. 'But you have made spells out of your husband's sin.' I turn to her husband, who is even more diminished by my sudden attention.

'Mrs Greer did not kill your son. He came upon you both and you chased him until he stumbled into a sleep he could never wake from.'

Mrs Greer hangs her head at this announcement while Mrs Ingram goes to her husband and tugs at his cloak. 'He is lying,' she insists. 'Tell them he is a liar.' She pulls her husband to his feet. Her husband frees himself from her grasp and leaves.

'You are witch, a demon!' Rush accuses. 'A spawn of Goetia hiding in plain sight. You commune with the dead.'

'Be careful,' I warn his men. 'If his words are true, then I am above your jurisdiction.'

I address the townspeople. 'At your invitation, the Devil has made himself at home. At his urging, you have lied about your neighbours. It is not too late to recant and drive him out.'

My proclamation is greeted with silence. If they will not speak, then the dead will. 'Mr Elwick. I told you I have no need of whispers,' I shout as he attempts to leave the church. 'Miss Lockton died after you gave her the wrong dosage. A drunken mistake, but one that cost an innocent girl her life. Will you forfeit Jane Foley's life instead?' He falters from the increased attention and then runs off. An older couple, Miss Lockton's parents, rush after him.

'Mr Turner.' He lunges at me, but a neighbour holds him back.

'You murdered your daughter,' I accuse.

'He's lying,' he denies, but his charm cannot withstand his neighbours' scrutiny nor his remaining daughter, who shrinks from his presence. 'He's lying,' he repeats, and attempts another lunge. A few more people place themselves between us. He leaves, his repeated denials worn thin.

I clutch my stomach and turn to Mr Wilson. 'Who told you to accuse Miss Althamia Hale?' He stutters and looks to Rush then back at me.

'Upon your word I will hang,' says Althamia.

Mr Wilson finds courage in the subsequent pause. 'Mr Rush told me to accuse her or face being accused myself,' he confesses, and half faints in his seat.

My words are a lash, each secret a torn strip of flesh. People flinch from me. 'Mr Keller,' I say once I've finished searching the throng. 'You have used your position to steal from the poor. You take girls by force and threats, and when Bess refused to submit, you accused her of witchcraft. Will you renounce the charge or face the girls in the light?'

Bess steps forward. Mr Keller laughs, a hearty sound that quietens when two unaccused women, or rather girls, step forward, one of them the servant who greeted Althamia and me at his home. Mrs Keller tries to hold her down, but the young girl sets herself apart from the family. Jane Foley places herself and her son next to Bess. Her oldest child is about twelve years of age. His eyes are blue, a colour shared by Mr Keller and his two young children.

'I renounce the charge,' says Mr Keller. 'I was misled.' He hurries out of the church with his wife behind him.

'Mr Powell.' I step towards the doctor. 'You were one of the first to welcome Mr Rush.' The secrets of the dead swirl in my head and Will breaks free from the dock to put a steady hand on my shoulder. 'You encouraged Mrs Gair to blame her husband's death on Margaret Greer's curse. You were fearful she would blame you.'

'I recant,' says Mr Powell.

Will places himself between us and warns Mr Gibbons off with a hard look.

'Mr Gibbons,' I say. 'Your wife was killed by lightning. Though she died a hundred times over whenever you felt moved to lay your hands on her.'

'No!' says Rush, but Mr Gibbons sags, all resistance gone, and turns away.

Enraged, Rush signals to his men and they surge forward, their hands pinning me in place as though I'm on a cross. The crowd draws in and I wonder if this is what Lady Katherine saw on the gallows: the indifferent stares, the excitement.

'He is a demon,' Rush shouts. 'Had I a rope, I would make you dance,' he whispers, his hands a tight embrace around my neck. I struggle to breathe, until slowly the pressure eases as his hands travel downwards to my wound. 'Evil has cast its net over this town,' he announces over Althamia and Will's protests. 'We must tear it apart.' His fingers probe my wound, opening up Grace's stitches, and he holds his bloody hands up in invitation.

No one makes a sound. With furtive looks they wait for someone else to begin the frenzy. Someone pushes their way towards us. Rush's lips spread, only for the man to walk past. 'Coward,' he calls after him. 'A witch crossed the threshold. I was defending myself,' he says, but all the crowd see is me, my flesh spread apart. 'Sheep,' he spits at the slow exodus of supporters. 'You knew exactly the type of man you made welcome and the methods I'd deploy. But now you shrink as though I am the demon and think to shoo me away.' His charm is now tarnished brass. 'I will not be shooed away. You are all monsters and I the method in which you work your malice. The truth of it will not change, no matter how many of you turn your back on me.'

I pull myself free when one of his men lets go of my arm and scurries off. The castle keeper and his men stand back. Will cuts through the thinning crowd while Althamia tends to the frail defendants. 'You have misjudged your audience,' Will tells Rush. 'The people of Rawton will keep their accusations and murders to hidden corners and behind closed doors.'

'Coward,' he repeats.

'You are right,' Will agrees. 'We are all cowards.' He turns to what remains of the crowd. 'Mr Rush is a fraud. He has threatened and bribed his way to influence. Your loyalty to him will lead you to ruin.'

His words are mutely received and perhaps it is the sight of my lips parting to reveal more of their secrets that causes them to disperse.

'There have been enough denouncements,' says Grace from a distance when Rush opens his mouth in protest. A truth conceded by a swift headcount of his remaining supporters and sight of the castle keeper closing in on him, shackles at the ready.

Rush's men stand aside when he rushes out.

'His hatred is an endless circle,' I tell Will when he tries to stop me from following. 'One I will break.'

'Nicholas,' warns Althamia, but I ignore her call and stagger after the fleeing Rush. He rides out of the courtyard, and I take the nearest horse and ride after him.

'I should have slit your throat,' he hisses when I catch up with him. He pushes my hands away from his reins and breaks into a gallop.

I clutch my stomach and urge my mount on.

'I will not let you go free,' I shout as we clear the town for the open countryside. The jolting of the gallop stains my chest with fresh blood.

'You have terrorised women,' I shout once I have caught up to him. The ground is rocky now that we are nearing Pendle Hill and I clutch at my ribs as though to hold myself together.

Rush's face is red. 'You have put self-interest above justice. But now you have fashioned yourself the hero and hold yourself above me. Why should I not have the same liberty? I am my own man after all.'

I slow down at the entrance of Pendle Hill and then urge my horse on with a gentle kick.

Rush is half shrouded by the mist, but I tense when he favours me with a backwards look. 'You revile me, but they will remember you when they speak of my work. Men like you are the thread of my story.'

'And Grace is your knot. Both can be undone.'

'You do not want to kill me,' he says when I unsheath my dagger.

'No?' I say, but he dodges my swipe and the next only inflicts a shallow cut.

'I have given you purpose. Without me you are nothing.'

'I will never stop hunting you,' I say as we near the top of the hill.

He chuckles, the sound smothered by the mist that settles on my face like a wet cloth. I stop and close my eyes and listen for the hooves of his horse.

'Rush,' I whisper, but my voice echoes as I circle round blindly.

I jump down and from the edge of the hill, the path before me is clear. 'Rush,' I shout. But I am greeted by silence.

Chapter Forty-One

The town of Rawton is a collapsed net in the wake of the Devil's abandonment. The remaining townspeople slip from underneath and gape at the space behind me in search of Rush. Meanwhile the Rawton witches cut a clear path into the waiting cart.

'We are safe,' shouts Althamia when I move to block the cart's progress with my horse. Amidst the castle keeper's curses, she raises her hands. They are unbound, as are the others' hands. 'The garrison commander has been sent for,' says Will. 'He will bring this matter to an end. We must reside in Lancaster Castle in the meantime.'

'There is sickness there,' I protest, with a look at the broken figure of Lord Carew.

'They will be given better lodgings,' says Grace from the church entrance and snags the loose string around her cloak.

Will, Althamia and I exchange a knowing look. More tricks, but one I am grateful for if it keeps them all safe.

Althamia holds me off with a look when Grace approaches to whisper in her ear. Their embrace ends when the castle keeper nudges the cart forward. I block him and move to grab the shackles about his waist. I could end this now, but my approach is halted by the castle keeper's raised cudgel.

Will is quick to intervene. 'Most of the people have already withdrawn their accusations. We should be freed soon.'

I draw back, though the castle keeper doesn't lower his weapon.

'Rush is gone,' I tell Will. 'He has disappeared and taken your freedom with him.' I had circled back on my trail but could find no sign of him.

Bess arches her head towards me. 'My testimony against you was coerced. I will withdraw it.'

'And my statement will clear your name,' Althamia finishes. She reaches out her hand towards me. 'It is over,' and the set to her face convinces me to give way.

'I will come to the castle every day until you are released,' I say. She nods and I ride after them for a short while until she sends me off with a wet smile.

I return to the church, where a waiting Grace stands near her horse.

'Where is he?' I demand.

Her eyes move to my restraining touch on her horse's reins. 'Gone,' she admits. 'Along with any hold I had over him. If indeed I had such a thing. Wherever he is, I do not have the power to stop him.'

She tries to jerk the reins away. 'Would you condemn me?'

'You have hurt so many people.'

She looks away. 'I have regrets. I would have acted differently had the times not made me so desperate.'

'You saw the accused today. They were desperate and suffering. Most of them will remain so even after they regain their liberty. An accusation of witchcraft is a dark mark. But you will soon have your freedom. Lord Carew has begun to sing.'

Her eyes close. 'I have time yet to press my cause. From a distance,' she says at my look. 'With pleading letters, not magic.'

'After everything you've done, you still find a way to get what you want.'

'I am sorry for it,' she says with a swooping look at our surroundings.

'You do not believe me. When I am older, I will think this a dream. That Rush was someone we all whispered in existence.'

'But it was your whisper,' I say. 'And one that you cannot undo. Whatever Rush does next, you are tied to him.'

'You too know what it's like to trade pieces of yourself away. Knot by knot.' Our eyes lock and reluctantly I step back. 'You should join me.'

'To seek out another stage?' I challenge.

'Weak as I am, I could never reject my power outright.' Her smile is a splintered confidence and she reaches out her hand. 'Witch-hunters are a knot. Today's events have no more than snagged its edges. You were brave to have so risked yourself, but the townspeople know you are not one of them and will hate you for it.'

'I have always been hated,' the confession enough to see her touch withdrawn.

Atop her horse she studies me. 'My aunt was like me, though marriage reduced her. The pretence is not easy. You will fare better with Althamia.'

She rides off before I have a mind to regret my clemency.

'You look well,' I tell Bess as we meet on the staircase. She traces the bruises across her face that have all but faded in the passing weeks.

She returns my inspection. 'You need more air. You should go to town.'

'And subject myself to people's stares?' Bess had shared the towns-people's whispers that I can snatch at their secrets with a single look. Not that I am troubled by their gossip. After Rush's disappearance and Grace's withdrawal, I had ridden to seek help. The garrison commander, possessing both an impatience for witchcraft and an over-adherence to rank, had promptly issued a pardon for Althamia, Lord Carew and the rest of the Rawton witches in the two days following the trial.

I'd paid for the prisoners too poor to afford the fines to cover their board during their forced imprisonment. The searching men and women were quick to dismiss their role in the witch-hunts to a coerced employment. It was an easy matter to persuade them and the rest of the townspeople to sign a certificate confirming the accused were not witches. But neither of these actions were enough to convince Jane Foley and her children, Mrs Greer and others to stay. The Rawton witches fled, or flew as the townspeople muttered. Of their number only Bess remained to accept Althamia's offer of a home.

Will's freedom had come two weeks later. The murder charge against him was dismissed following the withdrawal of Bess's testimony, the addition of Althamia's statement and the absence of Mr Rush, who has yet to be found.

Grace too has been granted her freedom. 'She has taken possession of her estates,' Althamia had shared soon after her release. Lord Carew had paid off Grace's fine, perhaps as an inducement to keep away. 'Let us hope she will satisfy herself with a quiet seclusion.' My reply was more of a prayer than anything else. Of her captivity, Althamia had said little at first, other than to reassure me that she had been left unharmed. Later she confided to me the stories Rush had told her, of the women he had tortured.

Bess's words pull me back to the present.

'You can stare back in turn as I do,' says Bess. Mrs Blake died last week. She delivered a dark mass, not a child. Mr Keller and Mr Turner remain at liberty, though their neighbours' watchfulness will prevent it from ever being a comfortable condition. 'Shame only bridles people for so long,' she adds with an elaborate curtsy and a warning look.

'I am grateful to you,' I overhear Althamia tell Will as I join them in the sun parlour. A sentiment her parents repeat only because they cannot say he will be missed. Instead they ply him with wine and biscuits while the carriage is readied for his departure.

Althamia holds herself still on the armless chair. She is beyond me now, caged as she is by the jewelled stomacher of her silver gown. A half-finished piece of embroidery sits on her lap. Grace's stuffed jackdaw is pinned on the wall behind her. Its dark feathers catch the afternoon light. We have hardly spoken since her parents arrived last week. I have been much confined to my bed, while Mrs Hale has seen to it that Althamia is kept busy helping to nurse Lord Carew. His song gets louder every day, though Mrs Hale and Althamia have settled in for a long stay. Lord Carew has not reneged on his decision to make Althamia his heir. Mrs Hale must wait out both her brother's death and Althamia's majority.

Hale looks at me, or rather at the clock above my head. He is dressed in one of Lord Carew's robes and sits in Grace's, or rather Lord Carew's chair. 'I envy your freedom,' he tells Will, 'I must soon leave to resume my duties in York.' Still, he eyes Lord Carew's possessions as though they are his.

'I did not have much choice in the matter,' says Will and brushes off Hale's apology. Broad had printed the pamphlet Althamia had sent him, and Will and I had built upon the sensation it created by writing to the major news-book to tell them all that occurred in Rawton. Parliament's response to a respected witch-hunter denouncing his profession as a fraud was swift, despite the clamour of support. Will was stripped of his post and leaves now to offer his services in the Royalist court in France. He has encouraged me to accept Dodmore's offer, though my slow recovery delays any decision on my part.

'Althamia and I will remain here in the meantime,' Mrs Hale finishes. The nervous flicker of her eyes betrays her discomfort at being home. Or perhaps it is my person that makes her so. She still wishes to keep Althamia from my reach.

A knock on the door. 'The carriage is ready for you, sir,' Bess announces.

Will hovers beside the carriage. His eyes blink under the bright sun.

'You could almost be living my life,' I tell him.

'It is a fortune I seek,' he says with a fleeting look at Althamia and her parents stationed near the entrance. 'A life is a different entity, one populated by people to care for.'

'I care for you,' I say, a truth he is unable to brush off despite his nonchalant expression.

'Whatever you decide, you will have better luck than me.' Despite my vagueness about my future endeavours, he had bequeathed me some funds a week earlier. A sum large enough that I could survive the withdrawal of my father's support.

'You must think my exile a reprieve,' he says after a while.

'I think nothing of the sort.'

'I do not mourn the loss of my post. I decided in the dungeon that, if I lived, I would go abroad and become someone entirely different. A foolish fantasy and one I have not earned.'

We are both rooted to the dying and the dead, but on him the weight is cumbersome.

'I am lifted,' he says when I grab his talisman and throw it to the ground along with my own. 'Perhaps I am leaving a piece of myself here.' His eyes dim at the sentiment. He spares another look at the entrance and I turn slightly to see Althamia remain even when Mr and Mrs Hale head inside.

'She is the knot I carry,' I say at his hopeful expression.

'You speak as though she is lost to you,' he says, his eyes move to my neck, now bare of Francis's knot.

'She would never be safe with me,' I say, a repeat of Mrs Hale's warning.

'Safety is a cage.'

'One I have no wish to fracture,' I say, with more finality.

A sighed farewell touch and he is gone, our talismans crushed by the carriage wheels. I wait until he is no more than a dot in the corner of my eye before turning. Althamia is still there and wordlessly offers her hand when I draw near.

'You are much in the shadows.' Althamia comes from the night, her eyes bright underneath a canopy of stars and her feet veiled by the subsiding mist.

'I could not sleep.' I had spent the rest of the day in my bedchamber after Will had left this morning. At Althamia's insistence, I had broken my self-isolation for dinner where Hale had been keen to confirm my intended departure by the week's end.

She shivers and pulls at her nightgown. 'Neither could I,' she says, with a sweeping look at the garden. The last time we were here, Will had interrupted with hands stained from Clements's blood.

Her eyes take in the sprawling estate.

'I hope you will be happy here,' I tell her.

She turns to me. 'I am four years away from my majority. I must convince myself of my happiness or count down the time in misery. Rawton is half dying, and I am frightened by the responsibility of tending to it. I have not lived enough to make a responsible mistress.'

'You are not Grace,' I reassure her. 'Your kindness will see this place restored.'

'In want of magic it must satisfy itself with that,' she replies.

I take her hands in mine. 'This is the spell.'

'You do not have to leave,' she says at my relinquished touch. 'You could seclude yourself here and write plays. You have sufficient material for a tragedy. Although I understand your father is eager for you return.'

I wince. My recovery has been plagued by my father's rants about *that business in Rawton*. He has greeted my silences with a terse summons to return home or face being disinherited.

'I am not for home.'

'Dodmore?' she asks.

I shake my head. I wouldn't have envisioned the choices available to me a few months before. But the answer now is clear even as I imagine an alternative life in each scenario.

'You are not for London or France. Witch trials have sprung up across the county. There is one ongoing investigation ten miles from here. You believe it is Rush?' she asks as the mist around her feet begin to rise.

'They are all Rush,' I say and brood over reports of witch-hunters across the country assuming the title of Witchfinder General. 'Men such as John Gaule are speaking up against them. I will add my voice to theirs in a fashion,' and hand her a letter from Broad.

Dear Mr Pearce,

Your words have started a frenzy. York's hunger for witches has been overtaken by a longing for witch-hunters and the men who hunt them. You have no doubt received offers of payment in return for further accounts of your exploits. I offer you more: a partnership in which you will have a dominant stake and control over the words you wish to see in print.

Yours
Mr Broad

'A Devil's bargain,' I murmur to Althamia once she's finished reading it, 'but one I hope will temper the ease with which witch-hunters peddle their lies.'

'But your mother's name,' she whispers.

'Gisla Maes.' The words leave my lips like a spell. 'Her name was always in my possession. Until you showed me the way, I never knew how to reach for it.'

'The knowledge lightens you. I am glad,' she confesses.

'I let go of my anger and will not burden myself with regret,' I say. When my work is done, I reach further and use what she has sung of to trace her remaining relatives.

A few steps are all that is needed to close the distance between us.

'Death is an outstretched hand to me. I have stopped flinching from it,' I tell her, even as she takes my hand and traces the outline of my scar.

'You are wrong. But even if it were true, I am unafraid.'

'Your parents would not approve.' Mrs Hale thought to escape her past. After everything that's happened, I wouldn't blame Althamia for wanting the same. 'I am set to be disinherited.'

'My father would think us an unequal pairing,' she concedes. 'Your youth and looks made you appealing, but your wealth made you eligible.' I blush to hear Will's words from our first day in York parroted.

'After this matter is done I could seek my fortune and come back.' A hesitant proposal, but one she answers.

'Or you could just come back.'

A flicker of light stops her falling into my arms. Hale stands on the garden steps. His eyes reflect the lantern he holds near his face. Althamia stares at me wordlessly before sweeping past her father. Hale appraises me for a moment and then closes the door behind him.

Chapter Forty-Two

Rawton, Lady Day, March 1645

Dear father,

My path is my own. I will walk it without your aid.

Your son,
Nicholas

I study the letter and add my mother's name to the top corner: Gisla Maes. The letter, once sent, will not be greeted with a reply. My father can only tie people to him with threats and bribes. I will not be bound by any of those measures and my father lacks the bravery to change his approach. I fold the letter and leave it on the desk for a servant to send. A revised goodbye but with none of the turmoil and doubt that shadowed the first. Beside it lies a longer letter to Stephens describing all that has transpired since I left London.

My thoughts are dismissed by a firm knock on my bedchamber door. 'It is strange to beckon a new year with a departure,' says Bess at the valise in my hand. We pause near the top stairs where I spy the hired carriage through the window.

'I will miss you,' she shares. 'You are like the tempest bringing change. My world is shaken whenever we meet. Each time I find my circumstances altered.' Her face wonders at it. 'I used to be a miss until my father drank away our family's reputation and Lord Carew fenced us from our lands. Since you've arrived, I've gone from a beggar to a servant . . .'

'And a miss if we meet again.'

'We will. And in the meantime I will say my goodbyes as Bess Heath, companion to Mrs Hale.'

I bow, and as she curtsies I wonder why Mrs Hale would need a companion. Bess snatches at my thoughts with a wry smile. She smooths down her new dress and skips down the stairs.

'He is late,' says Hale from the grand entrance, his back towards me.

'He is leaving,' Mrs Hale chides him. 'At one point you wanted him for Althamia.'

'When he was a merchant's son and Althamia—'

'Just a mayor's daughter,' Mrs Hale finishes.

'She is something more now, while Mr Pearce has squandered all his promise. I am glad of it, especially in the light of the whispers that surround him. Let him ride out to ruin, so long as our daughter is not spoiled by it.'

'The same whispers that plague my family,' comes Mrs Hale's calm reply.

He repeats his wife's earlier warning. 'Althamia would not be safe with him. She has nearly died twice while in his company.'

'I was wrong about him and our daughter. Althamia is capable of protecting herself.' A pause, then she adds a murmured, 'Besides, safe does not mean smothered.'

Their argument simmers when I cough an interruption.

'I hope you will relay my gratitude to Lord Carew for his hospitality. I am sad not to tell him so myself,' I say to Mrs Hale and her red-faced husband.

Mrs Hale's face is solemn. 'I will tell him.'

Bess appears and hovers a respectful distance behind Mr Hale.

'She is abed,' says Hale at my obvious attempts to catch a glimpse of Althamia.

'A headache,' adds Mrs Hale, kindlier.

I linger in the hope that Althamia will make an appearance. Hale grinds his jaw, but I do not move until the carriage driver arrives to say it is time.

I hand Mrs Hale my diary. 'I had hoped to give it to Althamia myself.'

Hale opens his mouth to refuse, but is tempered by the touch of his wife's hand on his.

She passes it back to me. 'She would find no purpose for it here.'

'Goodbye, Mr Pearce,' says Hale, and presses me back with such force I stumble. The door slams shut behind him and a waiting servant is quick to steer me into the carriage. By the time I've gathered my thoughts, it is too late. We are off. I look back at the manor and hold my diary close. I wish I had trusted Bess with its safekeeping.

'Why have we stopped?' I shout when the carriage grinds to a halt. I knock on the window but then the door is flung open, and a cloaked figure steps in. A moment later the carriage swiftly resumes its journey.

I start in surprise when Althamia lowers her blue hood. 'Your mother said you were ill.'

'A ruse we concocted together.'

She pulls the map from my valise and spreads it across both our laps. She studies it, her fingers tracing the thin line I've made across it. 'We were here, but this is our destination.'

'One of many,' I confirm. 'Which is why I must return you home. You cannot come with me,' I protest when she grabs my hand to stop me knocking for the driver's attention. 'It is dangerous,' I insist.

'I have survived far worse,' she argues. 'Besides, you need my help.

You have barely recovered. Your wound could fester and poison your blood. I know how to save you.'

'I will not help you to run away.'

'I am not running,' she says simply, and I cannot find the words to argue with her. For a runaway, she is remarkably determined and self-possessed.

'This is kindled ground I cover,' I warn.

'I have a light step,' she teases.

'I will come back for you once this over,' I promise.

'Nicholas,' she says softly, 'this will never be over. There will always be another war, another purge. We could live our lives waiting for the promise of an ending. Or we could live now.'

'Whatever you think I am, a happy ending is not one of them.'

'A happy ending is beyond most people, and yet I am willing to risk all for this one.'

'This is not proper,' I say, but I join our hands together.

'You are to become the scourge of witch-hunters. You cannot do it alone.'

'You wish to be my apprentice?' I tease.

'Your partner,' she corrects as I clasp our hands together.

'My wife?' I ask and knot her finger with a strand of thread from my cloak. She studies it a moment and then lifts her face to mine.

Her kiss leaves me breathless, and we break apart too soon. She leans back into my embrace, her attention soon taken by the map. The road to our destination is burdened by white shadows and the passing outline of Pendle Hill makes for a gloomy peace. My mood is lightened when Althamia rests her head on my arm.

'I am more for the dead than the living,' I tell her.

She breaks from plotting our course and eases my fears with kisses. 'And I have chosen you regardless.'

Author's Note

I wish I could say *The Revels* came together like a spell but that would be a disservice to the thousands of men and women who lost their lives to the witch-hunts that dominated early modern Europe.

The Revels was originally sparked by an interest in King James I, known for some of the following: unifying the Scottish and English crowns, his close relations with his handsome male favourites, his passion for hunting; and his paranoia that the Devil and his servants, witches, were out to assassinate him. James's fascination with witch-craft stems from a visit to Denmark where the witch persecutions were in full force. This fascination soon gave way to an obsessive paranoia when his return to Scotland with his wife Anne of Denmark was beset by storms in 1590.

The delay was blamed on witchcraft and James personally inter-rogated the suspected witches in what would later become known as the North Berwick witch trials. James's growing interest in the threat witches posed resulted in him publishing *Daemonologie* in 1597, a treatise on witchcraft. On his accession to the English throne, James introduced the Witchcraft Act of 1604 which made all forms of witchcraft punishable by death. However, his waning interest in this subject was prompted by a raft of false accusations, some of which he uncovered himself.

While a King is allowed to forget his obsessions, it's a different matter for the everyday person. One of the things I have to remind myself when reading seventeenth-century witch trial transcripts is just how embedded the fear of the supernatural was. Although King James didn't introduce this paranoia to England and Scotland, he did provide a platform which others used to their advantage. The most obvious would be the writers behind the widespread circulation of witchcraft pamphlets, based on real-life witch trials but prone to exaggeration. Indeed clerk Thomas Potts earned King James's approval and the keepership Skalme Park, for his transcription of the Pendle Witch Trials of 1612, which was published as *The Wonderful Discovery of Witches in the County of Lancaster.*

At the time my novel is set, witch pamphlets are still in vogue and many people would have heard of *A Most Certain, Strange, and True Discovery of a Witch,* a pamphlet which describes a group of Roundhead soldiers happening upon a witch dancing upon the River of Newbury and ending her merriment with a cascade of bullets.

Another group to benefit from King James's paranoia was the witch-hunters, in particular Matthew Hopkins. When I first read about Matthew Hopkins, I was shocked by both his youth and the number of alleged witches he killed. He was only in his twenties when he took up witch-hunting, even assuming the fake title of Witchfinder General to assert his authority. He was completely shameless in promoting himself and if he were alive today I could imagine him becoming a modern-day swindler in the vein of *Inventing Anna and The Tinder Swindler.* However, the chaos of the English Civil War provided Matthew Hopkins with a ripe environment to thrive in his chosen profession. Most of the alleged witches were elderly women, often resented by their neighbours for their poverty and reliance on parish relief. Witch-hunting was a convenient way to relieve the pressures on parish coffers and it's important to remember that Hopkins and his accomplish John Stearne were often invited by towns to undertake a witch-hunt. Hopkins and Stearne's successes, including the fees they demanded which were equivalent to a month's wage for a labourer or a foot soldier, proved to be their undoing. As did the rise of people speaking out against them, including puritan preacher John Gaule. Hopkins's attempt to deflect the criticisms with a pamphlet defending his methods and his fees, fortunately, did little to turn the tide against him. If you're interested in learning more about this period and Matthew Hopkins in particular, I highly recommend *Witchfinders: A Seventeenth-Century English Tragedy* by Malcolm Gaskill.

History is never stagnant and each generation finds a new way to engage with it. I'm pleased by the efforts being made to acknowledge the victims of the European witch-hunts, including the recent apologies made by the Church of Scotland and the German Church. I also hugely admire the organisations working to ensure that victims of the witch-hunts are never forgotten, including Witches of Scotland where Claire Mitchell QC and Zoe Venditozzi are leading a campaign to secure a pardon for the 4,000 people convicted of witchcraft, an apology and a national memorial.

Although inspired by true events, *The Revels* is ultimately a work of fiction. However, I do hope my book provides a path for readers to engage with this unique moment in history and find a modern-day resonance in my characters' stories.

Acknowledgements

When I first began writing *The Revels*, the idea of it being published seemed a distant dream. I am therefore eternally grateful to everyone who's helped to make it a reality.

To my wonderful editor Katie Seaman at HQ Stories – from our very first meeting, I was humbled by your passion for *The Revels*, your belief in what my story could be and your patience and advice in helping me to get there (even when I was convinced I couldn't!). I am so lucky to have you in my corner for this book and the next! Thank you x.

I also want to thank my amazing agent Liza DeBlock, queen of metaphors, soother of writer's doubts, etc for believing in my writing from the beginning. A huge thank you to everyone at Mushens Entertainment for your encouragement and support. You're all fantastic.

A book is more than just its author and I am so glad to be working with the team at HQ Stories to help get *The Revels* into readers' hands.

Janet Aspey – I could not have dreamed up a better launch for *The Revels*. Thank you for making me fall in love with my debut all over again. Sally Felton – Thank you so much for bringing the world of *The Revels* to life with your beautifully designed tarot cards.

I'd also like to thank Seema Mitra in editorial, Becci Mansell and Lucy Richardson in publicity, Kate Oakley and Andrew Davis for their design, Anne O'Brien for the amazing copyediting and Eldes Tran for a great proofread.

Clare Mackintosh – I always thought you were amazing, but it was only after you began to mentor me that I realised just how kind and supportive you are too. Your encouragement and advice in demystifying this whole author process mean more to me than you'll ever know ... thank you.

I wrote most of *The Revels* while studying with Curtis Brown Creative and I'm so grateful to my tutors and peers for their generous feedback: Simon Wroe (CBC tutor), Abhi, Jen, Barbara, Cathryn, Edward, Hannah, Julia, Lisa, Paula, Heidi, Daniel, Alice, Pip and Samantha. A special thank you to Cathi Unsworth (CBC tutor) for helping me to figure out the story I wanted to tell and making me feel like a writer from the very beginning.

Foday Mannah and Pim Wangtechawat – Thank you for being such wonderful beta readers of *The Revels*.

Kirsty Ridge (freelance editor and proofreader) – Your wonderful edits on an early draft of *The Revels* and a previous project were invaluable in helping me to become a better writer. Thank you!

Linda Bailey and Elliott Rae – Your friendship means so much to me as does your constant encouragement to go after my dreams. Thank you x

Alix Dunmore – Thank you for the villain monologues which came in handy when writing my antagonists.

Amy Mae Baxter, founder and editor-in-chief of *Bad Form Review* – You were the first person to provide me with a platform for my writing and was also so encouraging of *The Revels* at a time when I was still asking myself if the story was any good. Thank you!

I also want to thank Phoebe Morgan, Kathryn Cheshire, Sophie Churcher and Ayo Onatade for choosing *The Revels* as one of the winners of the HarperFiction Killing It Competition for Undiscovered Writers. Phoebe, I am so grateful for your belief in *The Revels* from the beginning and your support in demystifying publishing.

I'd also like to thank the writers and organisations who were generous with their time and for making me feel at that very early stage that my writing dream could be more than that: Jackson P Brown and Moyette Gibbons @BlkGirlWriters, Elane & Sarah @IAmInPrint, Davina Tijani, Cesca Major, Yaba Badoe, Bridget Collins, Sara Collins, Rowan Coleman, Laura Shepherd-Robinson, Stacey Halls, Jessie Burton and everyone in the @2023debuts and @debuts23 groups.

ONE PLACE. MANY STORIES

Bold, innovative and
empowering publishing.

FOLLOW US ON:

@HQStories